NIGHTWORLD

also by F. Paul Wilson

HEALER (1976)
WHEELS WITHIN WHEELS (1978)
AN ENEMY OF THE STATE (1980)
BLACK WIND (1988)
SOFT & OTHERS (1989)
DYDEETOWN WORLD (1989)
THE TERY (1990)
SIBS (1991)

The *Nightworld* Cycle (six volumes)
THE KEEP (1981)
THE TOMB (1984)
THE TOUCH (1986)
REBORN (1990)
REPRISAL (1991)
NIGHTWORLD (1992)

NIGHTWORLD

A Novel By

F. PAUL WILSON

DARK HARVEST
Arlington Hts., Illinois · 1992

ISBN 0-913165-71-9
NIGHTWORLD Copyright © 1992 by F. Paul Wilson
Artwork Copyright © 1992 by Ivan Skoric

Manufactured in the United States of America

FIRST EDITION

Dark Harvest / P.O. Box 941 / Arlington Heights, IL / 60005

The publishers would like to express their gratitude to the following people. Thank you: Ann Cameron Mikol, Stan and Phyllis Mikol, Dr. Stan Gurnick PhD, Greg MacIntyre, Raymond, Teresa and Mark Stadalsky, Al Zuckerman, Ivan Skoric, TypePlus, Ltd. and James Helms. And, of course, special thanks go to the author, F. Paul Wilson.

to Forrest J Ackerman

whose *Famous Monsters of Filmland* exposed a fascinated twelve year old to a gallery of monstrous creatures, demonstrated their wonders while allowing him to laugh at them, and set him on the road toward creating his own monsters as an adult.

Thanks, Forry. This one's for you.

Rasalom went to the mountain.

He is calling himself Rasalom these days because it seems he has always called himself Rasalom. It is not his birth name, the one his mother bestowed on him. He discarded that one back in the First Age when it was customary to keep one's True Name a secret. But he has used Rasalom so long it almost seems like his True Name.

From here atop Minya Konka, through a break in the clouds, much of what is now called China spreads out four and a half miles below him in the darkness. His birthplace is not far from here. It is bitterly cold on the mountaintop. Gale-force winds shriek and howl angrily as they swirl the frozen air about his naked body. Rasalom scarcely notices. The power within protects him, the ever-growing power, fed incessantly by the delicious woes of the world below.

The horizon brightens. Dawn does not break at this altitude—it shatters. Rasalom stares at the glint of brightness sliding into view and focuses the power he has been storing since his most recent rebirth. Millennia of frustration fall away as he begins the process to which he has devoted the ages of his existence. No gestures, no incantations, just the power, vomiting out of him, spreading out and up and around, seeping into the planet's crust, billowing into its atmosphere, saturating its locus in the universe.

Soon all of this shall be his. There is no opposition, no power on earth that can stop him.

He drops to his knees, not in prayer but in relief, elation.

At last, after so many ages, it has begun.

Dawn will never be the same.

PART 1

SUNSET

WEDNESDAY

1 • NICHOLAS QUINN, PhD.

Manhattan

On May 17, the sun was late.

Nick Quinn heard the first vague rumors of a delayed sunrise while filling his coffee mug from the urn in the lounge of Columbia University's physics department, but didn't pay them much mind. A screwed-up calculation, a missed observation, a malfunctioning clock. Human error. Had to be. Old Sol never missed appointments. It simply didn't happen.

But the rumor continued to echo through the halls all morning, with no offsetting rumor of explanation. So at lunch break, when Nick had settled his usual roast beef on rye and large cola on his tray in the faculty cafeteria, the first thing he did was hunt up Harvey Sapir from astrophysics.

Nick looked for the hair. Harv's hair was always perfect. It flowed back seamlessly from his forehead in a salt-and-pepper wave, so full and thick it looked like a toupee. But it wasn't. Close up, if you looked carefully, you could catch a glimpse of pink scalp through the mane. A running joke around the physics department was guesstimating how much time and spray Harv invested in his hair each morning.

Nick spotted him at a corner table with Cynthia Hayes. She was from astrophysics too.

Harv's hair was a mess.

Nick found that unsettling.

"Mind if I join you?" Nick said, hovering over the seat next to Cynthia.

The two of them were in deep conversation. Both glanced up and nodded absently, then immediately put their heads back together. Beneath his uncombed hair, Harv's face was haggard. He looked all of his forty-five years and then some. Cynthia, too, looked somewhat disheveled. She was closer to Nick's age— mid-thirties—with short, chestnut hair and glorious skin. Nick liked her. A lot. She was the main reason he'd put aside his coke-bottle lenses and got fitted for contacts. Years ago. Still hadn't found the nerve to ask her out yet. With his pocked skin and weird-shaped head, Nick felt like a warty frog who had no chance ever of changing into a prince, yet still he pined for this princess.

4

"What's all this I hear about the sun being late?" he said after swallowing the first bite of his sandwich. "How'd a story like that get started?"

They both glanced at him again, then Cynthia leaned back and rubbed her eyes.

"Because it's true," Harv said.

Nick stopped in mid bite and stared at them, looking for a smile, a twist of the lips, a hint of the put-on.

Nothing. Cynthia's expression was as deadpan as Harv's.

"Bullshit," Nick said.

Instantly he regretted it. He never used profanity in front of a woman, even though many of them had no reservations about swearing like sailors in front of him.

"Sunrise was scheduled at five-twenty-one this morning, Nick," Cynthia said. "It rose at five-twenty-six. Five minutes and eight-point-two-two seconds late this morning."

Her husky voice never failed to give him a warm feeling.

Except today. Her words chilled him. She was saying the unthinkable.

"Come on, guys", he said, forcing a laugh. "We set our clocks by the sun, not vice versa. If the clock says the sun is late, then the clock needs to be reset."

"*Atomic* clocks, Nick?"

"Oh."

That was different. Atomic clocks worked on nuclear decay. They were accurate to a millionth of a second. If they said the sun was late . . .

"Could be some sort of mechanical failure," Nick said hopefully.

Harv shook his head. "Greenwich reported a late rise too. Five minutes and a fraction late. They called us. I was here at four-thirty a.m., waiting. As Cynthia told you, sunrise was late here by exactly the same interval."

Nick felt a worm of uneasiness begin to work its way up his spine.

"Greenwich too? What about the West Coast?"

"Palo Alto got the same figure," Cynthia said.

"But do you know what you're saying?" Nick said. "Do you know what this means?"

"Of course I know what it means!" Harv said with ill- concealed annoyance. "This *is* my field, you know. It means the earth either temporarily slowed its rate of spin during the night or it tilted back on its axis."

"But either would mean cataclysm! Why, the effect on tides alone would be—"

"But it *didn't* slow. Not the slightest variation in axial rotation *or* axial tilt. Believe me, I've checked. The days are supposed to be getting progressively longer until the equinox in June, but today got shorter—or at least it started out that way."

"Then the clocks are wrong!"

"Atomic clocks? *All* of them? All experiencing precisely the same level of change in nuclear decay at the same time? I doubt it. No, Nick. The sun rose late this morning."

Nick's field was lasers and particle physics. He was used to uncertainties at the sub-atomic level—Heisenberg had seen to that. But on the celestial plane, things were supposed to go like . . . clockwork.

"This is all *impossible!*"

Harv's expression was desolate. And Cynthia's was frightened.

"I know," Harv said in a low voice. "Don't I know."

And then Nick remembered a conversation he'd had with a certain Jesuit a couple of months ago.

It will begin in the heavens . . .

Father Bill Ryan had returned to the city after five years of hiding in the South, and was still laying low. Only a handful of people knew he was back. After all, he was still wanted by the police.

Poor Father Bill. The years of seclusion had not been kind to him. He looked so much older, and he acted strange. Simultaneously jumpy, irritable, frightened, and angry. And he talked of strange things. No specifics, just cryptic warnings of some sort of approaching Armageddon. But with the Russians acting semi-civilized and the cold war over, that hadn't made much sense.

One thing Father Bill had been fairly positive about was where it all would start.

It will begin in the heavens.

He'd told Nick to keep his ears open and to let him know if he heard of anything strange happening in the skies, no matter how insignificant.

Well, something more than strange had happened. Something far from insignificant. Something impossible.

It will begin in the heavens.

The unease in Nick's spine stopped crawling and sprinted up to the back of his neck, spreading across his shoulders. He excused himself from the table and headed for the pay phone in the hallway.

2 • Father William Ryan, S.J.

"Ask him about tonight," Glaeken said, close by Father Bill's side. "Do they think the sun will set *ahead* of schedule tonight?"

Bill turned back to the phone and repeated the question. Nick's reply was agitated. Bill detected a tremor weaving through the younger man's voice.

"I don't know, and I'm sure Harv and Cynthia don't know, either. This is *terra incognita,* Bill. Nothing like this has ever happened before. All bets are off."

"Okay, Nick. Thanks for calling. Keep me posted, will you? Let me know about sunset."

"That's it?" Nick said. "Keep you posted? What's this all about? How did you know something was going to happen? What's it all mean?"

Bill sensed the fear, the uncharacteristic uncertainty in Nick, and wished he could say something to comfort him. But Bill had nothing comforting to say.

"You'll know as soon as I know. I promise you. Get back to me here tonight. I'll be waiting for you. Goodbye."

Bill hung up and turned to Glaeken, but the old man was over by the picture window, staring down at the Park. He did that a lot. Glaeken looked eighty-something, maybe ninety, slightly stooped, with white hair and deeply wrinkled skin; but he was a big man, and his frame blocked a good portion of the window. Bill had been living here in Glaeken's apartment for the past couple of months, helping him with his ailing wife, driving him around town while he did his "research," but mostly waiting.

The apartment was huge, occupying the entire top floor of the building, and filled with strange curios and even stranger paintings. The wall to Bill's left was mirrored and he started at the stranger facing him in the glass, then realized he was looking at himself. He'd shaved his beard and cut his hair and he missed his ponytail. He still wasn't used to seeing himself with bare cheeks. He wasn't used to looking so old. The gray hair had been there for years, but the beard had hidden all the lines on his face. He looked all of his fifty years.

Bill moved up to the window and stood beside Glaeken.

The wait, apparently, was over. He was glad for that. But an icy tendril of dread slithered through his gut as he realized he had traded one uncertainty for another. The apprehension of wondering *when* it would start had been replaced now by a greater worry of *what* was starting.

"You didn't seem too surprised," Bill said.

"I sensed the difference this morning. Your friend confirmed it. The Change has begun its march."

"You wouldn't know it from the looks of things down there."

Across the street and a dozen stories below, Central Park was a palette of greens in the light of the high spring sun as the various species of trees sprouted this year's crop of leaves.

"No," Glaeken said. "And you won't for a while. But now we must lower our watch. The next manifestation will occur in the earth."

"Like what?"

"I don't know. But if he follows his pattern, that is where he'll make his next move. And when he has reached his full powers—"

"You mean he *hasn't*?"

"There is a process he must go through before his power is complete. Plus, there's a purpose to playing with the length of our days. It's all part of his method."

"Not at full power," Bill said softly, his mind balking. "My God, if you're right about that, and he's able to alter the time the sun rises when he's *not* up to speed, what'll he be able to do when he is?"

Glaeken turned and pinned Bill with his deep blue gaze.

"Anything he wants. *Anything*."

"Nick says it's impossible for the sun to rise late," Bill said, grasping at straws. "It breaks too many physical laws."

"We'll have to learn to forget about physical laws—or any laws, for that matter. The 'laws' we have created to explain our existence and make sense of the universe around us are about to be repealed. Physics, chemistry, gravity, time itself will be reduced to futile, meaningless formulae. The first laws were broken at sunrise. Many more will follow until they all lie scattered about in ruins. As of this morning, we begin a trek toward a world and a time of no law."

An old woman's voice quavered from the master bedroom.

"Glen? Glen, where are you?"

"Coming, Magda," Glaeken said. He gripped Bill's upper arm and lowered his voice. "I don't think we can stop him, but there may be a chance to impede him."

Bill urged his spirits to respond, to lift, to cast off the pall of gloom that enveloped him. But his mood remained black.

"How? How can we hope to stand against a power that can alter the path of the sun?"

"We can't," the old man said sternly. "Not with that attitude. And that's just the way he wants us to react—with despair and hopelessness. 'He's too power-ful. Why even try to resist?'"

"Good question," Bill said.

"No." Glaeken tightened his grip painfully on Bill's arm. "*Bad* question. That way, he's already won, without a fight. He *may* win. In fact, I'm pretty sure we haven't got a chance. But I've fought him too long to sit around and simply wait for the end. I thought I could. I wanted to sit this out, sit everything out. That was why I took the name Veilleur. For once I'd be involved in nothing; I'd simply sit back and watch. And I have watched. And all the while I've waited for someone to come along with the power to stand in Rasalom's way. But no one's appeared. And now I find I can't sit by and let everything fall into his lap. I want that bastard to have to work for it. If he wants this world, he's going to have to *earn* it!"

Something in Glaeken's words, his manner, his flashing eyes gave Bill heart

"I'm all for that, but can we do enough to let him know he's even been in a fight?"

"Oh, yes. I'll see to it."

Magda's voice intruded again, trailing in from the bedroom.

"Doesn't anybody hear me? Isn't anybody there? Have I been left here alone to die?"

"I'd better go to her," Glaeken said.

"Can I help?"

"Thanks, no. She just needs a little reassurance. But I'd appreciate it if you could be around tonight while I go out. I've got a little errand I must run."

"If you need anything, I can—"

"No. This is someone I must meet alone."

Bill waited for Glaeken to elaborate, but no explanation was offered. He'd learned over the past couple of months that the old man played everything close to the vest, yielding only the minimal amount of necessary information, keeping the rest to himself.

"Okay. I think I'll stop in on Carol, then. To tell her it's started."

"Good. Do that. And keep emphasizing to her that none of what has happened or is about to happen is her fault."

"Will do." Bill started to turn away, then stopped. "Can we really give Rasalom a fight?"

"If I can gather together the proper elements, we may have ourselves a weapon."

"Really?" Bill was almost afraid to yield to the hope growing within him. "When do we start this gathering?"

"Tomorrow. Will you drive me out to Long Island? And would you wear your cassock?"

What a strange request. Why did Glaeken want him to look like a priest?

"I don't have one anymore. I . . . I don't believe in any of that anymore."

"I know. But I must be at my most persuasive. And the presence of a Jesuit at my side might lend some weight to my arguments. We'll fit you for a new cassock."

Bill shrugged. "Anything for the cause. Where on Long Island?"

"The north shore."

A familiar pang stirred within Bill.

"I grew up in that area."

"Yes. In the Village of Monroe."

"How did you know?"

Glaeken shrugged. "That's where we're going."

"Monroe? My home town? Why?"

"Part of the weapon is there."

Bill was baffled. *In Monroe?*

"It's just a little harbor town. What kind of weapon can you hope to find out there?"

Glaeken turned and walked down the hall to attend to his wife. He cast the reply over his shoulder.

"A small boy."

Over in the West Seventies, Bill knocked on an eighth-floor apartment door. A slender woman with ash blond hair, fine features and a pert, upturned nose opened it and stared at him. Carol. Her face was tight, her eyes haunted, her usual high coloring blanched.

"It's begun, hasn't it?" she said.

The afternoon sun filled the room behind her with golden light, giving her an almost ethereal quality. The sight of her disturbed once again the old feelings he tried to keep tucked away.

Bill stepped across the threshold and closed the door behind him.

"How did you know?"

"I heard about the late sunrise on the radio." Tears filled her eyes as her lips began to tremble. "I knew right away it was Jimmy's doing."

Bill reached out and folded her in an embrace. She was trembling as she leaned against him. Her arms locked around his back and she clung to him like a tree in a flood. Bill closed his eyes and let the good feelings wash through him. Good feelings were so hard to come by these days.

He'd been moving through a fog of black depression for the last couple of months, ever since the deadly events in February in North Carolina. Three times since 1968 his world had been all but torn apart. First there'd been the violent death of his old friend and Carol's first husband, Jim Stevens, followed by the bizarre murders in the Hanley mansion and Carol's flight to parts unknown; he'd recovered from that. Then five years ago there'd been his parents' deaths in the fire, Danny Gordon's mutilation and all the horrors that followed, capped by his own flight and years of hiding; he'd almost recovered from that when he'd had to face Renny Augustino's brutal murder, Lisl's suicide, and the exhumation of Danny Gordon's living corpse.

Bill wasn't bouncing back this time. He wasn't sure he had any bounce left in him. He'd dragged himself back to New York but it was no longer home. No place was home. In this entire teaming city, Nick Quinn and Carol Treece were the only people left alive from his past that he dared approach.

"You've got to call him Rasalom and stop calling him Jimmy, got to stop thinking of him as your son. He's not. There's nothing of you and Jim in him. He's someone else."

"I know that, Bill," she said, holding him tighter. "In my mind I know that. But in my heart is this feeling that if I'd loved him more, if I'd been a better mother, he'd have turned out differently. It's crazy but I can't get away from it."

"Nothing anyone could have done in his childhood would have made the slightest bit of difference. Except maybe strangling him as an infant."

He felt Carol stiffen against him and was sorry he'd said it. But it was true. "Don't."

"Okay. But stop calling him Jimmy. He's not Jimmy. Never was. His name is Rasalom and he was already who he was long before he took over the baby in your womb. Long before *you* were born. He didn't develop under your care. He was already there. You're not responsible."

He stood there in the middle of her tiny living room, holding Carol's thin body against him, breathing the scent of her hair, spying the streaks of gray nestling in the ash blond waves. Trickles of desire ran down his chest and over his abdomen. With a start, he felt himself hardening. He became aroused so easily these days. Sex had been no problem when he'd still considered himself a priest. But now that his lifelong beliefs had been reduced to ashes, buried with the charred remains of Danny Gordon, everything seemed to be inching out of control. Here he was, his arms wrapped around Carol Treece, formerly Carol Stevens, *nee* Carol Nevins. His high-school sweetheart, his best friend's widow, now another man's wife. Priest or ex-priest, this wasn't right.

Gently, Bill put some space between them. *Room for the Holy Ghost,* as the nuns used to say when he was a kid.

"Are we straight on that?" he said, gazing into her blue eyes. "You're *not* responsible."

She nodded. "Right. But how can I stop feeling like his mother, Bill? Tell me how I can do that?"

He saw the pain in her eyes and resisted the urge to pull her into his arms again.

"I don't know, Carol. But you've got to learn. You'll go crazy if you don't." They looked at each other for a moment, then Bill changed the subject. "How's Hank? Does he know yet?"

She shook her head and turned away.

"No. I haven't been able to tell him."

"Don't you think—?"

"You've met Hank. You know what he's like."

Bill nodded silently. He'd met Henry Treece a number of times; he'd even been over for dinner twice, but always as a priest and an old friend of the family. Hank was a straight arrow, a comptroller in a computer software firm. A man who dotted all his *i*s and crossed all his *t*s. A good man, a decent man, an *organized* man. The antithesis of spontaneity. Bill doubted whether Hank had ever done anything on impulse in his entire life. So unlike Jim, Carol's first husband. Bill couldn't see Henry Treece and Carol as a loving couple, but maybe that was because he didn't want to. Maybe Hank was just what she needed. After the way chaos had intruded repeatedly on Carol's life, maybe she needed the structure, stability, and predictability a man like Hank offered. If he made her happy and secure, more power to him.

But that didn't make Bill want Carol any less.

"How can I tell him what we know?" Carol said. "He'll never accept it. He'll think I'm crazy. He'll have me going to psychiatrists. I wouldn't blame him. I'd probably be doing the same if positions were reversed."

"But now with the sun playing tricks, we've got an indisputable fact on our side. Carol, he's got to know sooner or later. I mean, if you're going to be involved—"

"Maybe if he met Glaeken. You know how persuasive he is. Maybe he could convince Hank."

"It's worth a try. I'll talk to him about it." Bill glanced at his watch. "When's Hank due in?"

"Any minute."

"I'd better go."

"No, Bill." She took his hand and squeezed it. "Stay. Please."

Her fingers shot a bolus of tingling warmth up his arm.

"I can't. I've got a bunch of errands to run for Glaeken. Now that Rasalom's made his first move, the old guy's getting his countermoves ready. He needs me to be his legs."

Bill gave her a quick hug and fled the apartment. He hated lying to Carol. But how could he tell her that it ripped his heart out to see Henry Treece stroll in the door and give her his usual casual hello kiss? Didn't Hank realize what he had? Did he have any idea what Bill would give—*do*—to take his place?

And there was another reason he wanted to leave. He was afraid to get too close to Carol, afraid to care too much. First and most obvious: she was married. But more important was the fact that terrible things happened to the people he cared about. All his emotional investments crashed.

Bill began looking for a place where he could have a quiet beer and sit alone in the dark.

3 • REPAIRMAN JACK

They weren't making muggers like they used to.

Jack had been trolling for about an hour now and this was the second he'd found—or rather had found him. Jack was wearing his Hard Rock Cafe sweatshirt, acid-washed jeans, and an *I ♥ New York* visor. The compleat tourist. A piece of raw steak dangling before a hungry wolf.

When he'd spotted the guy tailing him, he'd wandered off the pavement and down into this leafy glade. Off to his right the mercury-vapor glow from Central Park West backlit the trees. Far behind his assailant he could make out the year-round Christmas lights on the trees that flanked the Tavern-on-the-Green.

Jack studied the guy facing him. A tall, hulking figure in the shadows, maybe twenty-five years, about six-feet, pushing two-hundred pounds, giving him an inch and thirty pounds on Jack. He had stringy brown hair bleached blond on top, all combed to the side so it hung over his right eye; the left side of his head above the ear and below the part had been buzzcut down to the scalp—Veronica Lake after a run-in with a lawn mower. Pale, pimply skin and a skull dangling on a chain from his left ear. Black boots, baggy black pants, black shirt, fingerless black leather gloves, one of which was wrapped around the handle of a big Special Forces knife, the point angled toward Jack's belly.

"You talking to me, Rambo?" Jack said.

"Yeah." The guy's voice was nasal. He twitched and sniffed, shifting his weight from one foot to the other. "I'm talkin' to you. You see anybody else around?"

Jack glanced around. "No. I guess if there were, you wouldn't have stopped me here."

"Gimme your wallet."

Jack looked him in the eye. This was the part he liked.

"No."

The guy jerked back as if he'd been slapped, then stared at Jack, obviously unsure of how to take that.

"What you say?"

"I said no. *En-oh.* What's the matter? You never heard that word before?"

Probably hadn't. Probably grew up in a home—"household" would no doubt be a more accurate term—where the parents were mere cohabitants, present now and then in body but hardly ever in spirit, who had endowed their offspring with their DNA and little else. A household in which no one gave enough of a damn to say no. Saying no meant you had to care about a kid. Saying no and meaning it meant you had to follow it up, be consistent. And that took effort. Or maybe he grew up in a place where one or both of his adult cohabitants beat the shit out of him every time he turned around, just for the hell of it, whether he was good or bad, till he didn't know which end was up.

You needed a license to drive a car, own a gun, dig a ditch, or sell hot dogs from a pushcart, but you didn't need a license to have a kid. The rationale for all the licenses was that those things affected public safety. Yet someone had popped this guy out a quarter of a century ago so he could spend his childhood being beaten or ignored or both, so he could grow up to spend his days sucking crack and his nights rolling people in Central Park. He was a loaded weapon. And *that* affected public safety.

So why didn't you have to have a license to be a parent?

Didn't matter where he started out—upper crust, middle class, poverty row—he'd left wherever he'd been, whether it was Boise or the Bronx, and had come here, to the Park, to be a menace, a walking time bomb waiting to go off. Didn't matter if he'd been abused or neglected as a kid, that was the past and Jack couldn't do anything about that. What did matter was that the guy was facing Jack here and now in the Park, and he was armed, dangerous, and lethal. That was what Jack had to deal with.

"You crazy?" the guy said, voice rising. "Gimme your wallet or I cut you. You wanna get cut?"

"No," Jack said. "Don't want to get cut." He reached into his pocket and pulled out a wad of cash. "I left my wallet home. Will this do?"

The guy's eyes all but bulged. His free hand darted out.

"Give it!"

Jack shoved it back into his pocket.

"No."

"You crazy fucker—!"

As the guy lunged at Jack, jabbing the bladepoint at his belly, Jack spun away, giving him plenty of room to miss. Not that he was worried about any surprises from the guy. Most of his type had wasted muscles and sluggish reflexes. But you had to respect that saw-toothed knife. It was a mean sucker.

The guy made a clumsy turn and came at Jack again, slashing high this time, at his face. Jack pulled his head back, grabbed the wrist behind the knife as it went by, got a two-handed grip, and twisted. Hard. The guy shouted with pain as he was jerked into an armlock with his weapon flattened between his shoulder blades. He kicked backward, landing a bootheel on one of Jack's shins. Jack winced with pain, gritted his teeth, and kicked the mugger's feet out from under him. As the guy went down on his face, Jack yanked the imprisoned arm back straight and rammed his right sneaker behind the shoulder, pinning him.

And then he stopped and counted to ten.

Jack knew it was at times like these that he was in danger of losing control. The blackness was there on the edges, beckoning him, urging him to go crazy on this guy, to take out all his accumulated anger, frustration, and rage on this one unlucky jerk.

Plenty accumulated during day to day life in this place. And every day it seemed to get a little worse.

The city had become ungovernable. Hardly anyone seemed to have any pride anymore, or possessed enough self-esteem to think anything was beneath them. Rip off an old lady's handbag or a toddler's candy bar. No item too small, no deed too low. Everything was up for grabs. Anything was okay if you got away with it. That was the operating ethic. "Mine" was anything I could take and keep. If you put something down and left it unguarded, it became mine if I could snatch it and make off with it. The civilized people were on the run. Those who could afford to were leaving, others were withdrawing, tightening their range of activities, limiting their hours on the street, in public. And those unfortunates who had to be out on the streets and on the subways, they were fodder. And they knew it.

On the way to the Park tonight Jack had passed car after car with "No Radio" signs in the windows. Every street was flanked with them. It was symptomatic of the city-dwellers' response to the predators. With no faith in City Hall's ability to make the streets safe, they took one more step in the direction they'd been heading over the past couple of decades—they retreated. They removed the radio when they parked their car and took it with them into the steel-doored, barred-windowed fortresses they called home. One more piece of ground surrendered. They'd pulled all their belongings in from the street a generation ago; after having the shrubs repeatedly dug up and carted off from the fronts of their apartment houses, they'd stopped planting them, and they'd chained— *chained*—the trunks of the few larger ones that remained.

Jack was fed up with retreating. He'd had it up to *here* with retreating. And when one of these creeps got within reach, like this doughy lump of dung, he wanted to stomp him into the earth, leaving nothing but a wet stain on the ground when he was finished. So when he felt that blackness rising, he did a ten count and willed it back down to wherever it lived. There was a thin line here, one he tip-toed along, one he tried to keep from crossing over. Spend too much time on the far side of that line and you became like them.

Jack let out his breath and looked down at the mugger.

He was whining.

"Hey, man! Can't you take a joke? I was only—"

"Drop the knife."

"Sure, sure."

The bare fingers opened, the big blade slipped from the gloved palm and clattered to the earth.

"Okay? I dropped it, okay? Now let me up."

Jack released his arm but kept a foot on his back.

"Empty your pockets."

"Hey, what—?"

Jack increased the pressure of his foot. "*Empty them!*"

"Okay! Okay!"

The mugger reached back and pulled a ragged cloth wallet from his hip pocket and slid it across the dirt.

"All of them," Jack said. "Everything."

The guy rolled left and right, pulled a couple of crumpled wads of bills from the front pockets, and dumped them by the wallet.

"You a cop?"

"You wish."

Jack squatted beside him and went through the small pile. About a hundred in cash, half a dozen credit cards, a gold high school ring. The wallet held a couple of twenties, three singles, and no ID.

"I see you've been busy tonight," Jack said.

"Early bird catches the worm."

"No, pal. You're the worm. This all you got?"

"Aw, you ain't gonna rip me off, are ya? I need that money."

"Your *jones* needs that money."

Actually, the Little League needed that money.

Every year about this time the kids from the local teams that played here in Central Park would come knocking on doors looking for donations for uniforms and equipment. Jack had made it a tradition over the past five or six years to help them out by taking up nocturnal collections in the Park. Repairman Jack's Annual Park-a-thon. Seemed only fair that the slimeballs who prowled the Park at night should make donations to the kids who used it during the day. At least that was the way Jack saw it.

"Let me see those hands," Jack said. He'd noticed an increasingly lower class of mugger over the past few years. Like this guy. Nothing on his fingers but a cheap pewter skull-faced pinky ring with red glass eyes. "How come no gold?" Jack pulled down the back of his collar. "No chains? You're pathetic, you know that? Where's your sense of style?"

"I'm a working man," the guy said, rolling a little and looking up at Jack. "No frills."

"Yeah. What do you work at?"

"This!"

The guy lunged for his knife, grabbed the handle, and stabbed up at Jack's groin. Jack rolled away to his left and kicked him in the face as he lunged again. The guy went down and Jack was on him again with his arm pulled up behind him and his sneaker back in its former spot on his back.

"We've already played this scene once," Jack said through his teeth as the blackness rose again.

"Hey, listen!" the guy said into the dirt. "You can have the dough!"

"No kidding."

"Just let me—"

He screamed as Jack shifted his foot into the rear of his shoulder and kicked down while he gave the arm a sharp twist. The shoulder dislocated with muffled pop.

The Rambo knife dropped from suddenly limp fingers. Jack kicked it away and released the arm. As the guy retched and writhed in the dirt, Jack scooped up the cash and rings. He emptied the wallet and dropped it onto the guy's back, then headed for the lights.

Jack debated whether to troll for a third mugger or call it a night. He mentally calculated that he had donations of about three hundred or so in cash and maybe an equal amount in pawnable gold. He'd set the goal of this year's Park-a-thon at twelve hundred dollars. Used to be he could clear an easy thousand on a single night on his annual spring troll but it didn't look like he was going to make that this year. Which meant he'd have to come back tomorrow night and bag a couple more. And exhort them to give. Give till it hurts.

As he was coming up the slope to Central Park West in the mid-Sixties, he saw an elderly gent dressed in an expensive-looking blue blazer and gray slacks trudging with a cane along the Park side of the street.

And about a dozen feet to Jack's left, a skinny guy in dirty Levis and a frayed Hawaiian shirt burst from the bushes at a dead run. At first Jack thought he was running from someone, but noticed that he never glanced behind him. Which meant he was running *toward* something rather than away. He realized the guy was making a beeline for the old man.

Jack paused a second. The smart part of him said to turn and walk back down the slope. It hated when he got involved in things like this, and reminded him of other times he'd played good Samaritan and landed in hot water. Besides, the area here was too open, too exposed. If Jack got involved he'd could be mistaken for the Hawaiian shirt's partner, a description would start circulating, and life would get more complicated than it was already. Butt out.

Sure. Sit back while this galloping glob of Park scum bowled the old guy over, kicked him a few times, grabbed his wallet, then high-tailed it back into the brush. Jack wasn't sure he could stand by and let something like that happen right in front of him. That would be another kind of retreat.

Besides, he was feeling kind of mean tonight.

Jack spurted into a dash of his own toward the old gent. No way he was going to beat the aloha guy with the lead he had, but he could get there right after him and maybe disable him before he did any real damage. Nothing elaborate. Hit him in the back with both feet, break a few ribs and give his spine a whiplash he'd remember the rest of his life. Make sure Aloha was down to stay, then keep right on sprinting across Central Park West and into yuppyville.

Aloha was closing with his target, arms stretched out for the big shove, when the old guy stepped aside and stuck out his cane. Aloha went down on his belly and skidded face first along the sidewalk, screaming curses all the way. When he stopped his slide, he began to roll to his feet. But the old guy was there, holding the bottom end of his cane in a two-handed grip like a golf club. He didn't yell "Fore!" as he swung the heavy metal handle around in a smooth wide arc. Jack heard the crack when it landed against the side of Aloha's skull. The mugger stiffened, then flopped back like a sack of flour.

Jack stopped dead and stared, then he began to laugh. He pumped a fist in the old guy's direction.

"Yes!"

Looked like he wasn't the only one in town who'd had enough.

Still smiling, Jack broke into an easy jog, intending to give the old dude a wide berth on his way by. The fellow eyed him as he neared.

"No worry," Jack said, raising his empty palms, "I'm on your side."

"I know that, Jack."

Jack nearly tripped as he stuttered to a halt and turned. The old guy had his cane by the handle again; he stepped over Aloha like he was so much refuse and strolled Jack's way as if nothing had happened. The guy had style.

"Why'd you call me Jack?"

The old man came abreast of him and stopped. Gray hair, a wrinkled face, pale eyes.

"You *are* Repairman Jack, aren't you?"

Jack scrutinized the man. Even though stooped, he was still taller than Jack. A big guy. Old, but big. And a complete stranger. Jack didn't like being recognized. It put him on edge. But there was something appealing about that half smile playing about the old dude's lips.

"Do I know you?"

"No. My name's Veilleur, by the way." He offered his hand. "And I've wanted to meet you for some time now. I came out here tonight to remedy that."

Jack shook his hand, baffled. "How did you—?"

"Let's walk, shall we?"

They crossed Central Park West and headed toward Columbus Avenue.

"Want to tell me what's going on?"

"The end of life as we know it."

"Swell." *A nut.* "Look, it was nice meeting you but I've got a few errands I've got to run and—"

"I'm not crazy."

"I'm sure you're not, but—"

"And I'd think that after your run-in with the rakoshi you'd be more open-minded than most about occurrences that the average person would write off immediately as madness."

As memories of that summer of death and horror swirled about him, Jack stopped and grabbed Veilleur's arm.

"Wait a sec. Wait a sec. What do you know about rakoshi? And *how* do you know?"

"I'm sensitive to certain things. I sensed their arrival. But I was more acutely aware of the necklaces worn by Mr. Bahkti and his sister."

Jack felt slightly numb. The only other people who knew about the rakoshi and the necklaces were the two most important people in the world to Jack—Gia and Vicki. And one other.

"Did Kolabati send you?"

"No. I wish I knew where she was. You see, it is Kolabati and those necklaces that I wish to discuss with you." He smiled at Jack. "Still have to run off on those errands?"

"They can wait," Jack said. "You like beer?"

"I love it."

"Come on. I know a place where we can talk."

$*\quad*\quad*$

"I like that sign over the bar," Veilleur said.

Jack glanced up at Julio's "Free Beer Tomorrow" logo. It had been there so long, Jack no longer noticed it.

"Yeah. Gets him in trouble sometimes."

They were each on their third pint of John Courage. Julio had put it on tap as a special favor to Jack but it had quickly become a favorite of the regulars. Unfortunately, its availability had attracted the attention of the area's abundant yuppy population, and for a while Julio's had seemed in danger of being overrun.

But it was relatively quiet here tonight and Jack and the old guy had the rear section pretty much to themselves. An arrangement Jack preferred on most occasions, but especially tonight. He wouldn't have wanted anyone he knew overhearing this Veilleur character's story. It was crazy. No, it went far beyond crazy. It was to crazy what a .45 prefragmented full load was to a BB.

But there was something about the old guy that Jack couldn't help liking and trusting. On a very deep, very basic, very primitive level he didn't understand, he sensed a solidarity with Veilleur, a subliminal bond, as if they were kindred spirits. He wouldn't lie to Jack.

But that didn't mean he wasn't a few bricks shy of the proverbial full load.

Yet he knew about the rakoshi, those dark, murderous, reeking demons from Bengali folklore, and about Kolabati and her pair of necklaces, with their power to heal and prolong life.

"I wore one of those necklaces for a while. Bati offered it to me."

"And you refused? Why?"

"Didn't like the price tag."

Veilleur nodded his approval and somehow that gave Jack a good feeling. What was it about this old dude?

"So this problem with the sun they've been talking about all day is really this guy Rasalom's doing? He made the sun rise *late*?"

"And set early. Apparently you haven't heard the evening news. Sundown was a little over ten minutes ahead of schedule."

The idea that the sun was no longer following its own rules gave Jack a queasy feeling.

"But assuming you're right, what it all mean?"

"I told you—"

"Right. 'The end of life as we know it.'" Jack was almost afraid to ask the next question. "Why were you looking for me?"

"I'm trying to locate Kolabati."

Kolabati . . . Jack was devoted to Gia, now more than ever. But there were times when memories of Kolabati and her long, dark, slender body floated back to him.

"Afraid I can't help you. I haven't seen her for years."

"Oh, I realize that. I'll find her eventually. And when I do, that's when I'll need your help."

"What for?"

"I need the necklaces."

Jack suppressed a laugh. "You don't know what you're asking. Kolabati will never give them up. Not in a million years. You might talk her out of *one*, but never both."

"I'll need both. And soon."

"Then forget it. The necklace keeps her alive, keeps her young. She's a hundred and fifty years old."

"Not quite," Veilleur said. "But close."

"Whatever. But she only looks thirty or so. All because of the necklace. Do you think she's going to give that up?"

"That's why I've contacted you. So you can convince her once I've located her."

"She'll die without it."

"I have faith in you."

Jack stared at him.

"You really are crazy, aren't you?" He rose and dropped a twenty on the table. "I don't think we can do business."

Veilleur reached into his breast pocket and produced a card.

"This is my number. Please take it. And call me when you reconsider."

Reluctantly, Jack took the card and tucked it away.

"You mean *if* I reconsider."

"Will you reconsider if Central Park shrinks?"

"Sure." That seemed a safe bet. "When Central Park shrinks, I'll give you a buzz."

"Fine," Veilleur said, smiling and nodding. "I'll be waiting."

Jack left him there, sipping his Courage. Nice old guy, but he'd developed a few loose wires in his old age.

As he walked home, he thought about Kolabati and wondered how she was. Where she was. And what she was up to these days.

4 • KOLABATI

Maui—upcountry

The wind stopped.

Kolabati put down her book and rose from her chair. Not sure at first what had happened, she took her coffee cup and stepped out on the lanai; she stood there for a moment, listening. Something was wrong. Too quiet. In her years on Maui she could not remember a truly silent moment. She had no neighbors to speak of, at least none within shouting or even bullhorn distance, but even when you were too far from the ocean to hear the surf, even when the birds and insects were silent, there was always the Maui breeze, child of the tireless tradewinds rolling from the northeast, a constant sussurant undertone varying in pitch but always there, perpetual, interminable, timeless, relentless.

But it paused now. The ceramic wind chimes hung silent on the corners of the unscreened lanai. The air lay perfectly still, as if resting. Or holding its breath.

What was happening? First the news of the late sunrise this morning, and now this.

Kolabati looked down the slope of Haleakala past the rooftops of Kula to the valley spread out below her in the late afternoon sun. A gently curved, almost flat span between the two volcanic masses that defined the island of Maui, the valley was a narrowed waist checkered with the pale green squares of sugar cane, the darker green of pineapple plants, the rich red-brown of newly tilled earth, and the near black of a recently burned cane field. She spent part of each day out here on the lanai, staring across the valley at the cloud-capped West Maui Mountains, waiting for her daily rainbow, or watching the cloud-shadows run across the valley floor thousands of feet below. But the shadows weren't running now. The streaming tradewinds that propelled the clouds had stalled. The clouds and their shadows waited.

Kolabati waited too. The air should have grown warmer in the wind's absence, yet she felt a chill of foreboding. Something was wrong. The perpetual Maui breeze occasionally changed its pattern when the kona winds came, but the air always moved.

Krishna, Vishnu, she said, silently praying to the ancient Indian gods of her youth, *please don't let anything spoil this. Not now. Not when I've finally found peace.*

Peace. Kolabati had searched for it all her life, and it had been a long life. She looked thirty, perhaps a youngish thirty-five, yet she had been born in 1848.

She had decided that she would cease counting her birthdays after the one hundred and fiftieth, which was fast approaching.

A long time to be searching for contentment. She thought she'd found a chance for it a few years ago with a man named Jack but he had spurned her and the gift of longevity she'd offered him. She'd left him sitting in a pool of his own blood, dying. He was probably dead, and the thought of that saddened her. Such a vital man . . .

But I'm different now. The new Kolabati would have stayed and helped Jack, or at least called a doctor for him despite the cruel things he had said to her.

Maui had helped make the difference in her. Maui and Moki. A place and a man. Together they had given her what peace there was in this world.

Here on Maui, clinging to the breast of Haleakala, the world's largest dormant volcano, she had all of the world within reach. If she tired of watching the valley below, cloud-dappled on sunny days, or lashed by rain and speared by lightning when storms marched through, she could travel to Haleakala's windward east coat and visit the jungles above Hana; further around on the south slope she could pretend she was in the savannahs of Africa or the plains of North America, grazing cattle and all; or she could travel across the valley and wander among the rich Japanese and American vacationers in the resorts at Ka'anapali and Kapalua, or travel into the Iao Valley and beyond to the rain-forests of the second wettest spot in the world, or return to Haleakala itself and walk the floor of its crater; there in the heart of desolation, she could wander among its thousand-foot cinder cones and imagine she was exploring the surface of Mars.

Wonders were close at hand too. Directly below the lanai her silversword garden grew. She had transplanted the seedlings from her wanderings on Haleakala's slopes and was perhaps unduly proud of her collection of the rare spiky clusters. Each would grow for twenty years before producing its one magnificent flower. Kolabati could wait. She had time.

She glanced down at the cup in her hands. Oh, yes. And coffee from the big island's Kona Coast—the richest coffee in the world. She sipped.

No, she could not see herself tiring of living here, even if she didn't have Moki. But Moki *was* here, and Moki gave meaning to all of it.

She could hear him in the back now, working in his shop. Moki—her *kane*, her man. He carved driftwood. Together they would scour the beaches and the banks of Haleakala's countless streams and waterfalls, searching for branches and small trunks, the long dead pieces, bleached and hardened by time and the elements. They'd bring these gnarled, weathered remains back to the house and set them up around Moki's workshop. There he would get to know them, live with them for a while. And gradually he would see things in them—the wrinkles around the eyes of an old woman's face, the curve of a panther's back, a lizard's claws. Once he had spied the form hiding within, he would bring his small ax and array of chisels into play, working *on* the wood and *with* the wood to expose the hidden form to the light of day.

Moki was modest about his work, never taking credit and refusing blame for the nature of the works he produced. His stock phrase: "It was already there in the wood; I just cleared away the excess material and set it free."

But he deserved far more credit than he took. For Moki wasn't content to leave his work as simple wood sculptures. They were Hawaiian wood carved by an almost full-blooded Hawaiian, but that wasn't quite Hawaiian enough for Moki. When each was finished he shipped it to the big island and carried it to the fiery mouth of Kilauea, the active crater on the southeastern slope of Mauna Loa. There he trapped some of the living lava, poured it into a shape that complemented his sculpture, allowed the lava to cool to a point where it wouldn't damage the wood, then set his sculpture into the gooey stone.

Kolabati had first seen Moki's work with its intricate cuts and swirls and unique lava rock bases in a Honolulu gallery. She'd been completely taken by them and had asked to meet the artist. She commissioned a piece, and visited Moki many times during its fashioning. She found herself as taken by the man as she was by his work. His intensity, his passion for living, his love of his native islands. He was complete. In that sense he reminded her a little of her dead brother, Kusum.

Moki wanted her, but he didn't need her, and that made him all the more attractive. Theirs was a relationship of passionate equals. She didn't want to own Moki, didn't demand all his passion. She knew some of his passion had to be funneled off into his art and she encouraged that. To dominate him, to possess him would risk destroying a wild and wonderful talent. Instead of having all of him, she would wind up with less than she had begun with.

Moki needed his art, needed to be Moki, and very much needed to be Hawaiian. He would have loved to have lived and worked on Niihau, the forbidden island, oldest of the Hawaiian chain, but had not been able to wrangle an invitation from the last of the pure-bred Hawaiians living there in the old, primitive ways. Like most Hawaiians, Moki was not pure-bred—he could find traces of Portuguese and Filipino in his bloodline.

But he remained pure Hawaiian in his heart, dressing the part around their *hale* or house, speaking the old language and teaching it to Kolabati. And together they moved to the side of Haleakala where he carved and sculpted his wood, and braved the heat of Kilauea to fashion his pieces.

The results, the graceful and the grotesque, were scattered about the islands, in galleries, museums, corporate offices, and on every available surface in their house. Kolabati loved the clutter, which was unusual for her. As a rule she preferred an ordered existence. But not in this case. The clutter was Moki. It put his stamp on their home, made it truly theirs. For there was no other place on earth quite like it.

And Kolabati did not want that to change. For the first time in her many years the persistent voice of dissatisfaction was silent within her. For the first time she no longer hungered for new people, new sensations, new feelings, the Next New Thing. Continuity—that was what counted most now.

"Bati! *Hele mai!*"

Moki's voice, calling from his workshop, telling her to come to him. He sounded excited. She started toward the rear of the house but he was already coming her way.

The old Kolabati used to tire of a man after two weeks. They were all the same; so few had anything new to offer. But even after two years with Moki, the sight of him still excited her. His long, wild, red-brown hair—he was considered an *ehu*, a red-haired Hawaiian—his lean, dark, muscled body, and his eyes as dark as her own. An artist, a sensitive man, as attuned to the mysteries of the wood he worked as to the mysteries within her own psyche. And yet he still retained an untamed quality, as witness the brief, loincloth-like *malo* he wore now. No two days were alike with Moki.

Which was why Kolabati called him her *kane* and allowed him to wear the other necklace.

And she loved his lilting accent.

"Bati, look!"

He held out his left palm to her. A ragged red line ran across it.

"Oh, Moki! What happened?"

"I cut myself."

"But you're always cutting yourself."

She looked at the cut. It was barely bleeding. He'd done worse to his hands before. What was so special about this?

"Yes, but this was a bad one. I slipped badly. I thought the chisel went half way through my palm. Blood started spurting a foot into the air—and then it stopped. I squeezed it for a few minutes, and when I checked again, it was half healed. And in the time it took me to come in from the workshop, it's healed even further. Look at it. You can almost see it closing before your eyes!"

He was right. Kolabati watched with uneasy fascination as the wound stopped oozing and became shallower.

"What's going on?" he said.

"I don't know."

He touched the necklace around his throat—a heavy chain of sculpted iron, each crescent link embossed with pre-Vedic script; centered over the notch atop his breast bone lay a matched pair of bright yellow elliptical stones, like thumb-sized topazes, each with a black center. Moki's necklace perfectly matched her own. They'd been in her family for generations . . . since before history.

"You said these things would help heal us, keep us young and healthy, but I never—"

"They don't work like this," Kolabati said. "They've never worked like this."

It was true. The necklace could heal illnesses, prolong life, stave off death from all but the most catastrophic injuries. But it worked slowly, subtly. Not like this. The healing of Moki's hand was crude, garish, like a sideshow trick.

Something was wrong.

"But they work like this now," Moki said, a wild light in his eyes. "Watch."

That was when she saw the wood knife in his other hand. He jabbed it through the skin on the underside of his left forearm and into the tissues beneath.

"No!" she cried. "Moki, don't!"

"It's all right, Bati. Just wait a minute and I'll show you what I mean."

Wincing with the pain, he dragged the blade upward until a four-inch wound gaped open. He watched the blood spurt for a moment, then squeezed it shut. He smiled crazily at her for a moment or two as he pressed the skin edges together, then he released it.

The wound had stopped bleeding. The edges were adhering as if they'd been sutured. And the light in his eyes was wilder than before.

"See? The necklace has made me almost indestructible. Maybe immortal. I feel like a god—like Maui himself!"

Kolabati watched in horror as Moki cavorted about the great room. First the sun, then the wind, and now this. She could not fend off the feeling of impending doom. Something was happening, something had gone terribly awry, and the necklaces were responding. Their powers were increasing, as if in preparation for . . . what?

And then she heard it—the ceramic tinkling of the wind chimes on the lanai. She turned and hurried to the railing. Thank the gods! The wind! The wind was back!

But it was the wrong wind. It blew from the west. The tradewinds came from the east, always from the east! Where did this wind come from? And where was it blowing?

At that moment Kolabati knew beyond a doubt that the world was beginning a monstrous change. But what? And why?

Then she felt rather than heard a deep seismic rumble. The lanai seemed to shudder beneath her feet. Haleakala? Could the old volcano be coming to life?

THURSDAY

WPLJ-FM
Hey! What's going on up there? It says here sunrise was late again this morning. C'mon, sun! Get your act together. You were over fifteen minutes late this morning. Get a new alarm clock already!

1 • THE VILLAGE OF MONROE

Bill barely recognized his home town.

He stared in awe as he cruised the morning-lit Monroe harbor front in Glaeken's pristine old Mercedes 240D. There were new condos on the east end, the trolley tracks had been paved over, and all the old Main Street buildings had been refurbished with nineteenth century clapboard facades.

"This is awful," he said aloud.

In the passenger seat, Glaeken straightened and looked around.

"The traffic? It doesn't look so bad."

"Not the traffic—the town. What did they do to it?"

"I hear lots of towns are trying to attract tourists these days."

"But this is where I grew up. My home. And now it looks like a theme park . . . like someone's idea of an old whaling village."

"I never saw a whaling village that looked like this," Glaeken said.

Bill glanced at Glaeken. "I guess you'd know, wouldn't you."

Glaeken said nothing.

Bill drove on, shaking his head in dismay at the changes. At least they'd left the old bricks on Town Hall, and hadn't changed the high white steeple of the Presbyterian church. He noticed with relief that Crosby's Marina was still there, and Memison's was still in business. *Some* of the old town was left, so he didn't feel completely lost.

But he'd come here today hoping for a burst of warmth, for a sense of belonging, a place to call home. He knew now he wasn't going to find it in Monroe.

Still, it was better than sitting around waiting, letting the unease within him bubble and stew. Probably nothing he could do would block out completely the growing dread, especially after hearing that sunrise had been late again this morning.

"I still don't know why you need me along, other than as a driver," Bill said.

He was uncomfortable wearing a cassock and collar again. The clothing fit him fine, but only physically. He no longer considered himself a priest, not in his mind, not in his heart, not in his soul.

"Your mere presence will help me."

"But you're going to do all the talking and what am I going to do? Stand around and look holy?"

"You may say anything you wish."

"Thanks loads. But I'll be afraid to open my mouth because I don't know what's going on. You're playing this too close to the vest, Glaeken. You ought to know by now you can trust me. And maybe if I knew a little bit more about what we're doing here, I might be able to help."

Glaeken sighed. "You're right, of course. I don't mean to keep you in the dark. It's just habit. I've kept so many secrets for so long . . ." His voice trailed off.

"Well?"

"We've come to Monroe for the *Dat-tay-vao.*"

Bill had to laugh. "Well! That clears up everything!"

"The name is Vietnamese. In truth, the *Dat-tay-vao* has no name. It is an elemental force, but it has wandered around Southeast Asia for so long that it's convenient to refer to it by the name the locals have used for centuries."

"*Dat-tay-vao.*" Bill rolled the alien syllables over his tongue. "What's it mean?"

"Loosely translated, 'to lay a hand on.' There's an old Vietnamese folk song about it:

It seeks but will not be sought.
It finds but will not be found.
It holds the one who would touch,
Who would cut away pain and ill.
But its blade cuts two ways
And will not be turned.
If you value your well-being,
Impede not its way.
Treat the Toucher doubly well,
For he bears the weight
Of the balance that must be struck.

It has better meter in the original language."

"A bit ominous, don't you think?"

"The song is a celebration and a warning. Twice a day, for an hour or so at a time, the one who possesses the *Dat-tay-vao*— or is possessed by the *Dat-tay-vao*, depending on how you look at it—can heal wounds, clear cancers, and cure illnesses with a touch."

Not too long ago, Bill would have scoffed. Today he remained silent, listening. He scoffed at nothing anymore.

"The *Dat-tay-vao* came to Monroe last year and became one with a local physician, Dr. Alan Bulmer."

"Sounds vaguely familiar. Wasn't he associated with Dr. Alberts for a while?"

"Possibly. He's on his own now. Out of practice since the *Dat-tay-vao* enabled him to heal with a touch."

"That's it. *People* did an article on him last summer. Hinted that he was a charlatan."

"He wasn't. And isn't. His cures were very real. He lives with Sylvia Nash and her adopted son now."

"Out on Shore Drive, you said?

Glaeken nodded. "Two-ninety-seven."

"The high rent district."

The Hanley mansion was out on Shore Drive. Bill repressed a shudder as memories of the horrors he'd witnessed there in 1968 flashed within his brain like distant lightning.

"The estate is called Toad Hall," Glaeken said.

"Never heard of it. Must be new."

But as soon as he saw Toad Hall, Bill knew that it wasn't new. Only the brass plaque on the right-hand brick gatepost was new. He recognized the place as one of the Preferred North Shore's most venerable mansions: the old Borg Estate. Three acres on the Long Island Sound surrounded by a stone wall and dense, insulating stands of white pines. The house itself was set far back, close to the water; a many-gabled affair, flanked by weeping willows. He hated the thought of someone renaming the old Borg place, but as he turned off the ignition and heard the briny breeze whisper through the swaying willow branches, he conceded that the new name might be right on target.

He accompanied Glaeken to the front door.

"It's a household of four," the old man said as they walked. "Mrs. Nash, Dr. Bulmer, a Vietnamese houseman named Ba, and Jeffrey, Mrs. Nash's adopted son."

"You said yesterday we're looking for a boy. Is he the one?"

Glaeken nodded. "He is. And his mother is not going to like what I have to tell her."

"Why? What's he got that—?"

The front door opened as they stepped onto the porch. A tall, gaunt Oriental towered in the doorway. This had to be Ba. His high-cheekboned face was expressionless, but his eyes were alert, active, darting back and forth between

Glaeken and Bill, picking up details, assessing, measuring, categorizing. Bill knew someone else with eyes like that: Glaeken.

"Yes, sirs." His voice was thickly accented. "May I be of service?"

"Yes, you may," Glaeken said, fishing a card out of his pocket. "My name is Veilleur. I believe Mrs. Nash is expecting me."

Ba stepped aside and ushered them through a marble-tiled foyer and into the living room. Doo-wop was playing softly through hidden speakers. A wave of nostalgia swept Bill away as he recognized "Story Untold" by the Nutmegs. He and Carol had danced to that song at CYO dances in the gym of Our Lady of Perpetual Sorrow, not a mile from here.

Ba's voice yanked him back to the present.

"I will tell the Missus that you are here. Do you wish coffee?"

They both agreed and remained standing by the cold fireplace as Ba turned and left them alone.

"That's one powerful looking fellow," Bill said. "I don't think I've ever seen a Vietnamese that tall."

Glaeken nodded. "A one-man security force, I would say."

A slender woman in her late thirties with short black hair, blue eyes, and finely chiseled features strode into the room. She wore loose black slacks and a white blouse buttoned all the way to her throat. She moved with complete self-confidence.

"I'm Sylvia Nash," she said. "Which one of you is —?"

"I'm Veilleur," Glaeken said, stepping forward and offering his hand. "And this is Father William Ryan."

Her handshake was as cool as the rest of her, Bill thought. A striking woman.

He was making connections now. He'd heard of her. Greg Nash's widow. Bill had gone to high school with Pete Nash, Greg's older brother. Greg had gone to Nam, come back in one piece, then he'd been killed trying to break up a convenience- store robbery. Sylvia had become a renowned sculptress. And obviously a very successful one if she could afford this place.

"Please sit down," she said, gesturing to the couch. She seated herself across from them. "You said you had something of a personal nature to discuss with me. I hope that wasn't a scam to get in here and try to sell me something."

Bill glanced up at Ba as he returned with a silver coffee service set on a huge silver tray; he almost pitied anyone who tried any tricks in this house.

"I assure you I have nothing to sell," Glaeken said. "I've come to talk to you about the *Dat-tay-vao*."

The big Vietnamese started as he was setting down the silver tray. He almost spilled the coffee pot but righted it in time. He stared at Glaeken but his eyes were unreadable. Bill glanced at Sylvia. Her face was ashen.

"Ba," she said in a shaky voice. "Please get Alan."

"Yes, Missus."

Ba turned to go but at that moment a man in a wheelchair rolled into the room. He was lean, pale, in his mid-forties, with gray-flecked brown hair and gentle brown eyes. He paused on the threshold, staring at Glaeken, a puzzled look on his face, then he came the rest of the way in. As the wheelchair came to a stop beside her chair, Sylvia reached over and grasped the man's hand. They shared a smile. Bill immediately sensed the powerful bond between these two. Sylvia introduced him as Dr. Alan Bulmer.

"They want to talk about the *Dat-tay-vao*, Alan."

Bill felt the weight of Bulmer's gaze as he stared at them.

"You'd better not be reporters." There was real loathing in his voice when he spoke the last word. The emotion seemed to arise from personal experience.

"I assure you, we're not."

Bulmer seemed to accept that. Glaeken had a way of speaking the truth in a way that *sounded* like the truth.

"What do you know—or think you know?" the doctor said.

"Everything."

"I doubt it."

"I know that your present condition is a direct result of your association with the *Dat-tay-vao*."

"Really."

"Yes. I know that the *Dat-tay-vao* left Viet Nam in late 1968 within a medic named Walter Erskine who couldn't handle the responsibility and became a derelict alcoholic—"

A flash of memory strobed Bill's brain. Five years ago . . . the parking lot of Downstate Medical Center . . . two winos, one was Martin Spano, the other a bearded stranger named Walter . . . "Walter was a medic once" . . . repeatedly asking, "Are you the one?" Could it have been . . . ?

"—but before he died, Walter Erskine passed the *Dat-tay-vao* on to you; that you used the power of the *Dat-tay-vao* to cure a great number of people—too many people for your own good. As a result—"

Bulmer looked uncomfortable as he held up his hand.

"Okay. Score one for you."

"May I ask if you regret your time with the *Dat-tay-vao*?"

Bulmer paused, then: "I've thought about that a lot, believe me. It left me half vegetable, but that appears to be only temporary. With therapy I'm working my way back to full function. My arms and hands are as good as they ever were, and my legs are starting to come around. The *Dat-tay-vao* helped me cure—*cure*—a hell of a lot of people with an incredible array of illnesses—acute, chronic, debilitating, life- threatening. And in the process Sylvia and I found each other. A year or two of rehab is a small price to pay for that."

Bill knew then and there that this man operated on a different plane than most people—and he liked him enormously for it.

"May I ask then—"

Glaeken stopped speaking and looked to his right.

A small boy stood in the living room entryway. He looked about nine; a round face, curly blond hair, and piercing blue eyes. He reminded Bill of another child from what seemed like another epoch . . . Danny.

The child's gaze roamed over the occupants of the room . . . and came to rest on Glaeken.

"Hello, Jeffy," Sylvia said. She obviously didn't want him listening to this. "Is anything wrong?"

"I came to see who was here."

He walked past Bulmer and his mother and stopped before Glaeken where he sat on the couch. For a long moment he stared almost vacantly into the old man's eyes, then threw his arms around Glaeken's neck and hugged him.

Sylvia found herself on her feet, stepping toward Jeffy and Mr. Veilleur who was returning the hug, gently patting the boy's back. This wasn't like Jeffy at all. He was usually so shy. What had got into him?

"Jeffy?" she said, restraining her hands from reaching for him. "I'm very sorry, Mr. Veilleur. He's never done this before."

"Quite all right," Veilleur said, looking up at her over Jeffy's shoulder. "I'm rather honored."

He gently pulled Jeffy's arms from around his neck, engulfed one of the child's little hands in his own, and sat him on the couch next to him.

"Want to sit here between me and Father Bill?"

Jeffy nodded, his eyes huge. "Yes."

"Good."

Sylvia sat down again but remained perched on the edge of the chair. She tried to catch Jeffy's attention but he had eyes only for Veilleur.

This whole scene made her uneasy.

"He used to be autistic," she said.

Jeffy had made such strides since his sudden release from autism, but he was still backward socially. He was learning, but he still wasn't sure how to act, so he wasn't comfortable with strangers. Until now, apparently.

"I know," Veilleur said. "And I know that Dr. Bulmer's final act with the *Dat-tay-vao* was to cure Jeffy of his autism."

Sylvia glanced at Alan. His expression mirrored her own alarm and confusion. How did this stranger know so much about them? It gave her the creeps.

"All right," Alan said, shrugging resignedly. "So you do know about the *Dat-tay-vao*. But I'm afraid you're too late. I don't have that power anymore. The *Dat-tay-vao* is gone."

"The *Dat-tay-vao* has left you, but it is not gone," Veilleur said.

Sylvia sensed Ba stiffen where he stood behind her. Why was he suddenly on the alert?

"That may be," she said. "But I still don't see what we can do for you."

"Not what you can do for me—for everyone. We are entering a time of great strife, of darkness and madness. The days are getting shorter when they should be lengthening. The *Dat-tay-vao* can help forestall that. Maybe even prevent it."

Sylvia glanced at Alan again. He nodded imperceptibly in agreement. This poor old man had blown a few fuses. She darted a glance at the priest. He was a good-looking man, a few years older than Alan, with heavily salted dark brown hair, a scarred face, and a nose that looked as if it had been badly broken. She wondered if he'd ever been a boxer. She also wondered how he could sit there with a straight face? Unless he was as crazy as the old fellow. Ever since yesterday's news of the sun's erratic behavior the kooks had been coming out of the woodwork, predicting the end of the world and worse. And to think she had let two of them into her house.

And then she saw something flash in the priest's eyes. A look of tortured weariness, as if he'd seen too much already and was dreading the time to come.

"But I told you," Alan said. "The *Dat-tay-vao* is gone."

"Gone from you, yes." Veilleur put his arm around Jeffy. "But it hasn't traveled far."

Sylvia shot to her feet, fighting the panic vaulting within her. She let anger take its place.

"Out! I want you out of here! Both of you. *Now!*"

"Mrs. Nash," the priest said, rising. "We mean no harm—to anyone."

"Fine," Sylvia said. "Good. But I want you both to leave. I have nothing to say to either of you, nothing more to discuss."

The priest pointed to Veilleur. "This man is trying to help you—help us all. Please listen to him."

"Please leave now, Father Ryan. Don't force me to have Ba eject you."

She looked at Ba. Over the years she'd learned to read his usually expressionless face. What she saw there now was reluctance. Why? Did he want them to stay? Did he want to hear them out?

No. It didn't matter what Ba wanted in this situation. She had to get them out of here. Now.

She strode through the foyer and opened the front door. With obvious reluctance, the old man and the priest made their exit. On the way out, Mr. Veilleur left a card on the hall table.

"For when you change your mind," he said.

He sounded so sure, she found herself unable to frame a reply. As she slammed the door behind them, she heard the sound of Alan's wheelchair rolling toward her.

"Kind of rough on them, weren't you?"

"You heard them. They're crazy." She stepped to one of the sidelights flanking the front door and watched the old man and the priest stand by their car in the driveway. "They might be dangerous."

"They might be. But neither of them struck me as dangerous. And that old fellow—he knew an awful lot about the *Dat-tay-vao*. All of it accurate."

"But his end-of-the-world talk . . . about a time of 'darkness and madness.' That's crazy talk."

"I recall someone who reacted exactly the same way when I told her that I had the power to heal with a touch."

Sylvia remembered how she'd thought Alan had gone off the deep end then. But this was different.

"You weren't talking about doomsday."

The priest and the old man were getting into the car. Thank God.

"True. But *some*thing's happening, Sylvia. It's spring, yet the days are getting shorter, and the scientists can't say why. Maybe we are heading for some sort of Armageddon. Maybe we should have listened a little longer. That man *knows* something."

"He doesn't know anything I care to hear. Certainly not doomsday nonsense."

"That's not what you're afraid of, is it, Sylvia?"

She turned and faced him. Sylvia still wasn't used to seeing Alan in a wheelchair. She *refused* to become used to it. Because Alan wouldn't be in it forever. The *Dat-tay-vao* had left him in a coma last summer, but he had fought back. And he was still fighting. That was why she loved him. He was a fighter. His will was as strong as hers. He'd never admit defeat.

"What do you mean?"

She knew exactly what he meant, and because of that she had trouble meeting his gaze.

"We've skirted around this for months now, but we've never really faced it."

"Alan, please." She stepped up beside the wheelchair and ran her fingers gently through his hair, then trailed them down to his neck, hoping to distract him. She didn't want to think about this. "Please don't."

But Alan wasn't going to be put off this time.

"Where's the *Dat-tay-vao*, Sylvia? Where did it go? We know it transferred from Erskine to me as he died. We know I still had it when it cured Jeffy of his autism. But when I came out of the coma in the hospital, it was gone. I can't cure anymore, Sylvia. The time comes and my touch is no different from anybody else's. So where'd it go? Where's the *Dat-tay-vao* now?"

"Who knows?" she said, angry that he was pushing her like this, forcing her to face the greatest fear of her life. "Maybe it died. Maybe it just evaporated."

"I don't believe that and neither do you. We've got to face it, Sylvia. When it left me it went to someone else. There were only three other people in the house that night. We know you don't have the Touch, and neither does Ba. That leaves only one other possibility."

She wrapped her hands around his head and pressed his face against her abdomen.

No! Please don't say it!

The possibility had kept her awake far into so many nights, and it skulked through her dreams when she finally did manage to drop off to sleep.

"You saw how Jeffy responded to Mr. Veilleur. He's attuned to him. So am I, I think. I just didn't happen into the living room earlier. I was *drawn.* And when I saw that old man I felt this burst of warmth inside me. I can only guess at what Jeffy felt."

She heard a noise over by the window and looked.

Jeffy was there, pressing his face and hands against the glass.

"I want to go with him, Mom. I want to *go!*"

Bill let the Mercedes' diesel engine idle a bit till it was good and warm. He was disappointed and found it difficult to hide his irritation. This whole trip had been for nothing.

"Well," he said, glancing at Glaeken, "that was a fiasco."

The old man was staring out the side window at the house. He did not turn to Bill as he spoke.

"It didn't go quite as I'd hoped, but I wouldn't say it was a fiasco."

"How could it have gone worse? She kicked us out."

"I expect resistance from the people I must recruit. After all, I'm asking them to believe that human civilization, such as it is, is on the brink of annihilation, and to put their trust in me, a perfect stranger. That's a difficult pill to swallow. Mrs. Nash's dose is doubly bitter."

"I gather you think this *Dat-tay-vao* is in Jeffy."

"I know it is."

"Well, then, I think you've got a real selling job ahead of you. Because it's pretty clear that not only does that woman not believe it, she doesn't *want* to believe it."

"She will. As the Change progresses she will have no choice but to believe. And then she will bring me the boy."

"Let's hope she doesn't wait too long."

Glaeken nodded, still staring at the house. "Let's hope that the *Dat-tay-vao* and the other components are enough to make a difference."

Bill fought the despondency as he felt it return.

"In other words, all this—everything you're trying to do—might be for nothing."

"Yes. It might. But even the trying counts for something. And I met the boy today. Contact with him has helped me locate someone I have been searching for. That was a good thing."

"He took to you like I've rarely seen a child take to a strange adult."

"Oh, that wasn't Jeffy himself responding to me. That was the *Dat-tay-vao* within him." Glaeken turned from the window and smiled at Bill. "We're old friends, you see."

Over his shoulder, in the window next to the mansion's front door, Bill spotted the little boy's face pressed against the glass, staring at them.

WFAN-AM

Well, for those of you keeping track of it, the sun set early again tonight. Should've gone down at 8:06 but it was gone by 7:35. That means the lights'll come on a little earlier tonight here at Shea Stadium as the Mets meet the Phillies. A lot of our listeners are concerned as to how that's going to affect the playing season . . .

Rasalom stands on the plot of grass in the heart of the city and looks up at the surrounding buildings. Their lights blot out the ever-changing stars overhead, nearly blot out the rising moon. He stares at the top-floor windows of a particular building in the nearest row to the west. Glaeken's building. Glaeken's windows.

"Do you see me, old man?" he whispers to the night. "Or if your feeble failing eyes can't penetrate the shadows, do you at least sense my presence? I hope so. I began in the sky where all could see. Now I move to the earth. Here. Under your nose. I don't want you to miss a thing, Glaeken. I want you front-row center until the final curtain.

"Watch."

Rasalom spreads his arms straight out on each side, palms down, forming a human cross. With a basso rumble, the ground begins to fall away beneath his feet, plummeting as if dropped from a cliff. But he does not fall. The opening widens beneath him yet he remains suspended in air as more earth, tons of earth crumble and tumble down,

down,
down out of sight.
Yet there is no sound of any of it striking bottom.
And when the hole has reached half of its eventual width, Rasalom allows himself to sink into the abyss. Slowly. Gently.
"Do you see me, Glaeken? Do you SEE?"

2 • THE FIRST HOLE

Manhattan

The city was getting nuttier by the minute.

Jack ambled past the darkened Museum of Natural History and headed south on Central Park West. On the corner of 74th there was a bearded guy dressed in sackcloth holding a placard. Straight out of a *New Yorker* cartoon. His sign was laboriously hand printed with a giant "REPENT!" at the top followed by a Biblical quote so long you'd have to stop and read for a good three minutes before you got it all.

So sunset had come even earlier tonight. Big whoop.

Jack was already getting used to the idea of the sun playing tricks with its own schedule; a little discomfiting, maybe, but hardly the end of the world. Things tended eventually to balance out on their own in nature. If the days were getting a little shorter here, they were probably getting a little longer in some other part of the world. The scientists said differently. In fact there'd been one on *Nightline* tonight just as Jack was leaving his apartment, claiming with barely repressed hysteria that the daylit hours were shrinking all over the globe. But the guy hadn't sounded too stable. The days *had* to be getting longer somewhere. They just didn't know where yet. Nature always found a balance.

It was people who didn't. People were always knocking things out of kilter. If they weren't, Repairman Jack would be out of work. Because when things got too far out of kilter, past the point of bearable, other people came to Jack to make it right again, to fix it.

But business was a little off at the moment, so Jack had decided to wind up this year's Park-a-thon tonight.

As he crossed Central Park West, he heard a deep rumble. Thunder? The sky was clear. Maybe a storm was gathering over Jersey.

He entered the Park at 72nd Street, got on the jogging path, and continued south. He expected to be alone, but was prepared to step off the path for any late runners coming through. As far as Jack was concerned, only an idiot would jog in the Park at night after what happened to that woman banker in '89. But then, joggers were a separate breed. When it came to a choice between risking death and, at the very least, permanent brain damage, or getting in a couple of extra miles before the end of the day, some of those folks had to stop and give the matter some serious thought.

He heard footsteps and heavy breathing ahead, coming his way. As he stopped under a lamp, a young teenage couple, certainly not seventeen yet, appeared, faces pale and strained, running like the girl's father was after them. They weren't joggers—weren't dressed for it. In fact, they seemed to be buttoning up their clothing as they ran.

"What's up?" Jack said, standing aside to let them pass.

"Earthquake!" the boy said, his voice a breathless whisper.

Jack walked on. He'd heard of making the earth move—he'd had it move for him a couple of times—but it was nothing to panic over.

Half a minute later another guy ran by and said the same thing.

"Where?" Jack said. He didn't feel anything.

"Sheep Meadow!"

"But what—?"

The guy was gone, running like a madman.

Curious now, Jack broke into a loping run and cut off the jogging path. He skirted the Lake until he got to the wide expanse of grass in the lower third of the Park called the Sheep Meadow. In the wan starlight he could make out a ragged, broken line of murmuring people rimming the area. And in the center of the meadow, what looked like a pool of inky liquid. But nothing reflected off its surface. A huge circle of empty blackness.

Jack paused. Something about that black pool raised the hackles on the back of his neck. An instinctive fear surged up from the most primitive parts of his brain. He'd experienced something similar when he'd seen his first rakosh. But this was different. This was a hell of a lot bigger.

He forced his feet to move, to carry him forward, toward the pool. He could make out the figures of a couple of people at the edge and they seemed all right, so he guessed it was safe.

As he neared the edge, Jack realized that it wasn't a pool at all. It was a hole. A huge sink hole, a good hundred feet across, had opened in the middle of the Sheep Meadow. The two guys there ahead of him were standing on the edge, laughing, jostling each other. Jack stopped behind them. He didn't want to get that close. This whole scene made him very uneasy.

One of the guys on the rim turned and spotted Jack. Jack could see that they were young, dressed in black, with spiky hair.

"Hey, dude, c'mon up here. You gotta see this. It's fuckin' *awesome*, man!"

"Yeah!" said the other. "The *mother* of all potholes!"

The started laughing and elbowing each other again.

Wrecked. Better to keep his distance from these two.

"That's okay," Jack said. "I can see all I want to from here."

Which was mostly true. In the wash of light from the tall buildings ringing the lower end of the Park, Jack could make out a sheer wall on the far side of the hole leading straight down through the granite. The edge of the hole was clean.

Jack had seen pictures of sink holes before on the news, from places like Florida where the underground water had been tapped out. But he'd never seen one so perfectly round. This looked like it had been made with a King Kong cookie cutter. And did sink holes occur in solid granite? He didn't think so.

The two kids on the edge were still fooling around, dancing on the edge, playing macho games. Jack was moving to his right, away from them, trying to get the light-bleed from Central Park South behind him for a better look into the hole, when he heard a yelp of terror.

One of the kids was leaning forward over the edge, his arms windmilling. Even from Jack's distance it was plain the kid was over-balanced and no longer fooling around, but his buddy only stood beside him, laughing at his antics.

But his laughter died abruptly with the first kid's scream as he toppled head first into the hole.

"Joey! Oh, shit! Joey!"

He lunged for his friend's foot but missed it, and Joey disappeared into the blackness. His scream was awful to hear, not merely for the blood-chilling terror it carried, but for its length. The cry seemed to go on forever, echoing up endlessly from below as Joey plummeted into the depths. It never really ended. It simply . . . faded . . . out . . .

His friend was on his hands and knees at the edge, looking down into the blackness.

"Oh, God, Joey! Where are you?" He turned to Jack. "How *deep* is this fuckin' thing?"

Jack didn't answer. Instead, he stepped to within half a dozen feet of the hole, got down on his belly, and crawled to the edge. Vertigo hit him like a gut punch as he looked down. There wasn't much to see, only a small section of the perpendicular wall; the rest was impenetrable blackness. But that same old something deep inside him that had reacted to the sight of the hole told him there was no bottom here, or if there was it was too far down to matter, and it wanted him gone from here.

Jack closed his eyes and hung on. And with his eyes closed he thought he could still hear Joey screaming down there. Way, way down there.

He felt a slight breeze against the back of his neck. Air was flowing into the hole. *Into* the hole. That meant it had to go somewhere, be open at the other end. Where could the other end of something this size be?

And then the earth began to slide away beneath his fingers, beneath his wrists, his forearms. Christ! The rim was giving way!

Jack rolled to his left and back, away from the edge, but he wasn't fast enough. A Cadillac-sized wedge of earth gave way and crumbled beneath him. He slid downward toward the black maw of the hole. With a desperate, panicky lunge he managed to grab a fistful of turf and hang on. His feet kicked empty air and for one breathless moment he felt eternity beckoning to him from below. Then the toes of his sneakers found the rocky wall of the hole. He levered himself up to ground level and scrambled away from the edge as fast as his rubbery knees would carry him.

When he'd gone a good fifty feet he heard a terrified cry and risked a look back. Joey's buddy was still back at the edge. Most of his body had dropped into the hole. Jack could see his head, see his arms and hands tearing at the grass in a losing effort to hold on.

"Help me, man!" he cried in a voice all tears and terror. "God, *please!*"

Jack started to unbutton his shirt, thinking he might be able to use it as a rope. But before he reached the last button, a huge clump of earth gave way beneath the kid and he was gone. Just like that. One moment there, the next gone, leaving behind only a fading high-pitched wail.

More earth sloughed off and fell away, narrowing the distance between Jack and the edge. The damn hole was getting bigger.

Jack looked around. The few people who had been scattered around the perimeter of the Sheep Meadow were now fleeing for the streets. A good idea, Jack thought. A *fine* idea. He broke into a headlong run and followed them.

And as he was running, it occurred to him that a big chunk of Central Park was missing. What was it that old weirdo had said last night?

Will you reconsider if Central Park shrinks?

Sure. Sure he'd reconsider.

Jack didn't remember his high-school geometry, so he didn't know the surface area of that hole in Central Park, but a helluva lot of square feet of the Sheep Meadow was missing. Which meant the Park was smaller by that many square feet.

. . . if Central Park shrinks . . .

Jack picked up his pace. He hoped he hadn't thrown out that old weirdo's number.

Arms limp at his sides, Rasalom floats within a tiny pocket in the granite, a pocket he has made. When he descended approximately a hundred feet into the pit, he stopped and hovered as a passage into the bedrock opened before him. He floated into the passage and followed it to this spot.

Yesterday he began the Change above. Now it is time to begin the Change within.

He hesitates. This is a step from which there is no return. This is a process which once begun cannot be reversed, cannot be halted. When it is complete he will have a new form, one he will wear into eternity.

He will be magnificent.

Still he hesitates. For the shape of his new form will not be of his own choosing. Those above—those puny, frightened creatures milling on the surface—will determine his countenance. He shall be an amalgam of all that they fear. For as their fear feeds him, so shall it shape him. His form shall be the common denominator of all that humanity loathes and fears most, the personification of all its nightmares. The deepest fears, from the darkest recesses of the fetid primordial swamps of their hindbrains. All the things that cause the hairs at the back of the neck to rise, make the flesh along the spine crawl, urge the bowels and bladder to empty. He shall be all of them.

Fear incarnate.

Rasalom's body tilts now until he is floating horizontally in the granite pocket. He spreads his legs and rams his feet against the stone wall and screams as they fuse with the living rock, screams as all the fears, the angers, the hatreds, hostilities, violence, pain, and grief from the vicinity surge into him. He stretches his arms and fuses his fists to the stone, and screams again. It is a scream of ecstasy as new power surges through him, but it is a scream of agony as well. For now the Change within has begun.

He swells. His skin stretches, then splits along his arms and legs, from his genitals to his scalp. As he continues to swell, the skin sloughs off and falls to the floor of the stone pocket like a discarded wrapper.

As the night air caresses his raw flesh, Rasalom screams again with what remains of his mouth.

FRIDAY

1 • IN PROFUNDIS

CNN:

—the sun's behavior continues to baffle astronomers, physicists, and cosmologists. We've been informed that it rose at 5:46 this morning, late again, this time by almost nineteen minutes.

And from New York City, startling news of a huge hole opening in Central Park during the night. We have a camera crew rushing to the scene now and we'll have live footage for you as soon as it is available . . .

Manhattan

Glaeken stood at the picture window and looked down on the hole in Central Park. Flashing red lights lit the tardy dawn as police cars and fire trucks ringed the lower end of the Park. A barricade had been set up around the entire Sheep Meadow to keep out the curious throngs. Television vans and camera trucks were there with miles of cable and lights that lit the area to noon brightness. Dominating the center of the scene was the hole. It had grown to two hundred feet across and stopped.

He closed his eyes to shut out the sight of it—just for a moment. He swayed with fatigue. He ached for sleep, but even when he lay down, it spurned his bidding.

So tired. He'd thought he'd freed himself from this, escaped the burden of responsibility for this war. But it wouldn't go away. Not till he'd found a successor. Only then would he truly be free.

But he had to have the weapon in order to pass it on. He'd expected some difficulty in reassembling its components, but the task was proving to be more formidable that he'd imagined. At least that fellow Repairman Jack was showing signs of turning his way. Jack had called in the wee hours this morning,

41

telling him about the hole and suggesting that they get together again and have a few more beers. Fine with Glaeken. That at least was a step in the right direction.

First the weapon, then the successor to wield it, then the battle. A battle which, from the looks of things, would be lost before it was begun. But he had to go through the motions.

Behind him he heard Bill hang up the phone and approach the window. Glaeken opened his eyes and rubbed a hand across his face. Had to appear calm and in control at all times. Couldn't let them see the doubt, the dread, the desperation that nipped at his heels. How could he exhort them to maintain belief in themselves if he didn't set the example?

"Finally got through to Nick," Bill said, coming up beside him. "He's coming down here with a team from the university."

"What for?"

"To find out what caused the hole."

"I can save him the trip. Rasalom caused the hole."

"That's not going to do it for Nick." He gazed down at the Park. "I guess this is what you meant when you said his next move would be in the earth."

Glaeken nodded. "And its placement is not random or haphazard."

"Really? Central Park has some significance for Rasalom?"

"Only so far as Central Park is located right outside my window."

You're going to rub my face in it, aren't you, Rasalom?

"It doesn't look real," Bill said. "I feel like I'm in a movie looking at one of those matte paintings they use for special effects."

"It's quite real, believe me."

"I do. They've got close-ups on the TV, by the way. Want to take a look?"

"I've seen these close up before, although never one this big."

"You have? When?"

"Long ago." *Ages ago.*

"How deep is that thing?"

"Bottomless."

Bill smiled. "No. Really."

Apparently he'd misunderstood, so Glaeken spoke slowly and clearly.

"There is no bottom to that hole," he said. "It is quite literally bottomless."

"But that's impossible. It would have to go all the way through to China or whatever's on the other end."

"The other end doesn't open on this world."

"Come on. Where then?"

"Elsewhere."

Glaeken watched the priest's eyes flick back and forth between him and the hole.

"Elsewhere? Where's elsewhere?"

"No place you'd ever want to visit."

"You can be a little more specific than that, can't you?"

"I wish I could, but the place has no name. And I don't believe there's any way to describe in human terms what the other end of that hole is like."

"I believe I'll change and go down there for a closer look."

"No need to rush. The hole isn't going anywhere. And it's only the first."

"You mean there's going to be more?"

"Many. All over the world. But Rasalom has honored me by opening the first outside my front door."

"I'll see if I can hook up with Nick down there and find out what he knows."

"Just be sure to be back before dark."

Bill smiled. "Okay, Dad."

"I'm quite serious."

His smile faded. "Yeah. I guess you are. Okay. Back before dark."

Glaeken watched Bill hurry to his room. He was fond of the man. He couldn't ask for a better house guest. Bill was always willing to help around the apartment or with Magda when the nurse wasn't around.

As if sensing her name within his thoughts, Magda called from the bedroom.

"Hello? Is anybody there? Have I been left alone to die?"

"Coming, dear."

He took one final look at the hole in the Sheep Meadow, then he headed down the hall.

Magda was sitting up in her bed. She'd been losing weight and her eyes were starting to retreat into her skull. Her face was as lined as his, her hair as white. But her brown eyes were bright with anger.

"Who are you?" she said, switching to her native Hungarian tongue.

"I'm your husband, Magda."

"No, you're not!" She spat the words. "I wouldn't marry such an old man like you! Why, you're old enough to be my father! Where's Glen?"

"Right here. I'm Glen."

"No! Glen's young and strong with red hair!"

He took her hands in his. "Magda, it's me. Glen."

Terror flashed across her face, then her features softened. She smiled.

"Oh, yes. Glen. How could I have forgotten? Where have you been?"

"Right in the next room."

Her expression hardened as her eyes narrowed.

"No you weren't! You've been out seeing other women! Don't deny it! You're out with that nurse! Don't think I don't know what the two of you are up to when you think I'm asleep!"

Glaeken held her hands and let her ramble on. He wanted to cry. After two years he'd have thought he could have adapted to anything, but he couldn't get used to Magda's dementia. None of her ravings were true, yet Magda fully believed her delusions as they passed through the expanding emptiness of her mind, truly meant the hurtful things she said as she spoke them, and that never failed to cut him deeply.

Oh, Magda, my Magda, where have you gone?

Glaeken closed his eyes and recalled Magda as she was when they'd met in 1941. Her soft, even features, her fresh pale skin, glossy chestnut hair, and wide dark eyes, filled with love, tenderness, and intelligence. It was the love, tenderness, and intelligence he mourned for most now. Even after her physical beauty had faded, his love for her had not. For she had remained Magda the poet, Magda the singer, Magda the mandolin player, Magda the scholar who so loved art and music and literature. Her compendium of Rumanian Gypsy music, *Songs of the Rom*, was still in print, still gracing the shelves of finer bookstores.

Three years ago Magda had started to slip away, to be infiltrated and irreversibly replaced by this mad, incoherent stranger. Her mental status had deteriorated first, but soon she had become physically enfeebled as well. She could not get out of bed by herself now. That made caring for her easier in a way because she could no longer wander at night. In the early stages of her decline Glaeken had found her searching the street below, calling for their pet cat, dead since 1962. After that he'd had to deadbolt the apartment door and remove the knobs from the stove to prevent her from "cooking dinner" at two in the morning.

There were still flashes of the old Magda. She couldn't remember what she had for breakfast—or if she'd even *had* breakfast—yet now and then she'd recall an incident in their life together from thirty or forty years ago as if it were yesterday. But instead of buoying him, the brief lapses in Magda's dementia only served to deepen Glaeken's depression.

It wasn't fair.

Glaeken had known and loved so many women through the ages, yet each relationship had ended in bitterness. Each in her own way had ended up hating him because she grew old while he stayed young. Finally there had been Magda, the one woman in his seemingly endless life that he would be allowed to grow old with. And they'd had a glorious life, a love that could not be tainted even by the pain of these past few years.

Maybe it was for the best. Magda would spend her final days immune to the horror stalking the world. Her body was as vulnerable as everybody else's, but her mind was impregnable to reality.

He glanced at Magda and saw that she'd fallen asleep again. This was her pattern—a reversal of day and night. Cat naps throughout the day, awake most of the night. Even with the hired nurse and Bill to help, Glaeken existed in a state of constant exhaustion. His heart went out to all the unfortunate spouses of Alzheimer's patients throughout the world who did not have his financial resources. Unless they had a large family of willing helpers, their lives were an endless nightmare.

Nightmare . . . soon everyone across the globe would know what it was like to live a nightmare.

Gently he lay Magda's head back down on the pillow and tucked the covers in around her. He would not allow a deterioration of her brain to lessen his commitment to her. If their conditions were reversed, she'd be at his side whenever he needed her. He was sure of it. And he would do no less.

All morning he had debated whether or not to warn the media about the hole. Finally, he'd decided against it. He didn't want to attract attention to himself. Besides, they'd write him off as just another doom-monger and ignore him. The end result would be the same: they'd have to learn the hard way.

FNN:

—on the commodities exchanges, prices are up sharply, especially in October beans and orange juice futures, in brisk trading around the globe due to uncertainties about the upcoming growing season . . .

Nick felt someone tugging at his arm. Reluctantly, he turned away from the hole to face one of the Park cops.

"You Dr. Quinn?" the guy said, shouting over the rattle and roar of the generators.

"Yeah. What's up?"

"Got a priest back in the crowd says you asked him here to say some prayers."

"Priest?" Nick said, baffled. "I didn't ask for any—" And then he knew. He almost laughed in the cop's face. "Oh, yeah. I've been waiting for him. Can you bring him over?"

The cop turned and waved to someone along the barricade. Nick saw a lone figure in black break from the crowd and approach at a quick walk.

He shook Father Bill's hand when he arrived. He'd seen the priest a couple of times since his return from North Carolina but still couldn't get used to how he'd aged during his five years in hiding. Before he disappeared, Nick had got to the point where he'd been calling the priest simply "Bill," but since his return he'd fallen back into the practice of prefixing the name with "Father." He pointed to the cassock and Roman collar.

"I thought you weren't going to wear that anymore."

"So did I. But I've decided the uniform has its uses. Especially when you want special treatment in a crowd."

"So what are you doing here?"

Father Bill smiled. "I came to perform the exorcism," he said in a low voice. "To close this thing up."

"Very funny."

The smile faded. "Seriously, Nick. I would like to get a close-up look at the hole."

"Sure. But stay on the platform. The dirt tends to crumble at the edges."

Nick felt the excitement build all over again as he led Father Bill to the edge. He still couldn't get over it. Something like this—a mysterious two-hundred-foot-wide hole appearing here, practically in his back yard. It was wonderful. He guided him to the railing at the edge of the wooden platform and together they looked down.

He heard Father Bill catch his breath.

"Incredible, isn't it?" Nick said. "I can't believe my luck. And that's all it is. Luck. If I'd been out getting coffee when the boys from Geology had called this morning, someone else might have picked up the phone and they'd be calling the shots here now instead of me. Being in the right place at the right time. That's all it takes."

But Father Bill said nothing. He seemed to be mesmerized by the hole.

Nick knew what the priest was feeling. He'd looked down into that hole a good hundred times since he'd arrived and still couldn't shake how unnatural it seemed.

The walls did it. Too sheer. They didn't look fallen away—more like *scooped* away. He could see the layers of earth and stone stacked like the cut edge of a trifle. When he'd first looked down he'd expected to see a sort of inverted cone with a rubble-filled bottom. But he couldn't see the bottom. The hole was much deeper than he'd imagined. Half a mile down, he guessed. Maybe deeper. Straight down into darkness. Maybe when the sun got higher they'd be able to see more, but right now it was night down there.

Nick had been to the Grand Canyon last summer and still remembered the vertigo he'd experienced standing at the edge of the look-out for the first time. The giddy, vertical descent of these walls gave him a similar sensation. But he'd been able to see a ribbon of water at the base of the Grand Canyon. Here, with the gentle downdraft flowing around him, he could see only blackness.

The downdraft had bothered him at first. Where could it be going? Then he realized that the air was probably flowing down into the cavity at the edges, and then turning upward and flowing out straight up through the center. That had to be the explanation. It couldn't all be flowing continually downward. There was no place to go.

He straightened up and turned to the priest.

"Well? What do you think of our little sand pit?"

The priest tore his eyes away from the hole and looked at him. He looked frightened.

"How'd it get here, Nick?"

"Don't know. That's for the geology boys to figure out. But already people are making comparisons to those crop circles in England. The tabloids will have a field day. I think *The Light* has got its whole staff here already."

"Any idea how deep it is?"

"We don't know yet. Geology rigged up a sonic range-finder first thing this morning and pointed it at the bottom, but couldn't get a reading."

"No bottom?" The priest's voice suddenly sounded a little dry.

Nick laughed. "Of course there's a bottom. It's just that echoes from the side walls were interfering with the readings. Geology was stumped, so they called Physics. We could wait till the sun hits zenith and do a sight measurement, but why wait? We've got a new laser that'll bounce a beam off the bottom of that hole and give us a distance reading accurate to within a centimeter."

Father Bill was staring into the hole again as he spoke.

"I have it on good authority that it's bottomless."

"It's deep," Nick said. "But not *that* deep." And then a thought struck him. "This authority wouldn't be the same one that told you about something happening 'in the heavens' now, would it?"

As Father Bill nodded, Nick felt a cold weight settle between his shoulder blades. He gestured toward the hole.

"Come on, now. Bottomless? You can't really believe that."

"I never believed the sun would be rising progressively later each day in mid-spring either. Did you?"

"No, but . . . "

Bottomless? That was patently impossible. Everything had a top and a bottom, a beginning and an end. That was the way things were. It couldn't be any other way.

Someone tapped him on his shoulder. He turned and found one of the grad students.

"We're ready to shoot."

"Great." He turned to Father Bill. "The laser's set. Wait here. In a few minutes we'll have a reading from the bottom— wherever it is."

Bill watched a moment as Nick hurried away toward some odd- looking contraption suspended on a boom over the hole. He was proud of him. He'd come a long way from the bratty little nine- year-old orphan he'd played chess with back in his early days at St. Francis Home for Boys. He was mature and self-assured—at least in the field of physics. He wondered how he was faring socially. Bill knew Nick was more than a little self-conscious about his appearance—the misshapen skull from when he was abused as an infant, the old acne scars. But a lot of worse-looking men had found the girl of their dreams and lived happily ever after. He hoped that would happen for Nick soon.

He turned back to the hole and stared into its black depths.

What was that Nietzsche quote? *If thou gaze into the abyss, the abyss will also gaze into thee.* That was how he now felt as he looked downward, as if he were gazing inward at his own reclusive darkness. The abyss expanded before him, beckoning. What mysteries, what horrors were sequestered in those misty, chaotic depths? For an instant he was gripped by a mad impulse to step off the edge and let himself fall. If it was truly bottomless as Glaeken had said, he would keep falling. And falling. Imagine the vistas, the wonders he'd see. What would he find? Himself? An endless voyage of self-discovery. How wonderful. How could anyone resist? How on earth could anyone with an iota of character refuse? How—?

"Better be careful, Father."

The voice jolted him out of the reverie. To his horror he found himself sitting astride the platform railing, readying to swing his other leg over. The depths loomed below. With a convulsive lunge, he hurled himself back onto the platform and squatted there panting, sweating, and shaking. He looked up and saw one of the city workers standing nearby, looking down at him.

"You okay, Father?"

"I will be in a minute."

"Hey, I din't mean t'scare ya, but I mean we built that railing as sturdy as we could, but it ain't gonna hold a guy your size, know what I mean?"

Bill nodded as he rose shakily to his feet.

"I realize that. Thanks for the warning." *Thanks more than you know.*

The workman waved and ambled off, leaving Bill alone on the platform. He pulled himself together and moved away from the edge.

What had happened a moment ago? What had he been doing sitting on that railing? Had he actually been readying to jump? What could he have been thinking?

Or had he been thinking at all? More like reacting—but to what? To the abyss?

Bill shuddered. Maybe coming down here hadn't been such a good idea. He'd seen the hole up close. He could watch further developments from Glaeken's window or on the tube. He looked around for Nick and saw him walking his way. His expression was troubled.

"What's wrong, Nick?"

" 'Technical difficulties,' as they say on TV. We'll have it straightened out in a few minutes."

Bill watched Nick's face closely. His upper lip was beaded with perspiration.

"You didn't get the reading you expected, did you."

"We didn't get *any* reading. A glitch in the receiver, that's all."

Bill allowed himself a quick shot of relief. He wanted very much for Nick to find the bottom of that hole. He wanted Glaeken to be wrong, just once. Not out of animosity or envy, but because Glaeken had been right about everything so far, and everything he was predicting was bad. Bill felt he'd be able to rest a little better at night if just once Glaeken was proven wrong.

And then a thought struck him like an icy wind, carrying off any sense of relief.

"Wait a minute, Nick. You said you didn't receive *any* signal. Isn't that what would happen if the hole was bottomless?"

"It's not bottomless, Fa—"

"*Isn't* that what would happen?"

"Well . . . yes. But that's not the only reason. There are scores of reasons why we wouldn't get a signal back."

"But one of them is that the beam didn't find anything to bounce off, and so therefore it never came back. Am I right?"

Nick sighed. "You're right." Suddenly he sounded tired. "But the hole's not bottomless. It can't be. Nothing's bottomless."

One of the grad students rushed up to Nick with a green- striped printout. Bill could tell from Nick's expression that he didn't like what he saw there. He handed the slip back to the student.

"Do it again. And do it right."

"But we are," the student said, looking offended. "Everything checks out a hundred percent. The beam and the receiver are working perfectly."

Nick tapped the printout. "Obviously not."

"Maybe something down there's absorbing the beam."

"Absorbing the beam," Nick said slowly. He seemed to like the idea. "Let's look into that." He turned to Bill. "I'm going to be tied up for awhile, Father, but hang around. We'll crack this yet." He winked and walked away.

Bill headed back to the apartment in mid-afternoon to grab a bite and make a pit stop before Nick started his descent.

He had to hand it to Nick—he was as inventive as he was stubborn. He wouldn't admit defeat. When Nick had heard there was a working diving bell on display down at South Street Seaport, he made a few calls and arranged to rent it. His plan was to get in that thing and ride it as far down into the hole as the cable would allow, then take another laser reading from down there. Bill wanted to be back in time to see him off.

He had to fight through the crowd on Central Park West. The area around the lower end of the park had become an impromptu street festival. Well, why not? The sun was out and the area was jammed with curious people. Anyone with anything to sell, from hot dogs to shishkebab, to balloons, to knock-off Rolexes was there. The air was redolent of a variety of ethnic foods wide enough to shame the U.N. cafeteria. He spotted someone hawking "I saw the Central Park Hole" tee-shirts, still wet from the silk screener.

In the apartment he found Glaeken, as expected, at the picture window.

"What have they decided down there?" the old man said without turning.

"They've decided that due to various technical glitches they can't figure out how deep it is at this time."

Even at noon, with the sun shining directly into the hole, they hadn't been able to see the bottom. The blackness had been driven further down, but it was still there, obscuring the bottom.

Now Glaeken turned. His smile was rueful.

"They've constructed these fabulous instruments for exact measurements, yet they refuse to believe the data they're receiving. Amazing how the mind resists the truth when the truth conflicts with preconceptions."

"I can't really blame them. It's not easy to accept the impossible."

"I suppose. But impossible is a useless word now." He turned back to the window. "What's that they're rigging up?"

"A derrick. Nick going down into the hole to—"

Glaeken spun and faced Bill. His eyes wide.

"You're talking about your young friend? He's going down into the hole?"

"Yes. As soon as the bell is set up."

Glaeken grabbed Bill's upper arms. His grip was like iron.

"Don't let him do it. You've got to stop him. Don't let him go into that hole!"

The look on his face made Bill afraid for Nick. Very afraid. He turned and ran for the door. Out in the hall, he pressed the elevator button. When the door didn't open immediately, he ran for the stairs. No time to wait for it. He made it down and out to the street in a few minutes, but there his progress came to a grinding halt. The crowd was even thicker. Pressing through them was like wading through taffy.

He fought a rising panic as he roughly pushed and shoved people aside, leaving an angry wake. He hadn't waited around to ask Glaeken what might happen to Nick down in that hole. The look on the old man's perpetually dead-pan face told him more than he wanted to know. He'd never seen Glaeken react that way.

As he inched his way toward the Sheep Meadow, he remembered Nick saying how lucky he felt to be here. But Bill couldn't help thinking what had happened to all those other people he cared about.

His gut writhed with the thought that perhaps luck had nothing to do with it.

"Lights, camera, action!" Nick said as the diving bell lurched into motion.

Dr. Dan Buckley gave him a wan smile and gripped one of the hand rungs. Buckley was an older gent, balding, white haired, sixty at least, from Geology. He had his video camcorder hooked up and directed out one of the forward ports; a 35mm Nikon hung from his neck. He was sweating. Nick wondered if Buckley was prone to panic attacks. The bell, named Trident, was the size of a small, low-ceilinged bathroom. Not a happy place for a claustrophobe.

His stomach did a little spin as the bell swung out over the hole. He'd never liked amusement park rides and this was starting out like one. He looked out the aft port to his right to double-check the laser range-finder mounted there. Everything looked secure. He glanced out the other port toward the crane and the crowd of cops and workers and various city officials and the other members of the teams from the university. He saw Father Bill push his way to the front and start jumping and waving and shouting. He'd been late coming back but at least he'd made it. Nick was glad to have him here to see this. He waved back and gave him a thumbs-up through the glass, then settled down for the ride.

This was great. This was fabulous. This was the most exciting thing that had ever happened to him.

"All set in there?" said a tinny voice from the speaker overhead.

"All set," Nick said. Buckley echoed the same.

There came a sick second of freefall, then they were on their way, lowered into the depths on a steel cable. They were soon out of the sunlight and into shadow. The alternating floodlights and spotlights ringing the bell's equator were already on, illuminating the near wall. Buckley was glued to his porthole snapping shot after shot of the passing strata with his Nikon.

"Can you hear us up there?" Nick said.

"Loud and clear, Trident," came the reply. *"How's it going down there?"*

"Smooth as can be. And fascinating. The city ought to consider buying this rig and making it into an amusement ride. Might keep taxes down."

He heard appreciative laughter from above and smiled. That sounded pretty cool and collected, didn't it? He hoped so. Cynthia Hayes was up there, watching and waiting with the others from the university. He hoped she'd heard it, hoped she was impressed. This little jaunt was going to make Nicholas Quinn, PhD. into a big name. The press would see to that. A mob of reporters was waiting up top, and he knew as soon as he stepped out of the bell they'd be all over him with a million questions. He'd be on all the news shows tonight, both the early and late. Maybe even the networks. Most guys in his spot would be figuring out how they could parlay this into a major step up in their career—

Nick could think of three from his own department right off. Nick almost laughed at his own narrow vision. He was wondering how he could parlay it into an opportunity to ask Cynthia out. If he was famous, how could she say no?

The intercom popped him out of a Cynthia daydream.

"You're at the half-way mark, Trident. How're you doing?"

"Fine," Nick said. "Can you still see us?"

"Yeah, but you're just a little blob of light down there now."

Half way. They had ten thousand feet of cable up there. Almost a mile down and still no bottom. This was incredible. What could have caused a hole like this? Could it be natural? Something extra-terrestrial maybe? Say, that was a thought. It did seem like an artifact. What if—?

Buckley's voice drew him back to reality again.

"Can we get these lights any brighter?" he said to the intercom.

"They're at max. What's the problem, Trident?"

"The wall's fading from view."

"You're out of sight now. Want to stop?"

Nick looked out his port. Black out there. The beams from the floodlights didn't seem to be going anywhere; the blackness swallowed their light within a few yards of the bulbs. The spots weren't doing much better—shafts of light poking a dozen or so feet into the darkness and then disappearing.

No, wait—ten feet into the darkness. No . . .

Nick swallowed hard. The darkness was edging in on the lights, overcoming, *devouring* the illumination.

"What's wrong with the lights?" Buckley said, his voice tremulous.

"I don't know," Nick said. His own voice didn't sound too steady either.

"They're losing power."

Nick didn't think so. It was the darkness out there. Something about it was overpowering the light, gobbling it up. Something thick and oily about it. The blackness seemed to move out there beyond the ports, almost seemed alive. Alive and hungry.

He shook himself. What kind of thinking was that?

But this blackness was certainly unusual, and probably the reason the laser signal had never returned. He smiled. Bottomless indeed! This weird old hole was deeper than it had any right to be, but it wasn't bottomless.

"We need more power to the lights!" Buckley said to the intercom.

It was pure black out there now. The lights were *gone*.

"You got it all, Trident. If there's an electrical problem we'll bring you back up and try again tomorrow."

"Not till I get at least one reading off the laser," Nick said.

He started flipping switches on the laser controls and noticed that his hands were trembling. It was suddenly cold in here. He glanced at Buckley as he fastened a flash attachment to his camera.

"You cold?"

Buckley nodded. "Yeah, now that you mention it." His breath steamed in the air. "You get your reading, I'll try a couple of flash shots through the ports, then we'll get back upstairs."

"You've got a deal."

Nick suddenly wanted very much to be out of this hole and into the sunlight again. He adjusted the laser settings, triggered it, and waited for the readout. And waited.

Nothing.

Buckley tried a few flash photos out his port while Nick rechecked his settings. Everything looked fine.

"This is useless!" Buckley said, irritably snatching his camera away from the glass. "Like black bean soup out there!"

Nick glanced out his port. The blackness seemed to press against the outer glass, as if it wanted to get in.

Nick fired the laser again. And again nothing. Nothing was coming back. Damn! Maybe the laser wasn't getting through the blackness or maybe the hole was indeed bottomless. Right now he was too cold to care.

"That does it." Nick said. "I'm through. Let's get out of here."

"Take us up!" Buckley shouted.

"Say again, Trident," said the speaker in the ceiling. *"We've got static on this end."*

Buckley repeated the message but no reply came through the speaker. The bell did not halt its descent.

Nick was frightened now. The walls of the Triton seemed to close in on him. And it was colder. And . . .

. . . darker?

"Did the lights just dim?" Buckley said.

Nick could only nod. His tongue felt glued to the roof of his mouth.

"Take us up, goddammit!" Buckley screamed, banging on the steel wall of the bell with his fist. *"Up!"*

"Okay, Triton," came the matter-of-fact reply. *"Will do."*

But they didn't stop, didn't even slow their descent. It was down, ever downward.

And it was getting darker by the second.

"Oh, my God, Quinn!" Buckley said in a hushed voice teetering on the edge of panic. "What's happening?"

Finally Nick found his voice. He tried to keep it calm as the cold and the darkness grew . . . and Buckley began to fade from view.

"I don't know. But one thing I do know is we've got to stay calm. Something's wrong with the intercom up there. But they've only got so much cable. They can only send us down so far, and then they'll have to bring us up. So let's just be cool and hang in there and we'll be okay."

Darkness had control of the Triton now, within and without. Nick couldn't see his hand in front of his face. He was losing his sense of direction, of up and down. His stomach threatened to heave.

"Quinn?" Buckley's voice seemed to come from some point outside the walls of the bell. "You still there?"

Nick forced a laugh. "No. I just stepped outside for a cigarette."

And suddenly there was more than darkness between them. Something solid. An entity, a *presence*. Beside him, around him, touching him. And it was cold and evil and filled Nick with an unnameable dread that threatened to kick his bowels loose in his pants. He wanted to cry, he wanted Father Bill, he wanted to go home, he wanted the drugged-up mother who'd tried to kick his head in when he was three-months old, *anything* but this!

And then Buckley's flash went off and they both screamed out their souls when they saw what had moved in to share the bell with them.

"Everything's fine. Don't reel us in yet. Play the cable out to the end."

Bill heard the voice over the loudspeaker and froze. That wasn't Nick's voice. And it wasn't the other scientist's either. It was a new voice—different.

He scanned the faces in the control area. No one was reacting. What was wrong with them? It was a different voice! Couldn't they hear that?

Something familiar about it too. He'd heard it before, but where? The answer was tantalizingly close. And then he heard it again.

"That's it," said the loudspeaker in that same voice. *"Just keep us going down."*

Suddenly Bill knew. And the realization nearly drove him to his knees.

Rafe! It was Rafe's voice! Rafe, Jimmy Stevens, Rasalom, whatever his name was, it was him! The one Glaeken called the Enemy. The one who was shrinking the daylight, who'd dug this huge worm hole in the earth. He'd tortured Bill for years in many forms and many voices, and the voice on that speaker was the one he'd used as Rafe Losmara. There was no mistaking it. Its sound still echoed through his dreams. The Enemy was in that diving bell—and God knew what he was doing to Nick!

Bill forced his wobbly legs into a run toward the control area.

"Bring them up!" he cried. "Bring them up *now!*"

The scientists and technicians started at the sound of his shouts. They looked at him as if he was crazy.

"Who the hell are you?" someone said.

"A friend of Nick Quinn's. And that wasn't his voice just then. Couldn't you hear that?"

"Of course it was Nick's voice," said a thirtyish woman with short brown hair. "I've worked with him for years and that was Nick."

Beside her, an older man with perfectly combed hair nodded in agreement. "That was Nick, all right."

"I'm telling you it wasn't. Reel them back up, dammit! Something's happening in there! Get them up!"

Someone grabbed his arms from behind and he heard a mix of voices talking over and under each other: *Who is he? ... Get security ... Says he's a friend of Nick's ... I don't care if he's Quinn's mother, get him out of here!*

Bill was hustled away from the control area. The security guards were going to take him back to the edge of the Sheep Meadow but he pleaded with them to let him stay near the hole, swore that he wouldn't say another word or go near the control area again. The Roman collar and cassock paid off again. They let him stay.

But it was torture to stand there and listen to that voice tell them to send the bell further and further into the hole. Did it sound like Nick to everyone else? Was he the only one who could hear the Rafe-voice? Why? Another game being played with his head?

Damn you!

He wanted to scream, to charge the derrick cab and wrest the controls from the operator and drag that bell back up to the light. But he had about as much chance of succeeding in that as he had of leaping to the far side of the hole itself. So he stood among the crowd of privileged onlookers and silently endured the clawed terror that lacerated the inner walls of his heart.

Finally, the cable reached its end. No matter what the voice told them, the bell could descend no further.

But the voice was silent.

Bill noticed a flurry of activity in the control area. He sidled in that direction through the crowd. He intercepted a student hurrying away from the area and caught his arm.

"What's happening?"

"The Triton—they're not answering!"

Bill let him go and stood there feeling cold and frightened and useless as the derrick reversed its gears and began to reel in the Triton at top speed. The rewind seemed to take forever. During the interval an ambulance and an EMS van roared into the Sheep Meadow with their howlers going full blast. Finally the bell hove into view again. When it was swung away from the hole and settled onto the platform near the edge, the people from the control area surged toward it.

Bill pushed his way to the front of the crowd until his belly pressed against one of the wooden "Police Line" horses that rimmed the area. He watched them spin the winged lug nuts on the hatch, swing it open, and peer inside.

Somebody screamed. Bill clutched the rough wooden plank of the horse and felt his heart double its already mad pounding. A flurry of activity erupted around the bell, people running for phones, frantically waving the EMS van forward. Good God, something had happened to Nick! He'd never forgive himself for not getting here in time to stop him from going down.

A pair of EMTs, stethoscopes around their necks, drug boxes and life packs in each hand, rushed forward as a limp figure was eased through the hatch. Bill craned his neck to see through the throng. He sighed with relief when he saw that the injured man was white haired and balding. Not Nick, thank God. The other one. They stretched him out prone on the platform and began pumping on his chest.

But where was Nick?

Bill spotted more activity around the hatch. They were carrying—no, *leading*—someone else out. It was Nick. Nick, thank God! He was on his feet, coming out under his own steam.

Then Bill got a look at his face. Red. There was blood on his face, on his lips. Blood dribbled down his chin. He'd cut his lower lip—looked more like he'd *chewed* it. But it was Nick's eyes that drove the air from Bill's lungs in a cry of horror. They were wide open and utterly vacant. Whatever he'd seen down there, whatever had happened, it had driven away all intelligence and sanity, sent it fleeing into hiding in the deepest, most obscure corners of his mind.

"Nick!" Bill cried.

He bent to slip under the barricade but one of the security cops was watching him.

"Stay back there, Father!" he warned. "You come through there an' I'll have to toss you in the wagon."

Bill ground his teeth in frustration but straightened up behind the barricade. He'd be no help to Nick in jail. And Nick was going to need him.

He stood quietly as they led a stumbling, drooling Nick Quinn to the waiting ambulance. Those mad, empty eyes. What had he seen down there?

And then, as Nick came even with him, his eyes suddenly focused. He turned his head to stare at Bill. Then he grinned—a wide, bloody-mouthed rictus, totally devoid of humor. Bill started in horror, pressing back against the people behind him. And then as suddenly as it had appeared, the grimace was gone. The light faded from Nick's eyes and he stumbled on, away from Bill, toward the waiting ambulance.

Bill watched a moment, weak, trembling, then he fought through the crowd and began to follow the ambulance on foot as it headed east across the grass. Finally he saw the name on its side: Columbia-Presbyterian. He ran for Fifth Avenue, looking for a cab to take him to the hospital, all the while fighting the feeling that he'd lived through this horror once already. He didn't know if he could survive a second round.

WNEW-FM:
FREDDY: *Bad news from Central Park, folks. Those two guys who went down into that big hole in a diving bell ran into some trouble.*

JO: *Yeah. One of them had a heart attack and the other got pretty sick. They're saying they think there was some problem with the air supply. We'll let you know more about it as soon as we hear.*

FREDDY: *Right. Meanwhile, here's a classic Beatles tune for all those people working out there in the Sheep Meadow.*

Cue: "Fixing a Hole"

"When's this other fellow arriving?"

"I'm not sure," Glaeken said.

He looked up from the couch at Repairman Jack standing at the picture window staring out at the Park. Everyone who came to his apartment was drawn to that window, including Glaeken himself. The vista had always been breathtaking. With that hole in the Sheep Meadow now, it was captivating.

Jack intrigued him. He wore slightly wrinkled beige slacks and a light blue shirt with the sleeves rolled half-way up his forearms. Average height, dark brown hair with a low hairline, and deceptively mild brown eyes. You would not pick him out of a crowd; in fact his manner of dress, his whole demeanor was geared toward unobtrusiveness. This man could dog your steps all day long and you'd never notice him.

Glaeken liked Jack, felt a rapport with him on a very fundamental level. Perhaps because Jack reminded him of himself in another era, another epoch, when he was that age. A warrior. He sensed the strength coiled within the man; not mere physical strength, although he knew there was plenty of that in his wiry muscles, but inner strength. A toughness, a resolve to see a task through to the end. He had the strength, too, to question himself, to examine his motives and actions and wonder at the wisdom, the sanity of the life he had chosen for himself.

Glaeken wondered if Jack might prove to be the one he was seeking.

He saw a downside to Jack, though. He was unruly and untamed. He recognized no master, no authority over himself. He followed his own code. And he was angry. Too angry, perhaps. At times the cold fire of his rage fairly lit the room.

Still, Glaeken desperately needed his services. Jack was the only one in this world who had any chance of retrieving the ancient necklaces. Glaeken knew he had to tread carefully with this man, and be at his most convincing.

"How long are we going to wait for him?" Jack said, turning from the window.

"He should be here by now. I have a feeling he might have been delayed by a sick friend."

Glaeken had watched on TV as the diving bell had returned from the depths of the hole. It continually amazed him how much one could experience through television without ever leaving the living room. When the first footprints were stamped into the surface of the moon, he had been there watching via television, just as he had been watching an hour or so ago when Bill's friend and the other scientist had been removed from the bell. The other man, a Dr. Buckley, was dead of cardiac arrest, and Dr. Quinn had been rushed to an emergency room in shock. Glaeken assumed that Bill had followed.

Too bad—for Bill's friend and because Glaeken had wanted Bill and Jack to meet, perhaps become friends. He'd have to save that for another time.

Jack dropped into a chair opposite Glaeken.

"Let's get on with it, then. You mentioned the necklaces again. You're not still set on getting ahold of them, are you?"

"Yes. I'm afraid they're an absolute necessity."

"To prevent 'the end of life as we know it,' right?"

"Correct."

Jack rose from the chair and stepped to the window again.

"I still say you're crazy," he said, looking down at the Park again. "But the damn Park *is* smaller, isn't it? I mean, it's lost whatever amount of surface area that hole swallowed. So it *has* shrunk, just like you said." He turned and stared at Glaeken. "How did you know that hole was going to open up?"

"Lucky guess."

"Yeah. Right. But you're going to need more than a lucky guess to find Kolabati and those necklaces."

"I've learned exactly where she is."

Jack sat down again.

"Where?"

"She's living on Maui, on the northwest slope of Haleakala, above Kula. And she has both necklaces with her."

"How'd you find that out? Two nights ago you hadn't the faintest idea where she was."

"I ran into an old acquaintance who happened to know."

"How convenient."

"Not really. I sought out this acquaintance."

Glaeken allowed himself a tight little smile and said no more. Let Jack assume that the acquaintance was a person. He could hardly tell him about the *Dat-tay-vao*, at least not at this juncture. He wasn't ready for it. But the truth was that when he had touched that boy Jeffy yesterday, he had made contact with the *Dat-tay-vao*, and in a flash that contact revealed the location of the necklaces. For the *Dat-tay-vao* always knew the whereabouts of the necklaces. They had been intimately linked once. Hopefully, with the co-operation of men like Repairman Jack, they would soon be reunited.

"And you want me to go there and convince Kolabati to give them up so she can turn into an old hag and die as a result."

"I want you to get them. Simply get them."

"Well, since she won't part with them willingly, I'll have to steal them. I'm not a thief, Mr. Veilleur."

"But you do steal things back for people, don't you?"

Jack leaned back in the chair and tapped his fingers on the arms.

"On occasion."

"Very well: those necklaces—or rather, the metal they were made from—originally belonged to me."

Jack shook his head slowly. "Uh-uh. That won't fly. I know for a fact that those necklaces date from pre-Vedic times, and that they've been in her family for generations. And believe me, hers is a family with *long* generations."

"Still, it is true. The source material was stolen from me long, long ago."

Jack's eyes narrowed. "You're telling me you're a couple of thousand years old?"

Glaeken sensed that he had pushed Jack's credulity to its limits. The whole truth might make him walk out again as he had from the tavern the other night. Probably wise to back off a step for now.

"Let's just say, then, that some time in the dim past a member of her family stole it from a member of mine. Will that do?"

Jack rubbed his eyes and shook his head as if to clear it.

"Why do I believe you?"

"Because I'm telling you the truth." *Or something reasonably close to it.*

"All right," Jack said after a lengthy pause. "I'll think about it. I'm not committing yet. I could use some detailed drawings of the necklaces, though. Got any?"

"I can have them for you tomorrow. Why?"

"That's my business." He rose to his feet. "You know my fee, and it doesn't look like you'll have any trouble meeting it, so—"

"Fee? I assumed you'd do this because you want to."

"Now why would I want to?"

"Your own self-interest. That hole out there is only the first. Many more holes will follow—*countless* holes. Those necklaces will go a long way toward stopping them."

Jack smiled. "Sure. Look, Mr. V. I'm in business, but it's not the business of saving the world. I'll be by tomorrow to pick up the drawings. *And* the down payment. See you then."

"It's almost sundown," Glaeken said as Jack headed for the door. "Go straight home."

Jack laughed. "Why? Vampires on the loose?"

"No," Glaeken said. "Worse. Do not go out after dark, especially near that hole."

Jack just smiled and waved at the door.

Glaeken hoped Jack heeded him. He truly liked the man; and he needed him. He didn't want him killed.

WPIX-TV

This is Charles Burge reporting live from the Sheep Meadow in Central Park. It's been quiet here since the tragedy this afternoon, but that doesn't mean nothing's been happening. If you look behind me you'll notice that the crowds are gone. That's because along about 5:30 or so, the downdraft that's been flowing into the hole changed to an updraft. And boy, let me tell you, it doesn't smell good here. A rotten odor permeates the air. Anyone who doesn't have to be here has gone. And I'll be going too. See you in the studio soon, Warren.

2 • DE PROFUNDIS

Washington Heights

"Physically, he checks out fine," the neurology resident said. "Overweight, cholesterol and triglycerides on the high side, otherwise, all his numbers, scans, and reflexes check out."

Bill swallowed and asked the dreaded question that had plagued him since he'd seen Nick's blank expression and empty eyes. It reminded him too much of a similar case five or so years ago.

"He's . . . he's not hollow, is he?"

The resident gave him a funny look. "*Hollow?* No, he's not hollow. Where'd you get an idea like that?"

"Never mind. Just a recurring nightmare. Go on."

"Right. As I was saying, he checks out physically, but"—he waved his hand before Nick's unresponsive eyes—"the Force is definitely not with him."

The name-tag read *R. O'Neill, M.D.* He wore an earring and his hair was braided at the back.

Not exactly Marcus Welby, Bill thought, but he seemed to know what he was about.

"He's in shock," Bill said.

"Well . . . shock to you isn't shock to me. Shock to me means he's prostrate, his blood pressure's hit bottom, his kidneys are shutting down, and so on. That's not our friend here."

Bill glanced over to where Nick sat on the edge of the bed. He'd trailed the ambulance up here to Columbia Presbyterian Medical Center. The emergency-room physicians and the consultants had unanimously recommended at the very least that he be kept overnight for observation. The university had wrangled a private room for him, very much like a sitting room, with a small picture window, a sofa, a couple of chairs, and of course, a hospital bed. Nick looked a lot better. His lower lip had been sutured; he'd been cleaned up and fitted into a hospital gown. But his eyes were still as vacant as a drive-in theater on a sunny afternoon.

"What's wrong with him, then?"

"Hysteria. Acute withdrawal. That's for the Psych boys to figure out. I'm here to say it's not medical, not neurological. It's the windmills of his mind—they aren't turning."

"Thank you for that astute observation," Bill said. "How about the other man who went down in the bell with him?"

Dr. O'Neill shrugged. "Haven't heard a thing."

"He's dead, you know."

Bill started at the sound. It was Nick. His eyes weren't exactly focused, but they weren't completely empty. And he wasn't grinning as he had before when they were leading him to the ambulance. His expression was neutral. Still, the sound of Nick's voice, so flat and expressionless, gave him a chill. Especially since there was no way Nick could know Dr. Buckley's condition.

"Great!" said Dr. O'Neill. "He's coming around already." He picked up Nick's chart and headed for the door. "I'll make a few notes and let Psych know."

Bill wanted to stop him, make him stay, but didn't know how. He didn't want to be alone with Nick. A moment later he was.

"Dr. Buckley's dead," Nick repeated.

Bill came around the bed and stood in front of him—but not too close.

"How do you know?"

Nick's brow furrowed. "I don't know. I just know he's dead."

The fact didn't seem to bother Nick and he sat silent for a a long moment. Abruptly he spoke again in that affectless voice.

"He wants to hurt you, you know."

"Who? Dr. Buckley?"

"No. *Him.*"

The room suddenly seemed cooler.

"Who are you talking about? The one you . . . met down there?"

A nod. "He hates you, Father Bill. There's one other he hates more than you, one he wants to hurt more than you, but he hates you terribly."

Bill reached back, found a chair, and lowered himself into it.

"Yes, I know. I've been told."

"Are you going to stay with me tonight?"

"Yes. Sure. If they'll let me."

"They'll let you. It's good that you're going to stay tonight."

Bill remembered the bespectacled nine-year-old orphan who used to be afraid of the dark but would never admit it.

"I'll stay as long as you need me."

"Not for me. For you. It's going to be dangerous out there."

Bill turned and looked out the window. The sun was down, the city's lights were beginning to sparkle through the growing darkness. He turned back to Nick.

"What do you—"

Nick was gone. He was still sitting on the bed, but he wasn't really there. His eyes had gone empty and his mind had slipped back into hiding.

But what *of* his mind? What did it know about Rasalom—the Enemy? And *how* did it know? Was Nick somehow tapped into a part of Rasalom as a result of whatever happened in that hole?

Bill shuddered and gently pushed Nick back to a reclining position on the bed. He didn't envy Nick if that were true. Simply to brush the hem of that sickness would mean madness . . .

And that was precisely where Nick was now, wasn't he?

Bill stood over Nick's bed, wondering if he should stay. How much could he do for Nick? Not much. But at least he could be here for him if he came around again, or came out of this mental fugue and wanted to know where he was and what had—

Something *splat*ted against the window.

Bill turned and saw what looked like a softball-sized glob of mucous pressed against the outer surface of the glass. It began to move—sideways.

Curious, he stepped closer. As he neared he heard an angry buzzing through the glass. The glob appeared to be encased in a thin membrane, red-laced with fine, pulsating blood vessels. It left a trail of moisture as it slid slowly across the glass. But the buzzing—it seemed to be coming from the glob.

Bill picked up a lamp from an end table and held it close to the window. He spotted a fluttering blur on the far side of the glob. Wings? He angled the lamp. Yes, wings—translucent, at least a foot long, fluttering like mad. And eyes. A cluster of four multi-faceted eyes at the end of a wasp-like body the size of a jumbo shrimp, lined with rows of luminescent dots. Eight articulated arms terminating in small pincers were stretched across the mucous-filled membrane.

"What the hell?" Bill muttered as he followed its progress across the pane.

He'd never seen or heard of anything like this creature. He felt his hackles rise. This thing was alien, like something out of a Geiger painting.

It reached the end of the picture pane and slid over the frame toward one of the double-hung windows that flanked it. Bill realized with a start that the side window was open. He was reaching out to close it when the creature lunged toward him. Bill snatched his hand away and watched as it buzzed furiously against the screen, as if trying to squeeze itself through the mesh. A foul, rotten odor from the thing backed him up a step. He slammed down the inner sash and watched through the glass. The creature hung on another minute or so, then dropped off, swooping away into the night, leaving a wet spot on the screen that steamed slightly in the cooling air.

Shaken, Bill shut the other double hung and turned down the lights. He pulled a chair up next to Nick's bed and readied himself for a long, uncomfortable night. He'd decided to take Nick's advice and stay. At least until sunrise.

WINS-AM

—now official that the sun set early for the third day in a row. It dropped below the western horizon at 7:11 p.m., robbing us of nearly two hours of daylight. The scientific community is becoming increasingly alarmed about the environmental effects of the shortened days. In a statement . . .

Sutton Square

"Sure," Gia said as she kissed him at the door to her townhouse. "Eat and run."

Jack returned the kiss and ran his fingertips through her short blonde hair.

"I've got an appointment at Julio's."

Her clear blue eyes flashed. "Another one of your customers?"

"Yeah. Another." She opened her mouth to speak but he pressed a finger across her full lips. "Don't start. Please."

In the past few years Gia seemed to have learned to accept the life he lived as Repairman Jack, but she still didn't like it, and she tended to let him know at every opportunity.

She kissed his finger and pulled it away.

"I wasn't going to say anything about that. I was just going to say that I wish you could stay."

"I do too. I wish we could move in together and—"

She smiled and pressed her finger against his lips.

"Don't *you* start."

Jack slipped his arms around her waist and pressed her slim body against him. Two people who loved each other should be able to live together. But Gia was hanging tough on her insistence that Jack find himself another line of work before she and Vicky moved in with him.

Vicky. The other bright spot in his life. The skinny little nine-year old who'd wormed her way into his heart years ago and refused to leave.

He ran his hands over Gia's back and noticed the muscles were tight. He knew she was a high-strung sort, but tonight she seemed unusually tense.

"Something wrong?"

"I don't know. I've feel jumpy. Like something's going to happen."

"Something already has. You saw the news: the sun set another couple of minutes early and a big chunk of Central Park fell all the way to hell."

"That's not it. Something in the air. Don't you feel it?"

Jack did feel it. A pervasive imminence in the still darkness at his back. The very air seemed heavy, pregnant with menace.

"It's probably all these strange things that've been happening."

"Maybe. But I don't want to be alone with Vicky tonight. Especially here. Can you come back later?"

Jack knew that the Sutton Square townhouse held both fond and frightening memories for Gia and Vicky. He'd convinced her to move in for economic reasons and because it seemed plain foolish to let such a beautiful home sit empty for all the years the Westphalen estate would be tied up in probate.

"Sure. Be glad to. I shouldn't be too—"

"Jack-Jack-Jack!"

Over Gia's shoulder Jack could see Vicky running down the hall, a piece of paper in her hand. She had her mother's blue eyes and her late father's brown hair, tied back in a long ponytail that flicked back and forth as she ran. Bony limbs and a dazzling smile that could pull Jack from his blackest moods.

"What is it, Vicks?"

"I drew you a picture."

Vicky had inherited her mother's artistic abilities and was heavily into drawing. Jack took the proffered sheet of paper and stared at it. A swarm of tentacled things filled the air over the Manhattan skyline. It was . . . disturbing.

"It's great, Vicks," Jack said, smiling through his discomfiture. "Is this from *War of the Worlds*?"

"No. It's raining octopuses!"

"Yeah . . . I guess it is. What made you think of that?"

"I don't know," she said, wrinkling her brow. "It just came to me."

"Well, thanks, Vicks," Jack said, rolling it up into a tube. "I'll add it to my Victoria Westphalen collection."

She beamed and flashed him that smile. "Because it's going to be worth a lot when I'm famous, right?"

"You got it kid. You're going to help me retire."

Jack gave her a kiss and a hug, then another quick kiss for Gia.

"I'll be back later."

Gia gave his hand a squeeze of thanks, then he was out on the street, walking west.

As he headed up 58th, Mr. Veilleur's final words of the afternoon echoed in his head.

Do not go out after dark, especially near that hole.

Why the hell not? The warning was like a waving red flag. And since he'd have to pass the Park on his way to Julio's . . .

The area around the Sheep Meadow looked deserted compared to this afternoon. The party was over.

Maybe it was the smell.

Jack caught his first whiff of it as he passed the Plaza. Something rotten, putrid. He wasn't the only one. The hotel guests emerging from their cabs and limos, or strolling down the steps from the entrances, wrinkled their noses as it struck them. He'd thought maybe a nearby sewer had backed up, but the odor had grown stronger as he entered the Park.

And here in the Sheep Meadow it was thick.

Banks of floodlights lit the hole and the surrounding area like home plate at Yankee Stadium. As he watched he thought he saw something like a pigeon fly up from the hole, darting through the light and into the darkness beyond. But it moved awfully fast for a pigeon.

Jack spotted a middle-aged woman crossing the grassy buffer zone between officialdom and the hoi poloi; he moved laterally to intercept her.

"Is that stink coming from the hole?" he said as she ducked under the barricade. The answer was obvious but it was a good opener.

She wore a plastic badge that flopped around as she walked. Her first name looked like Margaret; he couldn't make out her last but he caught the words "Health" and "Department" above it. Her tan slacks and blue blazer had a distinctly masculine cut.

"It's not coming from me."

Ooh, a friendly one.

"I hope not. Smells like something crawled into my nose and died."

She smiled. "That pretty well captures it."

"Seriously," Jack said, matching her stride as she headed toward the street. "When did it start? There was a downdraft into the hole last night."

She glanced sideways at him. "How'd you know about that?"

"I was here when it opened."

"We already have plenty of witnesses. If you want to make a statement—"

"I'm just curious about the stink."

"Oh. Well, the downdraft became an updraft shortly after sunset. We started noticing the odor about an hour later. It's almost unbearable at the edge."

"I thought I saw something fly out of there a few moments ago."

Margaret nodded. "There's been a few. We're toying with the idea of trying to net one, but we've got other concerns at the moment. We think they might be birds that flew in during the day. Maybe the smell is driving them out. But don't worry. The smell's not toxic."

"That's hard to believe."

"Believe it. We've checked it out eight ways from—"

Screams and shouts rose from behind them. They both turned. Jack saw a flock of bird-like things swarming in the air over the hole. No . . . not just swarming—swooping and diving at the people working along the perimeter.

"Oh, my God!" Margaret said and started running back toward the hole.

Jack kept pace. He wanted to get a closer look—but not too close. Those birds appeared to be going crazy, like something out of the Hitchcock movie.

Only they weren't birds. Jack realized that when they got to within fifty yards of the hole.

"Whoa!" he said, grabbing Margaret's arm. "I don't like the looks of this."

She pulled away.

"My reports! All my test data! They'll be ruined!"

Jack slowed his pace and hung back as she ran off toward one of the control tents. He stood in the shadows and tried to identify those *things* filling the air . . . more like insects than birds. They must have come out of the hole. He sure as hell hadn't seen anything like them around New York. Two kinds darting around on dragonfly wings, some with big, pendulous translucent sacks like water balloons filled with clear jello, looking too heavy and ungainly for flight, others that were mostly mouth, little more than giant, fanged jaws attached to lobster-sized, wasp-waisted bodies. Both had strips of neon-like dots along their flanks. They looked like those weird deep-sea fish that show up every so often in *National Geographic*, the ones from miles down where the sun never shines. Only these were right here in Central Park. And they were flying.

Screams of pain and terror drew his attention from the air to ground level. Suddenly everything was red in the false daylight of the lamps. Jack dropped to a frozen crouch when he saw what was happening along the periphery of the hole. The things weren't just buzzing the people stationed there, they were on the attack. People were scattering in all directions, swatting at the air like picnickers who'd disturbed a hornets' nest. But hornets would have been a blessing. The jawed things were like air-borne piranhas, swooping in, sinking their teeth into an arm, a leg, a neck, an abdomen, ripping a mouthful of flesh free, and then darting away. Blood spurted in all directions from a hundred wounds.

Amid the melee Jack saw a baldheaded man go down kicking and screaming under a dozen jaw-things; a second dozen joined the first, and then more until they covered him like ants on a piece of candy. Instinctively, Jack stepped forward to help him, then stepped back. There was nothing he could do. He watched helplessly as the man's screaming and kicking stopped, but the feeding went on.

Jack turned, ready to head for the street, when he noticed a bloated, distorted, vaguely human shape stumbling through the shadows in his direction. It gave off hoarse, high-pitched, muffled noises as it approached, its arms outstretched, reaching for him. At first Jack thought it was another sort of monstrosity from the hole, but as it drew nearer he realized there was something familiar about the swatches of tan fabric visible on its legs.

The horror slammed into Jack like a truck. Margaret—from the Health Department. But what—?

The other things from the hole, the ones with the jello sacks—she was covered with them. Wings humming, sacks pulsating, a good thirty or forty of the creatures clung to every part of her body. Jack leapt to her side and began tearing at the things, grabbing them by their wings and ripping them off, starting with the pair that clung to her face. Her scream of agony tore through the night and Jack stared in horror at the bloody ruin of her face. There wasn't much left of it. It looked melted, or corroded by acid. Her cheeks were eaten away, so deeply on the right that Jack spotted the exposed white of a tooth poking through.

He stepped back and looked at the two creatures squirming and writhing in his grasp, raking at his hands with their tiny claws. Their sacks were no longer clear. They were red—with Margaret's blood. He hurled them to the ground and stomped on them, rupturing their sacks. Crimson mucous exploded, smoking where it splattered his pants and sneakers, eating through the fabric and bubbling the rubber. Jack danced away from the mess and turned back to Margaret.

She was gone. He looked around. She couldn't have got far. Then he saw her, a still form face-down on the grass. He crouched beside her. As he reached toward her, one of the sack things lifted off her back, leaving a bloody patch of exposed ribs, denuded of flesh and muscle, and fluttered toward Jack. He tried to bat it away but it latched onto his forearm like a lump of epoxy glue. And the *pain*! Scalding—like boiling acid poured on his skin. It took Jack by surprise and he shouted with the sudden agony. He ripped it off his arm and as it came free he felt a layer of his skin peel away.

The pain nearly drove him to his knees, but he straightened up when he saw one of the jawed creatures winging toward him. He swung the sack thing at it, right into its jagged-toothed maw. The pair left a trail of steaming red as they went down in a tangle and rolled along the grass.

Jack glanced back at the perimeter of the hole. Nothing moving there but flocks of jaws and sacks swarming in the air. Many of the sacks were blood red. As he watched, a new drove rose from the hole and circled for a moment, then massed into a rough V-formation and took off toward the east side like a flying arrowhead.

East! Gia and Vicky were on the East Side.

As the remaining creatures spread out, some heading Jack's way, he took one last look at Margaret. The sack things were still massed on her. She looked deflated, like a scarecrow with the stuffing pulled out.

Jack headed for the trees, removing his shirt and wrapping it around the raw patch on his left forearm. He spotted the lights of the Tavern on the-Green and veered in that direction. When he reached the driveway, he saw a cab pulling away from the entrance. He flagged it down and hopped in the back.

"Sutton Square—quick! And roll up your windows!"

The driver turned in his seat and stared at Jack's arm. He was a thin black with dreads and a thick island accent.

"What hoppen to you arm, mon? If you in trouble—"

Jack rolled up the window on his right and began to work furiously on the one to his left.

"Roll up your goddam windows!"

"Look, mon. You don't come into my cab and tell me—Hey!"

Jack had leaned over the front seat and was rolling up the window on the passenger side.

"Are you crazy, mon?"

Just then one of the jaw-things caromed off the taxi's hood and slammed against the windshield. It's crystalline teeth worked furiously against the glass, scoring it in a dozen places at a time. A windshield wiper got caught in its maw and was ripped off its base.

It took the driver only a second or two to roll up his window.

"In the name of God, what is *that?*"

"I don't know," Jack said, slumping against the back seat and allowing himself to relax for a few seconds. "They came out of the hole—they're *still* coming out of the hole. The Park's loaded with them."

The jaw-thing continued its ferocious, mindless chewing at the windshield, trying to get through it. The driver stared at it in mute shock.

Jack slapped the back of the front seat.

"Come on! Let's get out of here. It'll only get worse. Sutton Square."

"Yes . . . yes, of course."

He threw the cab into gear and roared toward Central Park West. The jaw-thing's wings fluttered in the sudden rush of air. It slid off the hood but became air-borne, pacing the cab for about fifty yards, butting against the side windows a few times before it gave up.

"Persistent bugger," Jack said as it finally flew off.

"But what *was* that, mon? It looked like a creature from hell!"

"It just might be. Who knows how far down that hole in the Sheep Meadow goes? Maybe it popped through the roof of hell."

The driver glanced over his shoulder, real fear in his eyes.

"Don't say that, mon. Don't joke about something like that."

"Who's joking?"

They raced down to Columbus Circle, then east on Central Park South. The things from the hole were there ahead of them. People running, screaming, bleeding, dying, cabs careening out of control. Jack's taxi ran the gauntlet, dodging people and vehicles, screeching to a halt as a driverless Central Park hansom cab bolted in front of them, its horse galloping madly, eyes bulging in pain and terror, a sack-thing attached to its neck. And then they were into the calm and relative darkness of 58th Street.

The driver started sobbing.

"It's the end of the world, mon! Oh, I know it is! God's finally had enough. He's going to punish us all!"

"Easy, man," Jack said. "We're safe for the moment."

"Yes! But only for the moment! Judgment Day is here!"

He stopped at a red light and fumbled with something on the seat next to him. When his hand reappeared it held a joint the size of a burrito. He struck a wooden match and puffed furiously. As the cab filled with pungent smoke, he handed the joint back to Jack.

"Here. Partake."

Jack waved him off. "No thanks. Gave that up in high school."

"It's a sacrament, mon. Partake."

The last thing Jack needed now was to get mellow. He wanted every reflex at the ready. And he wanted to beat those things to Gia's place.

"The light's green. Let's go."

Two minutes later he was flipping the driver a ten and leaping to the front door of the townhouse. He rang the bell and slammed the brass knocker. Gia pulled the door open.

"Jack! What—?"

"No time!" He brushed by her. "Get the windows! Close and lock them, all of them! Vicky! Help us out!"

A lot of running, a lot of slamming, and all three floors were sealed up tight. Jack checked and rechecked each window personally. Then he gathered Gia and Vicky together in the library.

"Jack!" Gia said, clutching a very frightened Vicky against her. "You've got to explain this!"

He did. He told them all that had happened since he'd left here a short while ago, editing out the more horrific details for Vicky's sake.

"What does it mean, Jack?" Gia said, pulling Vicky even closer.

He thought of what Veilleur had said about hundreds, thousands of these holes opening up all over the world.

. . . the end of life as we know it . . .

"I'm not sure—at least not about the big picture. I do know that an old guy over on the West Side is going to get a Repairman Jack freebie."

He remembered that flock of hole creatures zooming off so purposefully toward the east. They hadn't come to Sutton Square. Maybe they'd continued further on. Where were they headed—Long Island?

Monroe, Long Island

"Mommy! Look at this bug!"

Sylvia heard Jeffy calling her from somewhere in the house. She tamped down the fresh soil around roots of one of her *bankan* bonsai—the one with the four-curved trunk—and followed the sound of his voice from the greenhouse to the kitchen, wiping the dirt from her hands as she moved. Bugs in the kitchen? She didn't like the sound of that. She became aware of an unsettling odor as she approached it.

She found a plate of cookies half-eaten on the butcher block kitchen table. Gladys, the cook and housekeeper, always left Jeffy a snack before she went home. Jeffy was standing at the back door, pointing up at the screen.

"See it, Mom? It looks like a giant booger!"

As much as Sylvia hated to admit it, Jeffy was right. What appeared to be a big glob of mucous with legs and buzzing wings was clinging to the outside of the screen.

She heard a growl. Old Phemus, their one-eyed mongrel, was crouched by the dishwasher, ears back, tail tucked under him, snarling at the thing on the screen.

"What's the matter, old boy?" she said, patting his head. "Never seen anything like that either, huh?"

As bizarre as the thing was, Sylvia was almost glad to see it. This was one of the few times since yesterday morning that Jeffy had shown any real interest in something besides that Mr. Veilleur. He'd talked about the man incessantly since his visit the other day. Jeffy seemed utterly infatuated with him, repeatedly asking when he was coming back or when Sylvia could take him to see the old man. Sylvia kept putting him off, saying "We'll see" instead of no, hoping the boy's fixation would pass. In the meantime, any distraction was welcome.

Sylvia wrinkled her nose. Whatever this creature was, it *stunk*. A part of her immediately loathed the thing, but her curiosity edged her forward. Some of its mucous appeared to be oozing through the mesh of the screen. She leaned closer and heard Phemus whine.

"It's all right, boy."

She reached out a finger to—

A hand grabbed her by the shoulder and pulled her back. She whirled and saw Ba. Sylvia stared in shock at the giant Vietnamese. He never touched her, not even to help her out of the car. He looked paler than usual, and he was sweating.

"Ba? What's wrong?"

"Please, Missus, no. Terrible sorry, but you mustn't touch it."

"I wasn't going to touch it, just get a better look."

"Please—let me close the door."

"What is it, Ba? I've never seen anything like it before. Have you?"

"No, Missus, but is an evil thing. You can tell by the smell."

The smell was bad, that was for sure, but if odor were a worthy criterion, Limberger cheese would be evil too. Ba was truly concerned, though, almost frightened. Sylvia had to respect that. An overt sign of emotion from the Vietnamese was an extraordinary event, not something to be taken lightly. And for him to show fear, that was almost unthinkable. Sylvia was suddenly a little afraid herself.

"Very well, Ba," she said, stepping away from the door. "We'll lock up if you think it best."

He smiled with relief. But as he reached for the door to swing it closed, something crashed into the screen. Another bug, but this one was different. A vicious-looking thing that seemed to be all mouth—but its jaws were lined with hundreds of transparent teeth that looked like tiny glass daggers. Some of those teeth had thrust through the metal mesh of the screen on impact. The creature gripped the screen with its tiny claws and began chewing, ripping an ever-larger hole in it.

Ba slammed the door shut as its head poked through.

"My God!" she cried. "What *are* those things?"

"What are what?" Alan said as he rolled his wheelchair into the kitchen.

"Chew bugs and booger bugs!" Jeffy said.

Sylvia felt him press against her leg, clinging to it. He seemed afraid now. She smoothed his blond hair and offered him what she hoped was a reassuring smile.

"Don't be afraid, Jeffy. They can't get in here."

"Yes, they can! They want to eat me!"

Just then another of the toothed insects buzzed against the screen of the casement window over the sink as Alan was passing. He stopped his chair and stared.

"What the—?"

As it began to chew at the screen, Ba stepped past Alan and tried to bat it away, but his efforts only seemed to enrage the thing. It buzzed more loudly, attracting another of its kind.

"Close the window!" Jeffy wailed as he trembled against Sylvia's leg. "Don't let them get me!"

Alan sat calmly in his wheelchair and stared at the creatures. He had to know he was directly in harm's way should those things get through, but nothing seemed to frighten him since his recovery from the coma last year. The only concession he made to the things was to pull a dish towel from under the sink and slowly wrap it around his right hand.

Ba glanced at her, a helpless look in his eyes. Sylvia saw the problem. If Ba wound the casement windows closed, the two things would be trapped between the glass and the screen. He'd be all but pushing them into the kitchen. But if more were coming, it might be better to shut them.

Apparently Ba came to the same conclusion. He wound the windows closed on the things. And none too soon—a third bounced off the glass seconds later. The confined space trapped their wings and stopped their buzzing, but not their chewing at the screen. What was he going to do with—?

She saw Ba pull open the knife drawer.

"Come on, Jeffy," she said, turning him away. "Those things haven't got a chance against Ba and Alan, so why don't we go upstairs and—"

"I'm scared, Mommy," Jeffy said. "I don't want to go upstairs. What if they come in those windows too?"

The upstairs windows. She'd left them open. Such a beautiful day, she'd wanted to air out the house. God, she had to get up there and close them!

"How about the basement?" she said. "No windows down there. Want to wait in the basement for a few minutes while I check upstairs?"

He nodded eagerly. There was a play room down there for him with a lot of his toys. He'd be safe, and what was more he'd *feel* safe down there.

"Want Phemus to come along?"

"Yes! That way he'll be safe too."

Sylvia ushered Jeffy and the dog down the hall to the basement door. When she flipped on the basement lights, Jeffy pointed down the steps.

"Look, Mommy. Mess is here too!"

She looked and saw the family cat huddled at the bottom of staircase, its pupils wide, fur standing out in all directions. It looked spooked. Phemus ran down the steps and waited next to Mess.

"Great. Both of your friends will be with you."

She waited for him to go down but he stopped on the first step and sat on the little landing inside the door

"Aren't you going down?"

He looked up at her with frightened blue eyes.

"Close the door and I'll wait right here."

"You're sure?"

He nodded solemnly.

"Okay," she said. "But I'll be right back. And don't you worry about a thing."

Feeling like some sort of abusive mother locking her child in a closet, she pushed the door closed. The click of the latch echoed in her heart like the clang of a jail cell door. But it was what Jeffy wanted. She'd never seen him so frightened. Granted, those things were vicious looking, ready to grind up anything that got in their way, but what made him think they were after him specifically? A carry-over from his years of autism?

She didn't want to think about that, didn't even want to entertain the possibility that he might slide back into his former impenetrable state.

She hurried back to the kitchen. There she found Alan in his chair by the sink, towel-wrapped fist held before him, and Ba leaning toward the window with a raised meat clever. One of the things broke through the screen just as she arrived. Faster than her eyes could follow, it launched itself into the kitchen with a furious buzz. Alan batted at it with his fist. The thing sank its teeth into the towel and bit down. Alan yelped with pain but held his hand steady while Ba's cleaver whizzed down and sliced through the creature just behind its head. The winged body dropped into the sink, then rose and flapped about the room, dripping orange fluid as it caromed off the walls and ceiling, leaving wet splotches wherever it impacted. Finally it flopped to the floor, twitched a couple of times, then lay still.

The head didn't relax its grip on Alan's hand, however. It clung there, its jaws weakly chewing, even in death. Finally it stopped.

Alan leaned in for a closer look. "Where the hell did you come from?" he said.

He pried the head off and dropped it into the sink. It left behind a shredded section of towel. Crimson fluid began to seep through from within.

Sylvia found her mouth parched but she managed to speak.

"Alan?" she said. "Are you all right?"

He winked at her and smiled. "Sharp teeth on those buggers. Only a scratch, though." He glanced at the second thing still caught between the screen and the window. "Better take cover before this one breaks through."

He wrapped a second towel around the first as he and Ba took their positions and waited.

"I'm going upstairs to close the windows," she told them.

"No, Missus," Ba said without taking his eyes from the window.

Alan glanced at her. "Don't risk it alone. Wait till we get this one, then we'll all go up together."

"I'll only be a minute," she said, and headed for the stairs.

"Sylvia!"

She heard Alan's call from the kitchen but she ignored him. She hurried through the front foyer and ran up the curved staircase. The lights were on in the master bedroom where she and Alan slept. She dashed from one window to the next, checking the screens for holes, slamming them closed. No holes, no booger bugs.

One room down, five more to go on the second floor.

She hurried down the hall to Jeffy's room. The door was closed. When she opened it and flipped the switch, nothing happened. The floor lamp in the corner was supposed to come on. Sylvia hovered on the threshold, afraid to enter. She held her breath and listened.

Silence. No . . . a faint tell-tale buzzing from the window near the corner. Silhouetted in the moonlight was a translucent globule clinging to the screen. Another booger bug. The one downstairs had seemed harmless enough. And anyway, it was outside.

Telling herself it was safe, Sylvia gritted her teeth and hurried across the darkened room. She was almost to the window when her foot caught on something. She went down on both knees with a bruising thud. She reached back and felt the beveled post of the floor lamp. It had been knocked over somehow. A breeze, or . . . ?

Suddenly afraid, Sylvia scrambled to her feet and fumbled for the lamp on Jeffy's end table, found the switch, twisted it.

Light. Blessed light.

She peered over at the window. The booger bug was still there alone on the screen, trying to strain itself through the mesh. It looked like it was making some headway too. Part of it had actually seeped through—

Sylvia's heart stumbled over a beat when she saw the jagged edges of the screen. My God, it wasn't seeping through the mesh, it was *bulging* through a jagged hole in it. She lunged for the window and slammed down the sash. Then she ran around the bed and closed the window on the other side.

But the question remained: had anything got in?

She stood and listened again. This time there was no buzzing. She let herself relax. She'd got here in time—*just* in time. But there were still other rooms to secure. Before heading further down the hall, she picked up the fallen floor lamp—

—and stopped, staring. The lampshade was chewn up, shredded, as if a teething puppy had been working at it for an hour. She dropped the lamp again and spun around, her skin rippling with fear. Nothing moved, nothing buzzed. But the door was open, and if something had got in, it could get loose in the house if she didn't close it.

Moving slowly, smoothly, as casually as she could, she stepped toward the door. Her heart was thumping madly. If one of those chew bugs came after her she knew she'd fall apart and run screaming for the hall.

Almost there. Half a dozen feet or so and she'd be home free. She just had to stay calm and—

Sylvia heard it before she saw it. A ferocious buzz from the other side of the bed, a machine-gun rattle of hundred- toothed jaws banging against each other as they chewed the air, then a blur hurtling over the bed toward her face. She ducked but not quickly enough. It caught her hair, twisting her head around with an incendiary blaze of pain from her scalp. She felt a patch of hair rip from its follicles as the thing yanked free and swooped around the room. As she crouched, watching it, she heard another sudden buzz from behind her and instinctively threw herself to the side. A second chew bug darted past her ear, jaws clicking dangerously close.

Two of them!

She stumbled in a circle, turned, felt something soft press against her calves, and then she was falling backward onto the bed. The mad clicking accelerated and the dissonant harmony of the buzzes rose in pitch as they came in together. Sylvia grabbed Jeffy's pillow and held it before her. The impact of the two creatures knocked her onto her back amid a squall of feathers. She could feel them wriggling, chewing their way into the pillow. She turned the pillow over, trapping them against Jeffy's bedspread.

"Got you!" She cried, and laughed. It was an awful sound, tinged with hysteria.

She glanced at the open door. With these things immobilized for the moment, she could make it. But just as she was about to ease her grip on the pillow, a pair of tooth-encrusted jaws burst through the case and snapped at her. She screamed and ran for the door, slipping on the feathers, scrabbling along on her hands and knees until she reached it. She rolled through, stretched up and grabbed the knob, and was just pulling the door closed when the two chew bugs hurtled through the air above her and dove toward the first floor.

"No!" she cried.

And even before they were out of sight she heard an angry shout from Alan in the kitchen. She got to her feet and ran downstairs where she met Alan and Ba in the foyer. Ba, cleaver in hand, looked like a mad oriental chef.

Alan's eyes widened when he saw her.

"Sylvia! What happened?" He was staring at her head.

"Why?" She touched the sore spot on her scalp. Her fingers came away wet and red. Some of her skin must have come away with her hair. "Two of those things upstairs—in Jeffy's room. They got away and came down here. Did you see them?"

"No. The second one in the kitchen window got past us. We were just looking for it."

"Listen, please," Ba said, holding up his cleaver.

They quieted. A rasping sound . . . from down the hall . . . like chisels working wood.

"Where—?" Alan began.

"Oh, God, I think I know!"

She turned and led them toward the cellar door. As she rounded the corner she skidded to a halt and bit back a scream. All three chew bugs were there, nose-on to the cellar door, gnawing at the wood in blind determination to get through to what lay beyond it.

And from the other side she heard the wail of a child's small, frightened voice.

"Mommy? Are you out there, Mommy? What's that noise? What's happening, Mommy?"

"Get them!" she said through her teeth in a controlled screech. *"Get them!"*

Ba leaped forward, Alan rolling behind him. Ba cut one in half, then another. As their body parts flopped and flew around, Alan reached out with his towel-wrapped hand and grabbed the third by its tail. He swung it against the floor, smashing its head. Glass-like teeth flew in all directions. The last chew bug lay still.

"Get the upstairs windows, Ba," he said. "I'll look after the ones down here."

As the two men hurried off in different directions, Sylvia opened the basement door just enough to slip through and step onto the landing, then quickly pulled it closed behind her.

Jeffy's face was ashen as he stared up at her.

"Don't let them get me, Mom!"

She took the boy in her arms and clutched him tight against her. Her mind raced.

Jeffy had been right. Those things *were* after him. But why?

"It's okay," she told him. "We've killed the bugs and as soon as the house is sealed up tight we'll get out of here."

A moment later she heard Alan's wheelchair on the other side of the door.

"Okay, gang," he said, pulling the door open. "The coast is clear. All the windows are down. No holes in any of the other screens."

She stepped out into the hall, carrying Jeffy. Alan was smiling but she noticed that his eyes were apprehensive as he looked at the boy.

"Why don't you and Ba go to the movie room while your mother and I get some hot chocolate. Then we'll all watch a movie."

The movie room? It was a converted over-sized pantry where they'd set up the giant screen TV. Perfect for movies any time of day because it had no windows. Was that why Alan was suggesting it?

Jeffy let go of her and went with Ba. He no longer looked afraid. What could possibly harm you when Ba Thuy Nguyen was holding your hand?

As soon as Jeffy was out of earshot she turned to Alan.

"What's wrong?" *Stupid question.* "I mean, what *else* is wrong?"

"They're all over the place, Sylvia," he said in a low voice. "A huge flock of them swarmed in just as we finished closing up. They're at every window, trying to get in. Listen."

She did. And she heard it. A cadenceless tattoo, as if a thousand people were outside bouncing tennis balls off the windows. It congealed her blood to think of how many of those creatures it took to make that kind of noise.

"Who do we call? The police, the fire company, who?"

"Nobody," Alan said. "The phone's out."

"Then we're trapped."

"I think we're safe for now. We'll see what the morning brings. But until then, let's keep Jeffy as calm as we can."

"They're after him, aren't they?"

Alan nodded gravely. "Sure looks that way."

She bit back a sob as she dropped into Alan's lap and flung her arms around his neck. She was afraid for Jeffy. If anything happened to him . . .

It was all she could do to keep from crying.

"Why, Alan?"

"I think Mr. Veilleur might know."

Sylvia said nothing. Mr. Veilleur . . . she'd thought of him too. But she didn't trust him. He was hiding too much. Besides, what could a feeble old man do against these hideous things?

She pulled away from Alan and stood up. She took his hand.

"We'll handle this ourselves. Let's make that cocoa."

So good!

The horror, the pain, the bloodshed, the ravenous, screaming FEAR soaks through from above, filtering through the tissues of the earth, through the living granite into the conduits of Rasalom's changed flesh.

His raw flesh has healed now, hardened into a tough new covering. His hands and feet remain fused to the walls of the granite pocket, reaching deeper and deeper into the rock, sending intangible feeder roots through the surrounding earth, searching for more nourishment. More.

And as he feeds Rasalom gains mass, grows larger, thicker. The granite walls of the pocket flake away to accommodate his increasing size. The chips slide to the bottom and collect there like shattered bones.

SATURDAY

1 • DAWN

Monroe, Long Island

It took her a moment or two to appreciate the silence, but shortly before dawn she realized that the incessant beating on the windows had stopped.

Sylvia was the first to know because she hadn't slept a wink all night. Jeffy had fallen asleep half way through his umpteenth viewing of *Pete's Dragon*. Alan dropped off a short while later in his chair. Ba had spent much of the night working on some sort of weapon—carving tiny niches into the wood of one of his billy clubs and fixing chew-bug teeth in them with Crazy Glue. But even he dozed now and then. Sylvia had sat by the door of the movie room, keeping it open an inch or two, listening at the gap.

Silence. She was almost afraid to believe it could be true. As she rose from her chair, Ba sprang up, instantly alert.

"Missus?" he whispered.

"It's all right, Ba. I'm just going to take a look outside."

"I'll come."

"That's okay. I'll just be—"

But he was already by her side, peering into the hall. When he was satisfied that it was safe, he stepped out and held the door for her. Sylvia sighed, smiled her thanks, and followed him.

She wondered if she'd ever get used to having someone around who was ready to lay down his life for her at any moment. How long had it been? Sometime around 1979 or 80 when she'd recognized Ba in a TV news story about the boat people arriving in the Philippines after crossing the South China Sea with nothing but the clothes on their backs. He'd stood out because he towered above his fellow Vietnamese; she'd dug out the picture her late husband Greg had once shown her, telling her about this huge South Vietnamese fisherman his Special Forces group had trained as a guerrilla, how they'd become friends. The man in the photo and on the tube were the same. She'd rushed to Manila, brought Ba and his wife Nhung Thi back here, and paid all of Nhung Thi's medical bills when the cancer hiding in her lung broke out and spread through her body. After her death, Ba had stayed on as driver, groundskeeper, and one-man security force. Sylvia had told him a thousand times that he didn't owe her a thing, but Ba didn't see it that way.

78

Now, as he glided ahead of her, as silent and fluid as a shadow in the pale light that filtered down the hall from the rooms on either end, his newly customized billy club poised at the ready, she was glad he'd never listened to her.

They entered the dining room and went directly to the windows. Sylvia pulled back the sheers and gasped. The screens hung in tatters, the panes were smeared and fouled, the mullions gouged and splintered.

But no bugs. Not a single chewer or booger bug in sight. It was as if they'd evaporated in the morning light—or gone back to where they came from.

"Let's take a look outside, Ba."

He led the way to the front door, motioned for her to stay back, opened it, then slipped outside. A moment later he returned.

"It is safe, Missus, but . . . "

"But what?"

"It is not nice."

Sylvia strode to the door and stepped outside. Down the steps, into the driveway, then she turned and faced the house.

"Oh . . . my . . . God!"

Toad Hall looked like a disaster area—as if it had sat empty for a decade, then been struck by a hurricane, a hailstorm, a horde of carpenter ants, and a plague of locusts all at once. Besides the shredded screens and splintered mullions on the widows, all the wooden siding looked *gnawed*. The chewers had left hundreds, thousands of their sharp, crystalline teeth in the wood. They gleamed like diamonds in the morning sun. And the trees—her beautiful willows! Half the branches, the ones facing the house, had been denuded of their leaves, as if the creatures had been so frustrated by their inability to get into the house that they'd attacked the trees in retaliation.

"Why, Ba? Why'd this happen? What's going on?"

Ba said nothing. He never offered opinions, even when asked. He stood beside her in silence, his tooth-studded club at the ready, his head swiveling as he scanned the grounds in a smooth, continuous motion, like a radar dish.

"Stay here," she told him. "I want to take a look next door."

Ba didn't stay, of course. He fell in behind her. It was a good fifty yards to the stone wall that ran three sides of Toad Hall's perimeter. When Sylvia reached it she fitted her foot into a crevice and pulled herself up to where she could see over. She peered through the shrubs at the house next door, a contemporary that had fallen into disrepair for a while after its previous owner, a golden oldies DJ named Lenny Winter, disappeared a few years ago, but the new owners had done a complete overhaul. She pushed a branch aside for a better look.

Her stomach turned. The house was untouched. Well, not completely untouched. She noticed a few ripped screens flapping in the breeze, and a wet smear or two on the cedar siding, but nothing near what had happened to Toad Hall. It was very possible the occupants weren't aware of the damage yet.

Weak and shaky, she dropped back to the ground. As she stared again at the violated exterior of her home, Jeffy's voice echoed in her brain.

They want to eat me!

He was right. They'd concentrated their attack on the house where he lived and they'd come after him when they broke into the house.

Why? Did it have anything to do with the *Dat-tay-vao?*

She couldn't let them hurt Jeffy. She'd risk anything to protect him. Even . . .

"Ba, do you remember that older man who was here the other day? He left a card on the foyer table. I told Gladys to throw it away. Do you know if she did?"

"No, Missus."

"Oh. Then I guess I'll have to wait until she arrives. I may just have to—"

She noticed that Ba was holding out a piece of paper.

"No, Missus," he said. "Gladys did not throw it away."

She took the card. *G. Veilleur* was embossed at its center.

She looked at him. She saw only devotion and fierce loyalty in his eyes. But she remembered the fear there last night when he'd pulled her away from that mucous creature. Alan wanted her to contact the old man, and Ba obviously agreed.

Now it was unanimous.

"Thank you, Ba."

With her heart weighing heavy in her chest, she headed for the backyard, toward the garage. She hoped the car's cellular phone still worked.

WOR-TV

Hello, I'm Alice Gray, and we interrupt our usual Saturday morning programming to bring you this special news report. Sunrise was late again for the fourth morning in a row. But it never rose for many of our fellow New Yorkers. As most of you are no doubt already aware, chaos reigned in Manhattan last night as the midtown area became the set of the world's goriest horror movie. Only last night the horrors were real. Real people died, hundreds of them, perhaps as many as a thousand. The police and emergency services are still counting at this time. And these are the killers.

roll tape of dead insects

From what we can gather, these creatures flew out of the hole in Central Park last night and attacked everyone in sight, leaving the streets littered with corpses. They were indiscriminate in their choice of targets, attacking men, women, children, even dogs and cats, creating a reign of bloody terror. But shortly before dawn they fled, forming swarms that streamed along the streets back to here . . .

roll tape of Sheep Meadow hole

Witnesses describe the smaller swarms gathering and mingling above the mysterious Central Park hole, swelling to a huge swirling mass before plummeting again into the depths of the earth where they originated.

back to tape of dead insects

But what are these things? No live specimens are available, but there are plenty of dead ones around. It appears that the ones that didn't make it back to the hole before dawn died in the daylight. People have already begun referring to them as "vampire bugs." Scientists from a variety of fields—biology, chemistry, even paleontology (that's the study of fossils)—are working at identifying the creatures and devising ways to combat them. State and federal authorities have already arrived and are conducting studies to find a way to prevent them from getting loose again. Talk of placing a huge metal mesh over the hole is circulating.

back to Alice

But that may prove futile. Chilling news just in from Long Island and New Jersey of other bottomless holes, identical to the one in our own Central Park, opening up in Bayside, Glen Cove, Hackensack, and other places. These reports are unconfirmed as yet, but we have a team racing to St. Ann's Cemetery in Bayside at this very moment and will bring you live coverage from Queens as soon as they arrive and set up . . .

2 • GATHERINGS

Manhattan

Glaeken handed the drawings of the necklaces to Jack and watched the younger man study them. These were xeroxes. He had the original drawings safely tucked away in a vault.

"These are good," Jack said, nodding appreciatively. "Great detail. Just what I need. Where'd you get them?"

"I've kept them in a series of safe places over the years," Glaeken said. "On the outside chance that I'd need them some day. That day is here."

"Yeah," Jack said glumly. He rubbed his gauze-wrapped forearm. "I guess it is."

He rose from the chair and began pacing the living room. Glaeken sensed the tension coiled within Jack, the frustration boiling just under the skin. Jack was used to solving problems, usually other people's problems. Now he himself was faced with a problem for which he had no solution.

"About your fee," Glaeken said, allowing a smile to show. "What made you change your mind?"

Jack stopped his pacing and faced Glaeken, his eyes flashing.

"Not funny, Mr. V."

Glaeken sighed. "You're right. The events of last night are nothing to take lightly. And call me Glaeken."

"Glaeken . . . that's a new one."

"No, it's a very old one. Not at all an uncommon name in the time of my youth."

His youth . . . images seeped up from the deep past . . . sunlit forests . . . laughing and running with other boys. It seemed almost inconceivable that there had ever been a boy called Glaeken, and that he had been that boy. So many names since then. But now he was an old man with no further need of pretense, so he might as well revert to his given name.

"Whatever," Jack said, folding the drawings of the necklace into a neat square as he began roaming the living room again. "All hell seems to have broken loose out there. I saw those things come out of that hole last night. And now there's rumors of others holes opening up all over the place."

"They're not rumors. I believe I told you—"

"I know," Jack said, slowing and stopping as he passed the window. "I know you told me." He pointed out toward the Park. "Thousands of those holes? *Thousands* of them?"

"I'm afraid so."

"What's going to keep one from opening up right under your building here and swallowing it up?"

"I doubt very much that will happen. That would be too quick—mercifully quick. The power behind these holes wants me to witness the death-throes of civilization before he comes for me. Besides, those holes cannot open just anywhere. They must locate at specific nexus points in order to connect with the . . . other place."

" 'The other place?' Sounds like seance talk."

"I don't know how else to explain it."

"But with swarms of those things pouring out from this 'other place' through thousands of holes, the whole planet will be overrun. I'm sure we can find ways to exterminate the bugs, but—"

"The belly flies and chew wasps are just the first wave. Worse things are on the way."

Jack was shaking his head slowly back and forth as he stared out the window.

"What could be worse than those little horrors last night?"

"*Bigger* horrors. But only during the hours of darkness. They must return to the holes before sunrise."

"Swell. I mean, that's a big comfort, isn't it, what with sunrise coming later and later each morning." Finally, he looked away from the window. "You said something before about 'the power behind these holes.' What did you mean? That somebody's in control here—causing the holes?"

"Yes. His name is Rasalom."

"Where do we find this guy? How can I get to him?"

"He won't be found unless he wishes to be. And he's not subject to your brand of solutions. You can't 'fix' him or undo his work by conventional means."

Jack held up the folded drawings of the necklaces.

"What about these? You're telling me these necklaces will help close up the holes?"

"They'll give us a chance. Without them we might as well quit right now."

"All right," Jack said, shoving them into the back pocket of his jeans. "Sounds crazy to me, but crazy seems to be in charge these days."

"Very true. But don't go yet. There are some people I want you to meet."

"The guy who didn't show up yesterday?"

"No. He had to accompany a sick friend to a hospital. I don't think he'll be back today."

Bill had called last night to explain his absence and to relate what had befallen his friend Nick. Glaeken had told him to do whatever he thought best for his friend.

But another call had come this morning—from Sylvia Nash. She told him what had transpired at her house last night. Glaeken had been shaken by the news. He had expected Rasalom's forces to home in on the *Dat-tay-vao* eventually, but not so soon. Certainly not on the first night. The news increased the sense of urgency simmering within him.

Mrs. Nash had wanted him to come out to Monroe and see the damage, but Glaeken had refused. He wanted her—no, not her, the boy—*here* where he could watch over him and protect him and the *Dat-tay-vao* residing within him. With obvious reluctance, she had agreed to meet him here today.

"I must tend to my wife for a few moments," he told Jack. "If the doorman announces a Mrs. Nash or a Mrs. Treece, tell him to send them up."

Jack tore his gaze away from the window. He seemed mesmerized by the hole in the Park.

"What? Oh, sure. You go do what you have to do. I'll take care of things."

Glaeken headed for Magda's room. He knew Repairman Jack was very good at taking care of things.

WXRK-FM
We've had a lot of requests for this next record here on K-Rock's All-Request Weekend. I guess it has something to do with what happened last night.
Cue: "The Night Has A Thousand Eyes"

"Maybe you'd better call and cancel us out of this little meeting," Hank said.

Carol glanced at him across the bedroom as she finished buttoning her blouse. He'd tested the lock on the bedroom window for the dozenth time, and now he was craning his neck this way and that, his quick hazel eyes scanning the street below and the sky above.

"We can't," she said. "It's too important."

Glaeken had called her early this morning and asked her to come over and meet the others who would be involved in his countermove against Jimmy.

No! Not Jimmy—Rasalom!

"I don't think it's safe. That's over by Central Park."

"Mr. Veilleur said we have nothing to fear in the daylight."

Hank quickly ran a hand through the thinning light-brown hair that he combed straight back from his receding hairline. That plus his prominent nose tended to give him a hawkish appearance. Carol had been trying to get him to soften his hairstyle. He'd comply for a while, then revert to his old ways. He'd been a bachelor for forty-five years when they met. She had no real hope of changing him into someone with a sense of style, but that didn't mean she'd stop trying. She liked challenges.

"Nothing to fear in the daylight? And what makes this Mr. Veilleur so sure about that when one renowned scientist after another claims to be completely baffled by that hole and these creatures?"

"He knows," Carol said. "Believe me, he knows."

"I don't like this, Carol," Hank said, wandering the tiny bedroom with his hands thrust deep into his pockets. "With all the awful things going on out on the streets, it seems to me the prudent thing to do would be to stay inside until everything's under control."

Carol shook her head and smiled softly as she pulled a skirt from its hanger in her closet. That was Hank, always weighing the pros and cons, measuring the liabilities, gauging the hazards to find the course of action with the lowest risk-benefit ratio. Always safe and sane, always planning ahead, that was Hank. And there was nothing wrong with that.

No . . . nothing wrong with that at all. Carol needed safe and sane in her life. She needed someone nearby who planned for the future. It helped Carol believe that there was going to *be* a future, and that it mattered.

Hank was so different from Jim. Her first husband had been a writer, living day to day, doing things on impulse, earning hangovers. Spontaneity and intemperance were not part of Hank's repertoire.

And yet there was much to be said for staid and stable. Her marriage to Hank might lack the heat and passion of her relationship with Jim, but it did have warmth and trust and companionship, and she needed those right now.

"I can't put it off," Carol said. "It's got to be this morning. There are people there he wants me to meet, and I want you to meet him and the others."

He looked at her. "You're determined to go, aren't you."

"Hank, I've got to."

"Well, I'm certainly not letting you travel across town alone today. So I guess we'll be paying a visit on Mr . . . "

"Veilleur. But he likes to be called Glaeken. And Bill Ryan will be there, so it won't be as if you won't know anybody."

"He's involved in this too? How long have you been meeting this Veilleur or Glaeken fellow? And why does it all have to be so mysterious? Why can't you tell me more about it?"

"I'm going to tell you all about it. I—I haven't told you everything about my past and I think it's high time you knew."

Hank stepped in front of her and gently slipped his arms around her.

"You don't have to worry about me. Nothing you can say will change how I feel about you."

"I hope so." *I hope you can handle what's coming.*

"But why can't you tell me first?"

"Because I want you to have the big picture first before I tell you my part in it. Glaeken knows more about it and can explain it better than I can." *He was there when it all started.* "He knows who's behind those things that came out of the Central Park hole last night."

Hank took a half step back from her.

"He does? Who?"

Carol bit her lip, wondering how much to say. Well, why not just blow the door off its hinges? Give him his first look into her locked room. Nothing would stay hidden long after that.

"My son."

Jack wasn't sure how long he'd been standing at the window, mesmerized by all the furious activity round the hole in the sheep Meadow, when the doorbell rang. He glanced down the hall where Glaeken had gone but there was no sign of him.

Well, he'd said to answer the door, so that was what he'd do. Obviously Glaeken was expecting company.

Jack opened the door and found the Odd Couple standing in the hall. A graying priest and a funny-looking younger guy with unfocused eyes, a stitched lip, and a dazed look on his puss. And was that drool in the corner of his mouth?

"Who are you?" the priest said. Obviously he'd expected someone else to answer the door.

"That's not what people usually say when they're on that side of the door," Jack told him.

"I live here," the priest said with a touch of irritation.

Jack wasn't going to argue with the man. He stepped out of the way.

"If you say so."

Jack checked out the priest as he passed. He was taller than Jack, maybe a dozen or so years older, but he looked fit. His face was battered and haggard and his blue eyes had a haunted look, the look of a guy who'd seen too much of a bad thing.

The priest led his shell-shocked companion into the living room and sat him on the sofa. He almost had to bend the guy's knees to get him to sit. Then he turned to Jack.

"Where's Glae—I mean, Mr. Veilleur?"

"He asked me to call him Glaeken, and he's back with his wife. My name's Jack, by the way."

"Oh, yes. I was supposed to meet you yesterday." He thrust out his hand. "Bill Ryan."

Jack shook his hand. "You the priest?"

"Used to be. I didn't catch your last name."

"Jack'll do." To steer the talk away from names, he pointed to the guy on the sofa, and yeah, that was drool on his chin. "What happened to him?"

"That's Dr. Nick Quinn. He's one of the scientists who went down into the hole yesterday. He's the one who survived."

Jack stared at Nick Quinn with new respect. "I saw what came out of there last night . . . "

Ryan put his hand on Quinn's shoulder. "I'm afraid Nick saw something much worse than those things."

"Yeah," Jack said, watching the poor bastard stare blindly into space. *Went down a rocket scientist, came back a geranium.* "I guess he did. Where'd you come from this morning?"

"Washington Heights."

"How do things look up there?"

"Not too bad. Mostly you'd never know anything happened until you get to Harlem. And even there, you could convince yourself they had nothing more than a bad storm last night. But from the Nineties down it looks like there was a riot or something. And around here . . . " He shook his head in dismay. "There's still blood on the pavement."

Jack nodded. "It was worse earlier when I walked through from the East Side."

His gut squirmed at the memory of that walk. He hadn't slept much last night. He'd spent most of the time standing anxious guard over Gia and Vicky and watching the tube for word from Central Park. There were news specials all night, but no visuals. Camera teams sent to the area were never heard from again. Shortly after sunrise he'd ventured out into the streets. Sutton Square was quiet, and early morning traffic was rolling uptown and down on Sutton Place as usual. No flying monsters anywhere about, so he'd jogged up the incline toward midtown.

Between Madison and Park he came upon police barricades. He slipped past and continued west. Fifty-ninth Street became a nightmare. Deflated, sunken-cheeked, desiccated corpses littered the pavements, body parts were everywhere—a limbless, headless torso on the sidewalk, a leg in a gutter, a gnawed finger atop a mailbox. The closer he got to the Park, the thicker the carnage.

Central Park South was the worst yet—dead people, dead horses still harnessed to their hansom cabs, overturned cars, a taxi half way through the front windows of Mickey Mantle's. Every emergency vehicle and meat wagon in the city seemed to have converged on the area to remove the bodies.

Live people were about, too. All on their way out. The cops weren't allowing cabs or civilian vehicles into the area, so the surviving members of the mink coat and tennis bracelet set were lugging their own suitcases out of the Plaza, the Park Lane, the St. Moritz, the Barbizon-Plaza and lugging them down the avenues to where they could get a ride to the nearest airport.

Jack had picked his way through the area and hurried home to find the old guy's phone number. Then he'd come here.

The intercom buzzed then and Ryan answered it. He seemed pretty much at home here. The doorman said that a Mrs. Nash had arrived. Ryan looked at Jack questioningly.

"It's okay," Jack said. "The old boy said she'd be coming."

Ryan said to send her up, then turned and looked back toward the bedrooms.

"Wonder what changed her mind?" he said to no one in particular. Then he shrugged and led Quinn to the kitchen. "I'm going to fix Nick something to eat. Want anything?"

"No, thanks."

Actually, Jack was hungry but too edgy, too unsettled to eat. Maybe later, at Julio's, over a pint of Courage. A *gallon* of Courage.

The doorbell rang. He opened it. The Addams family was outside.

At least they reminded him of the Addams family. There was a slinky brunette in a dark dress, a blond kid, and an Oriental Lurch. Only the guy in the wheelchair spoiled the picture.

"Is he here?" said the kid, his blue eyes wide and bright. He poked his head through the doorway and looked up and down the hall. "He's here! I know he's here!"

"Please, Jeffy," the woman said, placing a hand on his shoulder. She looked at Jack. "I'm Sylvia Nash."

Jack liked her voice. You could fall in love with that voice. But he was already in love.

"Hi," Jack said, stepping back and making way. "He's expecting you."

"Where's Mr. Veilleur?" said the guy in the wheelchair.

Jack pointed toward the living room.

"He's around. Come on in. Have a seat." Jack wanted to bite his tongue on that one. The guy already had a seat. "I'll tell him you're here."

Jack stood back and watched them as they all trooped toward the living room—all except the big Oriental whose eyes never stopped moving. He stayed with the group as far as the end of the hall but halted at the threshold of the bigger room. He gave the living room the once-over, then stepped to the side and stood with his back against the wall, his big hands folded in front of him. The drawstring of a plastic Lord & Taylor's bag hung from one of his fingers. Out on the street he might have passed as a tourist who'd been shopping, but Jack had spied the billy club handle protruding from the bag.

Jack admired the way he moved—smooth, silent, *graceful* for a guy his size. Everything about him said he'd been trained for hand-to-hand combat and security. As he studied the big guy, he realized the big guy was studying him.

Jack wandered over to where he stood. He put out his hand.

"My name's Jack."

The big guy bobbed a quick bow and gave Jack's hand a brief shake.

"Ba," he said in a deep voice.

While Jack tried to figure if that was a personal assessment or a name, he noticed that the big guy's eyes didn't stray from the living room for more than a heartbeat.

"It's safe here," Jack said. "You can relax."

Another bob from Ba and a fleeting, yellow-toothed smile. "Yes. I see. Thank you so very much."

Jack noted with approval that Ba did not relax one bit.

Bill Ryan came in from the kitchen then and greeted the newcomers. He waved Jack in and introduced him to Sylvia Nash, Dr. Alan Bulmer, and the boy, Jeffy. The kid seemed hyper. When Ryan went to get Glaeken, Jack wandered back to Ba.

"Where'd you train?"

"In my homeland—Viet Nam."

Jack wondered if he'd been a Cong.

"Army?"

His dark eyes never left the living room. "Special Forces."

Knew it!

"What's in the bag beside the billy?"

Ba glanced at him, his eyes searching his face for a moment, then he handed the bag to Jack.

Jack took it and loosened the drawstrings. From its weight he guessed there wasn't much more than the billy inside but he checked anyway. He pulled out the club and stared dumbfounded at the hundreds of tiny, gleaming, glass-like teeth protruding from the final ten inches of its business end.

"Good Lord," he whispered. "These are teeth from those—" What had Glaeken called them? "—chew wasps."

Ba said nothing.

Jack gave the club a few short test swings. He'd seen what those little teeth could do. A billy club studded with them made one *hell* of a weapon.

"How many did you kill?"

"A few," Ba said.

"How about the glob things? Get any of those?"

Ba shook his head.

"Watch out for them," Jack said. He lifted his partially eaten-away sneaker for Ba to see. "The glop in their bellies does this to rubber. It's even worse on skin."

Ba's eyes flicked to Jack's bandaged arm, then away.

Jack slipped the club back into the sack and held it out to him.

"Think you could make me one of those?"

Ba pushed the sack toward Jack. "You may have this."

Reflexively, Jack began to refuse. He didn't accept gifts from strangers. He didn't like to be indebted to anyone, especially someone he'd just met. But he caught himself. They'd met only a few moments ago, had spoken only a few words—Ba hardly any at all—yet he sensed a kinship with the other man. Something like this had happened only a few times in his life. A good feeling. Ba must have sensed it too. The big Oriental was making a gesture. Jack could not refuse.

"What about you? Won't you be needing it?"

"I will make myself another. Many, many teeth where I live."

"All right. I accept." Jack hefted the bag and tucked it under his arm. "Thank you, Ba. I have a feeling this might come in very handy."

Ba nodded silently and watched the living room.

Alan glanced over at where Ba was standing with the dark-haired, quick-eyed man who had been introduced simply as Jack. Something going on between those two, communication on a level he was not privy to. Odd . . . Ba related to almost no one outside the household.

Alan hauled his attention away from the pair and directed it toward Sylvia and Jeffy.

"He's here, isn't he, Mommy?" Jeffy was saying. He was bouncing on the seat cushion, his head swiveling this way and that. "Isn't he?"

"Yes," Sylvia said patiently. "That's what we were told."

"I bet he's in one of those rooms back there," he said. "Can I go back and see if he's—"

"Jeffy, please sit still," Sylvia said. "It's very bad manners to go wandering around someone's house."

"But I want to *see* him!"

She put an arm around the boy's shoulders and hugged him against her.

"I know you do, sweetie. So do I. That's why I'm here."

Poor Sylvia. She'd been having such a hard time with Jeffy since Veilleur had shown up two days ago. And now that he was here in the old man's home, the boy was like an overwound spring.

Alan could understand it. He too felt wired. Maybe it was the stress of last night, maybe it was all the coffee he'd poured down his throat this morning. But he had a feeling they were just a small part of it.

Veilleur was the major factor. For no good reason, something within Alan responded positively—no, *enthusiastically*—to the man. It had to have something to do with the months Alan had played host to the *Dat-tay-vao*. After reducing him to a comatose vegetable, the power—entity, elemental force, whatever it was—had deserted him. But it must have left some sort of residue within, whether clinging to his peritoneum, coating his meninges, or riding the neural currents along his axons, he couldn't say. All he knew was that he was drawn to this old man, trusted him; he still remembered the warm glow he'd felt at first sight of him.

And if that's how I feel, what must Jeffy feel?

For Alan had no doubt that the *Dat-tay-vao* had chosen Jeffy as its new residence.

He saw the priest, Father Ryan, return from the rear of the apartment. Mr. Veilleur followed him, wiping his hands on a towel as he walked in. And Alan felt that warmth again, glowing at his center, seeping throughout his torso and into his limbs.

And Jeffy . . . Jeffy was on his feet. He ran to the old man and clasped his leg in a bear hug. Veilleur stopped and smiled down at him as he smoothed the boy's hair.

"Hello, Jeffy. It's good to see you again."

The boy said nothing, merely looked up at Veilleur with glowing eyes.

Alan glanced over at the sofa where Sylvia, alone now, sat with a rigid spine and a tight, tense expression, chewing her lower lip as she watched the scene. Her eyes flashed with hurt—and anger. Alan knew the core of anger that coiled within Sylvia like a living thing. It had been quiescent in the past few months, but he vividly remembered how it used to bare its fangs and strike out at the unwary. He sensed it waking and stirring within her now.

His heart went out to her. She had taken Jeffy in when he'd been abandoned at age three by unknown parents who had been defeated by his autism. She had slaved over him with psychotherapy, physiotherapy, nutritional therapy, occupational therapy, butting her head and heart against the unyielding barricades of his autism without ever once entertaining the thought of giving up. And then, a miracle: the *Dat-tay-vao* smashed through his autistic shell and released the child trapped within. Sylvia at last had the little boy she had been seeking.

But now all that little boy seemed to care about was the mysterious old man who had appeared on her doorstep just two days ago.

Alan felt her hurt as if it were his own. He wanted to go to her side and put an arm around her to let her know he understood and was with her all the way, but he couldn't reach her with his hand and his wheelchair couldn't squeeze by the coffee table to get to where she was and these damn legs wouldn't carry him the lousy half-dozen feet to her side.

His legs. They infuriated him at times. Yes, they were getting stronger; slowly, steadily, he'd progressed to the point where he actually could stand for a few seconds. But that wouldn't help him now when Sylvia needed him. So he had to sit here, trapped in this ungainly, wheeled contraption and watch the woman he loved suffer. At times like this he—

A harsh voice broke through his thoughts.

"*You!*"

Alan twisted in his chair, searching for the source. He saw a tall, stoop-shouldered man with unruly dark hair standing in the hallway that led to the kitchen. His head was in constant motion, twisting back and forth, up and down, but his wild-eyed gaze remained pinned on Mr. Veilleur.

All around him was frozen silence. Even Jeffy fell quiet. The room had become a tableau.

"He *hates* you!"

Father Ryan came up behind him and gently took his arm, saying, "It's all right, Nick. Come back here with—"

"No." The man snatched his arm out of the priest's grasp and pointed a trembling finger at Veilleur. "He hates you *so!* He wants you to suffer!" He pointed to his head. "Here!" Then to his heart. "And here! And then he plans to make you suffer the tortures of the damned!"

Alan glanced at Veilleur and saw no sign of shock or fear in his wrinkled features. He looked like a man who was hearing exactly what he'd expected to hear. But his clear blue eyes narrowed ever so slightly.

"Come, Nick," Father Ryan was saying, trying to turn the man back toward the kitchen. "You're making a scene."

"Let him stay a moment," Veilleur said, stepping closer to Nick. Jeffy trailed along, clutching his leg. "This is your friend? The one who went into the hole yesterday?"

The priest nodded sadly. "What's left of him."

Into the hole? Alan had heard the news reports about yesterday's tragic expedition. A physicist and a geologist had been lowered into the depths, and the geologist had died in transit. Here was the survivor. What had happened to him down there?

"I've seen this before," Veilleur said to the priest. "On occasion, in the old days, one of the rare persons who survived a trek into a chaos hole returned sensitized to the Enemy." He turned to the man called Nick. "Tell me, my friend, do you know where Rasalom is?"

Nick stepped over to the picture window and pointed at the Park, at the hole down there. Alan had wanted to take a look through that window to see the hole from above but it had seemed like such a hassle to wheel his chair around all the furniture.

"He's down there," Nick said. "Way down there. I saw him. He opened his heart to me. I . . . I . . . " His mouth worked but he seemed incapable of describing what he had seen.

"Why?" Veilleur said. "Why is he down there?"

"He's changing."

For the first time, Mr. Veilleur appeared disturbed, and something deep inside Alan quailed at the thought of that man being afraid.

"He's started the Change already?"

"Yes!" Nick's eyes were wilder than ever. "And when the Change is complete, he's going to come for you!"

"I know," Veilleur said in a low voice. "I know."

The light suddenly died in Nick eyes. His gaze drifted and his shoulders slumped.

Father Ryan gripped his shoulder. "Nick? Nick?"

But Nick didn't answer.

"What's wrong with him?" Alan said.

He hadn't practiced medicine in over a year but he could almost hear the associations clicking into place. The man had lapsed into an almost catatonic state. Alan wondered if his behavior had anything to do with the cranial deformities he'd noticed as he'd watched the man. But that was unlikely. And they certainly wouldn't have sent a schizophrenic down into that hole.

"He's been like this since last night—since he came out of the hole."

"Has he been examined by a doctor?"

The priest nodded. "Scads of them. They're not sure what to do for him."

"Why isn't he in a hospital? He should be closely monitored until they work out an appropriate course of therapy."

Father Ryan looked at him a moment and Alan was jolted by the depth of the pain in his eyes. Then the priest looked away.

"Sorry, Dr. Bulmer, but it's . . . it's been my experience that modern medicine isn't really equipped to deal with Nick's sort of problem."

He took Nick's arm and the younger man docilely followed him into the kitchen, leaving Alan to wonder at what sort of hell that priest had been through.

"Well," Mr. Veilleur said, facing Sylvia and Alan. Jeffy still hung on his leg. "I'm expecting two more people any minute now; then our company will be complete." He pried the boy loose from his leg. "There now, Jeffy. Be a good boy and sit with your mother."

Reluctantly, Jeffy complied, seating himself next to Sylvia, but barely glancing at her. His eyes remained fixed on Glaeken.

"I'm glad you decided to come," Glaeken told Sylvia.

"You didn't leave us much choice," she said. "Not after what happened last night." Her voice slowed. "Strange . . . you show up at our house Thursday, I kick you out, and on Friday all hell breaks loose."

"No connection, I assure you, Mrs. Nash. I'm not responsible for any of this."

"So you say. But the area around your apartment building this morning looks like a slaughterhouse. And out on Long Island, way out in Nassau County, in the Village of Monroe, the same little monstrosities that did all the damage around here swarmed in and attacked one house. Ours. Why is that, Mr. Veilleur?"

"Call me Glaeken," the old man said. "And I believe you know the answer to your own question."

Alan caught the slightest tremor along Sylvia's lips; he noticed her eyes were suddenly moist. He ached for her. What she must be feeling to let even this much show. In all the years he'd known her, Sylvia had never once let her feelings show in public. Around the house she'd let her hair down with the best of them, but in public she was pretty much like Ba.

"Why would anyone want to hurt him?" she said in a small voice.

Alan noted how she avoided saying Jeffy's name.

The man who wanted to be called Glaeken smiled sadly and ruffled the boy's hair.

"He's not the target. It's what resides within him."

Sylvia leaned back and closed her eyes. Her voice was a whisper.

"The *Dat-tay-vao*."

Alan sagged with relief in his chair. Finally, after all these months, she'd admitted it. Now maybe they could get on with the problem of dealing with it.

"Yes," Glaeken said. "There's an instinctive enmity between the things from the hole and something like the *Dat-tay-vao*. That's why I'd like you to move in here with me."

Sylvia looked at him as if he'd just propositioned her. Before she could answer, the doorbell rang.

"Will you get that, Bill?" Glaeken called toward the kitchen. "I believe it's Mrs. Treece."

Father Ryan came out of the kitchen and headed for the door, tossing Glaeken a baffled look along the way.

A middle-aged couple entered, a trim, anxious-looking man, pale, with thinning light brown hair, and a slender, attractive ash blonde who had an immediate, bright smile for Father Ryan. The woman and the priest seemed to be old friends. Alan sensed that they might be more than just old friends.

Father Ryan introduced them around as Henry—"Hank"—and Carol Treece, then they seated themselves on the other section of the angled sofa. The priest stood behind them, but kept an eye on the entrance to the kitchen.

"Very good," Glaeken said. "Everyone is here. But before you can fully grasp *why* you are here, I must give you some background. It's a long story. Eons long. It begins—"

Suddenly there was screaming outside the window. Glaeken turned and Alan looked with the rest of them.

A woman was there—portly, middle-aged, dressed in a white blouse and a polyester pants suit—rising through the air a dozen feet beyond the window, twisting, turning, kicking, writhing, futilely reaching for something, anything that would halt her helpless ascent. Her face was a study in panic. Her terrified screams penetrated the double-paned windows.

We're twelve stories up! Alan thought as everyone but he, Ba, and Nick ran to the windows.

As quickly as she had appeared, she was gone, rising above the level of the windows and tumbling out of sight like a lost balloon.

Sylvia's face was white, her lips tight; Mrs. Treece's hands were pressed over her mouth. Her husband turned to Glaeken with an uncertain smile.

"It's a gag, right?"

The old man shook his head. "I'm afraid not. That woman is a victim of another kind of hole that will begin appearing at random intervals and locations—a gravity hole."

"Can't we do anything for her?" the priest said.

"No. She's beyond our reach. Perhaps a helicopter . . . " He sighed. "But please, all of you, sit down and let me finish. Perhaps it's a good thing this happened now. It's no accident that it occurred outside my windows. But even so, what I'm about to tell you will strain your credulity. I had little hope of any of you believing me before now. I hope, however, that the events of the past two days—the bottomless hole in Central Park, the depredations last night of the first wave of creatures from the hole, this unfortunate woman outside—have put you all in a more receptive frame of mind. It is important that you believe me, because our survival, the survival of most of the human race, will depend on the course of action we take from this day forward. And for you to act intelligently and get the job done, you must know what you are up against."

Alan glanced around the room. At the rear, Ba and Jack were listening intently. Nearby on his right, Sylvia wore her Go- ahead-and-this-had-better-be-good expression. Father Ryan hovered behind the sofa with a faraway look in his eyes; Alan got the impression that he'd already heard what Glaeken had to say. On the far side of the sofa, Carol's expression mirrored the priest's, while Hank's was frankly dubious.

Then Glaeken began to speak. He told of two warring forces existing beyond the veil of our reality—ageless, deathless, implacable, nebulous, huge beyond comprehension. One inimical to humanity, feeding on fear and depravity; the other an ally—not a friend, not a protector or guardian, an ally simply by circumstance, simply because it opposed the other force. He told of the endless war between these two forces, raging across the galaxies, across the dimensions, across all time itself; of the human named Rasalom who in ancient times aligned himself with the malign force, and of the other man, equally ancient, who'd had thrust upon him the burden of bearing the standard of the opposing force. And now the ages-long battle was coming to a close with only one army on the field. The outcome depended on this small group of people collected in this room. Unless they acted to muster an opposing force, all was lost.

"This is it?" the man named Jack said from where he stood by Ba. "This is *it*?" He shook his head as his eyes roamed the room. "I sure hope you're crazy. Because if you're not, we're in big trouble."

Emotionally, Alan believed Glaeken. Deep within he *felt* the truth of what Glaeken was saying. Perhaps that too was the result of his entanglement with the *Dat-tay-vao*. But intellectually he rebelled.

"Why are we so important to these . . . forces?" he blurted.

"So far as I know, we're not," Glaeken said. "It's almost impossible to divine the motives of such entities, but long experience has led me to conclude that we have not the slightest strategic value to either side."

"Then why—?"

"I think we amuse the side I've come to call, for obvious reasons, the Enemy. It is inimical to everything that gives our lives meaning, that makes life worth living. It thrives on what's worst in us, feeds on the misery and pain we cause each other. Perhaps it gathers enormous strength from our negative emotions. Or maybe we're only a potential snack."

Alan heard Jack mutter at the rear of the room.

"Swell! We're a cosmic McDonald's!"

"Whatever its reasons, it wants to be here."

"And this other power," Sylvia said, leaning forward. "It wants to protect us?"

"I doubt it. I very much doubt that the ally power cares a whit for our welfare. It has intervened only because the Enemy is interested in us or has some use for us."

"Where was it last night?" Alan said.

"It's gone," Glaeken said.

"Dead?"

"No. Just ... gone. Off to other battlefields, I imagine. My guess is that back in 1941 it thought it had won the little skirmish that our backwater world represented and so it turned its attention elsewhere."

"That's it?" Alan said. "This ally or whatever battles for eons, thinks it's won, then goes 'elsewhere'? Didn't it want to hang around and show off the prize, or maybe just gloat a little?"

Glaeken fixed him with his blue eyes and Alan felt the power behind them. He spoke softly.

"In chess, do you really *want* the other player's pieces for their intrinsic value? Do you have any plans for those pieces? After you've taken an opponent's pawn in a chess game, do you give it another thought?"

The room was dead quiet for a long, breathless moment.

From the back of the room, Jack said, "What you're telling us, I take it, is that in the old days we had some heavy back-up, but now we're on our own."

"Precisely. He glanced at Mrs. Treece. "Back in 1968 the ally made a subtle attempt to foil what it probably considered a half-hearted feint by the Enemy, then it deserted this sphere for good. We now know that Rasalom's transmigration was not a feint, but the ally power does not."

"So this is the Little Big Horn and we're not the Indians."

"You could put it that way. But we might have a chance of calling in the cavalry, so to speak."

"The necklaces," Jack said.

Glaeken nodded. "The necklaces, the right smithies, and ... " He gestured toward Jeffy. "This little boy."

"Would you mind being just a little more specific?" Sylvia said. She was speaking through her teeth. "Just what the hell are you talking about?"

Glaeken was unfazed by Sylvia's outburst. He smiled her way.

"To put it in a nutshell, Mrs. Nash: We need to let the ally force know that the battle isn't over yet, that the Enemy is still active here and about to take complete control of this sphere. We need to send the ally force a signal."

"And just how do we do that?" Sylvia said.

"We need to reconstruct an ancient artifact."

"A weapon?"

"In a way, but what I'm talking about is not so much a weapon as an antenna, a focal point."

"Where is it?" Jack asked.

"It was deactivated more than a half century ago when it supposedly destroyed the Enemy's agent in a Rumanian mountain pass outside a place called the keep."

Alan's mind continued to rebel against Glaeken's words, more intensely now than ever, but his heart, his emotions insisted that he believe.

"All right," Alan said. "Suppose we accept all this at face value." That earned him a sharp look from Sylvia. "How do we go about reactivating the focus deactivated in Rumania?"

"We don't," Glaeken said. "All the essences that made it a focus were drained off by the act of destroying Rasalom—or what appeared to be Rasalom's destruction. Only through a set of unfortunate circumstances—unfortunate for the rest of us— did he manage to survive. And the remnant of that instrument was reduced to dust when Rasalom started on the path toward rebirth back in 1968."

"If it's gone and we can't get it back," Jack said, annoyance creeping into his voice, "why are we jawing about it?"

"Because there were two. The other was stolen in ancient times and dismantled—melted down into other things. "

"Oh, jeez." It was Jack again. "The necklaces."

Glaeken smiled. "Correct."

"What are you two talking about?" Sylvia said. Alan sensed her anger edging closer to the surface.

"The other instrument—the other focus—was stolen and melted down. The melting process dislodged a powerful elemental force within the focus, releasing it to wander free. But a residue of that force remained in the molten metal. The metal was fashioned into a pair of necklaces which have been used for ages by the high priests and priestesses of an ancient cult to keep them well and to prolong their lives."

"And the elemental force?" Sylvia said, leaning forward, her face pale, her expression tight, tense.

The answer flashed into Alan's mind. He suspected Sylvia had guessed it as well.

"It wandered the globe for ages," Glaeken said. "It's been called many things in its time, but eventually it became known as the *Dat-tay-vao*."

Alan thought he heard a faint groan escape Sylvia as she closed her eyes and slipped an arm around Jeffy.

Just then a voice broke through from somewhere in the apartment.

"Glen? Glen!" It rose in pitch, edging toward panic. "Glen, I'm all alone in here! Where are you?"

As Glaeken glanced toward the rear rooms, Alan saw genuine concern and dismay mix in his eyes. It was the first time he had shown a hint of uncertainty. He took a hesitant step in the direction of the cries.

"Let me go," Father Ryan said, moving from his spot behind the sofa and slipping behind Glaeken. "She knows me by now. Maybe I can reassure her."

"Thank you, Bill," Glaeken said, then turned to his audience. "My wife is ill."

"Anything I can do?" Alan said.

"I'm afraid not, Dr. Bulmer, but I thank you for offering." Alan saw no hope in the man's eyes as he spoke. "She has Alzheimer's disease."

Alan could only say, "I'm sorry."

But Sylvia shot to her feet. "*Now* I get it!"

"Get what, Mrs. Nash?" Glaeken said. He appeared genuinely confused.

Sylvia was leaning forward, jabbing her finger toward him over the coffee table. Her core of anger was fully uncoiled, its fangs were bared, and it was lashing out.

"I should have known! Do you think I'm an idiot? You want Jeffy here so you can use him—or rather use the power you think is in him—to cure your wife!"

"Not at all, Mrs. Nash," he said softly with a slow, sad shake of his head. "The *Dat-tay-vao* will not work against a degenerative process like Alzheimer's. It can cure disease, but it can't turn back the clock."

"So you say."

Then Jeffy tugged at Sylvia's sleeve. "Don't yell at him, Mom. He's my friend."

That did it. Alan saw Sylvia wince as if she'd been jabbed by a needle.

"We're leaving," she said, taking Jeffy by the hand and guiding him away from the sofa.

"But Mrs. Nash," Glaeken said. "We need Jeffy to reactivate the focus. We need to reunite the *Dat-tay-vao* and the metal from the instrument."

"But you don't have the metal, do you."

"Not yet, but—"

"Then I see no point in discussing this further. When you've located this magic metal, call me. You have my number. Then we'll talk. Not before."

"But where are you going?"

"Back home. Where else?"

"No, you mustn't. It's too dangerous. It's better that you stay here. You'll be safe here."

"*Here?*" she said, stopping at the door. "This place is practically on top of that hole out there—all but falling into it. I'll take my chances in Monroe."

"This place is protected, in a way. It will be preserved until the end. You and Jeffy and your friends can share that protection."

"Why? What's so special about this place?"

"I'm here. I'm to be saved until the last."

. . . and then he plans to make you suffer the tortures of the damned!

Alan remembered Nick's words and wondered why the old man didn't look more frightened.

"Toad Hall will be protected too. Alan and I have already seen to that."

Alan turned his chair and wheeled it toward Sylvia and Jeffy. He'd got on the phone first thing this morning and called around until he found a contractor who could start installing steel storm shutters immediately. He'd offered a substantial bonus if the job was completed by sundown. Now he wondered if shutters would be enough.

Why not stay here? It might be a good move. Crowded, yes, but Alan felt at home with this group, had a feeling that there was safety here among this disparate, unlikely crew. Something going on here. A subtle chemistry, a subliminal bond.

But Sylvia seemed oblivious to all that. She got this way when her anger-core broke free and took the helm. She dug in her heels and refused to budge. Alan knew he couldn't talk to her when she got like this. Nobody could. He'd learned to recognize the signs and—when the storm came—to sit back and let it have its way with her. When the clouds and winds had blown past and she was cooler, calmer, she'd be a different Sylvia, and be able to discuss it. Later he might be able to change her mind. Sylvia's anger could be inconvenient, frustrating, even infuriating at times, but the anger was part of what made Sylvia who she was. And Alan loved who Sylvia was.

It was quite clear though that Jeffy wanted to stay.

"I don't want to go, Mom."

"Please don't argue with me, Jeffy," Sylvia said in a low voice. "It's time to go home."

Jeffy tried to pull away from her. "No!"

"Please obey your mother, Jeffy," Glaeken said softly.

The boy abruptly stopped struggling. The look Sylvia threw Glaeken was anything but grateful.

"There's something you should realize, Mrs. Nash," Glaeken said. "The creatures that attacked your house last night are active only in the hours between sunset and sunrise. They must hide from the sun during the day. However, as I'm sure you are all aware, the daylight hours are shrinking."

"But that can't go on forever," said an unfamiliar voice.

Alan turned and saw that Hank was on his feet, staring in turn at each person in the room. It was the first time he had opened his mouth since he'd been introduced.

"Can it?" Hank said.

"The pattern will continue," Glaeken said. "And accelerate. Sunrise was late again today. Tomorrow it will be even later. Sunset will keep coming earlier and earlier."

"But if that keeps up . . . " Hank's eyes widened. "Lord!"

Slowly he sank down next to Carol on the couch.

"You see the pattern? Shrinking daylight hours, lengthening periods of darkness. The hole creatures will have progressively longer time for their feedings, and shorter periods when they must be in hiding. And when daylight is gone completely . . . "

"They'll never stop," Jack said in a hushed voice.

Alan knew from looking at him that no matter what terrors he and Sylvia and Ba had experienced last night, Jack had seen far worse.

"Correct," Glaeken said. "We are headed for a world without light, without law, without reason, sanity, or logic. A nightworld from which there will be no dawn. *Unless* we do something."

"Call me when you get the metal," Sylvia said.

Alan reached out and shook hands with Glaeken as he passed, then wheeled himself to where Ba stood holding the door.

"Don't leave," said a strained voice.

Alan turned at the door and saw that Nick had stepped out of the kitchen. His eyes were bright and alive again. And there was genuine concern in them as he stared at Alan.

"Why not?" Alan said.

"If the four of you leave here today, only three will live to return."

A chill swept over Alan. He glanced out into the atrium and saw Sylvia, Ba, and Jeffy standing before the elevator. As he watched, the bell dinged and the doors slid open. Sylvia and Jeffy stepped inside. Ba stood waiting, restraining the doors with one of his big hands.

Alan was paralyzed for a moment. The three outside were waiting for him; the six people in the apartment were staring at him. He wanted to stay, but wouldn't—couldn't—stay without Sylvia. And no way was Sylvia moving in here. Not yet, at least.

He shrugged and flashed what he knew was a weak grin at the people in the apartment.

"We'll see about that."

Then he headed toward the elevator, feeling as if he was rolling himself toward an abyss as deep and dark as the one in the Sheep Meadow outside.

As the door closed behind Dr. Bulmer, Bill guided Nick back into the kitchen. The younger man's behavior disturbed him. He was acting like some sort of Delphic oracle, transmitting threats and predictions from beyond. Was it madness or had his brush with the abyss left him connected, as Glaeken had said, to the chaos that was encroaching on all their lives?

"Are you trying to frighten people, Nick?"

"No," he said as he resumed his seat at the kitchen table. His eyes were tortured. "They're in danger. One of them's going to die."

"Who, Nick? Which one?"

If Nick was actually tapped in to something, maybe Bill could get something concrete out of him before he went catatonic again. Those four people

from Long Island—the woman, Sylvia was a bit of a bitch, but he didn't want
to see harm come to any of them, especially the boy.

"Who's going to die, Nick? Who's in danger? Is it Jeffy, the boy?"

But Nick was gone again, his face empty, his eyes blank.

"Damn it, Nick!" Bill said softly. He gave the slumped shoulders a gentle
squeeze. "Couldn't you have held on a few minutes longer?"

No reply, of course. But he did catch a voice rising in the living room. He
went to see what was up.

"What are we doing here?" Hank was saying. He was on his feet again,
staring down at Carol where she sat on the sofa. He looked frightened. He
glanced at Glaeken, at Jack who had appropriated Sylvia Nash's seat, then at
Bill. "What do you want with Carol and me?"

"I brought you here so you could learn the truth," Carol said. "The truth
about me."

"What truth? What you said about your son before? I didn't even know you
had a son."

"Well, I do," she said, then looked away. "And I don't."

Bill caught a glimpse of the unfathomed pain in her eyes. He pressed his
shoulder against the edge of the wall and leaned into it until it hurt. It took all
his strength of will to hold back from rushing to her side.

"But what's that got to do with what's been going on in this room? Which,
quite frankly, I don't understand one bit."

"My son is behind it all," Carol said in a small voice, without looking up.

Hank looked around again. "Will someone please tell me what's going on?"

Glaeken stepped forward. "Let me try, Mr. Treece. If you remember, a short
while ago I told of a man named Rasalom who in ancient times sided with the
Enemy and became its agent here. That man was imprisoned in Eastern Europe
in the fifteenth century. He should have remained imprisoned forever, but the
German Army inadvertently released him in 1941. Before he could get fully
free, however, he was destroyed. Or at least appeared to have been destroyed.
Through luck and unique circumstances, Rasalom was able to incorporate
himself into the unborn body of a man who would grow to be James Stevens."

Bill noticed Hank glance sharply at Carol here—her last name had been
Stevens when he'd met her.

"But Rasalom was powerless within Jim Stevens," Glaeken continued. "He
could only watch the world pass by from within Jim's body. Until . . . Jim
married Carol Nevins and they conceived a child. Rasalom became that child.
He was reborn late in 1968. For decades he lay low while his new body matured,
soaking up power from the world around him, from the wars and genocide in
Southeast Asia, from the hatred in Africa and the Middle East, and from the
countless spites, acrimonies, antipathies, rancors, and casual brutalities of
everyday life as well. He was waiting for the proper time to make his move. A
few months ago he discovered that he was unopposed here. His first overt move

was with the sunrise on Wednesday morning. He has been steadily escalating since then."

Hank was staring at Carol. "Your son? I don't believe this. I don't believe any of it. Come on, Carol. I'm taking you home."

"This isn't going to go away, Hank," Carol said, meeting his gaze. "We've got to face it."

"Then we'll face it somewhere else. Anywhere but here. I can't think straight here."

Carol rose to her feet. "Okay. Somewhere else. But we've got to come to terms with this."

Bill wanted to stop them, make Hank believe, but it was not his place. He couldn't step between a man and wife, even if the wife was Carol.

Carol said goodbye, and thanked Glaeken. Hank said nothing. They left in silence.

Jack got up and walked over to where Glaeken stood.

"Do you hire out?" he said, clapping the old man on the back. "I mean, if I ever have guests I can't get to leave, will you come over and get rid of them for me?"

Glaeken smiled, and as concerned as Bill was about Carol, he had to laugh. It was good to laugh, especially since he wasn't sure when he'd have cause to laugh again.

3 • PREPARATIONS

"They're all crazy, aren't they?" Hank said as they turned left on 57th Street and walked east.

The police weren't letting anybody into Central Park, and they'd closed off the streets adjacent to it. There wasn't a cab to be had, so Carol and Hank had detoured south. The sun was high and warm and gleamed on Hank's scalp where his hair was thinning. Carol wished she'd worn lighter clothes.

"Who?" she said, though she knew very well who he meant.

"Your friends. They're nutty as fruitcakes. And they've infected you with their nuttiness."

Carol noticed how he watched her as he spoke. His expression was strained. He seemed desperate to hear her agree with him.

"Only Bill and Glaeken are my friends. I can only speak for them. And I assure you, Hank, they're not crazy."

"They're delusional, Carol. They've *got* to be!" It was almost a plea.

"Are the late sunrises and early sunsets delusions, Hank?" she said force-fully. She had to make him believe, make him understand. "Is that hole in Central Park a delusion? Were all those people killed last night another delusion?"

"Could be," Hank said. "We could all be suffering from mass hysteria of some sort."

"Tell me you really believe that."

"Okay. I don't. Just wishful thinking. But the world's rampant weirdness has no bearing on your friend Glaeken's delusions. I mean, just because the earth and the sky are acting crazy doesn't mean I have to swallow everything some demented old man has to say."

"Granted. But think about it: There's not a scientific authority in the world who can explain all the lunacy we've seen the past few days."

"More lunacy is not an explanation."

"It's *true*, Hank," Carol said. "I swear to you, it's true. I've seen too much that backs up what he says, things I wish I'd never seen. He's not crazy."

Hank's hazel eyes, paler that usual in the bright sunlight, searched her face.

"What sort of things have you seen?"

"Some other time. We'll sit down tonight with a bottle of wine and I'll tell you all the things I've been afraid to tell you."

They walked in silence awhile. Carol knew Hank was sifting and sorting everything he'd heard today. He was a scientist at heart. When he had it all filed in the proper slots, he'd be able to deal with it and come to a conclusion. It was the way he was. Not flashy, no dramatic epiphanies, but his insight was just as valid.

Screeching tires and cries of terror brought them up short. They turned and saw a yellow cab rising off the street, trunk first. The driver opened his door, hung by the seat belt, and dropped to the pavement.

"My God!" Carol cried when she saw the woman and child lean out the rear window and scream for help. "Can't somebody do something?"

She clutched Hank's arm and they watched in horror as the cab continued to rise, beginning a slow rotation as it cleared the tops of the surrounding buildings and kept on falling up.

Finally Hank pulled her away.

"Let's go. There's nothing we can do and I feel like some sort of vulture watching it."

Carol felt the same. The tragedy of the scene made her feel weak, yet there was a horrid fascination about it.

"Stay close to the buildings," Hank said. "That way we'll have something to grab on to if it happens to us."

They walked on in silence, stepping almost gingerly, wondering if a gravity hole lay in wait on the sidewalk ahead. But Carol could not help casting furtive glances over her shoulder. Each time, the taxi was higher.

When they reached Second Avenue they were supposed to turn uptown, but Hank stopped and squinted up at the sun. He was sweating. Finally he spoke.

"It doesn't look like it's traveling any faster."

Carol tried to look at it but it hurt her eyes.

"Do you think it is?"

"Something has to be moving faster." He turned and stared at her. His eyes were watering, the pupils tiny. "I mean, the sun doesn't move, *we* do. Earth's rotation on its axis—that's what determines the varying duration of daylight through the year. Shorter days would mean we're either rotating faster or the Earth's shifted on its axis. But the scientists say neither has happened. Yet the days *are* shortening. A paradox. The impossible is happening. If that's true, then the impossible—or the impossible-sounding—things Glaeken said could be true as well."

He's coming around, Carol thought as they turned up Second Avenue and put the sun to their backs. He wasn't getting there via an intuitive leap but by the only route he knew—a logical examination of the evidence at hand. He'd have made a good Sherlock Holmes.

"Do you really think it'll happen?" he said.

"What?"

"The 'nightworld' Glaeken was talking about. It's a real possibility, isn't it?"

"Yes, but not an inevitability if he can get some co- operation."

At first Carol had been furious with that Sylvia Nash woman. How could she talk to Glaeken like that? He was only trying to help everybody, and all he was asking was their co-operation to save their own hides. But Carol had to keep reminding herself that the truth was so difficult to accept—she remembered how she had fought it for years. Decades. And Sylvia Nash was afraid of something. Carol didn't know what, but she was sure she'd seen it in the younger woman's eyes as she walked past on her way out of Glaeken's apartment.

"Let's be optimistic," Hank said. "Let's say he gets the kind of co-operation he needs and he fashions and reactivates this 'focus' he was talking about. And let's even say he gets it to work and gets the sun to return to a normal pattern. That could take weeks, couldn't it? Maybe months."

"I don't know, Hank. What are you getting at?"

There was a strange new intensity about him, one she had never seen before. His eyes had taken on an almost feverish glow.

"Sunlight, Carol. What needs sunlight—regular, measured doses of sun-light—more than anything else?"

"Well . . . plants, I guess."

"Exactly! And right now, in the spring, sunlight is crucial for germination and seedling growth. If the daily dose of sunlight diminishes steadily over the next few weeks, there will be massive crop failures all across the globe."

"If Rasalom takes over, crop failures will be the least of our problems."

"But I told you, Carol: I'm thinking optimistically. I'm assuming Glaeken will win. But win or lose, we'll still be facing world-wide food shortages, maybe even famine."

The realization startled and sickened Carol. Even if they won, billions would starve in the aftermath. A Pyhrric victory was the best they could hope for. She wondered if Glaeken had foreseen this. She was tentatively proud of Hank. Tentatively . . . because his sudden agitation disturbed her.

"We've got to start making plans for that eventuality, Carol," he said. "Those who can anticipate the future can profit from it."

"Oh, no, Hank. You're not thinking of the stock market or anything like that, are you?"

"Of course not," he said. He seemed annoyed that she'd even suggested it. "If we lose much sunlight for any length of time, I don't see there even *being* a stock market, or a commodities exchange, for that matter. Grain futures might go through the roof, but what are you going to pay with?"

"I don't understand."

"Carol," he said, stopping and gripping her shoulders, "if we have worldwide crop failures, money—currency—won't be worth anything. It'll be just paper, and you can't eat paper. The only things that'll be worth anything are precious metals like gold and silver, probably diamonds and other jewels as well, and one other thing: food."

"How can you even think about something like that?"

"Somebody's got to think about it. Somebody's got to plan ahead. I'm thinking about *us*, Carol. When the crops fail and the grocery shelves are emptied, we're going to see food riots in this city—in every city. It's going to be a nasty time. And if we want to get through it alive, we'd better be prepared." He took her hand. "Come on."

They resumed their trek uptown, but at a faster pace now. Carol hurried to keep up. Hank seemed filled with urgent purpose. She'd never seen him like this. The mellow, laid-back number-cruncher was gone, replaced by a manic stranger.

As they neared their apartment, he led her into the Gristedes where she did most of her food shopping. He pulled two shopping carts free, rolled one in front of Carol and kept the other for himself.

"Hank, what are we doing?"

He glanced around nervously.

"Try to keep your voice down," he whispered. "We're stocking up—before the hoarding starts."

Carol started to laugh, mirthlessly, from shock.

"Do you hear yourself?"

"Come on, Carol. This is serious."

And she saw in his eyes then that he was afraid. I'm afraid too, she thought. She glanced down at the empty shopping cart before her. But am I *this* afraid?

"Just get canned and bottled goods, and things that will keep a long time, like pasta," he whispered. "Nothing that needs to be refrigerated. Load up as much as you can carry back to the apartment and put it on the Visa."

"Charge it? I've got cash."

"Save it. We'll charge everything to the limit. Who knows? If things get really bad, the credit card companies may not be around to collect."

"Why don't we go all the way, Hank?" she said, trying to keep her voice light. "Gristedes delivers. Why don't we just clear off the shelves and have them bring everything over later? Save us all the hassle of lugging heavy bags home."

"We've got to be discreet," he said, his eyes darting about again. "We can't let it get around that we've got a stockpile of food. People will be breaking down our door when things get tight."

She stared at him. He'd figured all this out during their short walk up from 57th Street.

"What a mind you have!"

"You'll thank me when the bad times come." He pointed to the left side of the store. "You go that way, I'll go this. We'll meet at the check-out."

And then he was on his way toward the canned goods section. Carol watched him in dismay.

It's the shock, she told herself. *He's been barraged with too much today. He must be reeling, confused, frightened. I've had since 1968 to adjust and I still can't quite accept it all. Poor Hank has had his whole belief system trashed in the past few hours.*

Carol headed for the pasta aisle. Okay. She'd play along. If stockpiling some food would allay some of Hank's fears, she'd help him out. It was the least she could do.

He'd come around. She was sure of it. She just hoped it was soon. She didn't like this new Hank.

CNN:

—same in country after country around the globe: gigantic holes, seemingly bottomless, averaging two hundred feet across, opening one after the other throughout the day. The governments of Iran, China, and Cuba deny the existence of any of such holes within their borders, but aerial reconnaissance says otherwise. And the question on everyone's mind is: Is each of these holes going to release a horde of vicious creatures like those that were loosed on Manhattan last night? And if so, what can be done to stop them?

In Manhattan, preparations are under way . . .

Jack sat behind the counter of the Isher Sports Shop—one of the few places left on the Upper West Side that spelled shop with one P—and watched the people passing by on the other side of the window. Amsterdam Avenue was sunny and only slightly less crowded than usual for a Saturday afternoon.

Like nothing's changed.

But everything had changed. They just didn't realize it yet. Jack had an urge to run out there and start grabbing people by the collar and shout in their faces that last night wasn't an isolated incident or bizarre aberration. It was going to happen again. And worse. Tonight.

Abe Grossman, the owner, bustled in from the rear of the store carrying two cups of coffee. He handed one to Jack and perched himself on the stool behind the cash register. Jack sipped and winced.

"Jeez, Abe. When did you make this?"

"This morning. Why?"

"It's not like wine, you know. It doesn't get better with age."

"I should waste it? With a microwave in the back, I should throw out perfectly good coffee because Mr. Repairman Jack suddenly has a delicate palate?"

The stool creaked as he adjusted the two-hundred-plus pounds he packed into a fifty-five-year-old, five-eight frame. He had receding gray hair and wore his usual black pleated-front pants, white shirt, and black tie. A bit of egg yolk from breakfast yellowed the breast pocket of his shirt; a red spot that looked like strawberry jelly clung to his tie; he had just finished sprinkling his entire shirt front with bits of finely chopped onion from the fresh bialies Jack had brought.

"*Nu?* he said when he was settled on his perch. "What have I been saying for so many years to the accompaniment of your derisive laughter? And now it's finally happening. The Collapse Of Civilization. It's all going to fall apart, right before our eyes, just as I've been saying."

Jack had expected this. He'd known that when he told Abe what Glaeken had said, he'd be in for an I-told-you-so lecture. But he had to let Abe know. He'd been Jack's friend, confidant, and arms supplier for most of his time in New York City. In fact it was Abe who had started calling him Repairman Jack.

"No offense, Abe, but you've been predicting an *economic* holocaust. You know, bank failures, runaway inflation, and so on. Remember?"

"And in Texas it almost happened back in—"

"This is different."

Abe stared at him over the rim of his coffee cup. "This Glaeken person's not a *meshuggener*, then? You really think this is going to happen?"

"Yeah," Jack said. "I really do."

Abe was silent a moment, then, "For some reason, I believe it too. Maybe because I've been preparing for this eventuality most of my adult life. Maybe because I'd feel like such a *schlemiel* if I'd been preparing for such a thing for so long and it never happened. But you know what, Jack? Now that the time has come, it's not such a vindication. Happy I'm not."

"You still have that hideaway?"

"Of course."

Abe, the world's dourest pessimist, had been preparing for The Collapse Of Civilization since the mid-seventies. Years ago he'd told Jack about his refuge in rural Pennsylvania, an overgrown farm with an underground bunker and deep stocks of water, weapons, and freeze-dried food. He'd said Jack was welcome there when the Big Crash came. He'd even told Jack where it was—something he'd never revealed to anyone else, even his own daughter.

"Go there, Abe. Get out of the city and hole yourself up there. Today, if possible."

"Today? Today I can't go. Tomorrow maybe."

"Not 'maybe,' Abe. If not today, then tomorrow for sure. For *sure*."

"You're really worried, aren't you. How bad we talking about, Jack?"

"Bad like you've never dreamed." Jack stopped and grinned. "Jeez, Abe. I'm around you half an hour and I start sounding like you."

"That's because you're part chameleon. But how bad is bad like I never dreamed? I dream pretty bad."

"Whatever you've dreamed, trust me: this'll be worse."

Scenes from the bloody carnage around the Sheep Meadow hole flashed before his eyes. And now there were more holes. Even if the predators from the holes remained limited to the two species he'd seen last night, the city would devolve into a nightmare. But Glaeken was saying that the things from the holes would get progressively bigger and more vicious each night.

Jack's mind shied away from envisioning the holocaust.

"But I'd like to ask a favor."

"Don't even ask," Abe said. "You show up here first thing tomorrow morning with Gia and that darling little girl of hers and we'll all head for the hills together."

"Thanks, Abe," feeling a burst of warmth for this dumpy gunrunner. "That means a lot. But I won't be coming along."

"I should go and you should stay?"

"There's a chance I can do something about the situation."

"Ah. The necklaces you mentioned. I remember the one you had. With the pre-Vedic inscriptions."

"Right. I need to get copies made. I was thinking about Walt Duran. What do you think?"

"Walt's as good as you could ask. A *shtarker* in the world of engraving. And he could use the work."

"Really? What happened?"

"Desktop publishing is what happened. Putting honest counterfeiters out of business."

Jack had heard about that. High-definition scanners and color laser printers were doing in minutes what used to take old-time counterfeiters months of grueling, painstaking labor at a cost of ruined eyesight and a chronic stiff neck.

Walt was a stand-up guy, a hard worker. If he'd put his talents to work in the jewelry industry, he'd probably have made more money in the long run and wouldn't have had to do that stretch in the joint. But even so, Jack was glad to hear he'd fallen on hard times. That meant he could be goosed into high gear by the lure of a bonus for early delivery.

Because Walt was as slow as he was good.

"Okay," Abe said. "What's the plan?"

Jack choked down the rest of his coffee and stood up.

"Here's my advice. Gas up that van of yours and garage it for the night. Pack up your stuff this afternoon and get back here before nightfall. Spend the night in your basement here. No matter what you hear upstairs, don't come up to have a look. *Stay down there.* I'll have Gia and Vicky here right after sunrise. Sound okay?"

Abe frowned. "Sounds like you think things will be going downhill fast."

"Downhill?" Jack said as he headed for the door. "I think they're going to run off a cliff."

Okay, Jack thought as he drove his black-on-white Corvair convertible toward the East Side. Walt's on the job. Now all I've got to do is convince Gia that she's got to leave town.

Walt had been glad for the work. Ecstatic, actually. He'd been reduced to living in a tiny tenement studio in Hell's Kitchen. Jack had shown him the drawings, told him he wanted two copies on a one-to-one scale, and given him a down payment so he could go out and get the raw materials. Delivery time was a problem, though. Walt had said no way could he get it done by Monday morning. But when Jack promised a ten-thousand-dollar bonus, Walt reconsidered. *Maybe* he could have them by then.

Jack drummed his fingers on the steering wheel as he cruised along. Getting those necklaces out of Walt by Monday morning would be a breeze compared to getting Gia into Abe's van tomorrow. And he didn't have all that much time to persuade her. The afternoon was already on the wane. But if Glaeken was right about tonight being worse that last night, maybe he wouldn't have to convince her. He could let the things from the hole do it.

He swung up toward the Park to see how the clean-up was going. Jack was amazed at the transformation. The barricades were still up to keep cars off Central Park South, but the corpses were gone, the wrecked vehicles had been cleared, the pavements were washed clean. Car were restricted, but not pedestrians. A *lot* of people were about on the sidewalks and the fringe of the Park, the curious of all ages, come to see the notorious Sheep Meadow hole and check out the stories of bloody carnage they'd heard on the news.

Jack checked his watch. He had a little time to spare so he double-parked and jogged toward the Sheep Meadow to get another look at the hole.

The crowd was thick there. Everyone seemed to be watching something going on down by the hole. Over their heads he could see cranes dipping up and down. He wove through the press until he got to a decent-sized tree. He shimmied up the trunk to where he could see the Sheep Meadow.

The southern half of the hole was covered with some sort of steel mesh. Work crews were in the process of screening over the rest of the opening. Jack watched for a moment, then slid back to the ground.

"How's it going?" someone said.

Jack turned and saw a well-dressed young couple standing nearby with a baby carriage. The guy was smiling warily.

"Better than half done," Jack said.

The woman sighed and squeezed her husband's biceps with both hands and looked at Jack with uneasy doe eyes.

"Do you think those things will come back?"

"You can count on it," Jack said.

"Will the net work?"

Jack shrugged. "Maybe. But this isn't the only hole."

"I know," the guy said, nodding. "But this is the one that counts for us." He put an arm around his wife's shoulders. "I'm sure we'll be all right," he told her.

Jack looked down at the baby in the stroller. Eighteen months at the most, all in pink, sandy-haired, grinning up at him.

"You got a cellar where you live?" Jack said, staring into those two innocent blue eyes. "Someplace with no windows?"

"Uh, yes we do. There's a storage area down by the boiler room where—"

"Move in there before sunset. Bring everything you'll need until morning. Don't go upstairs until sunrise."

He tore his eyes away from the child and hurried off.

Gia and Vicky. Dammit, even if he had to sling Gia over his shoulder and dump her in the back of Abe's van, he'd see to it that they were on their way out of town tomorrow morning.

Monroe, Long Island

Sylvia stood in the driveway and watched the workmen swarming along the scaffolding they'd set up against Toad Hall's west wall.

"I think we're gonna make it," said Rudy Snyder as he stood at her side.

Sylvia looked at the sinking sun, the long shadows. The day was ending too quickly, as if winter were approaching instead of summer.

"You promised me, Rudy," she said. She and Alan had called all along the North Shore this morning and had finally coaxed Rudy out of Glen Cove. "You guaranteed me you'd have every window shuttered before sunset. I hope I'm not hearing the sound of someone beginning to hedge on a deal."

She tightened her fists to hide her anxiety. She didn't think she could stand another ordeal like last night.

"No way, Mrs. Nash," said Rudy. He wore a peaked cap with *Giants* across the front; he was tall and fat, with red hair and a veiny, bulbous nose. When he aided the work crew, he did so at ground level only. "We'll have them all in, just like I said. But they won't all be wired."

"I don't care about the wiring. You can do that tomorrow. Just get those shutters in good and tight, then pull them down and leave them down."

"You really think all this is necessary?" he said.

She glanced at him, then away. He thought she was a nut, overreacting to some wild stories out of the city.

"You've seen all those little teeth in the siding?"

"Hey, I'm not saying you didn't have a problem last night, but do you really think they'll come back again?"

"Unfortunately, I'm sure they will. Especially since they don't have to come all the way from Central Park this time."

"You mean because of that hole that opened up in Oyster Bay this morning? Whatta y'think's goin' on?"

"Don't you know? It's the end of the world." *My world, at least.*

Rudy's smile was wary. "No . . . really."

"Please finish the job," she said. She didn't feel like talking about it. "Seal the house up tight. That will earn you the bonus I mentioned."

"You got it."

He bustled off and began shouting at his workers to get their asses moving.

Sylvia sighed as she stared at Toad Hall. The old place's carefully maintained look of faded elegance was gone, destroyed by the rolling storm shutters. But they were good, tight, with heavy-duty slats of solid steel. The best. During the day they could be rolled up into the cylinders bolted above the windows; at sunset they'd slide down along tracks fastened to the window frames. They'd be cranked down by hand tonight, but after they were fully wired up tomorrow, Sylvia would be able to roll them all up and down with the flick a single switch. This particular model was designed to withstand storms of hurricane force. Tonight they were going to have to withstand a storm of a different sort. She prayed they'd be enough.

"The back's done," Alan said, rolling toward her. "They're moving around here to help finish up this side." His gaze followed Sylvia's to the anachronisms being attached to Toad Hall. "A shame, isn't it?"

Sylvia smiled, glad to know their thoughts were still in synch, even after the uncomfortable silence of the ride back from the city. Especially when Alan had told her what that nut had said as they were leaving. *Only three will live to return.* What an awful thing to say.

"I feel like I'm witnessing the end of an era."

"It might be the end of a lot more than that," Alan said.

Sylvia felt all her muscles tighten under her skin. She said nothing. She knew where Alan was leading and didn't want to go there. She'd been dreading this conversation since they left Glaeken's apartment.

"Talk to me, Sylvia. Why are you so angry?"

"I'm not angry."

"You're coiled like a steel spring."

Again she said nothing. *I'm coiled, all right*, she thought, *but it's not anger. I wish it were. I can deal with anger.*

"What do you think, Syl?" Alan said finally.

You're not going to give up, are you?

"About what?".

"About Glaeken. About what he said this morning."

"I haven't had time to think much about anything since this morning, least of all that old crank's ravings."

"I believe him," Alan said. "And so do you. I saw it in your eyes when you were listening. I know your expression when you think you're being bullshitted. You weren't wearing it back in Glaeken's apartment. So why don't you admit it?"

"All right," she said through tight lips. "I believe him too. Does that make you happy?"

She regretted that last sentence as soon as she said it, but it seemed to roll right off Alan.

"Good. Now we're getting somewhere. So I've got to ask you: If you believe him, why did you walk out?"

"Because I don't trust him. Don't misunderstand me on that," she added quickly. "I don't think he's lying to us. I think he's sincere, I . . . just . . . don't think he's as much in control of his end of things as he thinks he is . . . or wants us to believe he is."

"Maybe not. He was trying to sell us—you, especially—on something none of us is prepared to accept. The only reason we *can* accept it is that we've already had our lives turned upside down by something that ninety-nine per cent of rational humanity would swear is impossible."

"The *Dat-tay-vao*," Sylvia said.

"Yeah. And if he says he needs the *Dat-tay-vao* to try to close up those holes and keep the days from shrinking to nothing and the world being overrun by those monstrosities from last night, why would you hold Jeffy away from him? Jeffy doesn't need the *Dat-tay-vao*."

"How do you know that?"

"Has it ever treated its carrier well? Look at Walter Erskine. Look at me. Remember the lines from the old song about the one who carries the Touch? '. . . He bears the weight of the balance that must be struck.' "

"But the *Dat-tay-vao* hasn't harmed Jeffy."

"Only because he hasn't used it—yet. He hasn't had an opportunity—yet. But what if he does find out, and does begin using it?"

Here it comes. She felt the pressure building up in her, edging past the point of control.

"And what if the *Dat-tay-vao*'s relationship with Jeffy is different? Special?" she said.

Alan's eyes were puzzled as he searched her face.

"I don't—"

"What if the *Dat-tay-vao*'s presence is keeping Jeffy like he is?" She tried to hold the tremor out of her voice but it grew, giving the words a jittery vibrato. "What if it's the reason he's been alert, responsive, laughing, singing, reading, playing with other kids—a normal boy—for the past year? Alan, what if that old man takes the *Dat-tay-vao* away for his focus or whatever he was talking about and Jeffy goes back to the way he was when I adopted him?" The tremor spread from her voice to her body now. She couldn't control the shaking in her hands and knees. "What if he becomes autistic again, Alan?"

Sylvia pressed her hands against her face, as much to hide as to catch the tears springing into her eyes.

"God, Alan, I'm so ashamed!"

Suddenly there was someone standing beside her. She felt a pair of arms slip around her and hold her close.

"Alan! You're standing!"

"Not very well, I'm afraid. But that's not the point. Watching you all morning, trying to figure out what's going on inside you, and never seeing how frightened you are. Christ, what a jerk."

"But you're standing!"

"You've seen me do it before."

"But not without the parallel bars."

"You're my parallel bars at the moment. I couldn't just sit there and watch you go to pieces and spout that nonsense about being ashamed."

"But I *am* ashamed." She twisted in his arms and clung to him. "If Glaeken's right, the whole world is threatened, billions of people in danger, and here I'm only worried about one little boy. I'm ready to let the whole world take a flying leap rather than jeopardize him."

"But that's not just any little boy. That's Jeffy—*your* little boy, the most important little boy in the world. Don't be ashamed of putting him first. That's where he should be. That's where he belongs."

"But the whole *world*, Alan! How can I say no?" Sylvia felt the panic well up inside her again. "How can I say *yes*?"

"I can't answer that for you, Syl. I wish I could. You've got to weigh everything. Got to figure that if Glaeken's right, and he can't get the *Dat-tay-vao* for the focus he was talking about, then Jeffy's a goner along with everybody else. There's nothing to say that he can't lure the *Dat-tay-vao* from Jeffy without harming him. If Glaeken can then turn all these horrors around, Jeffy will have a safer world to live in."

"But if Jeffy is left in autistic limbo again . . . "

"That branches into two possibilities. Glaeken succeeds and Jeffy's back to where he was a year ago and we deal with it and hope for a medical breakthrough in the treatment of autism. Or Glaeken fails despite Jeffy's sacrifice."

"Then it's all been for nothing."

"Not necessarily. If nothing else, Jeffy's relapse into autism will shield him from the living hell Glaeken's predicting. That might be a blessing."

Sylvia clung more tightly to Alan.

"I wish this wasn't up to me."

"I know. Too bad he's not old enough to be brought in on the decision."

Sylvia felt a vibration begin to shimmer through Alan's lean body. She looked down and saw that his left leg had begun to tremble. As she watched, it began to jitter and shake. Alan reached a hand down to steady it, but as soon as he let go, the tremors started again.

Alan smiled. "I feel like Robert Klein doing his old 'I can't stop my leg' routine."

"What's wrong?"

"Spasm. Happens when I'm on it too long. Used to be in both legs, now it's just my left. If I can't do Robert Klein, maybe I could try an Elvis imitation."

"Stop it. Nobody listens to Elvis anymore."

"I do. But only his Sun stuff, and pre-Army RCA."

Sylvia smiled. Alan and his oldies. Part of his therapy after the coma had been to rebuild his doo-wop collection. It had worked miracles with his memory linkages.

"Here. Sit down."

He eased himself back into the wheelchair. The leg stopped its jittering as soon as he took his weight off it.

"Uh-oh," Alan said, slapping the still leg. "There goes my new career."

Sylvia bent and hugged him around the neck.

"Have I told you that I love you?"

"Not today."

"I love you, Alan. And thanks."

"For what?"

"For standing up and holding me when I needed it. And for making things clear. I think I know what I'm going to do now."

"Missus?"

Sylvia started at the sound of Ba's voice. She wished he'd learn to make a little more noise when he moved about. He was like a cat.

He was standing behind her holding the new club he'd been working on most of the afternoon to replace the one he'd given to that Jack fellow; like its predecessor it was studded with diamond-like chew-wasp teeth.

"Yes, Ba?"

"Where is the Boy?"

Fingers of unease brushed her throat.

"I thought he was with you."

"He was in the garage with me. He wished to go outside. I knew the Missus and the Doctor were here so . . . "

Ba's voice trailed off as he did a slow turn, scanning the perimeter of the grounds.

"Maybe he's in the back."

Sylvia started toward the back yard. She never let Jeffy out alone by the water. Nightmares of dragging the Long Island Sound for his body . . .

"No, Missus. I watched him run around house to the front."

"Maybe he's inside, then."

"He is not, Missus."

The long shadows seemed to be reaching for her. The sun was a red glow behind the willows along the west wall. The fingers of unease at her throat stretched, reaching toward panic, encircling and squeezing.

Rudy came toward her across the lawn. "We're done!" he said, grinning.

"Have you seen Jeffy?" she asked. "My little boy?"

"The blond-haired kid? Not for while. Not for a few hours. But we've been kinda occupied with getting those shutters up on time. Now, about that bonus—"

"I'll pay you everything later—tomorrow. Right now we've got to find Jeffy!"

Alan said, "I'll check the waterfront. Ba, you beat the bushes along the wall. Sylvia, why don't you check the road?"

As Alan and Ba went their separate ways, Sylvia hurried down the driveway toward the front gate. When she reached the street she stopped, looking both ways, straining to see in the waning light.

Which way?

Shore Drive followed the curve of the Sound, running east toward the center of town and west toward Lattingtown and Glen Cove. Instinctively, she started east, toward the pale moon rising full and translucent in the fading light. Jeffy loved the toy shops and video arcades along the harbor front. If he was traveling Shore Drive, that was the way he'd go. Sylvia took a few steps, then stopped, suddenly unsure.

If I were Jeffy, she thought, which way would I go?

Slowly she turned and faced the other way, where the sun was on the horizon, sinking behind Manhattan.

Manhattan . . . where Glaeken was . . . where Jeffy and the power within him wanted to be . . .

Sylvia began running west. Her heart was a claustrophobic prisoner, trapped in her chest, pounding frantically on the bars of her ribs. Her eyes roved left and right, scanning the yards along the road. All the lots were big here, with as much frontage along the street as the shoreline. Unlike Toad Hall's, most of the other yards were open, their manicured grounds studded with trees and shrubs and free-form plantings. Jeffy could have followed a squirrel or a bird into any one of them.

He might be anywhere.

She slowed but kept moving. She didn't want to miss him. To her left a battered red pick-up truck squealed to a halt on the street. Rudy leaned out the window as the rest of his work crew sped by him in their own cars and trucks.

"Any sign of your boy?"

Sylvia shook her head. "No. Look, he's blond and we call him Jeffy. If you see him on your way—"

"I'll send him back. Good luck."

He sped off and Sylvia resumed her search, with increasingly frequent glances at the rapidly disappearing sun. Before she'd traveled a block—the blocks were long out here—the sun was gone.

My God, my God, she thought, the sun's down and those horrible insects could be rising out of that new hole in Oyster Bay and heading this way right now.

If she didn't get Jeffy back to the house soon those things would rip him to pieces. And if she stayed out here much longer, *she* would be ripped to pieces.

What am I going to do?

WCBS-FM

All right, everybody. It's official—the sun's gone down early again. It sank outta sight at 6:44. One hour and thirty-nine minutes early. If I were you I'd get off the streets. Now. Get indoors and keep it tuned here, to your favorite oldies station.

Manhattan

Carol rolled the two-wheeled shopping cart out of the elevator and down the hall. A big load—all the canned food and pasta it would hold, plus bottled water stacked on top—but it was her last trip of the day. And just in time too. It was getting dark out there.

Besides that, she was tired. She wasn't used to this kind of running around but she could handle the exertion. She stayed in shape, exercising regularly, watching her diet—her fifty- year-old body was trimmer, better toned, and younger looking than a lot of bodies in their thirties. This was a different kind of fatigue, arising not from the body but from the mind, from stress.

And it had been one hell of a stressful day.

She hoped Hank was home. She knew how out of character it would be for him to get caught out in the darkness, but he had become positively manic as the day wore on. She'd never seen him like this. Running in and out with five-gallon jugs of spring water, boxes of batteries, a propane stove, and food, food, food. Carol was almost afraid to open the apartment door.

She didn't have to. It opened as she came down he hall. Hank's worried face relaxed into a relieved smile.

"Thank God!" he said. "I've been worried about you." He stepped into the hall and took the cart from her. "Come on. Wait'll you see what I got on my last trip."

He ushered her in and closed the door behind her. Carol stopped and stared at her living room. She barely recognized it. Cartons of canned goods—*stacks* of cartons were arrayed along the walls. It looked more like a warehouse than a home.

"Hank . . . where . . . how?"

"I got smart," Hank said, beaming. "It occurred to me after I left you off at the A&P. Why think small? Why not go to the source? So I rented a van, looked up a distributor, and really stocked up. Backed it around back and brought everything up with this." He patted the hand truck leaning against the wall by the door. "But that wasn't my real coup." He headed down the hall. "Wait'll you see this."

"Oh, Hank. Not in the bedroom."

She suffered through visions of sleeping amid piles of Ronzoni macaroni until he returned lugging a pair of heavy canvas bags, one in each hand.

"I didn't know where else to put them," he said as he eased the bags down before her. They clinked inside as they settled on the floor. "They weigh almost fifty pounds each."

"What's in them?"

"Four thousand silver coins. Two whole bags of pre-nineteen-sixty-four quarters. All solid silver. Got the pair for under six grand at a coin dealer on Fifty-sixth. And you know what?" he said, his eyes dancing with glee. "I *charged* them! Can you believe it? The guy took Visa for them!"

"Hank, can we afford all this?"

"Sure! Sure we can. In fact, we can't afford *not* to buy all this. Because it won't matter what our Visa or Master Card balance is. Look, if daylight shrinks to nothing and things really start falling apart, there'll be nobody to collect on our credit cards. These coins are going to be like gold, like diamonds. I told you: If what that Glaeken fellow said really happens, paper money will be worthless. Each of these quarters could be worth fifty dollars apiece in buying power. Precious metals will be what matters. Gold, silver, gems, they'll replace government paper. But you know what'll be more valuable than any metal? Food, Carol. You can't eat gold or silver. In a world without sunlight, where nothing but mushrooms can grow, nothing will be more valuable than food. The man with the full larder will be king. Food, Carol. And we've got lots of it. And tomorrow we'll get even more."

Carol stared at her normally calm, quiet, rational husband. She'd never seen him like this.

"Hank . . . are you all right?"

"Carol, I've never been better. I feel like I'm on top of the world. You know, all my life I've worked my butt off for every cent I've put in my pocket. I've seen people around me invest in the stock market, invest in junk bonds or real estate and make killings. But not me. Whenever I tried, it was always too little too late. No matter what it was, I always got in on the wrong side of the curve. But this time is different. This is *my* time, when *I* get in on the ground floor." His eyes got a faraway look as he stared around at all the food. "One thing I know about is hunger, Carol. And I refuse to be hungry ever again."

"When were you ever hungry?"

"Hungry?" he said, his eyes focusing on her. "I didn't say anything about hungry."

"Yes, you did. You said you knew about hunger."

"Did I?" He sat on a stack of cases of Campbell's pork and beans and stared at the floor. "I didn't even hear myself."

Carol stepped to his side and laid a hand on his shoulder. The manic look had faded from his eyes. He was more like himself again. She wanted to keep him that way.

"I heard you. What did you mean? When were you ever hungry?"

He sighed. "As a kid. When I was about seven. My father was a precision machinist. He lost his job after the war when the weapons industry ground to a halt. A lot of machinists were out of work but they were picking up other jobs in other fields, doing anything to make ends meet. Not my father. He was a machinist and that was the only kind of work he would accept. Before too long we ran out of money. All I remember about those times was being hungry. Hungry all the time."

"But there were agencies, charities, welfare—"

"I didn't know about any of that. I was only seven. I found out later that my father wouldn't hear of taking a hand- out, as he called it. All I knew was that I was hungry and there was never enough food on the table for a good meal. I woke up hungry and went to bed hungry and was hungry every minute in between. I'd steal food from other kids' lunches in school. The only other thing I remember from that time besides hunger was fear. I was afraid we'd all starve to death. Finally he got a job and we could eat again." He shook his head slowly. "But, boy, that was a scary time."

Carol rubbed his shoulder and smoothed his thinning hair as she tried to picture Hank as a hungry, frightened little boy. She realized how little she really knew about this man she had married.

"You never told me."

"Frankly, I'd forgotten about it. I guess I've buried those days. And why not? They were the worst times of my life. I can't remember the last time I gave them a thought."

"Maybe they weren't buried as deeply as you thought. Look around you, Hank."

He glanced about at the stacked cases of food, then stood up.

"This is different, Carol. This isn't just survival. This is an investment in our future."

"Hank—"

"You know what I ought to do? I ought to take inventory. Right. Organize a list of what we have. That way we can spend tomorrow filling in any gaps."

"Hank . . . why don't we have dinner?"

He looked at her. "Good idea. I'm kind of hungry, come to think of it. But use the most perishable stuff we have. We'll finish that off first. We don't want to dip into our canned goods yet."

Carol watched in dismay as Hank picked up a pad and pencil and began going about the apartment making lists of their supplies. What was happening to her safe, sane Hank? Even though her husband was only a few feet away, she felt alone. Alone with a manic stranger.

4 • Nightwings

"There they are!"

Bill Ryan focused the binoculars on the hole in the Sheep meadow. An excellent set of field glasses—they brought the people below into sharp focus, seemingly within reach. But the people weren't what interested him.

"Right on time," Glaeken said from behind his right shoulder.

Bill watched the fluttering things begin to collect under the barrier that had been stretched over the hole, watched them straining upward against the steel mesh. Arrayed against them under the banks of lights was an army of exterminators sheathed in heavy protective gear and masks, wielding hoses attached to tank trucks equipped with high-pressure pumps. At a signal from somewhere down there, all the nozzles came to life, spewing out a golden fluid.

"What are they spraying?" Glaeken said.

"Looks like some sort of insecticide."

Glaeken grunted and turned away. "No toxins are going to hurt those things. They'd do far better simply with gasoline and a match." He turned on the television. "Here it is on the tevevision. You'll get a better angle here."

Bill stepped to his side and watched the scene below in living color. Apparently Glaeken was right. In the telephoto close-up on the screen, the insecticide was having no effect on the steadily increasing number of creatures massed under the mesh. They were getting wet and that was about it. He turned and looked at Nick, sitting on the sofa, staring at the wall.

"Think the net will hold through the night?" Bill said.

"It doesn't matter," Glaeken said with his predictable pessimism.

Bill shook his head. Perhaps being pessimistic was being realistic, but he couldn't suppress the thrill of hope that shot through him when he saw all those monstrosities from the hole trapped under the steel mesh.

"Why doesn't it matter? It shows we can contain them."

"Even as we speak, the holes in Queens, on Staten Island and out on Long Island are spewing out the very creatures they think they've defeated here."

"Then we'll cap those, too."

"Bigger things are coming," Glaeken said. "The speedy little flying things arrive first because they're the quickest. Then come the slower flying things. Then come the crawlers."

Crawlers . . . the very word made Bill's skin crawl.

"Then they've only bought a little time here," Bill said, his spirits palpably sagging.

"They haven't even bought that. And somewhere along the way . . . the leviathans will come."

Bill was about to ask for some elaboration on that when he heard a whining howl from the Park, loud enough to be audible through the locked and sealed windows. On the screen he noticed the exterminators and observers start to back away from the hole. The streams from the hoses seemed to be blowing back in their faces.

"Something's happening."

He returned to the window with the binocs. Down in the Sheep Meadow, a gale-force wind was roaring from the hole, bulging the heavy steel mesh upward as it crushed the insects against it.

"Looks like the hole is trying to blow the lid off!"

Glaeken came up beside him. "No," he said softly. "Something's coming. Something big."

Bill squinted through the binoculars as the wind howl grew louder. The exterminators had turned off their hoses but were still backing away. As he watched, a number of the steel girders anchoring the mesh at the south side were torn from the ground. That end of the mesh began to flap free, releasing a hoard of the killer insects. Panic took charge in the Sheep Meadow.

"Big?" Bill said. "How—?"

And then it happened. Something burst from the hole. Something beyond big. Something gargantuan, filling the two- hundred-foot diameter of the hole, something dark as the deepest cavern at the bottom of the Mariana Trench at midnight. It rammed through the steel mesh like a night train through a spider's web and kept hurtling upward, a monstrous, rough-hewn piling thrusting its seemingly endless length into the darkening sky.

Bill tore the glasses from his eyes and watched as it came free of the hole and continued upward. Awed, he pressed his face against the window pane and followed its course, wondering how far it could go before it lost its momentum and fell back to earth, his mind reeling at the thought of the resultant damage from something the size of a small skyscraper crashing down on the city.

Its rate of rise slowed, then stopped. For an instant it paused, a cyclopean column of black hanging vertically in the air. Then it began to tilt and fall to ₎arth. But as it fell it changed. Huge wings unfolded, unfurling like flags, spread, stretched across the sky, obscuring the emerging stars, blotting out most of the sky. It leveled itself and began to glide. It swooped over the Park, then banked to the east and was gone.

Thoroughly shaken, Bill turned to Glaeken.

"The leviathan you mentioned?"

Glaeken nodded. "One of them. There'll be more."

"But how's that thing going to get back into the hole at sunrise?"

"They don't have to. They can keep to the nightside and stay ahead of sunrise as they roam the skies. Or they can hide within storms on the dayside." He looked up at the stars. "Do you know the constellations?"

"Not really. The Big Dipper, maybe, but—"

"I do. And they've changed. Those aren't the same stars up there as last night."

Outside, another whining howl began to issue from the hole.

"Here comes another," Glaeken said.

Part of Bill wanted to pull the curtains, shut off the TV, and crawl under the couch. But another part of him had to watch. He dragged a chair up to the window and waited in horrid fascination to see what would happen next.

WINS-AM

Reports are filtering in from around the globe, especially from Europe where nightfall occurs hours ahead of ours. All the new holes that opened during the day are spewing forth swarms of creatures tonight, just like the ones that caused such devastation in our town last night. The reports also describe four species of bugs—two more than we saw around here. Some of the local reports say the infestation is particularly heavy on Long Island.

Monroe, Long Island

Trembling, Sylvia hurried through the growing darkness, crying out, screaming out Jeffy's name at the top of her lungs. But only the faint echo of her own voice answered. She was panting from the unaccustomed exertion.

Suddenly a red pick-up roared around the curve ahead. Rudy—and God could that be a little blond head peering through the windshield from the passenger seat? Sylvia ran into the street and narrowly missed being hit as the pick-up swerved into the curb.

"I hope this is him, Mrs. Nash," Rudy said, grinning as he hopped out of the cab and came around the front of his truck. "'Cause if he ain't, somebody's gonna have me up on kidnappin' charges sure."

"No, that's him," Sylvia said, weak kneed with relief and fighting tears. She pulled open the passenger door and reached for Jeffy. "I don't know how to thank you."

"Found him *way* down the road there, truckin' along like he had someplace real important to go."

Sylvia hugged the child against her. "Oh, Jeffy, Jeffy, you had me so worried!"

"I want to go see Glaeken," he said.

"You can't right now, honey. We've go to get back to the house so those chew-wasps don't get us."

"But Glaeken needs me."

Sylvia held him tighter. There was something unholy about this child's attraction to that old man.

Rudy laughed. "Kids. Aren't they somethin'? Who's Glaeken? A little friend of his? Must really want to see him bad. I damn near had to drag this little guy into my truck to get him back here. I guess you've drilled it into him not to—"

Something *whizz*ed between them. Rudy jerked his head back.

"What the hell was that?"

Sylvia cringed and wrapped her arms around Jeffy.

"It's a chew bug, Mom!" he wailed.

Another of the things sailed by, Rudy ducked but not quite fast enough. The creature knocked his Giants cap askew. He took it off and gawked at the piece bitten out of the beak.

"Christ!"

"Run, Jeffy!" Sylvia cried. "We've got to get home!"

Rudy grabbed her arm before they could get moving.

"Into the truck! I'll drive you back!"

Sylvia pushed Jeffy ahead of her into the cab of the idling truck, slammed the door behind her, and rolled up the window. Rudy hopped into the driver seat and yanked on the gear shift. The pick-up lurched forward.

"Better put up your window, Rudy."

He flashed her a lopsided smile. "It don't go up."

"Then I think you'd better plan on staying at our place tonight."

"Nah! Ain't no buncha bugs gonna keep me from goin' home. I don't care how big they are. They're only—what the fuck?"

He downshifted and the pick-up lurched to a slower speed. They were almost to Toad Hall, but up ahead something was floating across the road. A group of somethings, actually. They reminded Sylvia of the belly flies from last night, only these things were much bigger and carried their football-sized sacs atop their bodies like transparent balloons. Double dragonfly wings jutted out from their sides, and long gray tendrils dangled below. They looked like a school of air-borne Portuguese men-o'- war.

Rudy swerved to the right to try and go around the floating phalanx, but the balloon-like creatures banked left toward the pick-up. The front tire on the passenger side caromed off the Belgian block curb, violently bouncing Sylvia and Jeffy in the seat, and veering the truck toward the hovering men-o'-war.

The pick-up slammed into them, splattering the hood and windshield with ruptured sacks, broken wings, and gray fluid.

"Yeah!" Rudy shouted. "That'll show 'em!"

He hit the windshield-wiper switch but the wipers were jammed under the debris.

"Damn!" he said. "Can't see."

He slowed the truck to a crawl, stuck his head out the window, and reached around to the windshield.

"No!" Sylvia cried. "Rudy, don't—!"

His scream cut her off. He jerked his head and arm back but a mass of gray tendrils came with him. They were alive, writhing, twisting, curling, crawling along Rudy's arm to his shoulder, reaching for his face. Close up like this Sylvia could see that the tendrils were lined with tiny suckers, like octopus tentacles, except that these suckers were rimmed with tiny teeth, and in the center of each was a pale, curling tongue. The teeth were drawing blood as they moved, and the tongues were lapping it up.

Rudy looked at her, his eyes wide with pain and terror. He opened his mouth, whether to say something or scream again, Sylvia never knew, for another mass of tentacles swept through the open window and engulfed his head, the tips plunging into his mouth and worming into his nostrils. She had one last glimpse of his bulging eyes, and then he was pulled kicking and flailing through the side window.

As Jeffy's scream of horror mingled with her own, the pick- up stalled and jerked dead. Carol pulled the handle at her side and kicked the door. As it opened a mass of tentacles and broken wings slid off the roof. The tentacles reached for her as they fell past but she pulled back in time to avoid them. Then, grabbing Jeffy, she leaped out and they crouched beside the front wheel.

The darkening air was alive with flying things and with the low-pitched hum of their wings as they darted and swooped about the pick-up.

Sylvia rose warily and looked about for Rudy. She froze at the sight of a huge, ungainly, twisting shape rising slowly into the air on the far side of the hood. It was a group of a dozen or so men-o'-war clustered together, their float sacs bumping one another, their tentacles a writhing gorgonian mass, slithering about on—

Sylvia groaned as she recognized Rudy's boots and denimed legs protruding from the lower end of the mass, his dangling toes three or four feet above the pavement. His head and torso were engulfed in the hungry tangle of squirming, feeding tentacles. As she watched, the legs kicked feebly once, twice, then shuddered and hung limp in the air.

Rudy! Oh, dear God, poor Rudy!

Prompted by the breeze, the floating, feeding mass began a slow drift down the twilit street.

Sylvia swiveled around, frantically looking for a hiding place, wondering if they might not be better off in the cab of the truck. Across the street she spotted a corner of the wall that surrounded Toad Hall. Two hundred feet down the sidewalk the wrought iron gate stood open.

Jeffy was still crouched by the tire. She pulled him to his feet and pushed him around the front of the truck ahead of her.

"Run, Jeffy! Run for the wall!"

Crouching over him as a shield, she propelled him ahead of her across the street toward the wall; when they reached its base, they raced for the gate, hugging the wall as they ran. Belly flies and chewers circled about with another new species, similar to the chewers in size but equipped with a spear-shaped head. Most were winging overhead toward Toad Hall. Apparently the bugs hadn't spotted them in the shadows along the base of the wall. But that would change once they got through the gate. There was an open stretch along the driveway between the gate and the willows where she and Jeffy would be completely exposed. But she forced that out of her mind for the moment. She'd worry about it when the time came. First they had to reach the gate.

Something moved in her peripheral vision and she glanced right. Men-o'-war, three of them, in the middle of the street opposite the gate, gliding her way with graceful, deadly purpose, their long trailing tendrils curling and uncurling with hungry anticipation.

They've spotted us!

Stifling a scream, she caught Jeffy under the arms and lifted him, carrying him ahead of her as she threw every ounce of strength and will into her pumping legs. She had to reach the gate before those things cut her off. Suddenly a belly fly was swooping toward her face. She ducked, stumbled, scrambled back to her feet and kept running.

But the men-o'-war were closer. They were slower but they had the angle on her. Sylvia moaned softly as she realized she wasn't going to beat them to the gate.

Only three will live to return.

The words crawled across her mind. Were they going to prove true? Was she the one who wasn't going to make it? Or would it be Jeffy?

Her limbs responded to the horror of seeing Jeffy end like Rudy and she picked up speed. Her arms were throbbing, her lungs burned with the unaccustomed exertion, her legs wanted to fold under her, but she pushed it.

Almost there!

But so were the men-o'-war. Seeing them closing, Sylvia pushed her speed up a final desperate notch. They were so close she could smell their foul carrion odor. The tendrils swept forward through the air, reaching for her. She screamed in horror and despair of making it as she ducked and rounded the gatepost corner with only inches to spare.

A sob of relief was bursting free in her throat when something tangled in her hair and yanked her back. She pushed Jeffy ahead of her.

"Run home, Jeffy!" she cried.

He obeyed her, but glanced over his shoulder as he started to run. He stopped and screamed in terror.

"Mommy! It's got you!"

"Jeffy! Run for the house! Please!"

But he stood rooted to the spot, transfixed with horror.

Sylvia reached back and felt a clump of slimy tentacles tangled in her hair, worming toward her scalp. A few wrapped around her fingers and she felt the sharp bite of the suckers, the rasping licks of the tiny tongues before she snatched her hand free. To her right and left she saw other men-o'-war sailing her way, their hungry, questing tendrils extended toward her face. She had a sudden vision of herself as a floating corpse like Rudy.

It's me! she thought. I'm the one who's not going to make it!

She ducked as they closed in on her, her scalp blazing with pain as the thing tangled in her hair tried to hold her back. The tentacles of the others were only inches away now, reaching for her face. She put her hands up to swat them away but they became entangled and trapped. Frantically she yanked and twisted but she couldn't pull free. She felt the bites, felt her blood flow, felt the tiny tongues begin to lap. But she bottled her screams. She wouldn't let those tentacles reach into her mouth like they did Rudy's. As the tentacles climbed up her arm, her vision swam, darkened. The earth seemed to tilt under her—

She heard a *crunch* and suddenly the tentacles sheathing her right hand and forearm loosened their grip. She yanked free and stared.

The creature was sagging toward the driveway, its float sac ruptured, its wings broken and fluttering futilely. And then she realized she was not alone.

"Ba!"

He towered over her in the dimness, his clothes torn and bloody, swinging his razor-toothed billy club. Another crunch and the tentacles clutching her left hand spasmed and loosened their grip enough for her to pull free.

"Hold still, Missus," he said, and he swung his club at her head.

Sylvia winced instinctively, heard a third crunch behind her, and then her hair was free. Ba pulled her forward. She needed no further encouragement. She picked up Jeffy and started to run.

The air was alive with buzzing, soaring, biting *things*. Fully alerted to their presence now, the bugs were all around her and Jeffy. Wings brushed her face and hair, jaws clicked on empty air as they narrowly missed her. There would have been no hope for them without Ba. He took the lead, running tall, daring the creatures to attack him as he slashed left and right with his customized club. Sylvia clung to the back of his coat, awed by his reflexes, by the length of his reach, and by his seeming ability to see in the dark. Maybe he struck at the sound of the things. Whatever his method, he was clearing a path for them through the winged horrors.

Almost to the house. Another twenty feet and they'd be at the door. The *closed* door. What if it was locked?

Where was Alan? Good God, if he was still outside he was a goner, a sitting duck in that wheelchair.

Just then one of the chewers whizzed past her cheek and buried its teeth into Ba's shoulder. He grunted with pain but kept running, kept swinging his club ahead of him and clearing the path. Fighting her rising gorge, Sylvia shifted Jeffy's weight to one arm and reached up with her free hand; she forced her fingers around the chewer's body and gave it a violent twist. The body cracked and the teeth came free of Ba's back as cold fluid ran down her arm.

Ba turned and nodded his thanks, and at that instant, a writhing mass of tentacles dropped onto the back of his neck. He stumbled but managed to hold his balance and keep moving. And then they were at the door, Sylvia pulling whatever tentacles she could reach free of Ba's neck as he groped for the door knob. If the door was locked they were doomed. They'd die right here on Toad Hall's front steps.

But the door opened before Ba reached it. Light flooded out. She had a glimpse of Alan looking up from his wheelchair as he held it open. They tumbled through to the foyer and the door slammed shut behind them. Ba dropped his billy and sank to his knees, clawing at the tentacled monstrosity wrapping itself around his throat. Sylvia put Jeffy down and went to help him but Alan suddenly rolled between them and reached down to the floor.

"Drop your hands a second, Ba," he said.

As Ba obeyed, Alan lifted his hand. He held Ba's club. He swung at the man-o'-war, ripping its air sac and tearing its body open. The tentacles loosened their grip and Ba ripped it free, hurling it to the floor. As it tried to flutter-crawl toward Jeffy across the marble floor of the foyer, Alan ran it over with the big wheel of his chair. Twice. Finally the thing lay still.

Behind her, Jeffy was sobbing. From somewhere in the basement, Phemus was barking wildly.

Ba staggered to his feet. His neck was a mass of blood, his clothing shredded and bloody. He faced her, panting, ragged, swaying.

"You and the Boy are all right, Missus?"

"Yes, Ba. Thanks to you. But you need a doctor."

"I will go wash myself," he said. He turned and headed for the guest bathroom.

Sylvia looked at Alan. Tears streaked his face. His lips were trembling.

"I thought you were dead!" he said. "I knew you were out there and needed help and I couldn't go to you." He pounded his thighs. "God *damn* these useless things!"

Sylvia lifted Jeffy and carried him to Alan. She seated herself on Alan's lap and adjusted Jeffy on hers. Alan's arms encircled them both. Jeffy began to cry. Sylvia understood perfectly. For the first time today she felt safe. And that feeling of safety opened the floodgates. She began to sob as she had never sobbed in her life. The three of them cried together.

The Movie Channel
Joe Bob Briggs' Drive-In Movie:
        Night Of Bloody Horror (1969) Howco International

5 • CATACLYSM

Maui

The *moana puka* appeared around dusk.

Kolabati and Moki had been standing on the lanai watching the sun sink into the Pacific—earlier than ever. It was only a quarter to seven. They were also watching the airport. Neither of them could remember ever seeing it so busy.

"Look at them run," Moki said, grinning as he slipped an arm around her waist. "The shrinking daylight's got them all spooked. See how they run."

"It's got me spooked too," Kolabati said.

"Don't let it," he said. "If it sends all the Jap *malahinis* scurrying west back to their own islands, and all the *haoles* back to the mainland—preferably back to New York where they can fall into that hole in Central Park—it's all for the good. It will leave the islands to the Hawaiians."

She'd been fascinated by the news from New York of the mysterious hole in the Sheep Meadow. She knew the area well. Her brother Kusum had once owned an apartment overlooking Central Park.

"*I'm* not Hawaiian."

He tightened his grip on her waist. "As long as you're with me, you are."

Somehow, his arm around her was not as comforting as she would have wished. They watched the airport in silence for a while longer, then Moki released her and leaned on the railing, staring out at the valley, the sky.

"Something's going to happen soon. Do you feel it?"

Kolabati nodded. "Yes. I've felt it for days."

"Something wonderful."

"Wonderful?" She stared at him. Could he mean it? She'd been plagued by an almost overwhelming sense of dread since the tradewinds had reversed themselves. "No. Not wonderful at all. Something terrible."

His grin became fierce. "Terrible for other people, maybe. But wonderful for us. You wait and see."

Kolabati didn't know what to make of Moki lately. His behavior had remained slightly bizarre since Wednesday when the gash on his hand had healed so quickly. At least once a day he'd cut himself to see if the healing power was still with him. Each day he healed more quickly than the day before. And with each healing the wild light in his eyes had grown.

As the daylight began to fade, Kolabati turned toward the door, but Moki grabbed her arm.

"Wait. What is that?"

He was staring east, toward Kahului and beyond. She followed his gaze and saw it. Something in the water. White water, bubbling, roiling. A gigantic disturbance. With foreboding rising, ballooning within her, Kolabati grabbed the binoculars from their hook and focused on the disturbance.

At first all she saw was turbulent white water, giant chop, sloshing and swirling chaotically. But as she watched, the turbulence became ordered, took shape. The white water began to swirl in a uniform direction, counterclockwise, around a central point. She identified the center in time to see it sink below the surface and become a dark, spinning, sucking maw.

"Moki, look!" She handed him the glasses.

"I see!" he said, but took them anyway.

She watched his expression as he adjusted the lenses. His smile grew.

"A whirlpool! It's too close to shore to be from converging currents. It's got to be a crack in the ocean floor. No, wait!" He lowered the glasses and stared at her, his face flushed with excitement. "A hole! It has to be a hole in the ocean floor, just like the Central Park hole! We've got our own hole here!"

Together they watched the whirlpool organize and expand, Moki with undisguised glee, Kolabati with growing, gnawing unease. The troubles from the outer world, from the mainland, were intruding on her paradise. That could only bring misfortune. They watched together until it was too dark to see any more, then they went inside and turned on the TV to see what the news had to say about it. The scientists all agreed—the ocean floor had opened in a fashion similar to the phenomenon in Manhattan's Central Park. Already the locals had a name for it: *moana puka*—ocean hole.

Moki could barely contain his excitement. He wandered the great room, talking a blue streak, gesticulating wildly.

"You know what's going to happen, Bati?" he said. "The water's going to be sucked down into whatever abyss those holes lead to, and it's going to keep on disappearing into nowhere. And eventually the ocean level is going to drop. And if it drops far enough, do you know what will happen?"

Kolabati shook her head mutely. She had an inescapable feeling that she was witnessing the beginning of the end—of everything.

"I'll tell you what's going to happen: Greater Maui will be reborn." He went to the doorway that opened onto the lanai and gestured into the darkness. "Molokai, Lanai, Kahoolawe, even little Molokini—all of them were part of Maui before the Ice Age, connected to our island by valleys rather than cut off by channels of sea water. I see it happening, Bati. I see them all joined together again, reunited after ages of separation. A single island, as big as the Big Island. Maybe bigger. And I'll play a part in the future of Greater Maui."

"What future?" Kolabati said, joining him at the door. "If the Pacific Ocean drops that far we'll be looking at the end of the world!"

"No, Bati. Not the end. The beginning. The beginning of a new world."

And then the sky caught fire. All around them, like a sustained flash of sheet lightning, the night ignited. At the far end of the island she saw the Lahaina coast and the Iao Valley of West Maui light up like day. The same with the island of Lanai across the channel. Then a blast of superheated air, choked with flaming debris, roared overhead and to the sides, withering west Maui, searing Lanai, yet she and Moki remained in cool shadow, shielded by the enormous bulk of Haleakala.

"Shiva!" she cried in the Bengali dialect of her childhood. "What are you doing?"

And then came the sound. The floor shook and seemed to fall away beneath her as the night exploded with a rumbling, booming, deep-throated roar that shuddered through her flesh and shook every cell of her body, rattled the very core of her being.

As she tumbled to the floor she heard Moki's voice faintly above the din.

"Earthquake!"

He crawled to where she lay and rolled on top of her, using his body to shield her from the shelves and lamps and sculptures crashing down about them.

It went on forever. Kolabati didn't know how the house's cantilever supports managed to hold. Any moment now they were going to give way and send the house tumbling down the slope. Only once before in her life—when Jack had borrowed her necklace for a number of hours and all of her nearly 150 years had begun to assert their weight upon her—had Kolabati felt so close to death.

The earth tremors and shudders persisted but became quieter, muffled. Moki lifted himself off her and Kolabati struggled to her feet.

"*Pehea oe?*"

"All right . . . I think," she said, not bothering to reply in Hawaiian.

They clung to each other like sailors on a heaving deck. Kolabati looked around. The great room was in a shambles. His sculptures lay all about in pieces, their carved wood cracked and splintered, their lava bases shattered.

"Oh, Moki. Your work!"

"The sculptures don't matter." he said, clutching her tight against him. "They're the past. I would have had to smash them myself. Don't you see, Bati? This is it! The new beginning I told you about. It's here!"

He drew her to the trembling lanai where they leaned over the railing and stared up at the dark mass of Haleakala, toward her summit, rimmed now with fiery light.

"Look, Bati!" he said, pointing up the slope. "Haleakala is alive! After hundreds of years of dormancy, she's come back to life! For me! For us!"

Kolabati pulled away from him and fled back inside. She flipped one light switch after another but the room remained dark. She picked her way through the debris to the television but could not get it to work. The electricity was gone.

"Bati!" Moki called. *"Hele mai.* Stand with me and watch Haleakala. The House of the Sun has rekindled her fires. She's calling us home!"

Kolabati stood amid the shambles of their home—their *life*—and knew that her time of peace was at an end, that things would never be the same. She was afraid.

"That wasn't just Haleakala erupting, Moki," she said, her voice trembling like the floor beneath her. "Something else happened. Something far more violent and cataclysmic than an old volcano coming to life."

It's the end of the world, she thought. She could feel it in her bones and in the way the ancient necklace pulsed against her skin. The air about her screamed with tortured *atman*, released in sudden, violent death.

Haleakala had awakened, but what else had happened?

The pain is gone. Only the ecstasy remains now. And it grows. The night things run rampant in the dark sectors above. Rasalom senses the delirium of fear and pain and grief and misery they leave in their wake.

And then there was the convulsion of death and horror when the Pacific volcanoes roared back to life. The surge was almost unbearable.

As a result, the pace of the Change has picked up. He is so much larger now, and his granite womb has grown to accommodate him. The chips of sloughed stone have disappeared down the hole that has opened in the bottom of the chamber. Like the other holes that have opened around this globe, it, too, is bottomless. But it leads to a different place. A place of icy flame. Even now, a faint glow creeps up from the depths.

And the Change . . . his limbs have thickened, hardened to a stony consistency. His head has drawn into his trunk, concentrating his essence in a soft, bulbous core, a fleshy center in the hub of a four-spoked wheel.

He spreads his intangible feeders further and further afield, seeking more nourishment. He can never get enough.

SUNDAY

1 • SUNDAY IN NEW YORK

WCBS-TV

Good morning. This is a special edition of Sunday Morning. The sun rose late at 7:10 a.m. this morning and found not only a devastated New York City, but the entire world reeling from the events of last night . . .

MANHATTAN

What a night.

Jack stood yawning in the chilly dawn outside Gia's townhouse. He shivered and tugged the zipper on his windbreaker a little higher.

It's almost June, he thought. Isn't the weather supposed to be getting warmer?

Across the East River the sun was rising red and quick over Queens. He thought he could almost see it moving. Around him, Sutton Square had never looked so bad. The little half block of townhouses hanging over the F.D.R. Drive had been spared Friday, but last night had more than made up for it. Shattered glass on the sidewalks, lacerated screens hanging from the windows.

The chew wasps and the belly flies had been back, but other things—bigger, heavier things—had come as well. Luckily, the louvered wooden shutters flanking the windows of Gia's townhouse hadn't been merely ornamental. They were hung on real hinges and actually swung closed over the windows. The night had been long and tense, filled with hungry, predatory noises, but they'd passed it in safety.

Other places hadn't been so lucky. Jack was wondering whether he should check out some of the neighboring townhouses to see if anybody needed help when he noticed something hanging over the arm of the street lamp on the corner. Something big and limp.

133

He took a few steps toward it and stopped when he realized it was a corpse. Female, maybe, but so torn up and desiccated it was hard to tell.

But how had it got there? Twenty feet up. Was there a hole creature flying about at night big enough to fly off with someone?

It was getting worse faster than he'd thought.

Jack checked the 9mm Llama in his shoulder holster and the extra clips in his pockets, then went back and checked Ralph. The Corvair's black canvas convertible top had been shredded during the night, the antenna scored with teeth marks and bent almost double; the paint on the hood had been bubbled off as if it had been splashed with acid, and the windshield was fouled with some putrid-smelling gunk that Jack wiped off with a rag from his trunk.

"Eeeeuuuu! What happened to Ralph?"

Jack turned and saw Vicky standing in the townhouse doorway, dressed in bib-front overalls, a flannel shirt, a jacket, and her green-and-white N.Y. Jets cap. With the little suitcase in her hand, she looked like a country cousin arriving in the big city for a visit. But her blue eyes were wide with shock as she stared at the ruined top of the car.

"The things from the hole," Jack said, waving her forward to distract her from the corpse on the lamp post. "That's why I want you and your Mom to leave."

"Mom still doesn't want to go."

"I know that, Vicks." *Jeez, do I know.*

Gia didn't want to leave the city, thought she and Vicky could weather the wolf just fine in their brick house here on Sutton Square. Jack wasn't having any of that. He was willing to let her have her way in most anything unless he thought she'd be in danger. He'd been relentless last night, wearing her down until she'd finally agreed to leave the city with Abe first thing this morning.

"Is that why you and Mom were yelling last night?"

"We weren't yelling. We just had a . . . difference of opinion."

"Oh. I thought it was a fight."

"Your mother and I? Disagree? Never! Now come on, Vicks. Let's get you settled in Ralph."

As Vicky stepped down onto the sidewalk, Gia emerged behind her. She was dressed in jeans and a navy-blue V-neck sweater over a white turtleneck. Her eyes, the same shade of blue as Vicky's, went as wide as her daughter's when she saw the street. She ran her fingers through her short blonde hair.

"Oh my!"

"This is nothing," Jack said. "Wait'll you see the rest of the city."

He put his right index finger to his lips and pointed to the body on the lamp post. Gia started and staggered back a step when she spotted it.

"My God!"

"Still think you'll be safe here?" Jack said.

"We did okay last night."

Stubborn to the end.

"But it's going to get worse."

"So you've said—a thousand times."

"*Two*-thousand times. I get paid to know these things."

"And you're sure Abe's place is better?"

"Like a fortress."

She shrugged resignedly. "All right. I'm packed. Like I promised. But I still think this trip is overkill."

Jack ducked past her into the house to grab the suitcases before she changed her mind. He stowed some of the luggage in the front trunk and put the rest in the back seat with Vicky. Grumbling all the way, Gia reluctantly settled herself in the passenger seat. With the wind flapping through the shredded top, he zig-zagged down to 57th Street and started up the long incline toward Fifth Avenue.

It was bad, but not as bad as yesterday. Early Sunday morning is about the only time midtown Manhattan can be called silent, but there were even fewer cars on the streets than usual. And most of those were either police cars or emergency vehicles of one sort or another. All the streets were littered with sparkling glass fragments. Here and there along the way he spotted an occasional shrunken husk that had once been a human body. One or two dangled from high places, as if they'd been dropped or thrown there after being sucked dry. Jack kept glancing back at Vicky but she was slumped down in the back seat, engrossed in one of her Nancy Drew books, oblivious to her surroundings.

Good. He kept an eye on Gia, as well, watching her expression grow tighter, her face grow paler with each passing block. By Madison Avenue she was ashen. As he pulled to a stop at a red light, Gia looked at him with eyes even wider than before. Her voice was barely audible.

"Jack . . . I'm . . . what . . . ?"

She closed her mouth and stared ahead in silence.

Jack said nothing, but he was sure he wouldn't have any more resistance to the idea of getting out of town.

From the right came a sudden explosion of glass as a display case crashed through a corner jewelry store's only unbroken window.

A guy with glazed eyes and lank, oily brown hair, sporting a stained tee-shirt and torn jeans, followed it through the hole, laughing as he landed and rolled on the pavement. He was white but he had on enough gold chains and necklaces to qualify as a Mr. T runner-up. His fingers were stacked with so many rings he couldn't bend them. Another guy, heavier but dressed identically and sporting an equal amount of gold, made a more traditional exit through the door. They gave each other a metallic high five. Then they spotted the Corvair.

"Hey, man!" the first once said, smiling as he approached the car. "It's a ride!"

The heavier one followed him. "Yeah! Want some gold? We'll give you some gold for a ride downtown. We got plenty!"

Jack couldn't help laughing.

"Yeah, right. And like maybe I'll let you hold my wallet while I drive you around."

As the looters' disarming grins twisted into rage, he gunned the Corvair and pulled away through the red light. The thin one began running after them, screaming. For an uneasy moment Jack thought the guy might catch them. The Corvair was loaded down, its old engine was small, and it did not exactly leap up the slight incline toward Fifth Avenue. But it turned out to be just fast enough to leave a stoned looter behind.

Trouble was, Vicky was now sitting up and alert to her surroundings. After watching the looter through the scarred plastic of the rear window, she leaned forward between the bucket seats.

"Why didn't you give that man a ride, Jack?"

"Because he's one of the bad guys, Vicks. What's called a looter."

"But he just wanted a ride."

"I don't think so, Vicks. You know those silverfish we find crawling in the bathroom every so often?"

Vicky made a face. "Yuck."

"Yeah, well, looters are lower than silverfish. When the good folks are occupied fighting fires or helping earthquake victims or storm victims, looters sneak in and carry off anything that's not nailed down. Those guys didn't want a ride; they wanted Ralph."

"That's not fair!"

"Fair's not a word they care about, Vicks."

"Look!" she said, pointing to her left as they crossed Fifth Avenue. "More looters!"

She was right. Knots of people were jumping in and out of the broken windows all along Fifth, scampering off through the dim dawn light with jewelry, leather, anything they could carry. Someone had pulled a panel truck up on the sidewalk in front of Bergdorf's and was loading it with dresses. As Jack was pulling away, he saw a bearded, professorial type step through the open space that had once been the big front window of the Doubleday shop balancing a two-foot stack of books against the front of his tweed jacket.

"Everybody's getting into the act," he said. "Where the hell are the police?"

"It's anarchy, Jack," Gia said and he could hear the fear vibrating in her voice.

"Not yet. We've still got a police force—somewhere, I think—and we've still got electricity for lights, and we've still got gas to run the police cars. When the sun's all the way up these cockroaches will crawl back under the floorboards."

"But what happens when the gas and electricity go?" she said, reaching over and clutching Vicky's hand.

"Then they'll *own* the streets. That's when we'll see real anarchy."

"It's only been two days. I never dreamed . . . " Her voice trailed off.

"What? That things could fall apart this fast? This city's a sewer, Gia. All the garbage wandering around this half of the country seems to end up here. I've been watching it fall apart for years. Its veneer of civilization is about as thick as the layer of gold on the electroplated jewelry they hawk on the streets. A couple of good rubs against your jeans and the base metal underneath shows through."

"What about neighborliness and hanging together in times of trouble?"

"Maybe they'll have some of that out in Iowa where you grew up, and maybe there'll even be a pocket or two of it around here, but not enough to matter. The good folks will be driven into hiding and the slime will be free to do whatever they damn well please."

"I don't believe that. I don't *want* to believe that. And it disturbs me to know you believe that."

Jack shrugged. "In my work, you get to spend a lot of time hip-deep in slime. You—"

"Oh, my God!" Gia cried, craning her neck and staring up through the windshield.

Jack slowed and glanced up. Something bright in the sky. He struck his head out the window—and stopped the car to stare.

Vicky popped her head out behind him. "Ooooh neeeeat!"

"Jack!" Gia said. "What's happening? What *is* that?"

"Looks like an apartment building," Vicky said.

Half a mile up, probably over the West Side Highway or the midtown piers, was a heart-stopping sight . . . a building floating in the air. It hung as if suspended on an invisible wire, turning slowly, its roof canted slightly eastward, its torn underside westward. Light from the rising sun flashed off the few unbroken windows. Masonry that had broken away was floating up with it. Tiny figures leaned out the windows, waving shirts and towels in panicked attempts to attract the attention of the police helicopters that circled it like flies around a corpse.

"Jeez!" Jack said as he stared upward at the slowly dwindling shape. "It's still rising."

Those poor bastards trapped up there were doomed unless they could find a way of transferring to one of the helicopters.

At least now he knew where all the cops were.

"Let's get out of here," Gia said.

Jack flipped the little gearshift lever back into drive and they continued west. He refrained from saying *I told you so* as he ran red lights all the way to Amsterdam Avenue, then raced uptown to the Isher Sports Shop. Abe was outside, waiting by his panel truck in front of his store's smashed windows. So fixated was he on the flying building that he barely noticed their arrival. Jack screeched to a halt half a dozen feet in front of him.

That got his attention.

"Gevalt!" Abe said, cringing back. "You're trying to squish me or something?"

He was wearing a black jacket; his white shirt and black tie were clean. Obviously he hadn't had breakfast yet.

"Ready to go?" Jack said, pulling Vicky and a suitcase from the back seat.

"Yes, of course." Abe gave Gia a hug and Vicky a kiss on the top of her head. "I should want to keep two such beautiful young ladies waiting? Come with me. I've got coffee, juice, and not-so-fresh bagels in the front seat."

He opened the rear doors of the panel truck, then ushered Gia and Vicky around to the front. He returned as Jack was loading the last suitcase into the rear compartment. He pointed a trembling finger at the building in the sky.

"It's happening like you said, isn't it?" Abe's accent was gone, vanished without a trace. "All rules—man's and God's—*pffft!*"

Jack looked and saw that the building was considerably higher than before. When would it stop rising? *Would* it stop rising?

"Double-*pffft!*" Jack nodded toward the shattered storefront windows. "Looters?"

Abe shrugged. "Nothing's missing. Must have been those flying things. Haven't seen any looting."

"Plenty of it going on in the high rent district. They just haven't got this far yet."

Abe reached into his pocket and pulled out a set of keys. He thrust it into Jack's hand.

"Here. These are for the armory. They'll need a cannon to get in without them. You need anything, help yourself."

Jack hefted the keys and stuffed them in a front pocket. "The armory" was the basement of the Isher Sports Shop where Abe stocked his weapons—the illegal ones, plus the legal ones he sold illegally. He carried everything from blackjacks to Claymore land mines. It would be handy to maintain access to that sort of variety.

"I might move in," Jack said.

"Be my guest. You have the wavelength written down?"

"Yeah. Got the shortwave set on it. I'll be listening at seven a.m. and seven p.m. Don't forget to call in."

"Don't worry."

"Which way you heading out? The Lincoln?"

Abe nodded. "From what you say, the quicker we get out, the better."

"You know it. You carrying?"

Abe patted the heavy lump in the right side pocket of his jacket. "Of course."

"Good. But maybe I'll tail you down to the entrance anyway—just in case."

"You don't think I can protect your women?" he said huffily.

"I wouldn't be sending them off with you if I wasn't sure of that."

They stared at each other in silence a few seconds.

"Seems like we should say something here," Abe said. "I mean, two old friends at the end of the world. One of us should be able to come up with something meaningful."

"You're the guy with all the education. You do the honors."

Abe looked down, then smiled and thrust out his hand.

"See you soon, Jack."

Jack smiled as they shook hands. That just about said it all.

"Enough of this stuff," Jack said. "Get in the driver seat and I'll say my goodbyes to the ladies."

After a big hug from Vicky, Jack held Gia in his arms.

"Be careful, Jack," she whispered in his ear. "And thanks."

"For what?"

"For making us get out of town. I think you were right. The city's turning ugly. But *you* watch out."

He grinned. "Hell, I'm uglier than any city you can name."

"I'm not talking about that. I'm talking about *her.*"

"Oh."

He'd told Gia last night about how he was going to try to find Kolabati and get her necklaces for Glaeken. Gia knew a few things about Kolabati, but Jack had never quite got around to telling her that they'd been lovers for a brief time.

"Don't give me 'oh.' You got involved with her before and it almost killed you."

"That was my choice."

"She left you to die, Jack. This time she might finish the job."

"This time is different. I know what she is. I'll be careful. I've got a lot to come back for."

She kissed him one last time, long and deep, then she got back into the front seat of Abe's idling truck. Jack hurried back to his Corvair. He followed Abe over to West End and followed that downtown.

Along the way, the lights were against them. They'd gone out of synch for some reason and Abe stopped at every red. Jack knew why. He probably had enough weaponry in the back to overthrow a banana republic. He didn't want to get stopped and searched.

It happened at about where West End starts calling itself Eleventh Avenue. As Abe pulled to a stop at yet another red light, three guys leapt from a doorway and charged the truck, two running around to the driver side, one leaping up and reaching in the passenger window.

One of the guys on the left had a big hunting knife and the other had a lead pipe. As Abe tried to pull away the second guy began beating on Abe's window. Jack was already accelerating when the glass shattered and the guy started swinging the pipe at Abe.

The guy with the knife spotted Jack coming. He leapt out of the way as Jack sideswiped the truck, catching the pipe swinger hard in the backs of both calves. As he was spun and twisted between the two vehicles and tumbled to the pavement, screaming with the agony of two broken legs, Jack swerved at the guy with the knife and caught him head on with the Corvair's nose. But the car wasn't moving fast enough then to knock him sprawling. Instead he rolled up and over the hood and windshield and landed on the canvas top. He had to be hurt but he wasn't out of action yet. He rammed his knife through one of the slits and stabbed blindly at Jack. Jack ducked and grabbed the swinging wrist. He wrenched the knife free, and paused, wondering what to do. Then he heard Vicky scream.

Jack turned the guy's wrist and rammed the blade—honed side down—through the belly of the forearm, sliding it between the two bones and out the other side. Above on the roof the guy howled and flopped about and tried to pull his arm out. But the protruding edges of the point and grip caught on the sides of the slit, forcing the cutting edge of the blade to slice further down his arm. The guy screamed now.

Jack jumped out of the car and saw Abe holding his bloody scalp with his left hand, a .45 automatic in his right, and leaning toward the passenger door. Vicky was next to him, crying, but Gia was nowhere in sight and the passenger door was open.

Jack charged around to the far side and found another guy with a knife, but the point of this one was held at Gia's throat.

"All we want is the truck," he said, breathing hard. He wore a clean plaid short-sleeve shirt and beige slacks, white socks and running shoes; he looked almost preppy except for the tattoos on his arms. "Give us the truck and no one will get hurt."

"*We?*" Jack said, pulling the Llama from its holster and slowly, methodically working the slide for full effect. He'd have to play this very carefully. "*Us?* Your 'we' and 'us' are already down. They're out of the picture."

He paused to allow the guy to appreciate the wails and moans from his buddies on the far side of the truck and get a good look at the 9mm automatic in Jack's hand. He slid further behind Gia.

"You think you can get away with this?" Jack said softly.

"Yeah. I can get away with *anything*, man! All the rules are off! Don't you see that?" He stared for a moment into the sky over Jack's left shoulder. "We got buildings and people flyin' off into space during the day and monsters chewin' up everything in sight all night. I been through detox twice, man, and I ain't never seen shit like this, even when I was strung out like bubblegum. Anything goes, man. School is *out!*"

"Not my class," Jack said. "Let her go."

The guy pressed the knife blade to against Gia's throat. She winced at the sharp pressure.

"The truck or I'll cut her, man! I swear t'Christ I'll cut her fucking throat!"

Jack felt his heart begin to hammer in his chest. Gia's panicked eyes pleaded with him. He gave her a little nod of encouragement as he controlled himself. Had to be cool here. Had to go slow.

But if this bastard so much as broke her skin . . .

Jack settled the Llama into a two-handed grip and raised it until it was sighted at the guy's right eye where he peeked out from behind Gia's ear.

"You've been watching too many movies, turkey," Jack said softly. "This kind of thing doesn't work in real life. I've got a gun and you've got a knife. You cut her, you've lost your shield." Jack took a step closer. "Now, so far today you and your buddies have hurt a very good friend, deeply frightened a little girl I couldn't care for more if she were my own flesh and blood, and manhandled the woman I love." Another small step closer. "So I'm royally pissed. But I'm willing to work a deal. Drop the knife and you live. I'll let you walk."

The guy's laugh was flat and tremulous as he peeked out from behind Gia's head to speak.

"Don't try to bullshit me. I got your bitch here. I've got a knife at her neck. *I'm* callin' the shots!"

A car came by, slowed for a look, then sped away. Jack slipped forward another step.

"Maybe I didn't make it clear. Listen again. Drop it, you live. Spill one drop of her blood, you die—slowly. First I shoot off your right kneecap, then your left, then your right elbow, then your left. Then a gut shot. Then I take your knife and start cutting off pieces I decide you don't need anymore and feed them to you."

"Jack . . . please!" Gia said.

"Sorry. Just want to let this guy know what he's in for."

"You think that scares me?" the guy said, peeking out again. "I'll show you how scared I—"

As he increased the pressure of the blade against Gia's throat, Jack shot him in the eye. His head snapped back, a red mist blooming behind him for an instant before dissipating; his arms flung outward as he lurched back and collapsed on the pavement.

Jack leaped forward and encircled Gia with his arms.

"Don't look," he said, watching over her shoulder as a red puddle grew under the guy's head.

But Gia turned for a quick glance, and just as quickly turned away. Jack led her back to the truck and they spent a few minutes calming Vicky. When mother and daughter were tightly wound in each other's arms, Jack looked past them to Abe.

"You okay to drive?"

Abe nodded. "Only a scratch. But that guy on the roof of your car—what's his problem?"

"Oh, yeah," Jack said. "Almost forgot about him."

He went back to his car and found the other knifer lying on the roof, pale, sweaty, looking sick.

"Don't hurt me," he said in a weak voice. "I give up."

Jack wondered how the guy would respond if situations were reversed. How much mercy could he expect from him and his buddies? He decided it didn't merit much consideration.

He ducked inside the Corvair. The back seat was covered with blood.

"You bled all over my car!" Jack shouted.

Through the torn roof he heard the guy begin to whimper. Disgusted, Jack yanked the knife blade from the guy's forearm. A muffled scream from above as he jerked his arm from the hole and rolled off the roof to the street. A couple more cars passed as Jack went to the corner and dropped the knife through a sewer grate, then returned to the truck.

He gave Gia and Vicky one last hug, then slammed the door shut.

"Better get going, Abe. Traffic's picking up."

"Jack," Gia said as he started back to his car. Her face was pale and tear-streaked as she stared at him through the window. "Would you have let him go if he dropped the knife? You had that look in your eyes, Jack. I've seen that look before. I know what it means. You would have let him go like you said, wouldn't you?"

"Yeah," Jack said. "Sure."

He hoped he was convincing. Because he wasn't sure.

Pulling away from the scene, Jack glanced in the rearview mirror. One of their attackers lay in a pool of his own blood, staring skyward, another squatted on the pavement, moaning and cradling a bloody arm, while a third crawled toward the curb, dragging his broken legs behind him. Gia's question echoed in his head then and haunted him the rest of the way to the Lincoln Tunnel.

She knew him too well, damn it. Why'd she have to ask that question? He didn't like to think about that sort of thing. It wasn't necessary. The guy was dead. A part of Jack had taken immense pleasure in blowing his brains out the back of his head. But he'd learned to wall off that part of himself, to refuse to share in or even recognize the joyous partying in the dark corner behind the wall.

Would he have let the guy go? Abe bloodied, Vicky terrified, a knifepoint jabbed against Gia's throat—could he forgive that? Turn his back as the guy who'd caused it all sauntered off unscathed? Jack wasn't sure. Allowing someone who'd done damage to his friends to walk the streets with no pain or scars to remind him never even to think about doing something like that again . . . that might be too much to ask.

But if he'd said he'd let the guy go in exchange for dropping the knife, he'd have to do it. Or would he?

All the rules are off, man!

No. Not all of them. Some rules—at least the ones he had some say about—had to stay in effect.

He yawned. He hadn't had much sleep last night, and introspection was tough work.

Jack followed Abe's truck the rest of the way to the Lincoln Tunnel, watched and waved as it rolled down the ramp into the tiled gullet, then headed back uptown to Walt Duran's place. He hoped he'd made it through the night okay. And he hoped he was on schedule with his engraving. If not, Jack was going to have to induce him into a higher gear.

WNYW-TV

cut to Alice

Ladies and gentlemen, we are interrupting our special report from Central Park with catastrophic news from the Central Pacific. The island of Hawaii is gone. Less than an hour ago, the chain of eight islands that make up our fiftieth state was shaken by a cataclysmic explosion. At that instant, all communications with Hawaii, or the Big Island as it is called, were cut off. The mystery was quickly solved.

file footage of Hawaii

This is how the Big Island looked up until an hour ago. A lush volcanic island supporting four thousand square miles of paradise, including the world's longest steadily active volcano. But now . . .

run feed from Honolulu

. . . as we see here in a live aerial transmission from our affiliate in Honolulu on Oahu, the Big Island is no more. Less than an hour ago, the Big Island's active crater, Kilauea, along with supposedly extinct volcanoes Mauna Loa and Mauna Kea, simply blew up, taking the entire island with them. It is just dawn in the Central Pacific, but even so you can see that all that remains of the island of Hawaii is a flaming, steaming cauldron of bubbling lava. We can only show you the site of the Big Island's grave from the west. The plume of smoke, steam, ash, and debris that stretches far into the sky is drifting east. Meteorologists are presently calculating when the ash cloud will hit the West Coast. It is sure to affect weather around the globe.

You can't see it now but there are reports of a giant whirlpool situated off Maui, north of where the Big Island used to be. The whirlpool is believed to be the result of a hole similar to the one in our own Central Park, opening in the ocean bottom some nineteen thousand feet below the surface. Whether this has any relationship to the Big Island disaster is still a matter of speculation at this time.

Those flames you see now on the left of your screen are from another volcano. It's been confirmed that Haleakala, a formerly extinct volcano just seven miles away on the island of Maui, is active again. Although most of its

lava flow has been down its eastern flank, away from the heavily populated
areas, we've been told that the lovely town of Hana is no more. It was completely
submerged in an avalanche of lava during the night.
cut to Alice
Meanwhile, in Manhattan, the situation is rapidly deteriorating . . .

Glaeken stared at the TV screen in dismay, barely aware of the picture. But
he was listening intently, hoping for fresh news from Maui. As a geologist came
on, spouting his theory of how the hole in the channel between Hawaii and Maui
had destabilized the Pacific "hot spot" that had formed the Hawaiian Islands
over the ages, Glaeken hit the MUTE button on his remote control.

Apparently the doorman had rung while he'd been intent on the TV—he
saw Bill leading Jack into the room.

"Jack! I see you made it through the night. Did you take care of that
'business' you mentioned?"

Jack nodded, a bit glumly, Glaeken thought.

"Yeah. All taken care of."

As Bill returned to the kitchen to finish helping Nick with breakfast, Jack
dropped into a chair.

"Anything I can do?" Glaeken said.

Jack shook his head. "I sent some people off into the hinterlands. I'm just
hoping they get where they're going without any trouble. The city's already
starting to fall apart."

"So I've heard. I understand the National Guard is on alert but that fewer
than half of the Guardsmen are reporting in."

"Not surprised. They probably want to stay home and protect their own.
Who can blame them?"

"You should have had your people stay here. They're welcome."

"I thought about that after they left, but I think far from the city might be
better for them. However, I've got some other friends who could use this place.
Good people. You got room?"

"The building's practically empty."

"How come? It looks like a prime spot."

"I'm very choosy about my neighbors."

"Yeah, but—" Jack's eyes widened. "You mean—?"

"Yes. I own the building." As Jack rubbed a hand across his eyes, Glaeken
said, "You've heard about Maui, I presume?"

"No. What?"

Glaeken capsulized the news reports for him.

"You think she's still alive?"

Glaeken nodded. There's a good chance. She lives on the northwest slope. If she was home . . . " He asked the question that was uppermost in his mind. "When can you leave, Jack?"

"Tomorrow."

"No. You must leave today. Every moment counts."

"No way. The bogus necklaces won't be ready till tomorrow morning at the earliest. And I'm not going without them. They're my ace in the hole."

Glaeken considered that a moment. At the rate the situation was deteriorating, tomorrow might be too late. But he didn't see that he had much choice. He had no way of forcing Jack to leave today.

"I promise—I'll catch a flight out there first thing tomorrow—soon as those necklaces are ready."

"That may not be so easy. A number of airlines have grounded all flights."

"Why? Pilots not showing up?"

"Partly that. But a number of flights have disappeared. I should say, a *lot* of flights have disappeared. They take off but never land."

"Swell. What've we got now—holes in the sky?"

"No. Leviathans in the air, sweeping the planes from the sky. Pulverizing them."

Jack said nothing, simply sat and stared at Glaeken with a skeptical look.

"It's true," Bill said, leading Nick in from the kitchen.

Bill sat him in a chair that caught the last fleeting rays of the morning sun. Nick stared emptily at the wall.

"I've seen them," Bill went on. "Big. Big as towns, gliding through the night."

"At least we've got the days," Jack said. "The daylight time may be shrinking, but maybe this guy Rasalom made a mistake giving us some slack like this."

"Not at all. The days give us time to be at our worst. A constant onslaught might drive us together, bring out the best in us. But the respite offered by the daylight gives the terrors of the night before and the anticipated terrors of the night to come a chance to work on us. It allows fear a chance to demoralize us. Fear is the key to Rasalom's power. Fear is the great divider. From war and racism to the mundane vices of greed and gluttony—they're all rooted in fear. What is religion, after all, but a ritualized response to fear—fear of death, fear of the perversities of luck and happenstance that afflict every life at one time or another?" He pointed out the window. "Fear is rampant out there now. It's dividing us, hurting us, bringing out the worst in too many of us. It will be the end of us." He turned to Jack. "That's why you've got to get to Maui and retrieve those necklaces."

"I'll find a way," Jack said softly. "There's always a way."

Glaeken was sure Jack would find a way, and if he was successful in retrieving the necklaces, then what? Tension rolled out from Glaeken's chest along his limbs. He flexed his arthritic fingers to free it. What indeed? Knowing the source of the metal from which they'd been fashioned, he was almost afraid to be in the same room with those necklaces. What would happen if he touched them? Or even got near? Hopefully, nothing. But he couldn't risk it. He'd have to keep his distance when and if Jack brought them back.

Jack said, "You know, with the way things are going, I think I'm going to need some back-up on the trip."

Bill said, "I could come along if you wish."

At first, Glaeken was startled by Bill's offer. He glanced at the ex-priest and caught a desperate look in his eyes. Desperate for what? And then he understood. Bill felt lost, adrift, already a resident of the land to which most of humanity would soon be emigrating. Poor man. The New York City police records still listed him as a fugitive suspect in a capital crime, he had broken with his church, his family was dead, his last friend was sitting in the kitchen, lapsing in and out of catatonia, and Glaeken suspected that his feelings for Carol Treece ran deeper than he dared admit.

Small wonder he was feeling reckless.

Glaeken hoped Jack had the good sense not to take him up on the offer.

"Uh, nothing personal, Bill," Jack said after a long pause, "but I'm looking for someone with maybe a little experience in hand-to-hand work."

"If I were younger . . . " Glaeken said wistfully.

He remembered times when he had cursed the ages he'd spent in a body in its mid-thirties. Now, with the burden of eternity off him, there were moments when he would have relished tight muscles, mobile joints, and a supple back.

"Yeah," Jack said, smiling. "We'd have made a helluva pair, I think. But I was wondering about the big Viet guy from yesterday. Think he'd be up for it?"

"Ba? I don't know. I doubt he'd be willing to leave Mrs. Nash unprotected, but it wouldn't hurt to ask. I'll call if you like."

"Might be better if I go in person. Maybe I can sway him with my magnetic charm."

Bill laughed aloud. Jack gave him a sidelong look.

"Something funny, guy?"

Bill grinned. "I didn't know what to make of you at first, but I think you're all right."

"Which says loads about your character judgment. None of it good."

Glaeken gave Jack directions to Toad Hall and said he'd call ahead to let them know he was coming.

When he was gone, Glaeken reached for the TV remote control. Before he could resume the audio, Nick spoke.

"They won't be enough," he said in his monotone.

Bill squatted before him and looked into his eyes.

"What, Nick? What won't be enough?"

"The necklaces. They won't do the job. You'll need more to make it work. Pieces of something else. Pieces of the rest of it."

"What does that mean, Nick? Pieces of what?"

But he was gone again. Bill turned to Glaeken.

"Any idea what he's talking about?"

Glaeken sat numb and cold and sick as he stared at Nick.

"Yes, I'm afraid I do."

WXRK-FM

Well, the news keeps getting worse. Reports from the Midwest and the Plains States say that the nation's cattle herds were decimated by the bugs last night. Measures are being taken now to protect them but no one knows how successful they'll be. My advice: Enjoy your Big Macs and Whoppers today because pretty soon you won't be able to afford them.

And now, continuing with our K-Rock All-Request Weekend, we've got Marvin Gaye asking the question that's on everybody's lips.

Cue: "What's Goin' On?"

"Come on, Carol," Hank said. "We don't have much time!"

"We've got all day, Hank," she said, trying to hide her annoyance.

"But a day isn't what it used to be. Let's go!"

Carol joined him in the hall where he was holding the elevator.

"Where are we going now?" she asked when the doors had closed them in.

"You've got your list?"

"Yes," she sighed, fingering the handwritten sheet in her coat pocket. "I've got my list."

"We're going to split up," Hank said.

"I don't know if that's such a good idea."

"It's necessary," he said. "I've given it a lot of thought and that's the most efficient way to get everything done."

His eyes were feverish. He'd spent most of the night hours compiling lists of necessities they'd have to pick up today. He'd been up and down repeatedly, checking the windows. A few times he'd found one sort of monstrosity or another clinging to the screens, but for the most part it had been a quiet night.

"But there are warnings on the radio and TV—"

The elevator slowed to a stop at the fourth floor. The doors opened to reveal another couple outside in the hall, each weighted with a pair of suitcases. They looked pale, drawn, shaken. Carol recognized the woman—she'd seen her in the lobby a few times.

"Moving out?" she said, stepping aside to make room for them and their luggage.

The woman nodded glumly. "My sister's got a place in the Catskills. We're going to move in with her until this mess gets straightened out."

"What happened?"

"We had an awful night. Most of the lower floors did. They broke through our living-room windows and chased us through the apartment. We had to spend the rest of the night in the hall closet. Those things were right outside the door all night, clawing, chewing, scratching, trying to get in at us."

"How awful!" Carol said.

She realized then how lucky they were to have an apartment on an upper floor. They'd been spared last night. But what about tonight?

"Not as awful as what happened to the Honigs in four- twelve," her husband said. "Jerry lost his left hand and their little girl got carried off."

The woman's brave facade crumbled as she began to sob. "Poor Carrie!"

Carol's heart went out to the Honigs, whoever they were.

"If there's anything we can do for them—I mean, if they need food or—"

Hank nudged her. When she looked at him, he gave her a quick, tiny shake of his head.

"Hank—!"

"I'll explain later," he said under his breath.

The elevator doors opened onto the lobby then. The other couple hefted their luggage and moved out. Carol grabbed Hank's arm.

"Are you telling me we can't share any of our hoard with our neighbors if they need it?"

"Carol, please keep your voice down," he hissed, glancing around the empty lobby. "We can't let anyone know what we've got. *Anyone!* You tell one, she'll tell two who'll tell a couple more. Before you know it, the whole building—hell, the whole East Side will know what we've got. And then they'll be knocking on our door, begging. And if we give to one we'll have to give to more. And if we try to save some for ourselves they'll want that too. And when we don't give it to them, they'll break our door down and kill us and each other to get at it."

Shocked, Carol stared at him.

"God, Hank. What's wrong with you?"

"What's wrong with *me*? What's wrong with *you*? Can't you get it into your head that when things really begin to fall apart, our stock—our 'hoard,' as you like to call it—might be all that stands between us and starvation?"

She stared at him in wonder as a police car roared by outside with its sirens blasting.

Survival? Mere survival? At what cost? She couldn't see herself trading all her humane instincts and values for a full belly. And then an unsettling question wheedled its way into her thoughts: Would hunger—*real* hunger—put a whole new slant on her perspective?

She hoped the time never came when she had to deal with that question. But now, here, in the present, she had to deal with this strange new Hank. Maybe a more logical approach would work.

"But Hank, even with all we've put away, the time's going to come when that's going to run out too."

"No, no!" he said, a panicked look twisting his features for an instant. "A new order will be established after a while, and then we can begin trading for other things we need. We'll be in the catbird seat."

"Great, Hank. But we'll have had to pick our way through the starved corpses of our friends and neighbors to get there. Will that make you happy?"

"Dammit, Carol, I'm not talking about happiness—I'm talking about survival!"

Like talking to a wall, she thought dispiritedly.

"Fine, Hank. Keep on talking about survival. I need some fresh air."

She strode across the lobby and out to the street. Behind her she heard Hank call out.

"Don't forget your list! We need all that stuff by tonight!"

Carol wished she could have slammed the lobby door behind her.

CNN:

The Weekend Report continues with this just in from the White House. The President has declared a national state of emergency. Repeat: a national state of emergency. Reserve units of the Army are being activated. Congress has called an emergency session.

Monroe, Long Island

Sylvia recognized the old man's voice immediately. A wave of resentment surged through her.

"I hope this isn't about moving in with you in the city," she said, controlling her voice. "Pressure tactics won't work, Mr. Veilleur. I don't wear down very easily."

"I'm quite well aware of that, Mrs. Nash. And please call me Glaeken. That's my real name."

Sylvia didn't want to call him that. It was like a first name, and she didn't wish to be on a first-name basis with this man. So she said nothing.

"I didn't call to pressure you into anything," he said after a pause. "I merely wished to inquire as to how you and your household fared last night."

"We did just fine, thank you." *No thanks to you.*

She repressed the urge to tell him that the strange attraction Jeffy had developed for him had nearly cost the boy his life—and Ba's and her own as well; that if Jeffy hadn't become so fixated on Glaeken he wouldn't have wandered off last night. But in the back of her mind she knew Glaeken could crush her with the simple admonishment that a good mother should know the whereabouts of her child. She'd spent most of the night telling herself the same thing, berating herself for letting Jeffy wander off. If only she'd kept an eye on him, Rudy would still be alive and Ba wouldn't have dozens of healing wounds on the back of his neck.

"This is a tough old house," she said. "And with the metal storm shutters we installed yesterday, it's like a fortress."

The racket last night had been horrendous. Those things from the hole had pounded against the shutters incessantly until sunrise. Sealed in as they were, the silence from outside had been their only clue that daylight had arrived. She'd greeted the dawn with relief and exhaustion.

"Good," Glaeken said. "I'm very glad to hear that. I hope your defenses remain as effective against future assaults. But I called for two reasons. The other is to let you know that Jack, the fellow who let you in yesterday, will be stopping by later for a visit."

"I warned you about pressuring me."

"Have no fear, Mrs Nash. He's not coming to see you. He wishes to speak to Ba."

"Ba? What does he want with Ba?"

She vaguely remembered the wiry, dark-haired, dark-eyed man Glaeken had mentioned—a rather ordinary-looking sort. She had an impression of him and Ba standing at the back of the living room, speaking together in low tones. It was so unusual for Ba to speak at all to a stranger, she remembered wondering if they'd met before.

"Perhaps I'd better let Jack explain that himself," Glaeken said. "Good day, Mrs. Nash."

Jack arrived in the early afternoon. Sylvia heard him drive up and watched as he got out of a dented white Corvair convertible with a torn top. Since Ba was outside, reinforcing whatever weak points he could find in the houses defenses, and Alan was out in the back tossing a football to Jeffy, Sylvia went downstairs to let Jack in. He didn't come to the door, however. Instead, he walked around to the side of the house to where Ba was working.

What on earth could those two have in common? she wondered. She fought the temptation to tip-toe to one of the windows and eavesdrop. She'd know soon enough.

And sure enough, a few minutes later Ba was leading Jack into the house through the back door. Alan rolled in behind them and Jeffy brought up the rear, flipping his football from hand to hand.

"Hi, Mrs. Nash," Jack said, extending his hand. "We met yesterday."

She shook his hand briefly. "I remember."

"Can we all talk?" Jack said.

Alan looked at Sylvia and gave her a puzzled shrug. "Why don't we go into the den," he said.

Sylvia sent Jeffy upstairs to wash his hands and seated herself where she had a view of the stairs. If Jeffy came down, she'd see him. There'd be no wandering off this time. She was determined to know his whereabouts every minute of the day.

Jack seated himself across from her. Ba remained standing near Alan. She sensed tightly coiled tension in the tall Oriental and tried to read his expression, but as usual he was letting nothing show.

Jack said, "Do you remember Glaeken talking about a certain pair of necklaces yesterday?"

Sylvia nodded. "The ones supposedly made from the second focus."

"Right. Well, he's located them on Maui, and I'm going to head out there tomorrow to see if I can get them back."

"I see," Sylvia said, keeping her tone noncommittal. "What does that have to do with Ba?"

"I'd like him to come along."

"And what did Ba say?" She suspected the answer but wanted to hear it for herself.

"He refused. Said he couldn't leave you here unprotected."

Sylvia turned to the Oriental. "Thank you, Ba."

Ba gave her one of his little bows.

"I respect that," Jack said, "but I think it's shortsighted. When the light goes altogether, you're not going to get a break like this. Those things'll be at you nonstop. You won't get a chance to go out and repair the damage and shore up the weak spots. And I don't care how well fortified you are, Mrs. Nash, sooner or later they're gonna break through."

She glanced at Alan who was nodding silent agreement. And why not? The logic was unassailable.

"You can't do this alone?"

"I might be able to. I usually work alone, but this is different. Time is critical." He lifted his bandaged arm. "I've been out in the dark with those things. And I see by Ba's neck that he has too."

"So have I," Sylvia said.

Jack's eyebrows lifted. "Really? Well then, you know what it means to have someone watching your back."

Sylvia remembered the tentacles entwined in her hair, pulling her backward . . .

Repressing a shudder, she said, "How long have you known this Glaeken fellow?"

"A few days."

"And you're completely convinced?"

He shrugged. "I've seen a lot of scams—worked a few myself. This guy's for real. Besides, everything's going to hell out there at about a hundred and fifty miles an hour. After what I've seen in the past three days, I'm a believer."

Reluctantly, Sylvia admitted to herself that she, too, was becoming a believer.

"When would you be leaving?"

"Tomorrow morning. With any luck I'll have him back on your doorstep sometime Tuesday. Wednesday morning at the latest."

"Two days at the most. You're sure?"

"Pretty sure. Either I can get the necklaces back or I can't. I'll know fairly soon after I get there."

"Two nights," she said slowly. "Ba . . . .maybe you should reconsider."

"No, Missus," he said. "It is too dangerous here for you to stay alone."

Out of the corner of her eye she saw Alan stiffen—a barely perceptible straightening of his spine that would have passed unnoticed by a stranger. But Sylvia knew him too well. Ba would be devastated if he even suspected that his words had stung Alan. He'd never forgive himself.

"Glaeken's offer still stands," Jack told her. "Come into the city. Stay with him. He was right about his place being spared. He's practically hanging over that hole and he hasn't been bothered by a single bug."

"Out of the question," Sylvia said. "Alan and I are quite capable of handling the situation. We won't be driven from our home by these things." She turned to Ba. "We're safe in here, Ba. You saw that last night. Once we locked the doors and rolled down the shutters, we had no further problems. Tonight will be the same. And the night after that. And the night after that."

"Missus, I am not sure—"

"Neither am I, Ba. We can't be sure of anything anymore. Except perhaps that the situation will steadily deteriorate until we're all mad or dead."

"I vowed to protect you, Missus. Always."

"I know you did, Ba," she said softly.

Sylvia's heart warmed at his unflagging devotion. But that devotion could be a burden as well as a benefit. It was a great comfort to know she was protected, but she also had to *allow* herself to be protected. And that wasn't always easy.

Pulling away from the snug cocoon of that protection, even temporarily, was difficult—akin perhaps to leaving all the windows open in a storm. And knowing the distress it caused in Ba made the move all the more difficult for her.

She asked Jack, "What will the return of these necklaces do?"

He shrugged. "Only Glaeken knows. Set things right, I hope. Mother Nature's gone nuts. Maybe these things will go toward building something that'll give her some electroshock therapy."

"If that's true, Ba . . . if acquiring these necklaces will help end this nightmare, perhaps you would be adhering closer to the spirit of your vow by going with this man."

Ba stood silent for a moment, the center of attention. His eyes were tortured. "Missus . . . "

"Let's do it this way," Sylvia said, lighting on an idea. "We'll see how tonight goes. If Alan and I need your help to get through, then I'll ask you to stay. But if it turns out we can handle things ourselves, then I think you should go with Jack."

"Very well, Missus. If that is what you wish."

I don't know what I wish, she thought. But I know we can't spend the rest of our lives sealed up in Toad Hall.

"That is what I wish," she said.

"All right!" Jack said, clapping his hands once as he rose to his feet. "I'll be here first thing tomorrow morning— bright and early."

Alan said, "It probably won't be bright and it certainly won't be early."

Sylvia watched Jack go over to Ba and extend his hand.

"I respect where you're coming from, Big Guy, but believe me, this is our only chance to really *do* something about this— to maybe turn it around and stop it so we can all get back to our normal lives. That's worth risking a couple of days, isn't it?"

Ba shook his hand slowly. "I will go with you tomorrow."

Jack smiled. "Try to control your enthusiasm, okay?"

Then he waved and headed for the front door. When he was gone, Ba turned to her.

"Excuse me, Missus. I have work outside."

"Of course," Sylvia said. But as she watched him go, she caught her breath as that recurring phrase slipped into her mind.

Only three will live to return.

"Something wrong?" Alan said.

They were alone now and his gentle brown eyes were fixed on her.

"Is something right?" she said.

"You looked frightened."

"I was thinking about what that lunatic in Glaeken's apartment told you and wondering if I was sending Ba to his doom. What if he's killed on this trip? It will be my fault."

"I've never believed anyone could tell the future," he said. "And as for fault, that's a no-win game. If Ba goes off and gets killed, it's your fault. If you *don't* convince him to go and he gets killed around here, it's also your fault. But actually, neither scenario is anybody's fault. It's nothing but a mental trap."

"I guess you're right. I'm treating some nut's rant as if it's really going to happen. I must be as crazy as he is." She leaned over and kissed him. "Thanks, Alan. You're good for me."

He gave her a kiss of his own. "And thank *you.*"

"For what?"

"For saying, 'Alan and I are quite capable of handling the situation.' That meant a lot."

So . . . he *had* been stung by Ba's remark.

"Ba didn't mean anything."

"I know that."

"Ba admires you and respects you. He's forever in your debt for the care you gave Nhung Thi before she died. You're on his Good-Guy list."

"I'd hate to be on his Bad Guy list."

"Ba doesn't really have one of those. All the people he considers bad guys seem to disappear. And he'd be crushed if he thought he'd offended you."

"I wasn't offended."

Sylvia stared into his eyes. "Truth, Alan."

"Okay," he said, glancing away. "That crack about not wanting to leave you 'alone' did get to me. I mean, what am I— a houseplant? I know I'm in a wheelchair, but I'm not helpless."

"Of course you're not. And Ba knows that too. It's just that he's been my self-appointed watchman for so many years, he thinks he's the only one who can do the job. If I had the Eighty-second Airborne camping in with me, he'd still consider me unprotected if he wasn't at my side."

"It's funny," Alan said, staring at the wall. "You hear women complaining about being labeled as 'the weaker sex' and not given a chance to prove their competence and equality and maybe even superiority to men in business and industry. They don't see the flip side of the coin. The guys are saddled with the macho ethic. We're supposed to be tough, we're supposed to be able to handle anything, be cool in any situation, never back down, never surrender, never admit we're hurt, and for God's sake, never *ever* cry. It's not easy to handle even when you're at the top of your form; but when something happens to knock you off your feet, I tell you, Syl, it becomes a crushing burden. And sometimes . . . sometimes it's just plain murder."

Sylvia didn't know what to say to that. She simply reached over and held his hand. She hoped that said it all.

WWOR-TV

CAMERON: But Dr. Sapir, how exactly did you arrive at these figures?

SAPIR: I simply charted the times of sunrise and sunset and the resultant hours of daylight since Wednesday on a graph. Those figures yielded the curve you see here. I have merely continued that curve.

CAMERON: And that shows . . . ?

SAPIR: All you have to do is follow it. We'll have approximately eleven hours of sunlight today; slightly less than ten hours tomorrow, Monday; about eight hours and forty minutes of daylight on Tuesday, about seven hours on Wednesday, and—you see how steep the curve is becoming—four hours and forty-two minutes of light on Thursday.

CAMERON: And on Friday?

SAPIR: On Friday, nothing.

CAMERON: Nothing?

SAPIR: Correct. If the curve holds true, the sun will set at 3:01 p.m. on Thursday and will not rise again. There will be no sunrise on Friday.

Manhattan

Bill Ryan sat stunned before the TV in Glaeken's study. He'd turned on the show to see if the sight of his old colleague would shock Nick back into the real world. Instead it was Bill who had received the shock.

No sunrise on Friday? It seemed impossible, but Dr. Harvey Sapir was a world-renowned physicist from Columbia University.

"Nick," Bill said, turning to the younger man. "What's going to happen? You've been coming on with all sorts of predictions lately. How's all this going to turn out?"

Nick didn't answer. His vacant gaze remained fixed on one of the curlicues in the wallpaper design.

Bill closed his eyes and tried to keep from shouting in frustration. Nothing was right. Especially Nick. Because every time he looked at Nick he was reminded of all the people who had suffered because they were close to him, because he'd cared for them. His parents, little Danny Gordon, Lisl, and now Nick. All of them either dead or mad. And to what end? To isolate him? To make him doubt himself? To make him afraid to get close to anyone, or care for anyone again?

Hello, down there! he thought, looking out the study window at the Sheep Meadow hole, a dark splotch in the afternoon light. Guess what? It's working.

What the hell good was he? Of what use was he to Glaeken? If anything, he was a Jonah. Why did the old man keep him around?

Answerless questions. Glaeken wasn't even home. He was somewhere in the building helping Jack's friends move into the deserted apartments. Bill would have liked to help—the physical activity might do something to dispel this lethargy weighing upon him—but someone had to stay with Nick. And Bill felt responsible for Nick.

The doorbell rang.

Strange, he thought as he headed for the door. You needed a key to get up here. Who'd come this far and then ring the bell?

He was startled when he saw the woman standing in the atrium.

"Carol! I didn't know you were coming."

Bill's lethargy was swept away in the flood of warmth that gushed through him at the sight of her. Already his spirits were lifting.

"Neither did I," she said. "Glaeken sent me up."

Immediately he knew something was wrong. He looked at her more closely and saw how prominent were the lines in her face. Carol had always looked younger than her years, but today she showed every birthday.

"Come in." He glanced out into the atrium as she passed. "Where's Hank?"

"Who knows?"

"Want to talk about it?"

"Yes," she said, then quickly shook her head. "No. I mean . . . " She sat down on the couch. "Oh, Bill, Hank's acting so strange I don't know what to say or what to do."

She told him about the abrupt change in Hank's personality, about the hoarding, the lists, the other obsessive behavior.

"You're obviously upset," he heard himself say. "Have you tried to talk to him about it?"

Without realizing it, he had slipped into his old priestly, family-counselor role. He pulled back from it. This wasn't a parishioner, this was Carol. Someone he knew. No, not just knew, but—he could admit it now—*loved* for almost forty years. It was silly to try for emotional distance where Carol was concerned. He'd never make it.

"Sure I've tried," she said, "but it's like talking to a wall. Is he having a breakdown, do you think?"

Bill sighed. "I don't know if 'breakdown' is the right word. He's not behaving irrationally—in fact, what he's doing makes a lot of sense self-preservation-wise. He's frightened and stressed-out, like most everybody else."

He felt the depression begin closing in again.

"I know that. And he's not doing anything terrible, not hurting anybody. He's a good man. Really. But he's got this crazy look in his eyes."

"Do you love him, Carol?"

The words slipped out and immediately he wanted to call them back. He began to tell her she didn't have to answer, then realized that she knew that. So he let it hang. The question had plagued him since his return to the city a few months ago. He wanted to know, damn it.

"Yes. In a way. Not like I loved Jim. Nothing like that. But he's a good man, gentle and kind—at least he used to be kind. Now he's just . . . I don't know."

"Why did you marry him?"

He couldn't believe he was asking these questions. But here in the darkening room, with Carol becoming a silhouette against the dying light outside, he felt he could. Should. He didn't reach for a lamp. That would break the mood set by the half light.

"I guess I was lonely, Bill. When I came back to New York, I knew no one. Mostly, I wanted it that way. I wanted a fresh start. I didn't want to go back to Monroe and look up old friends. Too much time had passed. They'd just remind me of Jim and the life we had there. And they'd want to know where I'd been all these years, they'd want to know why I left, and they'd want to know about . . . the baby. I didn't want to talk about any of it. It would be too much like reliving everything. I wanted to create a new Carol."

"I can understand that. Perfectly."

"Can you?"

"Sure. I did it myself in North Carolina. Even changed my name to Will Ryerson. But for different reasons. Strange, isn't it? We were a thousand miles apart but we were both trying to remodel ourselves, and at just about the same time."

"Well then maybe you can understand how lonely it can be. At least you have your religious beliefs—"

Bill shook his head slowly. "Had. *Had* my beliefs. They're gone now." *Like just about everyone or everything else in my life I've cared about.* "But go on. Please."

"This isn't an easy city to build relationships in. Not if you're my age and unconnected. You get hit on by younger men who think you're an easy mark who'll be so grateful for the attention you'll hop into bed with them right off, or you're pursued by older ones who've already got a couple broken marriages behind them and think nothing of trying a third, or others who are simply looking for someone to take care of them. That's why Hank was so refreshing."

"What was he looking for?"

"Nothing. He was self-sufficient—a lifelong bachelor who knew how to take care of himself. He wasn't on the make, and neither was I. So we wound up feeling very comfortable with each other. No pressure. Just companionship—real companionship."

Bill made no comment. He'd heard far worse reasons for marriage.

"Companionship led to a . . . um . . . closer relationship, which led to us moving in together. After a while we decided to make it legal." A soft laugh in the growing darkness. "Not the stuff that makes for a hot romance novel, but it worked for us. Until now."

"I wish I had some brilliant advice for you, Carol. All I can say is . . . " the words tasted bitter on his tongue. . . "hang in there a little longer. If Glaeken can buy us some time, Hank will probably come around. If Glaeken fails . . . well, you just might be very glad you have all that food."

"'Hang in there,'" she repeated. "It won't be easy, but that's what I was going to do anyway. I owe him that. I just needed a little pep talk." Suddenly she stiffened and turned to look out the window. "My God, it's almost dark! I'd better get going."

She shot to her feet and Bill rose with her. It seemed like the day had just begun.

Carol started for the door. Bill followed. She was reaching for the knob when Glaeken opened it and stepped inside. Jack was with him.

"Carol?" he said. "You're still here?"

"Yes, I'm late. I've got to hurry. It's almost sunset."

"It *is* sunset," he said. "You can't go out now. You'd never make it to the other side of the Park, let alone to your apartment."

"But I've *got* to go. Hank will be worried."

"Call him," Glaeken said. "The phones were still working last time I checked. Tell him you're all right and you'll be safe here tonight."

Bill guided her back to the phone. He empathized with her distress at being cut off from her home, but try as he might, he could not douse the gleeful elation that sparked within him at the prospect of having her near all night.

WINS-AM

This just in: The New York City Department of Corrections has reported a massive jail break from Riker's Island less than an hour ago. When approximately eighty-five per cent of guards on the third shift called in sick, the second shift refused overtime pay and walked off.

The Police Commissioner reports similar third-shift problems in most of the city's precincts.

Almost done.

Hank had started an hour ago. He'd used the bolt cutters to snip all the pieces of cyclone fencing to size in one shot, and now he was nailing the last piece to the frame of the bathroom window. When the last nail was in place, he stepped back and surveyed the job.

"There!" he said aloud. "That oughta keep them out."

It was a good bet those monsters would reach the upper floors tonight. If they did, he was ready for them. Even if they tore out his screens and smashed the panes, nothing bigger than two inches around was getting through that fencing. But just as important as the fencing on the windows was the bar on the door. He'd bolted the steel brackets into the door frame; they were heavy, sturdy, and designed to hold a four-by-four oak bar. Nobody was getting into this place unless Hank said so.

He had to admit, though, it looked like hell. Carol would probably have a fit when she got back.

Carol!

He stepped to the window and peered out. The sun was down. Soon the air would be filled with those monstrosities. She should have been home by now. Where was she?

The phone rang then. Hank ran to answer it.

"Carol?" he said as he jammed the receiver to his ear. Relief flooded him at the sound of her voice.

"Oh, Hank!" Carol said. "I'm so glad you're home."

"Where are you? Don't you know it's almost dark?"

"That's why I'm calling. I'm at Glaeken's. I'm okay, but I can't get home."

"I see," he said. Now that he knew she was safe, annoyance seeped though. "Did you get the things on your list?"

"No."

"What? You know I was counting on you."

"I'll get them tomorrow."

"You can't! It's like a jungle out there. The stores were selling out when I started this morning. They're all empty now. Dammit, Carol! I can't do all this alone!"

She'd let him down. He tried to hide his hurt.

"I needed to talk to somebody, Hank. So I stopped by here to see Bill."

"Talk?" His heart kicked up its rate. "What did you talk to him about?"

"Us. I wanted to straighten a few things out in my head."

"Did you tell him about the—about our supplies?"

"Yes. But I just—"

"Carol! How could you?" He felt as if he'd been stabbed. "Didn't I tell you not to mention them to anybody? Those are for us!"

"Okay, Hank. Okay. We'll talk about that when I come home. I'll be there first thing tomorrow morning."

"Fine!" he said, feeling a cold wind stirring up and blowing through his heart. "Stay the night with your priest friend. Talk your little heart out. Good night!"

He slammed the receiver down, waited a couple of seconds, then lifted it again and left it off the cradle. Then he stepped to the door and dropped the big four-by-four bar onto its brackets.

The receiver began to howl. He jammed a cushion over it.

Carol . . . how could she do this to him? Why was she blabbing about their supplies all over town? Why was she trying to undermine his plans? It didn't make sense. He'd put all this together for the two of them. He was her husband. It was his duty to look out for her. And that was just what he'd been doing.

But apparently Carol didn't care. No, it was worse than not caring—she was actively sabotaging him. Her big mouth was going to ruin everything. And there was no way he could stop her.

Or was there?

He couldn't make her go around and tell everyone that she'd been lying. Even if he could, it wouldn't work. But he could *make* her story a lie.

All he'd have to do was move their supplies.

And he knew just where to take them: the Jersey Shore. During a long span of his bachelor years he used to rent a bungalow every summer at places like Chadwick Beach or Seaside Heights. Most of them were little more than plywood boxes, but he knew a couple of places that were fairly sturdy, equipped with storm shutters and heat. They'd be empty now, the beaches and boardwalks all but deserted, waiting for the summer renters— renters who wouldn't be coming. A perfect locale.

He got to work arranging all the cases of food in four-foot stacks by the door—the maximum load he could handle with his hand truck. At first light tomorrow he'd cover each stack with a sheet and hustle it down to his rented van still parked below.

Hank took a blanket and huddled down behind his walls of food and began counting the hours till dawn.

As Carol listened to the busy signal for perhaps the dozenth time, she watched Jack and Glaeken in huddled conversation on the far side of the living room. Jack had arrived earlier, jubilant that he'd heard from someone named Gia over the shortwave. Apparently she and her daughter had made it safely to a hideaway in Pennsylvania. Now, as he and Glaeken conversed, they'd occasionally glance her way, but she realized they were really looking at Bill, and that made her uneasy.

She hung up and dialed her home phone number again. *Still busy.* She wanted to scream at it to ring. She had to speak to Hank, straighten things out. She didn't like the thought of him spending the night alone in that apartment thinking she'd let him down. She'd tried the operator but her rings were never answered. NYNEX seemed to be running on its computers alone. She wondered how long they'd hold up. She hung up the phone and looked at Bill.

"Still busy. Do you think anything's wrong?"

"Sounds like he's in some sort of snit. He'll get over it."

"I hope so. Snit's a perfect word. I can't believe he's acting like this. Do you think he'll be all right?"

"I'm sure he'll be fine. I just wish he was as concerned about you as you are about him."

How true, she thought. Why isn't he calling to see how I'm doing?

Jack came over and rested his hand on the phone.

"Mind if I make a call?"

"Go ahead," she said. "It's not doing me any good."

She and Bill moved away to make room for him. They gravitated to the picture window overlooking the Sheep Meadow. Carol saw lights and bustling figures below.

"What's going on?"

"I'm not sure," Bill said. He lifted a pair of binoculars from a nearby table and peered through them. "They were dropping some sort of depth charges in it earlier today. Looks like they're going to try spraying them with insecticide again." He passed the glasses to her. "Take a look."

The Sheep Meadow swam into focus through the lenses. Carol remembered watching a similar scene on TV last night, a scene that had ended in bloody horror.

"I can't believe they're going to try this again," she said. "Those men down there must be either very brave or very crazy."

"I'd venture they're neither," Bill said. "They're doing their job. Everybody else can go nuts, throw up their hands and say nothing matters anymore, the world's coming to an end so screw everything and let's party, let's go wild, let's do all the things we never allowed ourselves to do when we knew there'd be a price to pay. Let's get drunk, get stoned, rape, pillage, kill, destroy, burn everything to the ground just because we feel like it. But there will always be a certain small percentage out there who'll go on doing their jobs, people with an overriding sense of duty, of responsibility, of obligation to try to keep things running, to ignore the end-of-the-world *zeitgeist* and just keep going. People who know that to let yourself go crazy is to say that your day-to-day life has been a sham, that you've been a hypocrite, that your lifestyle has been little more than play-acting for other people; like saying, 'Hey, you know everything

I've said and done up till now? It's all been a lie. *This* is the real me.' No matter what Rasalom throws at that small percentage of humans, they aren't going to back down. Some of them are down there around that goddam hole right now."

Carol found herself staring at Bill, a lump in her throat, tears in her eyes. *And I know you're one of them.* The sound of applause made her turn. Behind them, Jack and Glaeken were clapping.

"I bet you used to give some wicked sermons," Jack said.

Bill looked sheepish. "Sorry. I got a little carried away."

"Don't apologize. You've just demonstrated one of the reasons Rasalom hates you so. The type of person you describe is the only threat to his supremacy. Unfortunately, there aren't enough of them. If the percentages were reversed, however—if there were as many people sticking to their posts, holding on and refusing to allow fear to rob them of everything they believe in, everything they've lived for, as there now are people falling victim to their fears—Rasalom wouldn't have a chance. But the opposite is true. The violent anarchy growing outside feeds his power, helps him shorten the days even further, which increases the fear and irrationality, which in turn makes him stronger, and around and around it goes until he is victor."

A flash of light from below caught Carol's attention. She turned and stared out the window.

"Oh, look!"

The others joined her at the window as she raised the glasses and watched as the men around the Sheep Meadow hole sprayed fire at the things winging up from the depths.

"I'll be damned!" Jack said from over her left shoulder. "Flame throwers! King Kong flame throwers!"

"I think it's working!" Bill said.

And sure enough, the fire did seem to be working. The things flying out of the hole were caught in the crossfire. Arcs of flame streamed inward from all sides of the hole. Powered by the pumps on the trucks around the rim, they crisscrossed over the opening, waving back and forth, catching the winged things as they tried to escape into the night. Doused with gasoline, or whatever the hoses were spraying, they caught fire and hurtled out of control into the darkness, twisting, turning, tumbling, fluttering up and down and about like windswept embers from a fresh-lit campfire.

A thrill ran through Carol. The things were dying! They could be contained! Here was the spark of hope they'd all been looking for!

"Do you know what this means?" she said, lowering the glasses and turning to the others. "If they can set up flamethrowers around all the holes—"

"Hey, what's going on down there?" Jack said.

Carol peered through the glasses again. The arcs of flame were wavering, faltering, some dropping, falling, pouring straight down into the hole; others were backing away from the edge, spraying the ground along the rim with liquid fire. And then Carol saw why.

"Oh, no!"

The flying things weren't the only creatures leaving the pit tonight. Through the lenses she saw other shapes—bulbous creatures with hard, shiny, black bodies; sinuous, multi-legged crawlers as long as a man and as thick around as a muscular thigh, and more—moving along the rim, crawling over the edge, worming their way onto the grass. They leapt upon the men directing the flame throwers, began tearing them to pieces.

Carol snatched the glasses from her eyes and held them away from her. Jack took them, watched for a moment in silence, then handed them to Bill.

"Every night some new horror is added to the others," Bill said after a moment. His voice was dry, quavering.

"And each night is longer than the last," Glaeken said. "But come away from the window for now. We have something to discuss."

Carol was glad to retreat to the lighted space of the living room. She sat next to Bill—huddled next to him, actually. It was warm in the apartment but she felt cold. She almost wished he'd put an arm around her and hug her close. She felt so alone tonight.

Jack sat across from them. Glaeken remained standing.

"Jack is leaving for the Central Pacific tomorrow. The object of his mission is crucial to our survival. However, even if he's successful in retrieving the necklaces, I fear they won't be enough. We need something else. One more constituent. And to obtain that, someone must travel in the opposite direction. Jack can't do both—there's not enough time. I need a volunteer to go the other way."

A sick feeling grew in the pit of Carol's stomach as she noticed both men staring at Bill.

"How . . . how far in this 'other direction'?"

"Rumania."

Carol grabbed Bill's hand and squeezed. *No!*

"How can I get there? The airlines—"

He's already decided! Carol thought. They didn't even ask him and he's already making travel plans.

"I know some pilots," Jack said. "A couple of brothers. I did some work for them once. They run an executive jet service out on Long Island. They owe me."

"They're still flying?"

Jack smiled. "You know the kind of people you were talking about before— the ones who keep on keepin' on, no matter what? Frank and Joe Ashe are two of those. They don't back down—I don't think they know how."

"Frank and Joe," Bill said. "They sound like the Hardy Boys. They owe *you*. Will they fly me?"

Jack nodded. "For a price. I just spoke to them. They're not crazy about flying into Eastern Europe, but for the right price—in gold—they'll do it."

"Gold?" Bill said. "I don't—"

"I have plenty," Glaeken said. "Are you willing to make the trip?"

"Of course," Bill said.

"Bill!" Carol said, giving his hand a hard squeeze. "Maybe you should think about this."

"What's to think about?" he said, his blue eyes clear and untroubled as they stared into hers. "Somebody's got to do it. Might as well be me. I want to be useful, Carol. I'm tired of feeling like a fifth wheel. I want to *do* something. Hell, I'm not needed for anything else around here."

I need you! she thought. The intensity of the emotion behind that thought startled her.

"You could be killed."

"We'll all be dead if we don't do what we can now," he said, then looked at Glaeken. "When do I leave and what am I supposed to get?"

"You leave tomorrow morning—"

"Oh, no!" Carol couldn't help it.

"—and you'll be searching a rocky ravine for scraps of metal, shards from a sword blade that shattered there half a century ago."

"Do I have to get them all?"

"Just a few. Just a sampling is all that is needed. You must—"

An explosion rattled the apartment windows. Carol followed Glaeken, Bill, and Jack to the picture window.

Below, in the Sheep Meadow, flames billowed high into the night air. One of the tank trucks supplying the gasoline for the flame throwers had exploded. In the flickering light of the flames, even without the binoculars, Carol could see that the entire Sheep Meadow was now acrawl with the new horrors from the hole. They were on the move, spreading out into the city streets in a glistening, worming, undulating carpet.

Carol glanced up and saw the moon rising huge and orange over the rooftops of the city. But there was something . . . different about it tonight.

"What's wrong with the moon?" she asked.

The others stared along with her. It was Jack who noticed first.

"The face—the Man in the Moon face is gone. Jeez—even the moon's been changed!"

"Not changed," said a flat voice by her shoulder.

A small cry of surprise escaped Carol as she turned and saw Nick standing directly behind her. But he wasn't looking at her. His attention was focused on the moon.

"It's the same moon," he said. "It's just been turned. You're looking at what used to be the dark side of the moon."

Carol turned back and stared up at the vaguely threatening orb that had been a symbol of romance for ages.

Even the Man in the Moon has turned his back on us.

"Take me with you tomorrow," Nick said to Bill. "You won't find anything without me."

Carol watched Bill stare at Nick, then look questioningly at Glaeken.

After a pause, Glaeken nodded. "He's right, I think. He may help shorten your trip. And right now anything that saves time is worth a try."

Feeling colder than ever, Carol turned back to the window and leaned against Bill. As she stared at the pale, unfamiliar ridges of the moon's new face, she gasped. Something dark, hideous, and mind-numbingly huge was sweeping across the sky, blotting out the light of the rising moon. It passed slowly, like a floating shroud, casting a chill over everything in its enormous shadow, and then it moved on and the moon was visible again.

She shuddered and felt Bill's arm slip around her shoulders. But even that could not dispel the chill of foreboding that had insinuated its way into her bones.

The Movie Channel
Joe Bob Briggs' Drive-In Movie—A Special All-Nite Edition.
Up From The Depths (1969) New World
The Fly (1958) Twentieth Century Fox
Return Of The Fly (1965) Twentieth Century Fox
Curse Of The Fly (1965) Lippert/Twentieth Century Fox
Night Creatures (1962) Hammer/Universal
Not Of This Earth (1956) Allied Artists

3 • CEREMONIES

MAUI

"It's a gift, Bati! A sign from Pele herself!"

Moki's voice was barely audible over the blast-furnace roar of the volcano. Dressed only in his *malo*, he stood near the ruins of the visitor center on the crater rim of the newly awakened Haleakala. Perspiration coated his skin, giving it a glossy sheen as red and orange light from the fires below flickered off the planes and curves of his taut, muscular body, making it glow against the inky night sky.

The two yellow stones in his necklace seemed to glow with internal fires of their own. And why not? The necklace had been working overtime on Moki.

Only moments ago he had emerged from the crater with second-degree burns blistering most of his body. But the blisters had shriveled and the damaged skin had peeled and sloughed away to reveal fresh, unmarred flesh beneath.

Kolabati backed away from the heat and worried about Moki. He'd changed so drastically. He was no longer the man she'd loved and lived with for the past few years. He was a stranger, a deranged interloper fashioning his own delusions out of the madness around him.

Yesterday she had been afraid for him. But now she was afraid *of* him. The cataclysm that had destroyed the Big Island and reawakened Haleakala seemed to have pushed him over the edge.

And tingeing Kolabati's fear, coloring it a deep, dull red, was anger. Why? Why now? Why did all of nature choose this time to go mad? Was it coincidence? Or was it fate? Was her enormous karmic burden—and she knew too well the extent to which the deeds of her 150 years had polluted her karma—finally catching up to her?

"What does it mean, Moki?" she called back, humoring him. "What kind of sign would the fire goddess be sending you?"

"She didn't want me leaving Maui to gather lava from Kileau, so she destroyed Kileau and brought her fires to my back yard."

Kolabati shook her head in silent dismay. Didn't Moki's mania admit any limits? How many countless thousands had died on the Big Island when it had exploded? How many more here on Maui in those areas not shielded from the blast by Haleakala? But Haleakala herself had gathered her share of lives. Hana was gone, as were the Seven Sacred Pools, buried under the tons of ash and dirt from Haleakala's explosive awakening and sealed over by the initial gush of lava that had filled the Kipahulu Valley and burst through into the Waihoi Valley, running down to the sea. According to the news, the whole southeast corner of the island, from the Kaupo Gap to Nanualele Point, was a seething bed of molten lava.

All so Moki wouldn't have to leave Maui on day trips?

Fortunately the lava had flowed along its old paths. If Haleakala had erupted through its northern wall instead, the heavily populated central valley would have become a graveyard. Moki even had an explanation for that: Pele wished to spare Moki and his *wahine.*

So Moki had changed, and with his transformation Kolabati recognized unwelcome changes within herself. The inner tranquility had been shattered, the peace broken, and she found her thoughts traveling along old familiar ways, the cold, calculating paths of the past.

Kolabati shivered in the chill wind. Shielded as she was from the heat of the crater, it was cold up here nearly two miles above the ocean. She wanted to flee, but where to? The news from the mainland was frightening. It might be safer here on the islands, but not with Moki. He was an explosive charge, ready to detonate at any moment and destroy everything and anyone nearby. Yet she could not leave him. Not while he wore the other necklace. That belonged to her, and she would not leave without it.

Yet how to retrieve the necklace? How to unbell the cat?

She had considered removing it from around his neck while he slept but had not yet dared to try. Since the madness had come upon him, Moki hardly slept at all. And if he awoke from one of his short naps to find the necklace gone, he would track her down, and then only the goddess Kali knew what he might do to her. He might even rip her own necklace from around her throat and watch as a century and a half caught up with her. He of course would not age noticeably without his necklace, for he had worn it only for a few years. But Kolabati would grew old and crumble into dying ashes before his eyes.

She could not risk that. So she kept quiet, acted supportive, and waited for her chance.

With a start, Kolabati realized that they were not alone on the crater rim. A group of perhaps sixty men of varying ages in traditional Hawaiian dress had joined them. Led by their *alii*, an elderly man in a chieftain's feather robe and headdress, they were approaching Moki where he stood watching the fires. The *alii* called to him and he turned. She caught snatches of traditional Hawaiian chattered back and forth but had difficulty grasping the gist of what was being said.

Finally, Moki turned and walked down the slope toward her. The others remained up near the rim, waiting.

"Bati!" he said in a low voice, his grin wide and wild, his eyes dancing with excitement. "Do you see them? They're the last of the traditional Hawaiians. They sailed all the way from Niihau looking for Maui."

"They found it," Kolabati said. "What's left of it."

"Not the island—Maui the god. You know the story."

"Of course."

Before dawn one day long ago, Maui the mischievous Polynesian demigod crept to the summit of Haleakala, the House of the Sun, on a mission of filial love. His mother had complained that the days were not long enough to allow her to finish her tasks of cooking, cleaning, and drying tapa cloth, so Maui decided to do something about it. When the first ray of the sun appeared over the summit, Maui snared it with his lasso, thus trapping the sun. The sun pleaded for freedom but Maui would not release it until it promised to lengthen the days by slowing its trek across the heavens.

"The Niihauans say the shorter days show that the sun has broken its promise and so they've come to aid Maui when he returns to recapture the sun. They want to know if I've seen him! Can you believe it?"

Kolabati looked past Moki at the grown men dressed in feathers and carrying spears, and pitied them.

"What did you tell them?"

"I temporized. I wasn't sure what to say. But now I do."

Kolabati didn't like the look in his eyes.

"I'm almost afraid to ask."

His grin widened. "I'm going to tell them *I'm* Maui."

"Oh, Moki, don't toy with them. Aren't things bad enough already?"

"Who's toying?" he said. "I feel a strange power in me, Bati. I have a feeling I just might *be* Maui, or at least his avatar. I tell you, Bati, I'm here in this place at this time for a reason. Perhaps this is a sign as to why."

Kolabati grabbed his hand and tried to lead him down the slope.

"Moki, no. Come back to the house. Work on that new sculpture you started."

"Later," he said, pulling free. "After I've told them who I am."

She watched him stride back up to the rim and face the Niihauans, saw him pound his chest and gesture to the fires below and then to the night sky above. The traditional Hawaiians stepped back from him and whispered among themselves. Then the *alii* gestured to one of the younger men who stepped forward and drove his spear into Moki's chest.

Kolabati screamed.

His consciousness is fuzzy, but he still has control.

Rasalom is in solution now. All his tissues—his bones, brains, organs, nerves, intestines—have liquefied. All that he was resides in a sack suspended from the hub of the four-spoked wheel that was once his body. The spokes have grown thicker, longer, and the stony womb has enlarged to accommodate his increased size. It is a cavern now, stretching downward into the infinity where the cold fire burns. The icy glow from below chills the sack where he grows, where his constituents reorganize into his new form. The petrous columns that arch across the cavern act as conduits for the fear, the violence, the pain, the misery they siphon from the surface, feeding him, shaping him.

His new form shall be ready by the undawn on Friday.

But now it is time for the next step—to deny them the sight of the sun.

Part II

TWILIGHT

MONDAY

1 • FELLOW TRAVELERS

FNN:

In case you haven't heard, we are witnessing a global collapse of the world's stock markets. The Nikkei Exchange has crashed. All stocks from Hong Kong, throughout Europe, and in London are in freefall. There is no reason to expect that the U.S. exchanges to fare any better when they open in New York this morning. We are witnessing the greatest financial cataclysm in history.

Precious metals, however, are a different story. Gold opened in Hong Kong at twelve hundred and fifty-one dollars an ounce and went through the roof from there. Silver opened at an astounding eighty dollars an ounce and hasn't stopped rising. No price seems too high to bid on these metals.

MANHATTAN

Suddenly Hank was awake. A sound from the bedroom. Breaking glass. Bugs—spearheads most likely—were ramming themselves against the windows, smashing the panes. They'd be swarming in and eating him alive now if not for the cyclone fencing. He listened for a while as they battered futilely against the metal links, then fluttered off, heading for redder pastures.

It used to be the nights were never long enough for Hank. His head would hit the pillow and before he knew it, the clock radio would switch on and *Imus In The Morning* would be bitching and complaining through the bedroom.

Now the nights were too long. He'd fallen into an exhausted sleep soon after stacking the cartons by the door, and now he nestled down into his blanket and tried to find sleep again. At various times during the night he heard screams from next door, thudding footsteps in the hallway. At one point a woman pounded on his door, crying about bugs in the hallway, begging for *somebody* to let her in. Hank's first impulse had been to open up—he actually reached for the bar—but then he'd wondered if it might be a trap, someone who'd spotted him bringing in his supplies and was trying to trick her way in. So he'd crouched there with his hands pressed over his ears and his teeth clamped down on his lips, waiting for her to go away. A sudden, agonized scream broke through the seal of his palms and he snatched them away to listen. No further screams, but violent thrashing just beyond the door, then muffled, gurgling sobs that were hideous to hear. Then silence.

Thoroughly shaken, Hank was about to turn and crawl back to his blanket when he saw the blood leaking under the door and pooling on the floor by the threshold. He gagged and ran for the bathroom.

Later on, when he could stomach it, he made coffee. With the sound down so low he could barely hear it, he watched the tube. The picture flickered now and again, but he never totally lost power. He had a battery-powered portable ready if needed. About the only things on were preachers and news— disastrous news.

The President had proclaimed a state of national emergency but the armed forces were proving ineffective against an enemy of such overwhelming numbers so intimately mixed with the population they were meant to protect. Those with wives, children, parents, were staying home to protect their own. The remainder were vastly outnumbered. For every hole they plugged with explosives—in the instances where they could safely use explosives—two more opened up elsewhere. People were quickly losing confidence in the government's ability to manage the situation. The whole social fabric was unraveling.

The news footage only steeled Hank's resolve to get out of the city as soon as the sun rose. In fact, why wait till dawn? The sky was getting lighter now. Those things should be on their way back to the hole already if they wanted to make it before sunrise. Maybe he could get a head start on loading the van.

The first stack was already draped and loaded on the hand truck. Hank lifted the bar and opened the door for a quick peek.

Someone was out there. Down the hall to his left a still form lay curled on its side near the elevators. No one else was in sight. Hank stepped outside his door, locked it behind him, then hurried down the hall, pushing the loaded hand truck ahead of him, following the long trail of smeared blood that ran from his doorway to the still form.

It was a woman. Or had been. Hank forced himself to look. He didn't recognize what was left of her. Her body was shrunken, wizened, all her exposed skin was shredded, chewed up but strangely bloodless. He bit back a surge of bile and told himself that it was a good thing he hadn't opened his door last night; if he had he might be as dead as she. He repeated that a couple of times as he turned his back to her and waited for the elevator to arrive.

Hank whirled as an angry buzz came from far down the hall to his left. A couple of the ceiling fixtures were smashed down at that end so it was dark there. He couldn't see anything, but he knew that buzz. Wings. Big, double, dragonfly wings. He'd heard plenty of it these past nights. And then he heard another sound—the gnashing teeth of a chew wasp.

Terror rammed a fist down hard on his bladder. Too early! He'd left the apartment *too damn early*!

His first impulse was to run for his apartment but a vision of himself standing before the locked door, fumbling for his keys while the chew wasp zeroed in on his neck kept him where he was, pounding on the DOWN button, the UP button, *anything* that would get the elevator here.

The buzz became louder, angrier, closer. And then he saw it as it came into the light, hurtling down the hall at a level of about five feet, directly at him. The grinding of the teeth picked up tempo. Frozen with terror, a scream building in his throat, Hank watched it come for him.

And then another sound—the opening of the elevator doors. Hank ducked inside, yanking the hand truck after him as he hit the DOOR CLOSE button. The chew wasp veered toward him but couldn't make the turn. It slammed into the edge of the open door and fell to the floor with a bent and twisted wing. It flopped and thrashed and buzzed furiously on the hallway carpet while Hank frantically pressed the LOBBY button. As the doors began to close, it straightened its wing and launched itself at the elevator. Hank ducked but the doors slid closed before the thing reached him.

Pressing both hands over his quaking, churning stomach, Hank leaned against the back wall of the sinking elevator in a sweaty, gasping squat. He didn't want to move. He wanted to stay in this windowless steel box and wait for day. But he pushed himself to his feet. The elevator was on its way down and he had to get out of the city. He had to get these supplies transferred to the van before everybody else who survived the night was out and about.

The elevator light dimmed and the car lurched, paused. Oh, Lord! Was he going to be stuck here?

Then it started down again.

No question about it: He had to get out now. Who knew how long the power would last?

When the doors slid open on the lobby, Hank peered out. Dim out there. All the lights either out or broken. More than lights were broken. Off to his right, in the faint predawn light, he saw that the thick glass of the front door and windows was smashed, blue-green shards scattered all over the tiled lobby floor. And something else there by the remains of the door.

Hank squinted into the faint but growing light. Another body. He listened for the sound of wings. Quiet. Taking a deep breath, he tilted the hand truck and rolled it ahead of him as he hurried toward the door. He slowed by the corpse. This one was male, hardly chewed up at all, but very pale, very dead. He didn't recognize him, either. Hank realized how few of his fellow tenants he knew. Maybe that was for the best. He looked down at this fellow's wide, glazed eyes and shuddered.

How did you die, mister?

As he turned away, he heard a sound, something between a cluck and a gurgle. It seemed to come from the corpse. As he stared, he saw the throat work, the jaw move. But he couldn't be alive—not with those dead eyes!

And then the man's mouth opened and Hank saw something moving inside. No, not inside anymore, slithering out. A flat, wide, pincered head, dark glistening brown where it wasn't bloody red, followed by a sinuous six-foot body as big around as a beer can, powered by countless fine, rubbery legs, all dripping red.

Some sort of giant millipede, squeezing out the corpse's gullet and coming right for him. And it was *fast*.

Hank yelped and backpedaled across the lobby. He kept going until the backs of his legs hit the edge of the settee against the wall, then he hopped up on it and tried to climb the wall.

But the thing wasn't interested in him. It veered toward the doorway and raced over the shattered glass, heading for the street. Heading for the nearest hole, no doubt.

He'd never seen anything like that before. It had to be the latest addition to the bug horde.

Realizing that he looked like an old maid who'd seen a mouse, Hank jumped down from the settee, ran to the doorway, and looked out.

Monday morning. The sky looked funny. Not quite sunrise yet, but the streets should have been jumping by now, clogged with cabs and cars and delivery trucks. But nothing was moving. No, wait. Up the street he spotted a garbage-can-size beetle with a wicked set of mandibles spread wide before it, scuttling by at the corner, heading toward Central Park; an occasional flying thing whizzed through the air, also heading west. Except for those, the street was empty. Where had the giant millipede gone? How could it have got around the corner so fast?

Didn't matter. He had to get moving. He ran back into lobby, his feet slipping and crunching on the glass, and pulled his hand truck out to the van. He quickly dumped all the cases into the back, then hurried back to the elevator. Had to keep moving. He was going to have to make a lot of trips before he got everything transferred.

WFAN-AM

DAVE: And now our next caller on sports radio is Rick from Brooklyn. What's on your mind, Rick?

RICK: Yeah, hi, Dave. I just want to say that I really love your show, and I'd like to talk about the commissioner's canceling all games indefinitely.

DAVE: What's wrong with that, Rick?

RICK: It's not fair to the Mets. They've got one of their best teams ever. They was headin' for the Pennant for sure. I think it's a dirty trick. And you know what else? . . .

"Isn't the sun coming up?" Bill said, looking out the window. The sky was getting lighter but there was no sun, just a strange yellow light.

"Looks overcast," Jack said, coming up beside him.

"But those aren't clouds up there, or even haze. It's like . . . I don't know what it's like. Looks like a yellow scum of some sort's been poured over the sky."

"Whatever," Jack said. "We've waited long enough. The boogie beasts have called it a night and it's time to roll. You ready?"

"Soon as I take Carol back home."

"All right. I've got a couple of stops to make, then I'll be back to pick up you and the Amazing Criswell and we'll all head out to the Ashe brothers' airfield."

"Okay. I'll be ready."

"Don't get lost. There's not a lot of time to spare." He turned to go, then turned back. "How you getting there?"

"Glaeken's car."

Jack reached into his belt and pulled out an automatic pistol. He held it out to Bill, grip first.

"Better take this."

Bill stared at the thing. Its dark metal gleamed dully in the diffuse light from the window. It seemed as if some sort of alien creature had invaded the apartment.

"A gun? I wouldn't know what to do with it."

"I'll show you. First you—"

"I couldn't use it, Jack. Really."

"It's bad out there, Bill. People have been calling this city a jungle for years. They thought it was bad before the first hole opened up. They had no idea how bad it could get. There's not much trouble right around here—the creeps are no more anxious to get near that hole than anyone else—but you get too far up- or downtown and you'll run into spots that would make a jungle look like a Sunday afternoon drive. Take the gun. Just for show if nothing else."

"All right," Bill said. He took the pistol and was surprised by how heavy it was. "But what about you?"

Jack smiled. "Plenty more where that came from. Besides, I never carry just one."

As Jack hurried off, Bill slipped the pistol under his belt and pulled his sweater down over it. Then he went to the study where Carol had spent the night. She was on the phone. She hung up when he came in.

"Still busy," she said. "And I still can't get hold of an operator."

"I'll drive you over. I'm sure he's all right."

In the strange, shadowless yellow half-light that was passing for day, Bill skirted the Park to the south and headed east across town. No road blocks and no traffic to speak of. No police to speak of, either, and that concerned him. He came to First Avenue and was about to turn uptown when he glanced at the Queensboro Bridge.

"Carol!" he said as he screeched to a halt. "Look at the bridge."

"Oh, my God!" she whispered.

The center section of the span had broken up and now floated in the air in sections, tethered to the rest of the bridge by the suspension cables.

"A gravity hole," Carol said. "And it was such a beautiful bridge."

"The engineers have been saying for years what poor shape the bridges were in. Now we know how right they were."

He turned up first and drove along the middle of the street. It seemed as if almost every window in the city had been broken—except for those in Glaeken's building; not a pane had been so much as cracked there.

He eased to the left and upped their speed when he spotted a mob clustered around the front of a grocery on their right.

"Hank and I shopped there two days ago," Carol said.

Nobody was shopping now. Pillaging was more like it. People were jumping in and out of the broken door and windows, looking for anything remotely edible. But there didn't seem to be anything left to pillage. The enraged mob was tearing out the empty shelves and hurling them into the street. Three men were brawling over what looked like a can of tuna fish.

Further on, groups of tight-faced people hung about on the glass-bejeweled sidewalks, clustered in tense circles, glancing nervously over their shoulders this way and that with their fear- haunted eyes. He saw three women standing around a doorway sobbing as a sheet-covered body was being carried out. The people on the streets looked like ghosts.

"It's falling apart," Carol said, her arms crossed in front of her chest as if to ward off a chill. "Just like Hank said it would."

As Bill was slowing for a red light at 63rd—habit, pure habit—somebody shot at them. The bullet punched through the rear window and smashed the right rear side pane on its way out. Bill floored the gas pedal and sped uptown, ignoring traffic lights the rest of the way.

He double parked in front of Carol and Hank's apartment building and led her toward the shattered front door.

"The van's gone," she said, looking up and down the street.

"What van?"

"The one Hank rented."

"Maybe he had to move it."

Bill doubted that Carol believed that; he didn't believe it himself. He had a bad feeling about this: Carol was going to get hurt this morning.

They hurried inside. Carol gasped when she saw the body on the floor. Someone had covered it with a drape from one of the ruined windows.

"Do you think it's—?" she said, looking at Bill with terror in her eyes.

"I'll see."

He knelt by the still form and lifted a corner of the sheet. He dropped it quickly when he saw the white, agonized face, open mouth, and dull, staring eyes.

"Not Hank," he said, taking her arm and leading her away.

The elevator ride was slow and rough, as if the motors weren't getting enough power. As soon as the doors opened on her floor, Carol bolted from the car and ran down the hall. Bill noticed some drying brown stains on the carpet and what looked like a trail of the same leading to her apartment but he said nothing. She had her door open by the time Bill caught up with her. He stayed close behind her as she entered.

He bumped up against her back when she stopped dead inside the threshold.

"It's empty!" she cried. "He's gone!"

"Empty?" Bill said.

He glanced about. Hank might have been gone but the place didn't look empty. Except for the cyclone fencing over the windows, everything was just as it had been last time he'd come by. The furniture looked the same, nothing was—

"The food and the rest of his precious hoard. It's gone!" Her voice edged toward a sob. "He'd never leave without it. He's taken it and left me."

Bill did a quick search of the apartment. He found the note on the dresser in the bedroom.

Dear Carol

I've taken our supplies and gone looking for a safer place. I think I know of one. I can't say where it is right now, but when I get set up there, I'll come back for you. Wait for me.

Love,
Hank

Love. Right.

Carol seemed to crumble as she read the note. Bill knew it wasn't because Hank had taken the food and run off. The food didn't matter. It was simply that

Hank had shown her without a doubt where she ranked in his scheme of things. Bill put his arms around her quaking shoulders and held her tight against him.

And damn it all, he was glad Hank had taken off. Because it was one less barrier between them. He loathed himself for that. But he wanted her. God, how he wanted her.

He forced himself to pull back and take her arm.

"Come on. We're going back."

"No, Bill. I've got to wait to hear from Hank."

"*Hank*?" he said, suddenly furious with her, with Hank, with everything. "Hank won't be calling." He went to the sofa and yanked the telephone receiver from under a cushion and dangled it before her. "That's how much Hank wants to talk to you!"

Carol's shoulders slumped. She turned and walked out the door. Bill hurled the receiver to the floor. Now he was angry with himself. He ran after her and caught up with her at the elevator.

"I'm sorry," he said. "That was uncalled for. But I hate him for running out on you. Because he ran out on *us* too."

Carol stared at him, teary eyed. "Us?"

"All of us. Now's the time when we have to stick together, help each other through this catastrophe. Doing what Hank did, that just makes Rasalom stronger. It's another brick in the walls going up between people. Don't you see what's happening? All the intangibles that link us are being destroyed. Love, trust, brotherhood, community, camaraderie, neighborliness. The simple everyday things that make us human, that make us more than just a collection of organisms, that make us larger than ourselves—they're all going up in smoke."

"It's fear, Bill. Everyone's afraid. Death is everywhere. Up is down, down is up—nothing's sure anymore."

"That's *outside*," Bill said. "Rasalom's wrecking everything outside. He's calling all the shots out there. But inside" . . . he pounded on his chest . . . "inside you've got who you are, and you've got the bonds you've formed with other people. That's where those bonds are anchored. Rasalom can't get inside unless he's *allowed* in. You let that fear in and it will destroy those bonds. And that's the beginning of the end. For without them we divide up into small, suspicious enclaves, which soon deteriorate into warring packs, which finally degenerate into a bunch of back-stabbing lone wolves."

"Hank would never—"

"Excuse me, Carol, but I believe you've got a knife in your back. One with Hank's fingerprints all over it. As far as I'm concerned, running off like this is aiding and abetting the enemy."

"He'll call, Bill."

Bill didn't trust himself to respond directly to that.

"You'll be safer at Glaeken's," he said. "Hank knows the number. He can reach you there."

Carol didn't argue.

The elevator doors opened. They rode down in silence and they didn't talk much on the ride back. There was more traffic about now, but scattered and fitful. Bill headed west toward the Park on 72nd. As he slowed for a passing truck on Madison, three tough-looking blacks, either high or drunk or both, stepped in front of the car.

"A Mercedes," the biggest of them said, slurring his words. "Always wanted me a Mercedes."

Bill pulled out the pistol and pointed it through the windshield at one of the men, hoping the bluff would work. He knew he couldn't pull the trigger. The big man smiled sheepishly, held up his hands, and the three of them staggered away. Bill glanced at Carol and found her staring at him.

"A pistol, Bill?" she said. "*You?*"

"Jack's idea," he said. "I don't even know how to fire it."

Carol held out her hand. "I do. I spent fifteen years roaming around the South with Jonah and . . . that boy."

She took the gun, flicked a little switch on its side, worked the slide back and forth once, then held it up in plain view next to her window.

Speechless, Bill drove on. They had no trouble the rest of the trip back.

WNEW-FM

JO: Hi, this is Jo and Freddie. Yeah, I know we're early but we're the only ones left at the station. No one knows where the other guys are.

FREDDIE: Headed for the hills, if they're smart.

JO: Yeah. But we're not smart. We're sticking this out. In fact, we're moving into the station. We're living here, man, and we're staying on the air as long as they let us. And since nobody else is around, that could be a long time.

EDDIE: Yeah. Jo and Freddie all day and all night.

JO: Right. So let's get this started. It's Monday morning, May twenty-second. The sun rose at 7:40 a.m. According to the Sapir curve, it will set at 5:35 this afternoon, leaving us with a measly nine hours and fifty-five minutes of sunlight today.

FREDDIE: So do what you have to do quick and get home soon. And be careful out there, folks. Be good to each other. We're all we've got left.

THE NEW JERSEY TURNPIKE

Clear sailing on the open blacktop. Hardly any other cars. Hank had most of the six southbound lanes to himself.

He wondered why more people weren't on the move, then realized that gas was probably in short supply—all the service areas he'd passed so far had been deserted. And where was there to go? According to the news reports, hell was everywhere. It might be a horror show where you were, but you could be fleeing into something far worse. And what if dark fell before you made it to where you were going? Better to stay where you were, hunker down, and try to hold on to what you had.

As he drove he couldn't help thinking about Carol. Strange it had taken a crisis of these apocalyptic proportions to make him realize how little they had in common, how shallow their relationship was. He should have seen it long ago.

He wasn't deserting her, though. He was nothing if not loyal. He'd come back for her when he'd found a place for them down the Shore. But he'd make sure she didn't know where they were going until they got there. That way she couldn't yap about it to anyone.

He saw the sign for Exit 11 - Garden State Parkway. That was his. The Parkway would take him down the coast to Seaside Heights. Just past that sign was another for the Thomas A. Edison Service Area. Under that, sitting on the curb, was a sheet of plywood, hand painted:

WE HAVE GAS

DEISEL TOO

Yeah, but can you spell?

Hank checked his gas gauge: half a tank. They were probably charging an arm and a leg per gallon, but who knew when he'd get another chance to buy gas—if ever?

Ahead he saw a beat-up station wagon turn off the road onto the service area approach. Hank decided to follow.

As he approached the gas lanes he saw one of the two overalled attendants leaning in the passenger window of the station wagon. He straightened up and waved the wagon on.

Probably doesn't have enough money, Hank thought.

He smiled and clinked his heel against the canvas bags stowed under the front seat. He had something better than money. Silver coins. Precious metal. Always worth something no matter what the times, but worth more in bad times. And the worse things got, the more they were worth.

He slowed, reached down and pulled out a handful of coins; he shoved them into his pocket, checked that both door locks were down, then headed for the gas lanes.

The two attendants were clean cut and clean shaven, one blond, one dark, both well built, each about thirty. The blond one came around to Hank's side.

"You've got gas?" Hank said, rolling his window down a couple of inches.

The fellow nodded. "What've you got for it besides plastic or paper?"

Hank pulled out his quarters. "These should do. They're all pre-1964—solid silver."

The blond stared at the coins, then called to the dark- haired one.

"Hey, Ray. He's got silver. We want silver?"

Ray came up to the passenger window. "I dunno," he said through the glass. "What else you got?"

"This is it," Hank said.

"What you got in the back?" the blond one said.

A trapped feeling had begun to steal over Hank. He reached for the gear shift.

"Never mind."

His hand never reached it. Both side windows exploded inward, peppering him with glass; a fist came in from his left and smashed against his cheek, showering cascades of flashing lights through his vision. He heard the door open, felt fingers clutch his hair and his shoulder, then he was dragged from behind the wheel and dumped onto his back on the pavement.

Pain shot up and down Hank's spine as he writhed on his back, trying to catch the wind that had been knocked out of him. Above him, he was dimly aware of one the attendants reaching into the cab and turning off the engine, then taking the keys around to the rear doors. He heard the doors swing open.

"Holy shit!" It was Ray's voice. "Gary! Take a look! This guy's loaded!"

Hank struggled to his feet. He was terrified. A part of him wanted to run, but where? For what? To be caught out in the open when dark came? Or to starve to death if he did find shelter? No! He had to get his supplies back.

He staggered to the rear of his van and tried to slam the nearest door closed. "That's mine!" he shouted.

The fair one, Gary, turned on him in red-faced fury and lashed out with his fists so fast, so hard, so many times in rapid succession that Hank barely knew what hit him. All he knew was one moment he was on his feet, the next his head and abdomen were exploding with pain and his face was slamming against the asphalt drive.

He began to sob. "It's not fair! It's mine!"

He raised his head and spat blood. As his vision slowly cleared, he saw a white car speeding toward them from the Parkway. He blinked. Something on top of the car—a red-and- blue flasher bar. And the state seal on the door. A Jersey State Trooper.

Thank God!

Groaning, he forced himself up to his knees and began waving with both arms.

"Help! Over here! Help! Robbery!"

The police unit screeched to a halt behind Hank's van and a tall, graying, bareheaded trooper, resplendent in his gray uniform and shiny Sam Brown belt, hopped out and approached the two thieves still leaning inside the back doors.

"Yo, Captain," Ray said. "Look what we found."

"Fucking supermarket on wheels," Gary said.

The trooper stared at the stacks of cartons.

"Very impressive," he said. "Looks like we caught us a live one."

"Officer," Hank said, not quite believing his ears, "these men tried to rob me!"

The trooper swiveled and looked down at Hank, fixing him with a withering glare.

"We're commandeering your hoard."

"You're *with* them?"

"No. They're with me. I'm their superior officer. I set up this little sting operation to catch hoarder scum and looters on the run. You have the honor of being our first catch of the day."

"I *bought* all that stuff!" Hank said, struggling to his feet. He stood swaying like a sapling in a gale. "You have no right!"

"Wrong," the trooper said calmly. "I have every right. *Hoarders* have no rights."

"I'll report you!"

His smile was white ice. "Move away, little man. I'm the court of last resort around here. Be thankful I don't have you shot on the spot. Your hoard is about to be divided up among those who'll make the best use of it. It'll see us through until the time comes for us to restore order."

Hank couldn't believe this was happening. There had to be something he could do, someone he could turn to.

And then he saw Gary rip open a carton and pull out a cellophane envelope.

"Hey, look! Oodles of Noodles. My favorite!"

Something snapped inside Hank. Screaming, waving his fists, he charged at Gary.

"That's mine! Get your hands off it!"

He never made it. The captain stepped in front of him and rammed his forearm into Hank's face. Hank reeled back, clutching his shattered nose.

"Get running, little man," the captain said in a tight, cold voice. "Run while you still can."

"I can't!" Hank said, mortally afraid now. "There's no place to go! We're in the middle of nowhere! I've got two bags of silver coins under the front seat. You can have them. Just give me back my van. Please!"

The captain reached for the revolver in his holster. He didn't pause or hesitate an instant. In one smooth, swift motion he pulled it free, ratcheted the hammer back with his thumb as he raised it, and pointed it at Hank's face.

"You just don't get it, do you?"

There was nothing in his eyes as he pulled the trigger. Hank tried to duck but was too late. He felt a blast of pain in his skull as the world exploded into unbearable light, then collapsed into fathomless darkness.

WXRK-FM

Stay out of the water, everybody. In fact, stay away from the water. There are things in the rivers and apparently they don't go into hiding during the day. We've just received a confirmed report of a fisherman being pulled off a dock in Coney Island and eaten alive before the eyes of his horrified family.

Don't go near the water, man.

MANHATTAN

"W'happen t'yer car, buddy?"

The drunk had been staggering along the glass-littered sidewalk; he'd veered toward Jack's Corvair as it pulled into the curb in front of Walt Duran's apartment building.

"Ran into some bugs," Jack said as he got out.

The drunk stared at the torn top. He was fiftyish, overweight, and needed a shave; he wore a gray wool suit that looked to be of decent quality, but it was filthy. A liter bottle of Bacardi Light dangled from his hand. His complexion was ghastly in the yellow light.

"Tore her up bad, didn't they," he said, then his face screwed up and he began to sob. "Just like they tore up my Jane!"

Jack didn't know what to do. What do you say to a crying drunk? He put a hand on the guy's quaking shoulder.

"Hang around. Maybe I can help you out."

The guy shook his head and stumbled off down the sidewalk, still sobbing. Jack hurried up the steps to Walt Duran's apartment house. He pressed the button for Walt's room but got no answering buzz. The glass panel in the front door was broken. Maybe the buzzer was too. Jack reached through the shattered pane and turned the inside knob. Then he hurried up to the third floor.

Despite repeated knocks, Walt didn't answer his door. Concerned now, Jack pulled the piece of clear, flexible plastic he kept in his back pocket, slipped it between the door and the jamb, and jimmied the latch. The door swung open.

"Oh, jeez," Jack said as he viewed the carnage within.

The front room was a shambles of shattered glass, torn upholstery, and broken furniture. Jack dodged through the wreckage and hurried to the bathroom where he'd installed Walt last night. Empty, damn it. He went to the one remaining place to look, the tiny bedroom.

Blood. Blood on the sheets, on the floor, on the transparent daggers remaining in the frame of the smashed bedroom window.

"Walt," Jack said softly, staring at the dry brown streaks on the glass. "Why didn't you come back with me last night? Why didn't you stay locked up like I told you?"

Angry and sad, and not sure which to give in to, he wandered back to the bathroom. Walt's metal-working tools were set up across the rust-stained tub. But where were the necklaces? He probably hadn't finished them, but Jack knew he'd started them.

And what was Jack going to do without the copies?

Then he spotted something silvery gray and serpentine in the tub, under the work board. He dropped to his knees and reached in. Out came a necklace.

Jack cradled it in his hands and stared at it. The sculpted, crescent-shaped links, the weird engraved inscriptions, the pair of topazes with dark centers. The look of it, weight of it . . . a deluge of memories, most of them bad, engulfed him. He especially remembered the night he had worn the genuine article, how it had kept him alive when he should have died, how removing it had damn near killed him.

He shook off the past and felt a lump form in his throat for the man who had made this.

"Walt," he whispered. "You were the best."

He reached into the tub and found the second necklace. But when he got a good look at it, he groaned. It was only half a necklace. The links on the left side were blank. Walt hadn't got around to engraving them before . . . well, before whatever had happened to him.

One and a half necklaces wasn't going to cut it. Jack's plan required two phonies to get the two real ones.

He got to his feet and stuffed the completed necklace into his pocket. He'd have to come up with a new plan.

Out on the street again, he looked around for the drunk and spotted him sitting on the curb at the corner. He called to him, but the guy was absorbed in staring down at the sewer grate beneath his feet. Jack walked toward him.

"Hey, fella!" he called. "I'll get you to a safe place where you can sober up."

The guy looked up. "Somebod's downair," he said, pointing into the sewer. "Can't see'm but I hear'm movin' 'round."

Jack wondered if people were hiding in the sewers from the night things.

"Swell. But I don't think you'll fit through that opening, so—"

"Probly c'use a drink," the guy said and reached down to pour some of his rum through the grate.

Something flashed up from the sewer, something long and thick and brown whipped out and grabbed the drunk by his neck and yanked him down face first onto the grate, nearly breaking his spine in the process. Then it began tugging him into the opening in the curb face. Not slowly, smoothly, inexorably, but with violent heaves, accompanied by sprays of blood and frantically but futilely flailing arms and legs. Three heaves did it. Before Jack could recover from his shock and take a single step forward to help, the man was gone. All that remained behind were splashes of blood and a bottle of rum on its side, slowly emptying its contents into the sewer after its owner.

Jack backed up a few steps, then turned and ran for Ralph. There weren't people hiding in the sewers from the night things, there were night things—*big* night things—down there hiding from the day.

Am I going to lose you too? Carol thought as she stood next to Bill in his bedroom and helped him pack a small duffel bag with some extra clothes for the trip.

Why was it always she who was left behind? Jim had died and left her—although that certainly wasn't of his choosing. And her son—at the time she had thought of him as her son—had left her. Hank had run off last night, and now Bill was preparing to fly to Rumania.

"What are your chances of getting back?"

"I don't know," Bill said. "Not great, I think."

"Oh." Carol couldn't manage any more than that.

"Do I sound brave?" Bill said, straightening and looking at her. "I hope so. Because I sure as hell don't feel brave. I mean, I want to do this, but I don't want to die or even get hurt doing this. But I've got to do *some*thing."

"Can I go with you?"

Anything would be better than being left behind again, especially now when she had nothing else to do but sit around and wait for Hank's call. A call she was sure would never come. And that certainty hurt. She and Hank hadn't had the romance of the ages, but to pack up everything and sneak off like that . . .

Even if he did call, she wouldn't go back to him. She didn't want to be with somebody who'd do that to her. And then there was the matter of that crazed look in his eyes. She had to face it: She no longer trusted her husband.

"To Rumania?" Bill said, staring at her. "It's too dangerous."

"Is anyplace safe anymore?"

Even the daytime was no longer safe. A rather shaken Jack had returned a short while ago with a story of horrors hiding in the sewers and storm drains.

"This place is. And Glaeken seems to want you around."

"But why? What can I do besides help him take care of Magda? Not that I mind, but what else?"

"I don't know. Maybe you're part of the equation. I don't pretend to understand why he's doing what he's doing. Sometimes I wonder if *he* knows why he's doing what he's doing. But he's all we've got. And if he says we need these bits of metal from Rumania and I'm the only one left who can get them, then I'll try to get them. And if he says you're important to the solution to what's happening to the world, then I'll go along with him. He hasn't let us down yet."

" 'Part of the equation,' " she said, her throat constricting around the words. "I've been part of some sort of equation since I got pregnant and provided the little body that allowed this . . . this *monster* back into the world!" Her voice cracked. "He took my baby, Bill! He kicked out whoever my real baby might have been and took over his tiny body. And now he's going to take you!"

She felt Bill's arms go around her shoulders and pull her tight against him. His flannel shirt smelled lightly of detergent, and as its rough surface pressed against her cheek, the thought that he really should use fabric softener wafted inanely across her mind. She slipped her arms around his waist and pulled herself closer. If she could just hold him here like this, it soon would be too late for him leave, and then she wouldn't lose him.

And she realized then how much she wanted him. Not like the last time, not like back in '68 when the beast within twisted her into trying to seduce Bill from his vows. That had been lust, induced lust. This was something else. This was love. An old love, following a long and winding road from the puppy love when they'd dated in their teens, to something deep and real. In a way, perhaps she'd always loved Bill. And now that he'd turned away from his church and his old beliefs, now that the cocoon of the priesthood had been unraveled from around him, he seemed real again, flesh and blood again. She wanted to tell him how she felt but the decades-old memories of that degrading scene of attempted seduction still echoed around her and held her back. And yet, if she didn't tell him now, would she ever get the chance again?

Jack's voice shattered the moment: "Time's a-wastin', Bill. We've got to make a stop in Monroe on the way."

Monroe . . . her home town. Bill's too. Where Rasalom had usurped her child's body at conception. The torrent of memories was cut off as Bill pulled free of her arms.

"Got to go, Carol."

He went to kiss her on the forehead. Impulsively, Carol lifted her face and kissed him on the lips. From the way he pulled back and the way he looked at her, she knew that he hadn't forgotten 1968 either.

"Come back to me, Bill," she said softly. "I don't want to lose you too."

He swallowed, nodded. "Okay. Yeah." His voice was sandpaper dry. "I'll be back. We can talk more about this then." He picked up his duffel and started for the door, then stopped and turned. "I love you, Carol. I can't think of a moment when I didn't."

And then he was gone. But his final words lingered after him, filling Carol with a bewildering mix of emotions. She wanted to laugh with joy; instead she sat on the edge of the bed and cried.

WINS-AM

—and at sea, the QE2 appears to be missing. She was last heard from Sunday evening. It is feared she is sunk. If she had hit one of the gravity anomalies she would have radioed for help. The single air-sea rescue plane that was sent out has found no survivors.

LONG ISLAND

It took Jack longer than he'd planned to get to Monroe. A lot of traffic outbound on the Long Island Expressway. Maybe they thought it would be better out on the Island. He'd talked to Doc Bulmer on the phone this morning, and from what he'd said, things didn't seem a whole hell of a lot quieter out here.

So he did the best speed he could as the wind fluttered and whistled through the rips in the top. Nick sat in the back seat, his zombie stare fixed straight ahead. Bill wasn't much better as company. He sat in the passenger seat and said nothing, just gazed out the window, lost in a world of his own. Jack wondered what was going on between him and that Mrs. Treece. Her husband had run off and left her. Was Bill moving in? He'd been a priest for most of his life. He had a lot of lost time to make up for. Jack couldn't blame him. She was attractive, even if she had a good ten or fifteen years on Jack. But he sensed there was more to it than opportunity knocking. Those two seemed to go back a long way.

So Jack played the radio. A number of stations were gone, nothing but static in their slots on the band, but a few DJs and newsfolk were hanging in there, still playing music, still broadcasting the news, keeping their listeners informed to the best of their ability as to what was fact and what was merely rumor. He had to hand it to them. They had more guts than he would have given them credit for.

He clicked it off. He wasn't in the mood for music.

"So, Bill," he said, jerking his thumb toward the back seat. "How are you going to handle Edgar Cayce back there?"

Bill turned from the window and fixed Jack with a stare.

"Don't make fun of him. He's an old friend of mine and he's a victim, just like a lot of other people these days."

Jack instinctively bristled at the sound of someone telling him what to do, then realized that Bill was right.

"Sorry. I didn't know him before he . . . before he went down into the hole."

"He was brilliant. Hopefully he'll be brilliant again. A mind like a computer, but a good heart too."

"Bit of a spread in age between the two of you. How'd you meet?"

"I was his father for a few years."

When Jack shot him a questioning look, Bill went on and explained about his years as director of a Jesuit orphanage in Queens, and how a certain little boy had died and how he'd spent five years on the run as a result. The story fascinated Jack. He'd been seeing this guy every day lately and never guessed what kind of a man he was, or the hell he'd been through. How could he? Bill seemed to have built a wall around himself, as if he was practicing being a nobody.

But now that Jack had got a peek over that wall, he decided he liked Bill Ryan.

And besides that, the story made the trip pass faster. Here they were already, in Monroe, on Shore Drive.

Ba must have been watching from one of the windows. He stepped out the front door as they pulled in the driveway. He approached the car with only a Macy's shopping bag dangling from his hand. The Nash lady, Doc Bulmer, and the kid, Jeffy, were all clustered at the front door to see him off, like the Cleavers sending an Oriental Wally off to war.

"I'd better get in the back," Bill said. "He'll never fit."

As he shifted to the rear, Jack got out, waved to Ba, then trotted to the front door.

"Glaeken wants me to 'urge' you folks—his word—to come stay with him in the city. He says it's going to get a lot worse out here."

"We'll be okay," the doc said. "We've got our own protection."

Jack glanced around at all the steel storm shades. The place looked like a fortress.

"Maybe you do," he said, nodding. "But I promised him I'd ask."

"You've kept your promise to Glaeken," the Nash lady said softly, and Jack thought he saw tears in her eyes. "Now keep one to me: You bring Ba back, okay?" Her voice sounded like it was going to break. "You bring him back just the way he left, you hear?"

"I hear you, Mrs. Nash," he said.

Jack was touched by her show of emotion. No doubt about it, she genuinely cared about Ba. Had real feeling for the guy. Maybe he'd misjudged her. Maybe she wasn't quite the hardcase she pretended to be.

"Either we both come back," he added, "or neither of us comes back. You've got my word on that."

"I'll hold you to it," she said, her eyes steely blue.

As Jack hurried back to the car he figured he'd damn well better get Ba back safe and sound.

The sign atop the hanger read TWIN AIRWAYS in bold red letters. Tension coiled around Bill's gut as they bumped toward it along a rutted dirt road. Where were they? Somewhere off the Jericho Turnpike was all Bill knew.

And the Ashe brothers. Who were they? He'd never heard of them and didn't know a thing about them and yet he was going to get into a jet and let one of them fly him across the Atlantic. And why? Because this fellow named Jack—who had about a dozen last names and had an immediate avoidance response to anything labeled Police, who carried two or three pistols and God knew how many other weapons at all times, who called his ancient Corvair Ralph and drove it like a maniac—had said the Ashe Brothers were "good guys."

Glaeken, old boy, he thought as Jack skidded to a halt beside the hanger, I hope this trip is worth it.

Two reed-thin, blue-eyed men in their mid-thirties with fair, shoulder-length hair came out to meet them. They might have been mirror images had not one of them sported a stubbly beard and the other a long, droopy mustache. Both wore beat-up jeans so low on their hips they looked ready to fall off; the bearded one wore a purple paisley shirt tucked in behind a Jack Daniels belt buckle. The one with the mustache had on a fringed buckskin jacket over a tee-shirt.

"They look like holdovers from the sixties, Jack," Bill said softly out of the corner of his mouth.

"It's okay. They sort of think they're the Allman Brothers. Not really, of course. I mean, Duane being dead and all. But soul-mates, so to speak. They *are* from Georgia and they do like the blues, but trust me: You're looking at two of the best damn pilots going. Not a place in the world with an airport they haven't been."

Bill wondered if he had that much trust left in him.

Jack introduced them as Frank and Joe. Joe had the beard and the JD buckle and he was going to be Bill's pilot. But Bill's flight seemed to be of secondary importance. The big concern seemed to be getting Jack and Ba into the air as soon as possible. After payment was made—a sack of gold coins transferred from the Corvair's front-end trunk to the Ashe brothers' office safe—Joe left Bill and Nick in the tiny office while he went out to help get his brother's Gulfstream air-borne. Twenty minutes later, Bill heard jet engines whine, then roar off into the western sky.

"Shouldn't we be hurrying too?" Bill said when Joe returned to the office.

"I reckon," he said with a heavy drawl. "But it's not as critical for us as for them. If Frank hustles his ass he's got a damn good chance of staying in daylight all the way to Hawaii. Not us. We're heading east—right into the dark. It's about 6:00 p.m. in Rumania now. Already past sunset."

His expression showed how little he relished the trip.

"How did you wind up with us?"

"We flipped a coin."

"And you lost."

Joe Ashe shrugged. "Six o' one, half a dozen of t'other. We're talking round trips here. Frank'll have to fly east on the way home while we're flying west." He frowned. "Maybe I should say it's four of one and half a dozen of the other. We'll have a shorter daylight window on the way back." He grunted. "Shit. I *did* get the short end of this stick. That Frank's always tricking me. That boy's my evil twin, he is."

Great, Bill thought. I've got the slow one.

"You want to back out?" Bill said, almost hoping he'd say yes.

Joe Ashe grinned. "Nah. Said I'd do it and so it's a done deal. Unless o' course you've changed *your* mind."

Bill shook his head. "I'm afraid we're stuck with each other."

"Guess so. But what about your friend there. He's lookin' right poorly, I'd say."

"He's . . . he hasn't been well lately."

"Bummer. Maybe you ought to leave him behind. Things could get a mite hairy on this little jaunt."

"I know. I wish I could leave him, but I need him along."

"You don't say." Joe studied Nick's blank face a moment, then turned to Bill. "What the hell for?"

"I don't know yet." *But Glaeken assures me I will.*

Joe let out a soft, low whistle through his teeth.

"Okay, pal. You're the boss. Let's roll. I've got the flight plan all worked out. We've got a ten- to eleven-hour trip ahead of us, and a seven-hour time difference between here and Ploiesti."

"Ploiesti? I thought we were going to Bucharest."

"Ploiesti's a little further north, closer to the Alps where this pass you're headed for is supposed to be. I couldn't find it on any of my maps."

Bill handed Joe the packet Glaeken had given him.

"You'll find it on these."

Joe took the packet. "Good. I'll check them out on the way. Get your friend there moving now. Time to rock 'n' roll."

The Movie Channel

Joe Bob Briggs' Drive-In Movie—A Special All-Day Edition.

Beginning Of The End (1957) Republic

The Last Days Of Man On Earth (1974) New World

The Monsters Are Loose (1965) Hollywood Star

Fear In The Night (1947) Paramount

Horror Of The Blood Monsters (1970) IIP

Destroy All Monsters (1968) Toho/AIP

I Drink Your Blood (1971) Cinemation

Jaws Of Death (1976) Selected

Night Of The Blood Beast (1958) AIP

The Day The Fish Came Out (1967) International Classics

Target Earth (1954) Allied Artists

The Blood Suckers (1971) Chevron

OVER THE ATLANTIC

Flying west, night came especially early. As darkness engulfed them, the sky cleared, became a crystal dome that revealed the foreign face of the moon set amid alien constellations.

Bill left Nick sleeping back in the passenger compartment and headed forward to take the co-pilot's seat next to Joe. As he gazed out at the night, he was glad for the lack of clouds and excellent visibility in the moonlight. He could find no sign of anything like the air leviathans he'd seen swooping from the Central Park hole Saturday night. No sign of anything in the air, but the water below seemed *alive*. It churned with shadows and swirled with phosphorescent flashes.

He turned back to the stars, studying them, trying to make sense of them, or find a familiar pattern.

"Where are we?" he said, wondering aloud.

"Over the Atlantic," Joe replied from his left.

"Thanks. I mean where in space? The sun's fading away, the moon's been turned around, and the stars have been shifted into new formations."

"Not just new formations," Joe said, stroking his beard as he craned his neck to see the stars. "Notice that there's *fewer* stars up there? And every night there's even less than the night before. I wonder if some night soon I'll take a peek and find there's no stars at all."

The stars do look kind of sparse up there, Bill thought.

"It's almost as if the planet's been moved to a different part of the universe."

"Cosmic, man," Joe said, eyes widening. "Maybe it has."

"No," Bill said. "That would be too logical an explanation, and easier to accept than what we're going through."

"Magnetic north's changed too," Joe said. "Compasses have been pointing anywhere they damn well please for the past couple days."

"Really? I hadn't heard that." And then something occurred to him. "If the stars are changed and compasses no longer point north, how do you know where you're going?"

"Radio beacon. I'm homing in on a signal from the English coast. We're not headed for England, but it's on the way."

"Where are we—good God!"

Bill had glanced off to his right at what had looked like a lone cloud in an empty sky. It wasn't the cloud that had startled him, it was what was under it.

Joe was leaning over his shoulder, squinting into the darkness.

"Shee-it! What the hell is that?"

Far to the south, a huge pillar had risen from the sea. It was made of some grayish substance that gleamed dully in the moonlight and streamed with lightning-like flickers of phosphorescence. Bill guessed it was hundreds of feet across and thousands of feet—maybe *miles*—high. Its top disappeared into the dark cloud growing above it.

So alien, so Cyclopean in its size, the sight of it gave him a crawling feeling in his gut.

Joe must have felt it too. His voice was hushed.

"Almost looks like it's holding up the sky."

Bill said, "Do we have enough fuel to maybe—?"

"No way, José!" Joe straightened in his seat and checked his instruments. "Even if we had plenty to spare, I wouldn't get a foot closer to that thing than I absolutely had to. And I don't have to get any closer than I am now, thank-you-very-much."

As they continued east, Bill's eyes remained fixed on the giant column. The dark gray cloud above it continued to grow, and as it grew it began to sink around the column, eventually obscuring it completely from view.

"I'll be damned!" Joe said. Bill turned in his seat and found him pointing north. "There's another one!"

Bill wished the moon was brighter so he could get a better look at it.

And then the moon went out for a second.

"What was that?" Joe said.

Bill's mouth was suddenly dry. "Something big."

"Yeah? How big?"

"Very big. A body two hundred feet across and square miles of wing."

Joe glanced at him with raised eyebrows, then scanned the night.

"I see it," he said after a moment. "Or rather I don't see the stars where it's cruising. It's—shee-*it*! It's coming this way!"

Joe threw the Gulfstream into a screaming dive that jammed Bill back into his seat. And then the world got darker as something swooped through the air where they had been only seconds before. The jet bucked and rocked in the backwash from the monstrous wings. Bill craned his neck back and forth looking for the behemoth as Joe continued the dive. He saw it, off the south, banking around, coming back to make another run at them.

"Never seen anything so goddamned big in my life!" Joe said.

And still he held the jet into the dive. The black water was looming up below them.

"Joe," Bill said. "Aren't you getting kind of low?"

"Not low enough yet," he said.

And still they dove. Not till Bill was ready to shout with terror that they were going to plunge into the sea did Joe level off. They raced along at fifty feet above the surface.

"You see it?" Joe said.

Bill twisted around. "Yeah. I can see its right wing. It's on our tail, coming up fast. Oh, God it's coming fast!"

"Tell me when it's almost on us. Don't tell me too soon— and f'God's sake don't tell me too late. Just wait till you think its about to chomp us, then give a shout."

It wasn't long. The thing was moving faster than the Gulfstream. Bill barely had time to wonder how something so big could move so fast when suddenly it was almost upon them.

"Now, Joe! Now! NOW!"

Abruptly the Gulfstream banked a sharp left, rocking Bill against his safety belt. And suddenly the ocean was exploding with white water.

"What happened?" Bill said.

"It hit the water," Joe said, grinning. "Simple aerodynamics, boy. You want to make a sharp turn in flight, you've gotta bank. You bank at this altitude with wings that size, the downside one's gonna catch the surface. And then it's cartwheel time."

Bill leaned back in the seat and wanted to throw up. But he swallowed hard and held out his hand to Joe.

"You are one hell of a pilot."

Joe slapped his palm. "I don't argue that."

"When's day?" Bill said.

Joe glanced at his watch. "Not for a long while. Sunrise won't come till 7:21 Greenwich meantime. Still some daylight left back home, I'd guess. Though not much.

WNEW-FM

FREDDY: It's 5:15, folks. Twenty minutes to sundown.

JO: Yeah. Everybody inside. Get inside NOW.

Hank didn't know how long he'd been phasing in and out of consciousness, but eventually he felt strong enough to move. His head felt three times its normal size and throbbed viciously, but he forced it off the pavement to look around. The movement triggered an explosion of pain through the left side of his skull as the world spun around him. He choked back the vomit that surged into his throat, squeezed his eyes shut, and held still. And while he held still, he tried to remember what had happened.

He recalled loading the van, driving down the Turnpike, turning in for gas—

Oh, Lord. The State Trooper. The pistol. The shot.

Hank reached up and gingerly touched the left side of his head. A deep wet gash above his ear there, clots and soft crusts all up and down the side of his head and neck.

But he was alive. The bullet had glanced off his skull and plowed a deep furrow through his scalp. He was weak, sick, dizzy, hurting like he'd never hurt before, but he was alive.

Hank opened his eyes again. He was looking down. A puddle of coagulated blood was pooled on the pavement a few inches below his nose. Keeping his eyes fixed on the blood, he pushed himself further up, pulled his knees under him, then straightened. The vertigo took him for another twirling ride, but when it stopped, he took his bearings.

Green metal bins on either side of him—garbage dumpsters. Framed between them he could see the rest stop gas pumps a hundred or so feet away.

Deserted now. No phony attendants waving cars forward. To his left was the stuccoed side of a building. The restaurants. Bob's Big Boy. Roy Rogers. TCBY.

They must have dragged him over here out of sight and left him for dead while they lay in wait for the next hapless traveler.

Clenching his teeth against the pain and the nausea, he pulled himself to his feet and peered over the dumpsters. The whole rest stop was deserted. Beyond the pumps the Turnpike stood quiet and empty. The cars he'd seen parked over here earlier were gone now.

So was his van.

Hank wanted to cry. Robbed. By state cops, no less. Lord, what was happening to this world? The human monsters acrawl during the day were as bad as the inhuman ones that ruled the night.

Night! He glanced at the sky, at the horizon. Good Lord, it was getting dark. In a few minutes those horrors would start flying and crawling from their holes. He couldn't be caught out in the open.

He hobbled to the door on the near flank of the restaurants. Locked. He made his way around to the front entrance. The glass double doors were chained shut from the inside. He peered through. A shambles within. It looked as if the place had been ransacked and looted before it had been locked up. No matter. He wasn't worried about food now. All he wanted was to get to shelter.

He looked around in the failing light for something to break the glass—a rock, a garbage can, anything. He found a heavy, stuccoed trash receptacle nearby but no way could he lift it.

Near panic now, he circled the rest stop, desperate to find a way in. He was half way around the back when something whizzed by his head, its jaws grinding as it passed. Then another. He couldn't see them in the dusky light but he didn't have to. Chew wasps. Here already. There must be a hole nearby.

In a low crouch he ran for the dumpsters on the far side of the building. Maybe he could hide in one of them—crawl inside and pull the top down over him. Maybe he'd even find some scraps of food among the refuse.

When he reached the dumpsters he hoisted himself up the side of the first and saw that its hinged top was gone. Same with the other. Now what?

As he eased himself back down his foot caught in a slot in the pavement. A storm drain. His foot rested on the rusty grate.

Try it! he thought, bending and yanking on the grate. It was square, a couple of feet on each side. No problem getting through if he could pull it free.

Another bug whistled by—close enough to ruffle his hair. A spearhead.

Ignoring the throbbing in his skull that crescendoed toward agony with the effort, he put all of what little strength he had left into lifting the grate. The metal squeaked and moved a quarter inch, then half an inch, then screeched free of its seat. Hank pushed it aside and slid through the opening into the darkness below. Four feet down, his feet landed in a puddle. No problem. Not even an inch deep. He reached up and slid the grate back over the opening. When it clanked into its seat, he slumped into a crouch and looked up at the sky.

Dark up there, but still lighter than down here. As he watched a lonely star break through the dispersing haze, a huge belly fly plopped onto the grate directly over Hank and tried to squeeze through. Its acid sack strained against the openings, bulged into the slots, but it was too wide. Buzzing angrily, it lifted off and flew away.

He should have been relieved, happy he'd found a safe haven. Instead, Hank found himself sobbing. Why not? No one around to see. He was alone, hurt— still bleeding a little—cold, tired, hungry, no food, no money, no ride, and now he was hiding in a storm drain with dirty, stagnant water soaking through his sneakers. He'd really hit bottom now.

He forced a laugh that echoed eerily up and down the length of the drain. If nothing else, he could soothe himself with the knowledge that things couldn't get worse.

Something splashed off to his right.

Hank froze and listened. What was that, oh Lord, what was that? A rat? Or something worse—something much, much worse?

He eased his feet out of the water and inched them up the far side of the pipe until he spanned its diameter. If anything was moving through the water, it would pass under him. He peered into the darkness to his right, straining ears and eyes for some sign of life.

Nothing there.

But from his left came a furtive scurrying, moving closer . . . countless tiny clicks and scratches as something— no, some*things!*—with thousands of feet slithered toward him along the concrete wall of the drain.

More splashing from the right, bolder now, *lots* of splashes, hurried, anxious, eager, avid, frantic splashes coming faster, racing toward him. The storm drain was suddenly *alive* with sound and movement and it was all converging on him.

Hank whimpered with terror and dropped his feet back into the water as he slammed his palms against the grate above and levered it up from its seat. But before it came completely free a pair on tong-like pincers vised around his right ankle. He shouted his terror and agony but kept pushing. Another set of pincers lanced into his left calf. His feet were pulled from under him and he went down to his knees in the stagnant water.

And then in the faint light through the grate above he saw them. Huge, pincer-mouthed millipede creatures, like the one he'd seen wriggling from the throat of the corpse in the lobby this morning. The pipe was acrawl with them, five, six, eight, ten feet long. The nearest ones raised their heads toward him, their pincers clicking. Hank slapped at them, trying to bat them away, but they darted past his defenses and latched onto him, digging the ice-pick points of their mandibles into his arms and shoulders. The pain and horror were too much. His scream echoed up and down the hungry pipe as he was dragged onto his back. His arms were pulled above his head and his legs yanked straight as he was positioned along the length of the pipe. Cold water soaked his clothes and ran along his spine. And then more of the things leaped upon him, all over him, their countless clawed feet scratching him, their pincers ripping at his clothing, tearing through the protective layers like so much tissue paper until every last shred had been stripped away and he lay cold and wet and naked, stretched out like a heretic on the rack.

And then they backed off, all but the ones holding him who continued to pin him there in the water. The drain grew quiet. The sloshing and splashing, the scraping of the myriad feet died away until the only noise in Hank's ears was the sound of his own ragged breathing.

What did they want? What were they—?

Then came another sound, a heavy, chitonous slithering from the impenetrable darkness beyond his feet. As it grew louder, Hank began to whimper in fear. He began to thrash in the water, struggling desperately to pull free but the pincers in his arms and legs tightened their grip, digging deeper into his already bleeding flesh.

And then in the growing shaft of light from the rising moon he saw it. A millipede like all the rest, but so much larger. Its head was the size of Hank's torso, its body a good two feet across, half-filling the drain pipe,

Hank screamed as understanding exploded within him. These other, smaller horrors were workers or drones of some sort; they'd captured him and were holding him here for their queen! He renewed his struggles, ignoring the tearing pain in his limbs. He had to get free!

But he couldn't. Sliding over the bodies of her obedient subjects the queen crawled between Hank's squirming legs until she held her head poised over his chest, staring at him with her huge, black, multifaceted eyes. As Hank watched in mute horror, a drill-like proboscis extruded from between her huge mandibles. Slowly, she raised her head and angled it down over Hank's abdomen. Hank found his voice and screamed again as she plunged the proboscis deep into his abdomen.

Liquid fire exploded at his center and spread into his chest, it ran down his legs and his arms, draining the strength from them.

Poison! He opened his mouth to scream again but the neurotoxin reached his throat first and allowed him to give voice to little more than an especially loud, breathy exhalation. Hank's hands were the last things to go dead, and then he was floating. He still lay in the water but could not feel its wetness. The last thing he saw before tumbling into a void of blessed darkness was the queen horror with her snout still buried in his flesh, sucking greedily.

CNN:

News from NASA: We have lost contact with most of our higher orbiting satellites. The communication satellites are still operational—otherwise you would not be watching this broadcast—but the rest are simply . . . gone.

OVER THE PACIFIC

They got in and out of Bakersfield in record time. Or so Frank said. Jack would have to take his word about the record part, but it sure as hell had been fast. The main reason was that Frank's plane was one of only a half dozen scheduled in and out of there today.

It hadn't been Bakersfield, actually, but a small airstrip just outside it. Frank seemed to know everybody in sight; there weren't too many of those, but they all were impressed that he was still on the job. Especially impressed that he was making arrangements to get refueled here on his return flight.

"Yer gonna be fly'n' inna dark comin' back, y'know," the old guy who ran the place had said as the wing tanks were filling.

He was the one who'd pocketed a stack of Glaeken's gold coins for the fuel. He was wrinkled and grizzled and looked old enough to have been Billy Rickenbacker's wingman in the Lafayette Escadrille.

"I know," Frank said from the pilot seat. He had his Walkman earphones slung around his neck and was playing with one of the drooping ends of his mustache.

Jack sat beside Frank in the pilot's cabin—he'd called it the "cock-pit" earlier and had been corrected—while Ba sat in the passenger compartment, adding more teeth to his billy clubs.

"Lotsa planes disappearin' inna dark these days, Frankie. Go up, neva come down."

"So I've heard."

"Some are even disappearin' inna day. Inna *day*! So nobody's flyin'—nobody with any sense, that is. Scared to get off the ground. 'Fraid they won't come back. Don't want you t'be one a thems that don't come back, Frankie."

"Thanks, Pops," Frank said. "Neither do I."

"Where's Joe?"

"On his way to Bucharest."

"*Hungary?*"

"No. Rumania."

"Same difference. Shit! What's the matter with you two? You need the money that bad? Hell, I can lend you—"

"Hey, Pops," Frank said. "It's not the bread. I'm a pilot, man. I fly folks places. That's what I do. I ain't changing that, okay? Not for any body or any bugs. Besides, we once like promised this here dude that any time he really needed to get somewhere, we'd take him. You can dig that, can't you?"

"No, I can't dig nothin' of the sort. Where y'goin'?"

"He says he's got to get to Maui and back real bad."

Pops stared past Frank at Jack like he was looking at a lunatic. Jack smiled and gave him an Oliver Hardy wave.

"Got to see my girl. It's her birthday."

Pops rolled his eyes and started to turn away.

"Real weird kind of weather you got around here," Frank said, glancing up at the lid of gray overhead.

"All that shit from Hawaii." Pops wiped his finger along the fuselage and held it up to demonstrate the coating of gray ash. "Just like your name, Frankie. And you're headed straight into it. Tops off at twenny thou, though. Watch yer intakes."

"Will do."

Pops went back to check on the refueling. A few minutes later they were air-borne. Jack sniffed the air that leaked into the cabin at the lower altitude.

"Smells burnt."

"It is," Frank said. "It's *vog*—a mixture of like water vapor, smoke, and fine, fine, super-fine volcanic ash. Under normal conditions it would give us awesome sunsets all over the world. But now . . . hey, who knows? We don't seem to get real sunsets anymore."

Jack felt closed in, trapped by the formless grayness pressing against the windows of the jet. It was difficult even to tell if they were headed up. He'd have to trust Frank on that.

Which was probably one of the reasons he didn't like to fly. He liked to be in control of a situation. Up here he was at Frank's mercy. He didn't know which way they were headed, and if something should happen to Frank, Jack didn't have the faintest idea of how to get them down safely. It had scared the hell out of him when Frank had put the controls on autopilot over Denver and made a trip back to the head. He'd returned soon, but it hadn't been anywhere near soon enough for Jack.

Suddenly the grayness darkened as if a curtain had been drawn, and the jet wobbled.

"What's up?" Jack said as calmly as he could.

"Don't rightly know," Frank said.

"Those are three little words I do not want to hear from my pilot."

Jack held on to his seats arm rests and knew if he looked down at his hands he'd see two sets of white knuckles.

"We'll be okay," Frank said.

"Good. A much better choice of three words."

"Be cool, Jack. Some weird air currents out of nowhere, that's all."

The grayness lightened as abruptly as it had darkened. Jack began to breath easier. He was leaning against his window, staring out into the unrelieved grayness, when the plane passed through a brief break in the vog. His throat closed and his hands renewed their chokehold on his armrests. Directly below the wings he saw a broad flat surface, smooth and black as new asphalt, spanning off in all directions until it disappeared into the gray. He was about to shout to Frank that they were going to crash when he saw the eye: Far off to his right, perhaps a quarter-mile away, cathedral-sized, huge and yellow with a slit pupil, it sat embedded in the black surface, staring back at him like a lab tech eying a microbe.

Jack slammed back in his seat, gasping for breath.

"My God, Frank!" he said, his voice a croak. "What *is* that?"

Frank glanced past him. "What's what?"

Jack took another look. The vog had closed in again. Nothing there now but gray.

"Nothing."

Jack remembered Glaeken mentioning winged leviathans big as towns cruising the skies, but he'd said they'd keep to the nightside. Looked like he was wrong. At least one of them had made itself at home in the dense vog from Hawaii. Maybe more than one.

His mouth was dry. "How long till we get above this junk?"

"Any minute now."

Sure enough, two minutes later they broke into clear air. But no sign of the sun. The whole sky was now some sort of tinted filter, a ground-glass lens that wouldn't allow direct sunlight through. Right now, Jack didn't care. They were out of the vog, out of reach of that thing in the clouds falling away beneath them.

He looked down. As far as he could see, nothing but a smooth dome of gray cloud. Plenty of room for a bunch of leviathans down there. Frank said they were over the Pacific; for all Jack knew they could be headed back toward New York.

The pilot's cabin suddenly seemed too small. Jack decided to head back and see what Ba was up to. He slapped Frank on the shoulder.

"Get you anything?"

"A hefty J would be super right about now. I've got a lid of bodacious—"

"Frank, don't even kid about that."

"Who's kidding, man? It's the only way to fly. Hell, I recall the time I jumped the Himalayas and coasted into Kathmandu totally wrecked. It was—"

"Please, Frank. Not on this trip."

Six miles above the Central Pacific with a blitzed pilot. Not Jack's idea of Friendly Skies.

Frank grinned. "Okay, man. Another coffee'd be good."

"Not getting sleepy, are you?"

"Not yet. I'll let you know when. Then you can take over the controls."

"*Two* coffees coming right up! An *urn*, already!"

Jack spent a few hours with Ba, trying to get to know him. It wasn't easy. He did learn a few things about Sylvia Nash which cast her in a different light—about her dead husband, Greg—"the Sergeant", as Ba called him—a Special Forces non- com who'd made it through Nam in one piece only to go out one night for a pack of cigarettes and get killed by an armed robber when he tried to break up a 7-11 heist.

He learned about Jeffy, the once autistic kid, and about the *Dat-tay-vao* that had inhabited Dr. Bulmer for a while and left him a cripple, and now lay dormant in Jeffy, waiting. He learned about the powerful love between Sylvia and Doc Bulmer, how they were soulmates who locked horns and butted heads on a regular basis but whose karmas were so intertwined that one could not imagine life without the other.

Jack learned all that, but he learned very little about Ba, other than the fact that he grew up in a poor Vietnamese fishing village and was intensely devoted to the Sergeant's wife— referred to simply as "the Missus"—and how that devotion extended to anyone who mattered to her.

When Jack ran out of questions, they sat in silence, and Nick Quinn's words to Alan Bulmer came back to him. *Only three of you will return.* He brushed the words away. Nick may have met this mysterious Rasalom down in that hole, but he'd yet to prove that he had any powers of prediction. He talked in riddles anyway.

When Jack noticed the plane banking to its left, he headed back up front to see what was going on.

"We almost there?" he said as he stepped into the pilot's cabin.

Frank was bouncing around in his seat, listening to his earphones. The volume was so high Jack could recognize "Statesboro Blues" from where he stood. He sniffed the air. No trace of herbal-smelling smoke. He tapped Frank on the shoulder and repeated his question when Frank pulled off the head-phones.

"We're past it," Frank said. "Got to come around to make our approach from the west."

Jack strapped himself in the co-pilot's seat and peered out the window. The vog was gone. The air was clear all the way to the pristine blue of the Pacific below. Off the upturned tip of the right wing an irregular patch of lush green, spiked with mountains and rimmed with white sand and surf, floated amid the blue.

"Maui?" Jack said.

Frank shook his head. "Oahu. Pearl Harbor's down there in that notch. Hang on. We're coming around toward Maui now." A moment later the plane leveled off and three islands swung into view. "There. That's Molokai on the left, Lanai on the right, and Maui's dead ahead."

Jack had been studying the maps Glaeken had given him. They were approaching from the northwest. Molokai looked okay, and the resort hotels along Maui's Ka'anapali Bay were intact but deserted. Inland, the tops of the western mountains were tucked away within a wreath of rain clouds.

But as Frank banked southward, Jack saw that there was nothing left of the old whaling town of Lahaina—everything burned, blackened, flattened. To their right the whole southern flank of Lanai was scorched and smoking. And then Jack's stomach lurched, not so much from the movement of the plane as from what he saw ahead of them. He felt as if he'd been thrown into any one of a dozen prehistoric island movies of the *Lost Continent/Land That Time Forgot* type.

Maui looked swaybacked from here, as green as Oahu but with mountains at each end and a broad flat valley between. But the big mountain that took up most of the eastern end, Haleakala, was belching fire and pouring gray-black smoke into the air. The old volcano's sides, however—at least from Jack's vantage—were still lush and green.

And somewhere on the slope of that chimney flue to hell dwelt Kolabati and her necklaces.

Jack studied the scene, wondering what the hell he'd got himself into. Maui looked so fragile, like it could blow any minute. Just like Hawaii on its far side.

"Frank," he said, "can we swing around the island? I'd like to get the lay of the land before we touch down."

"I don't know, Jack. It's getting late. And we'd have to fly low to see anything. Air currents could be tricky on the far side. I mean, with the wide temperature variants between the ocean and the lava and the vog, we could hit some weird thermals. I don't like to do that when I'm straight."

"Okay," Jack said casually. "If you don't think you can hack it, I'll find somebody at the airport to take me up after we land."

Frank grinned. "You're a rotten, despicable, evil dude, Jack, and I hate you very, very much. May your karma turn black and fall into the void. Hang on."

Frank swung the jet out and banked around the western flank of the reactivated Haleakala to the south end of the island. The scenery changed abruptly from lush green to scorched black, as if a giant flame thrower had been played over the terrain. The eastern slope, however, was a scene from Dante's *Inferno*. Molten lava streamed down the broken-out side of the cone, cooling black crusts rode inexorably downward on the crests of crimson flame-waves, throwing up immense clouds of salty steam as they wiped out in the sea.

Frank skirted the turbulent clouds for a few miles. On the right was the immense bubbling, boiling cauldron of ocean where the Big Island of Hawaii had once stood, the source of the lid of vog that covered much of the Eastern Pacific.

Frank turned to Jack. "You sure you want to go all the way around?"

Jack nodded. "All the way."

"Okay. Strap in and don't say I didn't warn you."

He banked a sharp left and gunned the jet into the roiling steam. Water sluiced off the windshields like rain as the craft was buffeted about by updrafts and downdrafts and mini-vortices of air, but Frank guided her through with a clenched jaw and steely-eyed determination. When they broke free into the light again, Frank relaxed his grip on the controls and half-turned to Jack.

"Aw*right!* Far freaking out! Let's try that again. Maybe we can— Jesus H. Christ!"

Jack had already seen it. His stomach was fluttering in awe. The news reports had mentioned it and he'd seen photos, but nothing had prepared him for the reality of it.

A whirlpool. A maelstrom. A swirling, pinwheeling, ten- mile-wide mass of water, spread out below him like the planet's navel. Its perimeter moved slowly where it edged into Kahului Bay, but quickly picked up speed as the water progressed inexorably toward the whirling center where it funneled down into a black hole somewhere far below in the ocean floor.

Both Jack and Frank stared dumbly through their windows on the first two passes, then Jack began noticing details.

"Frank!" Jack said, staring down on the third pass. "It looks like—"

He grabbed the binocs from the clamp in the ceiling panel and focused in on the colorful specs he'd spotted below, riding the rim of the maelstrom, then darting in toward its swirling heart and out again.

"What's doing?" Frank said.

"Windsurfers! There's a bunch of nuts down there windsurfing along the edge of the whirlpool!"

"That's Ho'okipa Bay, Jack. Windsurfing capital of the world. Those dudes live for that shit. I know where they're comin' from. So do you, I reckon."

"Yeah, I can dig it," Jack said, nodding slowly. *Jeez, I'm starting to sound like Frank.* "But one little slip and you're gone."

"Yeah, but what a way to go!" Frank said dreamily. "If I've gotta go, I want it to be in right here, strapped into my jet. Stoked to the eyeballs and Mach one straight down into the earth so's after we hit me and the plane are so tangled and twisted up they can't tell Frank Ashe from Frank Ashe's plane and so they bury us together. Or better yet, straight down into one of those holes until I run into something or run out of fuel. Whatta trip that'd be! Might even try that one straight. Whatcha think?"

"Drop me off first," Jack said. "It's getting late. I think it's time to land."

Frank grinned. "Aw. And just when we was starting to have some fun."

He radioed down to Kahului airport for clearance; they told him the winds were out of the west and that they'd cleaned off the runway. All was clear and he'd better land fast because once it was dark, the hangers would be locked and wouldn't be opened for anyone.

"'Cleaned off the runway?'" Frank said to Jack as he started his approach. "What's that mean?"

They found out after they landed and opened the hatches. From off to the east came a dull roar, the low, gurgling rumble of uncountable tons of water being sucked down through the ocean depths. Looming behind them, Haleakala smoked and thundered. The steady breeze was warm and wet, and it stunk.

"Sheesh!" Jack said as he stepped down onto the tarmac. The ripe, putrid odor clogged his nose and throat. He shifted the strap of his duffel bag on his shoulder and glanced around at the deserted runways and empty buildings, searching for the source. "What *is* that?"

"Dead fish," said Ba, debarking behind him. "I know that smell from village where I grew."

"You get used to the *pilau* after a while," said the tractor driver who'd come out to tow their jet into a nearby hangar.

"Don't tell me Hawaii always smells like this."

"Hell no. Didn't they tell you? It's been raining fish for the past two nights."

"Fish?"

"Yeah. You name it: tuna, squid, crabs, blues, mahi mahi, everything. Even a few dolphin. Raining out of the sky. And first thing every morning I've got to go out with the plow and clear them off the runways. Don't know why. Nobody's flying much these days anyway since all the tourists upped and went home."

"But raining fish?"

"It's the *puka moana*. It backs up at night."

With that he jumped on his tractor and started towing the jet toward the hanger, leaving Jack wondering how a whirlpool could back up. It wasn't as if it was a toilet. Or was it?

Frank led them toward the terminal building.

"Let's see what we can do about getting you guys a car."

The main terminal building looked like an Atlantean relic raised from the sea. Its windows and skylights were smashed, rotting fish and seaweed draped its roof and walls. Inside it was worse.

"Shee-it!" Frank said, waving his hand before his face. "Smells like a fish market that's run out of ice."

They trooped through the gloomy, deserted building, looking for someone, anyone. Finally they ran across a dark, middle-aged fat guy squeezing into a wrinkled sports jacket as he hurried toward them down a ramp. His badge read "Fred" and he looked part Hawaiian.

Jack waved him down. "Where are the car rentals?"

"There ain't. All closed up. Nobody to rent to."

"We need a car."

"You're outta luck, I'm afraid."

Jack looked at Ba. "Looks like we'll have to wait till morning, Ba. What do you say?"

Ba shook his head. "Too long away from the Missus."

Jack nodded. He knew Ba was feeling the time pressure as much as he; maybe more. He grabbed the guy's arm as he tried to squeeze by.

"You don't understand, Fred. We *really* need a car."

Fred tried to pull away but Jack tightened his grip on his flabby upper arm. Ba stepped closer and looked down at him.

"I can't help you, Mister," Fred said, wincing. "Now let me go. It's after five. It'll be getting dark in half an hour. I've got to get home."

"Fine," Jack said. "But we're new around here and you're not. And since you seem to be the *only* one around here, we've elected you to find us a car. And if you can't help us out, we'll be forced to take yours. We'll pay you a generous rental price before we take it, but we *will* take it. So where do they keep the cars around here?"

Fred stared at Jack, then up at Ba, then at Frank who stood behind them. Jack felt a little sorry for the guy, but there was no time to play nice.

"Okay," Fred said. "I can do that. I can show you to the rental lot. But I don't know about keys or—"

"You let me worry about keys. You just get us there."

"All right," Fred said, glancing up through one of the broken skylights. "But we've got to hurry!"

They could have walked. The rent-a-car lots were only a couple of hundred yards from the terminal. Jack used his Semmerling .45 to shoot a link out of the chain locking the gate to the Avis lot. The lot was littered with rotting fish—on the cars, between the cars, in the lanes—and so the stench was especially vile here. Fred's tires squished through the fish, sending sprays of rotting entrails left or right whenever he ran over a particularly ripe one. He drove them around the return area until they found a Jeep Laredo. Jack was ready to hot-wire it but didn't have to. The keys were in the ignition. It started easily. The fuel gauge read between half and three- quarters. That would be enough. Jack went back to where Ba and Frank waited with Fred in his car. He pulled out the Maui road map Glaeken had given him and pointed to the red *X* drawn above a town called Kula.

"What's the best way to get here—to Pali Drive?"

"You want to go upcountry? On Haleakala?" Fred said. "Now? With night coming? You've got to be kidding!"

"Fred," Jack said, staring at him. "We've only known each other for a few minutes, but look at this face, Fred. Is this face kidding?"

"All right, all right. I've never heard of Pali Drive but this spot you've got marked here is somewhere between the Crater Road and Waipoli Road. You take Thirty-seven, it runs right out of the airport here. That'll take you upcountry. You turn left past Kula, keep to the left onto Waipoli Road, and it looks like it'll be somewhere off to your right. But there's nobody up there . . . except for the *pupule kahuna* and his witch woman."

Jack grabbed Fred's wrist. "Witch woman? Dark, Indian looking?"

"That's the one. You know her?"

"Yeah. That's who we're going to see."

Fred shook his head. "Lot's of strange stories coming down hill. Now I'm *real* glad you're not taking my car up there. Because you ain't coming back."

"We'll see about that," Jack said.

After Fred rushed off to drop Frank at the hangar where he planned to spend the night in his plane, Jack pushed a half dozen dead fish off the Jeep's hood, unzipped his duffel bag, and began laying out its contents.

"Okay, Ba. Name your poison."

He laid out the chew-wasp-toothed club Ba had given him, plus a .45 1911, a Tokarev 9mm, a couple of TT9mm nine-shot automatics, two Mac 10 assault pistols, and a pair of Spas-12 pump action assault shotguns with pistol grip stocks and extended magazines.

Ba didn't hesitate. He picked out the 1911 and one of the shotguns. Jack nodded his approval. Good choices. Jack already had his Semmerling; he added the toothed billy, the Tokarev, and the remaining shotgun to his own armament, then tossed a fifty- cartridge bandoleer to Ba.

"You ride shotgun."

Ba pumped the Spas-12, checked the breach, then handed it to Jack.

"No," he said, his face set in its usual mortician's dead pan. "I am a far better driver than you."

"Oh, really?" Jack repressed a smile. This was the longest piece of spontaneous conversation he'd been able to elicit from Ba all day. "What makes you say that?"

"The drive to the airport this morning."

Jack snatched the offered shotgun from his grasp.

"Fine. You drive. And try not to wear me out with all this empty chatter as we go," Jack added. "It distracts me."

They'd gone about half a dozen miles or so on Route 37—some of the signs called it "Haleakala Highway"—driving on stinking pavement slick with the crushed remains of countless dead fish. The outskirts of a town called Pukalani were in sight when Jack glanced back at the lowlands behind them. It was fairly dark below; lights were few and scattered; the airport was completely dark. He glanced beyond the coast to the strange-faced moon peeking huge and full above the edge of the sea, but when he saw the sea itself, his heart fumbled a beat and he squinted through the thickening dusk to confirm what he thought he saw.

"Whoa, Ba," he said, grabbing the Oriental's shoulder. "Check out the whirlpool. Tell me if you see what I see."

Ba braked and looked over his shoulder.

"There is no whirlpool."

"Thank you," Jack said. "Then I'm not crazy."

He wished he'd thought to bring the binocs so he could get a better look, but even from this distance in the poor light it was plain that the huge pinwheel of white water in the sea off Kahului Bay was gone.

Had the hole in the ocean floor closed up?

"I don't understand any of this," he muttered. "But then, I'm not supposed to. That's the whole point."

He was about to tell Ba to drive on when he noticed a white area of boiling water bubbling up where the center of the whirlpool had been. The bubbling grew, became more violent, and finally erupted into the night. Not volcanic fire, not steam, just water, a huge thick column of it, hundreds of feet across, geysering out of the ocean and lancing into the sky at an impossible speed. It roared upward, ever upward, ten thousand, fifteen thousand, twenty thousand feet in the air until it plumed into billowing cumulus clouds at its apex.

And it kept spewing, kept on pouring unmeasured thousands of tons of water into the sky.

"My . . . God!" was about all Jack could manage in the face of such a gargantuan surreal display.

"It is as the attendant said," Ba said. "The whirlpool backs up at night."

He threw the Jeep back into gear and continued up the highway. They had the road to themselves.

Three or four miles uphill from Pukalani heavy drops of seawater began to splatter all around them. Jack rolled up his window as the shower evolved into a deluge, forcing Ba to cut his pace.

A few minutes later, a blue and green parrot fish bounced off the hood with a nerve-jarring *thunk*. Then a bright yellow butterfly fish, then they were being pelted with sea life, banging on the hood, thudding on the canvas top, littering the road ahead of them. The ones that didn't burst open or die from the impact flopped and danced on the wet pavement in the glare of the headlights. A huge squid splatted against the windshield, momentarily blocking Ba's vision; when it slid off he had to swerve violently to the right to avoid a six-foot porpoise stretched dead across the road.

And then fish weren't the only things in the air. Chew wasps, spearheads, belly flies, men-o'-war, and a couple of new species Jack hadn't seen before, began darting about. Ba accelerated. Jack was uneasy about traveling at this pace through pelting rain and falling fish over an unfamiliar road slick with dead or dying sea life. But the headlights and speed seemed to confuse the winged predators, and Ba plowed into the ones that wouldn't or couldn't get out of the way.

After they passed through Kula, Jack spotted the turn-off for 377. Ba slid the Jeep into the hairpin turn as smoothly as a movie stuntman, downshifted, and roared up the incline.

Jack had to admit—silently, and only to himself—that Ba was indeed the better driver.

The Waipoli Road turn-off came up so quickly that they overshot it. But Ba had them around and back on track in seconds. And then the going got really rough. The pavement disappeared and devolved into an ungraded road that wound back and forth in sharp switchbacks up a steep incline. The slower pace allowed the night things to zero in on the Jeep. They began battering the windows and gnawing at the canvas top.

I had to choose a jeep.

But soon the headlights picked out a brightly painted hand- carved sign that read *Pali Drive*. Ba made the turn and the road narrowed to a pair of ruts. They bounced along its puddled length until it ended at the cantilevered underbelly of a cedar- sided house overlooking the valley. Ba stopped with the headlights trained on a narrow door in the concrete foundation.

Jack rechecked his map and notes by the dashboard light.

"This is it. Think anybody's home?"

Ba squinted through the windshield. "There are lights."

"So there are. I guess that means we've go to go in."

A spearhead rammed its spike through the canvas top then, narrowly missing Jack's head. Hungry little tongues wiggled through the openings behind the point and lapped at empty air. As it pulled back, sea water began to pour in through the hole.

"Let's go," Jack said. "Shotguns and clubs?"

Ba nodded and picked up the other Spas-12.

"Okay. We meet at the front bumper and head for the house back-to-back. Use the shotgun only if you have to. Go!"

Jack kicked open his door, leapt into the downpour, and dashed-splashed toward the front of the Jeep. Something fluttered near his head; without looking he lashed out at it with the wasp-toothed billy. A crunch, a tear, and whatever it was tumbled away. He met Ba in the glow of the headlights and they slammed their backs together. A spearhead darted through the light, low, toward Jack's groin, while a belly fly sailed in toward his face. The falling sea water stung the healing area on his arm where the first belly fly had caught him. He didn't want to let this one in close. He swung the club at the spearhead and shredded its wings while ramming the muzzle of the shotgun into the belly fly's acid sack, rupturing it.

"Let's move." Jack shouted. "I'll lead."

Like a pair of Siamese twins fused at the spine, they moved toward the door, Jack clearing a path with his billy and shotgun, Ba backpedaling, protecting the rear. When he reached the door, Jack began pounding on its hardwood surface, then decided he couldn't wait. He handed Ba his billy and pulled the plastic strip from his pocket, all the while congratulating himself for bringing Ba along. The big guy was faced into the headlights now, a club in each hand, batting the bugs away left and right. Fortunately, the bugs weren't nearly as thick here as they'd been in New York, but even so, without Ba, Jack would have been eaten alive as he faced the door.

Jack quickly slipped the latch and they burst into a utility room. He spotted a sink and a washing machine before they slammed the door closed behind them and stood panting and dripping in the safe quiet darkness.

"You okay?"

"Yes," Ba said. "And you?"

"I'm just groovy. Let's go see who—"

Suddenly the overhead lights went on. A tall, dark-skinned man with reddish hair stood in the doorway. He was dressed in a loin cloth and a feather headdress and Jack might have laughed except that he was pointing a Marlin 336 their way.

"Who are you?" he said.

Jack put his hands up. "Just travelers seeking shelter from the storm."

"No shelter here for *malihini.*" He stepped forward and raised the rifle. "Get out! *Hele aku oe!*"

"Easy there," Jack said. "We're looking for Miss Bahkti, Kolabati Bahkti. We were told she lived here."

"Never heard of her. Out!"

Even if the guy hadn't flinched at the sound of her name, the necklace around his neck, a perfect match to the copy Jack carried in his pocket, would have proved him a liar.

Then Jack heard a woman's voice call his name.

"*Jack!*"

Kolabati had followed Moki down to the lower level to see who was pounding on the door; she'd hung back in the dark hallway, watching the scene in the utility room over Moki's shoulder. Two wet and weary men there, one white, the other a tall Oriental. Something about the smaller man, the dark-haired, dark-eyed Caucasian, had struck her immediately as familiar. But she didn't recognize him until he spoke her name. It couldn't be! But even with his hair plastered to his scalp and down over his forehead, even looking tired and older as he did, he could be no one else. Her heart leapt at the sight of him.

She brushed past Moki and ran to him, arms outstretched. Never in her life had she been so glad to see someone.

"Oh, Jack, I thought you were dead!"

She threw her arms around his neck and clung to him. Jack returned the embrace, but without much enthusiasm.

"I am," he said coolly. "I just came back to see how you were doing."

She stepped back and stared at him.

"But when I left you, you were—"

"I healed up—my own way."

Kolabati sensed Moki close behind her. She turned and was relieved to see that he had lowered his rifle. She manufactured a smile for him.

"Moki, this is Jack, a very old and dear friend."

"Jack?" he said, his gaze flicking between her and the newcomer. "The Jack you said you once loved but who died in New York? That Jack?"

"Yes," she said. A glance at Jack's face revealed a bewildered expression. "I . . . I guess I was wrong about his being dead. Isn't that wonderful? Jack, this is Moki."

Kolabati held her breath. No telling how Moki would react. He'd become so unpredictable—*unbalanced* was a better word— since the changes had begun.

Moki's jaw was set and his smile was fierce as he thrust his hand open toward Jack.

"*Aloha*, Jack. Welcome to my kingdom."

Kolabati watched the muscles in Moki's forearm bulge as he gripped Jack's hand, a wince flicker across Jack's features before he returned the smile and the grip.

"Thank you, Moki. And this is my good friend, Ba Thuy Nguyen."

This time it was Moki's turn to wince as he shook hands with the Oriental.

"You're both just in time," Moki said. "We were just about to leave for the ceremony."

"Maybe now that they're here we should stay home," Kolabati said.

"Nonsense! They can come along. In fact, I *insist* they come along!"

"You're not thinking of going outside, are you?" Jack said.

"Of course. We're heading uphill to the fires. The night things do not bother us. Besides, they seem to avoid the higher altitudes. You shall have the honor and privilege of witnessing the Ceremony of the Knife tonight."

Moki had told her about the ceremony he'd worked out with the Niihauans, a nightly replay of last night's bloody incident. She wanted no part of it, and Jack's arrival was a good excuse to stay away.

"Moki," Kolabati said, "why don't you go alone tonight. Our guests are cold and wet."

"Yeah," Jack said. "How about a raincheck on that? We're kinda beat—"

"Nonsense! The awakened fires of Haleakala will dry your clothes and renew your strength."

"Go yourself, Moki," Kolabati said. "After all, the ceremony can go on without us, but not without you."

Moki's glare spelled out his thoughts: *Leave you here with your reborn lover? Do you take me for a fool?* Then he faced Jack.

"I shall be insulted if you do not come."

"A guest must not insult a host," the tall Oriental said.

Kolabati noticed a quick look pass between Jack and Ba, then Jack turned to Moki.

"How can we refuse such an honor? Lead the way."

Kolabati held on as Moki bounced their Isuzu Trooper up the rutted jeep trail toward Haleakala's fire-limned summit.

"What sort of a ceremony is this?" Jack said from behind her.

"You'll find out soon enough," Moki said.

"I mean, is it traditional, or what?"

"Not entirely," Moki said. "It has its traditional aspects, naturally—ancient Hawaiians often made sacrifices to Pele— but this variation is one of my own devising."

Jack and his silent Oriental companion were two jouncing shadows in the rear as Kolabati turned from the front seat to face him.

"Pele?" said Jack's shadow.

"Hawaii's Goddess of Fire," Kolabati told him. "She rules the volcanoes."

"So what are we doing—throwing some pineapples and coconuts over the edge?"

Moki laughed as he turned onto Skyline Trail. "Pele has no use for fruits and nuts. She demands tribute that really matters. *Human* tribute."

Jack's laugh was low and uncertain.

Kolabati said, "He's not joking."

Jack said nothing then, but even in the dark Kolabati could feel the impact of his gaze. She heard his silent questions, asking her what she had come to, what had brought her to this. She wanted to explain, but she couldn't. Not now. Not in front of Moki.

The quality of the road improved as they approached Red Hill and the observatory. Moki pulled to a stop a quarter mile from the summit and the four of them walked under the cold gaze of the unfamiliar moon to the crater's edge.

And there, half a mile below them, a sea of fire. The boiling center of the crater, the terminus of an express delivery tube from the planet's molten core, was alive with motion. Bubbles rose on the storm-tossed surface and burst convulsively, splattering liquid rock in all directions. Geysers of molten lava shot like whale spume, hurling red-orange arcs a thousand feet into the air. And governing the chaos was a steady downward flow to the sea in a wide fan of fiery destruction.

Even here, thousands of feet above, with the reversed tradewinds blowing cold against their backs, the fire stroked them with its heat. Kolabati watched Jack hold out his hands to warm them, then turn his wet back toward the fire. The wind had an icy bite at 10,000 feet. He must have been freezing. The Oriental, too, rotated his wet clothing toward the heat.

"I've figured out why Pele is so *huhu*," Moki said, shouting above Haleakala's roar. "She's seen her people abandoning the old ways and becoming *malihini* to their own traditions. She's sent us all a message."

Jack was staring down into the fire. "I'd say she's one very touchy lady."

"Ah!" said Moki, glancing off to their right. "The other celebrants arrive. The ceremony can begin."

He strode away toward the approaching Niihauans. Their elderly *alii* raised his feathered staff and they all knelt before Moki.

Kolabati felt a cold hand grip her arm. It was Jack.

"He's just kidding about this human sacrifice stuff, isn't he? I mean, I keep expecting Bob Hope, Bing Crosby, and Dorothy LaMore to show up."

Kolabati could barely meet his eyes. "I wish he were, but he means it. The group over there, the ones wearing the feathers and such, they're the last of the pure-bred traditional Hawaiians from the forbidden island of Niihau. Moki confronted them last night and told them he was Maui."

Jack's eyes widened. "He thinks he's an island?"

"No. He's mad but he's not *that* mad. Maui was a god who came up here ages ago, right where we're standing, and trapped the sun and forced it to make the days longer. When Moki told them he was Maui, the Niihauans didn't believe him. One of them stabbed him in the chest with a spear."

Jack glanced over to where Moki stood talking with the Niihauan *alii*.

"You mean *tried* to stab him in the chest."

"No. The spearhead sank to its full length right here."

She reached out and touched a spot over Jack's heart. She'd been wanting to touch him since her first sight of him, to assure herself that he was really here, truly alive. He was.

Jack gave her a quick look, then stared again at Moki.

"The necklace?"

Kolabati nodded.

"It didn't work that way when I wore it."

"It's never worked that way for anyone. Something's happened to it. It's been activated, *stimulated* in some way that I don't understand."

"I do," Jack said, still staring at Moki.

"You do? How can you—?"

"That's why I'm here. I need that necklace. There's someone back in New York who might be able to set the world right again. But he needs the necklace to do it."

The thought of giving away the second necklace to a stranger jolted Kolabati. She turned to look at Moki and held her breath as she saw a middle-aged Niihauan rise and step toward him with a raised knife. Moki stood firm, showing no fear. In fact, he gestured the man forward. The Niihauan stepped closer, and in a blur of motion raised the knife and plunged it into Moki's chest.

Jack cried, "Jesus Christ!" while Ba stiffened and muttered something unintelligible.

Kolabati watched the rim with fatalistic distaste as Moki staggered back a step, then straightened. He grasped the knife handle with both hands, and slowly, deliberately, his body shaking convulsively, withdrew the bloody blade from his chest. The Niihauan looked on in open-mouthed amazement, then raised his face and arms toward the sky. Moki gave him a moment, then rammed the dripping blade into his heart.

As the man screamed in agony, Jack turned away, cursing angrily under his breath. Kolabati continued to watch. Human sacrifices had been part of her childhood. When you are born to a priest and priestess of a temple where humans were regularly thrown to the rakoshi, it became a matter-of-fact event. It was a necessity—the rakoshi had to be fed. But this was different. This was obscene, serving no useful purpose other than feeding Moki's delusions.

As she watched Moki lift the Niihauan's corpse and hurl it into the fire, a sacrifice to the false goddess, Pele, Jack turned to her.

"How the *hell* did you get involved with this maniac?"

"A long, sad story, Jack. Believe me, he was nothing like this before the sun and the earth began to betray us."

Inside she mourned for the Moki who had been, the Moki she sensed was irretrievably lost to her.

"I'll take your word for it," Jack said. "But right now he's got to be stopped. And one way to stop him is to get that necklace from him."

"More easily said than done when you're talking about a man who heals like Moki."

"I might have a way." His eyes bored into hers. "Will you help?"

She nodded vigorously. "Of course."

But don't expect to walk out of here with Moki's necklace when we get it back.

TUESDAY

1 • PASSAGES

WNEW-FM

JO: Hi. We're back. You probably thought we jumped ship just like most everybody else in town, didn't you. But we didn't. We lost our power for a bit there. As we're sure you already know, the whole city's dark.

FREDDY: Yeah, but we've got a generator going now so we're staying on the air, just like we promised.

JO: Trouble is, we won't be able to bring you much news. The papers can't roll their presses and the wire services are shutting down. But we'll stay on the air and do the best we can.

FREDDY: Yeah. You're stuck with us.

DINU PASS, RUMANIA

"I think we're lost, Nick," Bill said.

They were tipping and grinding and scraping along what passed for a road in these parts as Bill fought the wheel of the Rumanian equivalent of a Land-Rover. It was rust streaked, its odometer was in kilometers, it had creaky, ratchety steering, failing brakes, and a leaky exhaust system. But it seemed damn near indestructible, and its thick glass seemed impervious to the bugs that had swarmed over them in the Ploiesti area. Not too many bugs around here, though. Maybe because there weren't many humans or animals in these parts to feed on.

Bill squinted ahead. Sheer mountain walls towered on either side, closer on his left, but the formerly seamless blackness beyond the flickering, dancing headlights was showing some cracks. Morning was coming. Good. Although traveling east had made the night mercifully short, he was tired of the darkness. He had a blinding headache from the carbon monoxide-tainted air as well as the tension growing in his neck, his left leg and right arm burned from fighting the

213

creaky clutch and stubborn gear shift, and he was sure they'd missed a crucial turn about ten kilometers back.

And he'd begun talking to Nick. Nick hadn't deigned to reply yet, but the sound of his own voice gave Bill the feeling that he wasn't completely alone out here in a remote mountain pass in the heart of a benighted country where he spoke not a word of the native language.

"We'll never find our way back home again," he said. "Unless it's in a pine box."

Joe Ashe had piloted them across the Atlantic and Northern Europe in great time, riding the jet stream all the way. The field at Ploiesti had been deserted except for one of Joe's East European pilot buddies—apparently the Ashe brothers had a global network of kindred spirits—who had this beat-up old land- rover waiting for them. They'd assumed Bill would wait until daylight before setting out. But dawn, such as it was these days, had been nearly three hours away. And three hours seemed like a lifetime. Sure, it was 6:02 a.m. local time, but the clock in Bill's body read only midnight. He was too wired to sleep, so why not put the time to good use? The Rumanian land-rover looked sturdy enough—more like a converted half-track mini-tank than a car—so he'd loaded Nick into the passenger seat and headed out into the darkness.

A foolish mistake. Bill realized that now. He glanced at his watch. Eight o'clock. They'd covered thirty miles in two hours—the majority of them coast-ing along the road north from Ploiesti, the last few crawling along this ridge road. According to the Sapir curve, dawn was due at 8:41, after which there would be eight hours and thirty-eight minutes of sunlight today. Which was about half an hour shorter than the shortest day of the year in the dead of all the Decembers that had preceded the celestial changes.

Bill shivered. A new kind of winter had come. A winter of the soul.

"I know what you're going to say, Nick," he said. "You're going to say, 'I told you so.' And maybe you did, but I guess I wasn't listening. Doesn't matter now, though. We're stuck out here in the middle of nowhere and we'll just have to wait until the light comes and hope to find somebody who can tell us how to get to this keep place."

Nick, ever polite, refrained from an I-told-you-so.

Bill scanned the terrain ahead for a level place to park and noticed the road widening. Great. He could pull to the side and wait for the light. Then he saw the white shapes ahead. As he got closer he realized they were houses. A cluster of them. A village.

"Maybe there is a God after all, Nick," but he knew Nick didn't believe that. Neither did he.

Bill almost wished again for the old days when he did believe. Because he'd be praying now for help, for direction, for the Lord to inspire his hands on the wheel to guide them to the right road and lead them to their destination.

But those days were gone. His god was dead. Mumbled words would not bring help from on high. He was going to have to do this just the way he'd always done things—by himself.

As he followed the road on its winding course among the houses, he felt no lessening of his sense of isolation. What had appeared to be a village was really no more than a collection of huts, and those huts looked beat up and run down. As the headlight beams raked them he saw how their white stucco walls were scarred and chipped, noted the gaps in the shakes covering their roofs. Hard times had come to this place. He didn't have to search the huts to know the village was deserted.

"Now we're really lost," he told Nick. The fatigue was settling on him like a ratty blanket. "Lost in the middle of nowhere. If there is a God, he's forsaken this place."

Then he saw the flames. On the far side of the village, flickering fitfully in the fading darkness. It looked like a campfire. He drove toward it, steadily picking up speed.

A fire meant people and that meant he wasn't completely lost. Maybe there was still hope of salvaging this trip.

But suddenly there was nothing ahead—no road, no grass, no earth, only emptiness. He stood on the brakes, tumbling Nick into the dashboard as the rover swerved and skidded to a stalling halt at the edge of a precipice. A hole, dammit! Another one of those bottomless holes!

No, wait. To his left, vague and dim, an ancient bridge of some sort, with stone supports plunging into the pit. It coursed two hundred feet across the emptiness—a rocky gorge, he saw now; not a hole—toward the campfire. And now that he was closer and the sky was lighter, Bill realized that the campfire wasn't outside. It was *inside*, glowing through a tall open gate set within a massive stone wall that seemed to spring from the mountainside. He could make out human forms standing around it. Some of them might even be staring back at him. On the structure's leading edge, a thick, sturdy tower rose a good forty or fifty feet above the top of the wall. The whole thing looked like a small castle, a pocket fortress. He felt a smile spread over his face—how long since he'd really smiled?

He was here. He'd found it.

The keep.

Bill let out a whoop and pounded the steering wheel.

"We made it, Nick!"

He restarted the vehicle and headed for the causeway, intending to drive across. But when the headlights picked up the worn and ragged timbers, he stopped, unsure if he should risk it.

"What do you think, Nick?"

The question was rhetorical, but Bill noticed that Nick seemed more aware than he'd been a few moments ago. Had the impact with the dashboard jostled his mind? Or was it something else?

Maybe it was all the bugs swarming around the keep. He hadn't noticed them before, but he could see now that the air was thick with them. Perhaps because the only people in the pass were clustered around that fire inside. But why were the doors open? And why weren't the bugs running rampant through the keep, chewing everybody up?

One thing Bill did know was that walking across the causeway now was impossible. They'd be ground beef before they'd traveled fifty feet. Of course, they could wait. But Bill couldn't wait, not another minute. He hadn't come this far through the dark simply to sit here with his destination in sight and wait for dawn. Screw the bugs. He was going across. Now.

"All right, Nick," he said. "Here goes nothing."

He went slowly, keeping his eyes glued to the timbers directly ahead. Not so easy with the bugs batting against the vehicle with increasing frequency. A bumpy ride, but smoother than the ridge road they'd been traveling. A glance ahead showed a group of figures clustered in the gateway of the keep, watching him.

"Stop."

Bill slammed on the brakes. It was Nick. His face was pressed against the side window. His voice was as lifeless as ever, but Bill sensed real emotion hidden within it—almost excitement.

"What is it, Nick? What's wrong?"

"I see them. Down there. Little pieces of the sword."

He was pointing down to his right, below the base of the tower, down to where its rocky foundation melted into the gorge, fifty feet below. Bill could barely make out the floor of the gorge. How could Nick see little pieces of metal?

"I don't see a thing, Nick."

"Right there. They glow with bright blue fire. Are you blind?"

Bill strained to see but could find only darkness below.

"I guess so. But as long as one of us can see them, we're in business."

Bill was congratulating himself on how smoothly this mission was going when the rear window cracked and bellied inward as one of the bigger bugs hit it like a stone. It held, but for how long? Because suddenly they were under full-scale attack as the bugs launched a blitzkrieg on the rover, scraping, gnawing, pounding, and slapping against every square inch of the vehicle's surface, as if the approach of dawn had driven them into one final feeding frenzy before they'd be forced to return to the hole from which they'd sprung.

Bill shifted into first but held the clutch. He couldn't see. With all the chew wasps, belly flies, spearheads, men-o'- war, and other things clustered against the windshield and the other windows, the outer world had become a squirming mass of gnashing jaws, writhing tentacles, and acid-filled sacks. He'd be driving blind. No guardrail, and fifty feet of empty air awaiting them if the rover strayed more than three feet left or right.

Then the rear window bulged further inward with the weight of the onslaught and he knew he had no choice. Even going over the side was preferable to sitting here and being eaten alive when that window gave way.

Taking a deep breath, Bill eased up on the clutch and they started to move. He found that by looking down through his side window he could catch an occasional glimpse of the causeway's edge. He used that as a guide.

As they rolled forward, he heard a noise, faint and indistinct at first, but growing steadily in volume. It sounded almost like human voices—*cheering* voices. It was. The sound reached into the rover and touched him, warmed him. Using it as a beacon, he increased his speed, homing in on it.

And suddenly—like driving under an overpass in the heart of a cloud-burst—the bugs were gone. Swept away, every last one of them. Silence in the rover. Except for the voices. Instead of bugs the vehicle was now surrounded by cheering people. Men and women, middle aged and older with rugged peasant faces, coarse clothing, sheepskin vests, woolly hats. They pulled open the rover's door and helped him out, all the while shaking his hand and slapping his back. Bill returned the smiles and the handshakes, then glanced back along the causeway. The bugs crowded the air outside the arch of the gateway, but not one ventured through.

He turned back to the people and saw children and goats wandering around behind them. And beyond those, on the stone block walls, crosses. Hundreds of crosses. *Thousands* of crosses.

What sort of place was this? And why did he feel as if somehow he'd returned home after a long journey?

With the coming of day the bugs fled back to the darkness where they lived and the peasants trooped out of the keep with their children and animals, crossing the causeway to what was left of the real world, leaving Bill and Nick and their vehicle behind with the ashes of the night fire.

Bill knew he should head down into the gorge with Nick to search for the shards of the shattered sword, but he could not leave this place. Not just yet. The keep took him in, wrapped him in the arms of its walls, and demanded his attention.

It was the crosses, he knew. How could he spend thirty years of his life in the priesthood and not be taken in by a place so thoroughly studded with crosses? Not dull, dreary, run-of-the-mill Latin crosses, but strange thick ones, with brass uprights and nickel crosspieces set high, almost at the top. Like a tau cross or what was called St. Anthony's cross.

Not all of the villagers left. An ancient, white-bearded gent—eighty if he was a day—named Alexandru remained behind. He spoke as much English as Bill did Rumanian, but they found common ground in German. Bill had studied the language in high school and college and had been fluent enough to read *Faust* in the original text. He found he remembered enough to communicate with Alexandru.

The old man showed him around the structure. His father, also named Alexandru, had been the keep's last caretaker in the days before World War Two. It could have used a caretaker now— a whole crew of them. Snow, wind, rain, drought, heat, and cold, all had left their mark on the keep. All the upper floors within the tower had collapsed, leaving nothing but a giant, rubble- choked stone cylinder. Yet although crumbling and in sad disrepair, it still exuded a certain power.

"It used to be a bad place," Alexandru said. "Now it is a good place. The little monsters will not come here. All around they fly, but never in here."

He went to the gate and gestured off to the left. Bill's gaze followed the pointing arm to a black circular area, hundreds of feet across, marring the verdant floor of the pass.

A hole.

"That is where they come from, the little monsters."

"I know," Bill said. "The holes are everywhere."

Alexandru then led Bill to the keep's cellar and showed him the opening in the stone floor there. He told of how the Germans had camped in the keep in the spring of 1941 and nearly wrecked the place, of how something immeasurably evil had awakened and slaughtered all the soldiers, of how it had almost escaped before it was destroyed.

Alexandru looked at Bill with watery blue eyes.

"At least we *thought* it was destroyed. Now I am not so sure."

"How was it destroyed?"

"A red-headed stranger came and slew it with a magic sword—"

...a magic sword ...

"— then he limped off with a Jewish woman from Bucharest and was never seen again. I wonder whatever happened to him."

"He's old and gray like you now," Bill said, wondering what Glaeken had looked like in his prime. He must have been magnificent. "And he and the woman are still together."

Alexandru nodded and smiled. "I am glad. He was a brave man, but terrible to see when he was angry."

With the aid of Alexandru's directions, Glaeken's notes, and a flashlight, Bill led Nick down through the utter blackness of the subcellar to the lower segment of the tower. A narrow stairway wound down to the base where an iron ring was set in the stone block. Bill pulled. Part of the wall separated from the rest and swung inward. Light flooded the base of the keep's tower. Bill wondered when was the last time sunlight had shown on these stones.

"All right, Nick," he said, leading him outside. "Do your thing. Where are they?"

Nick stood blinking in the light. Thin, and paler than ever, he didn't look well. And he'd crawled back into himself.

Bill scanned the ground, looking for the shards Nick had said he'd seen. It was like river-bottom here, fist-sized stones jumbling down a gentle slope to a sluggish stream. Bill looked to his right up at the mountains soaring skyward behind the keep. This gorge was probably all water in early spring when the snows melted. Half a century had passed since the sword blade had shattered here. How could anything be left? How could they hope to find the remnants even if any still existed?

"Well, Nick?" he said. "Where are they?"

Nick said nothing, only stared ahead.

Desperate, Bill knelt and picked among the stones and gravel. This was impossible. He'd never find anything this way.

He straightened up and brushed off his hands. It had been earlier, in the dark, when Nick had said he'd seen the pieces, glowing "with bright blue fire."

Maybe he could only see them at night.

"Damn!"

He'd risked their lives rushing to get here so he could get back to Ploiesti as soon as possible so they could start their homeward journey in the light. Now he was going to have to wait until dark.

He turned and aimed a kick at the tower's granite-block hem. The keep, a dark, brooding, lithic presence looming over him, took no notice.

Bill led Nick back inside the tower to a gloom as deep and dark as his spirits. The delay meant it would be Wednesday before he got back to Carol. He wondered how she was doing, and if she'd heard from Hank?

Where had he run off to, anyway?

The Movie Channel
Joe Bob Briggs' Drive-In Movie—A Special All-Day Edition.
Eaten Alive (1976) New World
Day Of The Nightmare (1965) Herts-Lion
Nightwing (1979) Columbia
Raw Meat (1972) AIP
The Devils of Darkness (1965) Twentieth Century Fox
Tentacles (1977) AIP
Phase IV (1974) Paramount

It! The Terror From Beyond Space (1958) United Artists
They Came From Beyond Space (1967) Amicus
The Last Days Of Planet Earth (1974) Toho
The Flesh Eaters (1964) CDA
They Came From Within (1975) TransAmerica
The Earth Dies Screaming (1964) Lippert/Twentieth Century Fox

THE NEW JERSEY TURNPIKE

Hank wasn't sure if he was awake or dreaming. He seemed to be awake. He was aware of noises around him, of a stale, sour odor, of growing light beyond his eyelids, but he could not get those eyelids to move. And he could *feel* nothing. For all he knew, he no longer had a body. Where was he? What—?

And then he remembered. The millipedes . . . their queen . . . a scream bubbled up in his throat but died stillborn. How can you scream when you can't open your mouth?

No. That had been a dream. It had all been a dream—the holes, the flying horrors, storing up the food, deserted by Carol, the rest stop, the trooper, the gun, the bullet, the millipedes—a long, horrible nightmare. But finally it was at an end. He was waking up now.

If he could just open his eyes he'd see the familiar cracks in the ceiling of their bedroom. And then he'd be free of the nightmare. He'd be able to move then, to reach out an arm and touch Carol.

The eyes. They were the key. He concentrated on the lids, focusing all his will, all his energy into them. And slowly they began to move. He didn't feel the motion but he saw a knife-slit streak of light open across his eyes, pale light, like the glow on the horizon at the approach of dawn.

Encouraged, he doubled his efforts. Light widened around the horizon as the edges of his lids stretched the gummy substance that bound them, then burst through as they broke apart. Not the blaze of the rising sun, but a wan, diffuse sort of light. He forced his lids to separate further and the light began to take form through the narrow opening, breaking down into shapes and color. Vague shapes. A paucity of color. Mostly grays. His pupils constricted, bringing the images into sharper focus.

He was looking down along a body. His own body, lying in bed, naked atop the sheets. Hazy, but he knew his own body. Thank God, it had all been a dream. He tried to turn his head to the left, toward the light, but it wouldn't move. Why couldn't he move? He was awake now. He should be able to move. He slid his eyeballs leftward. The bedroom window was over there somewhere. If he could just—

Wait . . . the walls—rounded. The ceiling—convex. Concrete. Concrete everywhere. And the light. It came from above. He forced his eyelids open another millimeter. No window—the light was coming through a grate in the concrete ceiling.

The stillborn scream from a moment ago came alive again and rammed up against his throat, pounding at his larynx, crying to be free.

This wasn't the bedroom. It was the pipe—the drainage pipe! It hadn't been a dream. It was real. *Real!*

Hank fought the panic, beat it down, and tried to think. He was still alive. He had to remember that. He was still alive and it was daytime. The things from the holes were quiet in the daylight hours. They hid from the light. He had to think, had to plan. He'd always been good at planning.

He shifted his eyes down to his body. His vision was clearer now. He saw the gentle tidal rise and fall of his sparsely haired chest, and further down, on his belly, he spotted the bloody wound where the queen millipede had spiked him and injected him with her poison. The neurotoxin was still working, obviously, paralyzing his voluntary muscles while it let his heart and lungs go on moving. But it didn't have complete control of him. He'd managed to open his eyes, hadn't he? He could move his eyeballs, couldn't he? What else could he move?

He pulled his gaze away from his abdominal wound and searched for his hands. They lay flopped out on either side, palms up. He checked out his lower limbs. They were intact, slightly spread with the toes angled outward. He could have been a sun bather. His body was the picture of relaxation . . . the relaxation of complete paralysis. He returned his gaze to his arm and followed it down to the hand. If he could move a finger—

And then he noticed the webbing. It was all around him, running in all directions, crisscrossed like gauze. It curved away from each arm and leg like heavy-duty spiderweb and ran out to the wall of the drain pipe where it melted into a glob of some sticky looking gelatin smeared on the concrete. He looked down as much as his slit perspective would permit and realized that he wasn't lying in the pipe, he was *suspended* in it. From the horizontal lie of his body he guessed that he was resting on a hammock of web across the diameter of the pipe.

Hank marveled at the coolness of his mind as it analyzed his position. He was trapped—not only paralyzed, but effectively and securely bound in position. The web hammock, however, was not entirely without its advantages. Long, uninterrupted contact with the cold concrete would have made it difficult for his body to maintain its temperature; the webbing also kept him out of the water, thereby preventing his flesh from breaking down in the constant moisture.

So in a very real sense he was high and dry, but also bound, gagged, and paralyzed.

Hung up like a side of beef.

That last thought impacted with the force of a sledgehammer. That was it! He was food! They'd shot him full of preservatives and stored him away alive so he wouldn't decompose. So when pickings got slim above ground, they could come down here and devour him at their leisure.

He willed down the rising panic. Panic wouldn't help here. They'd already paralyzed his body. Allowing fear to paralyze his mind would only make matters worse. But that one cold hard fact battered relentlessly at his defenses.

I'm food!

That rogue cop lieutenant would get a good laugh out of that: The hoarder becomes the hoard. Even Carol would probably appreciate the irony.

But I'm alive, he told himself. And I can beat these bugs.

He knew their pattern. They'd probably stay dormant all day and crawl up to the surface to hunt during the dark hours. That was when he'd get free.

But first he had to regain control of his body. He already controlled his eyeballs and eyelids. Next was his hands. If he was to get free he'd need them the most. A finger. He'd start with the pointer on his right hand, concentrate all his will and energy into that one digit until he got it to move. Then he'd proceed to the next, and the next, until he could make a fist. Then he'd switch to his left.

He glared at his index finger, narrowing his vision, his entire world to that single digit, channeling all his power into it.

And then it moved.

Or had it? The twitch had been almost imperceptible, so slight it might have been a trick of the light. Or wishful thinking.

But it *had* moved. He had to hold onto that thought. It *had* moved. He was regaining control. He was going to get out of here.

With climbing spirits, he redoubled his concentration on the reluctant digit.

WFAN-AM

            dead air

MONROE VILLAGE, LONG ISLAND

Alan rolled his wheelchair along the network of cement paths that encircled Toad Hall, heading from the back yard to the front. Off to his left, to the west, he saw smoke rising over the trees. Not near smoke, from the Shore Drive neighborhood, but further away. From downtown Monroe, most likely. He'd heard stories of roving gangs, looting, burning, raping. They hadn't shown up out here, but perhaps that was just a matter of time.

Strange how things had worked out. He'd always imagined that if the world ever descended into anarchic nihilism, the violence and chaos and mob madness would occur at night, screams and flames hurtling into a dark, unseeing sky. But given the current situation, human violence was confined to the daylight hours. The night was reserved for *in*human violence.

Alan turned from the smoke and inspected Toad Hall. The old mansion had absorbed another merciless pummeling last night but, like the valiant, indomitable champion that she was, she remained on her feet.

The injuries were accumulating at an alarming rate, however. Her flanks were cut and bruised and splintered, her scalp showed through where her shingles had been torn up. She could still open her eyes to the dwindling daylight, though. Most of them, at least.

Which was why Alan was out here now. A couple of the storm shutters had refused to roll up this morning. Even from the inside Alan could see that they were deeply dented, more deeply that he'd have thought possible from a bug attack, at least from any of the bugs he'd seen so far.

Which meant there might be something new under the moon, something bigger than its hellish predecessors and consequently more dangerous to the little fortress Toad Hall had become. He coasted to a halt and stared as he rounded to the front.

The dents in the steel shutters were deeper than he'd realized. And they'd been scored by something sharp and heavy, with the weight and density of a steel spike.

But it was the rhododendrons under the shuttered windows that bothered him more.

They'd been trampled flat.

Alan rolled across the grass for a closer look. These were old rhodos, maybe fifty years old, with heavy trunks and sturdy branches, kept thick with healthy deep green leaves through Ba's magical ministrations. Tough wood. Alan remembered that from the times he'd cut back the rhodos around his old house before it burned down.

These hadn't been cut, though. The trunks and branches had been crushed, and their splinters pressed into the ground. Something awful big and heavy—or a number of big and heavy somethings—had been outside these windows last night banging and scraping at the shutters.

But they hadn't got in. That was the important thing.

As Alan pushed his left wheel forward and pulled the right backward to turn and roll back to the path, he saw the depression in the lawn. His stomach lurched. He hadn't noticed it before; he'd been too intent on the shutters and the ruined rhodos. But from this angle you couldn't miss it.

The fresh spring grass, overdue now for a trimming, had been crushed in a wide swath that angled in from the front gate, around the willows, and directly to the house. Alan tried to imagine what sort of creature could leave such a trail but all he could come up with was a thirty-foot bowling ball. With teeth, most likely. Lots of them.

He shuddered and rolled back to the path. Each night it got a little rougher. One of these nights Toad Hall's defenses were going to fail. It was inevitable. Alan prayed he'd be able to persuade Sylvia to move out before that happened, or that Glaeken would be able to assemble the pieces he needed to call for help.

Alan could feel it in his bones: they were all going to need help. Lots of it. And soon. Otherwise, if the Sapir curve was correct, they had two sunrises left. Then the sun would set for the last time at three o'clock on Thursday afternoon. And the endless night would begin.

MAUI

Even the coffee tasted like fish.

Jack knew the water was pure—he'd watched Kolabati draw it from the water cooler—but it still tasted fishy. Maybe because everything *smelled* fishy. The air was so thick with the odor of dead sea life he swore he could taste it when he breathed.

He was standing on the lanai, forcing the coffee down, looking out at the valley below and at the great whirlpool spinning off Kahului. It would have been heart-stoppingly beautiful if not for the stench. Behind him, sounds of chopping, chipping, sawing, and hammering drifted through the door from the house's great room.

Kolabati joined him, coffee cup in hand, and leaned on the railing to his right. She wore a bright, flowered muumuu that somehow enhanced her figure instead of hiding it. Jack's eyes locked on the necklace. He tried to be casual but it wasn't easy. There it was, half the reason for this hairy trip, a couple of feet away. All he had to do was reach out and—

"My silverswords are all dead," she said, looking down at a wilted garden beneath the deck. "The salt water's killed them. I'd hoped to see them bloom."

"I'm sorry."

She gestured with her cup toward the giant maelstrom.

"There's no point to it. It sucks water and fish down all day, then shoots it miles into the air at night."

"The point," Jack said, remembering the gist of Glaeken's explanations, "is not to have a point. Except to mess with our minds, make us feel weak, impotent, useless. Make us crazy with fear and uncertainty, fear of the unknown."

Jack noticed when he said "crazy" Kolabati stole a quick glance over her shoulder at the house.

"And speaking of points," he said, "what's the point of Moki? How'd you get involved with a guy like that? He's not your type, Bati."

As far as Jack could see, Moki was nobody's type. The guy was not only out to lunch, but out to breakfast, dinner, and the midnight snack as well. A homicidal megalomaniac who truly believed he was a god, or at least possessed by one: Maui, the Polynesian Prometheus who brought fire to humanity and hoisted the Hawaiian Islands from the bottom of the sea with his fishing pole. After last night's ceremony the four of them had returned to the house where Ba and Jack spent the night in the garage, the only place in the house secure from the bugs. Moki and Bati were never bothered by the creatures—more proof of Moki's divinity. He'd kept them up most of the night elaborating on his future plans for "Greater Maui" and the rest of the remaining Hawaiian Islands. And running under it all Jack sensed a current of hatred and jealously—aimed at him. Moki seemed to see Jack as a threat, a rival suitor for Kolabati's affections. Jack hadn't planned on any of this. He spent his time wondering how he could use that jealousy to get to the necklace Moki wore, but so far, except for the simple act of putting a bullet through his skull, he'd come up blank.

"How do you know my type?" Kolabati said, eyes and nostrils flaring. "What do you know of me?"

Jack studied her face. Kolabati had changed. He wasn't sure how. Her wide, dark, almond-shaped eyes, her high, wide cheekbones, full lips, and flawless mocha skin were the same as he remembered. Maybe it was her hair. She'd let it grow since he'd last seen her. It trailed long over her near shoulder and rustled in the sour wind like an ebony mane. But it wasn't the hair. It was something else, something inside.

Good question, he thought. What *do* I know about her?

"I know you don't hang out too long with people who don't see things your way."

She turned and stared down at the valley.

"This is not the real Moki—or at least not the Moki who shared my life up to a week ago."

Shared her life? Jack was about to make a crack about the ability of this one hundred and fifty year old woman to share anything when he saw a droplet of moisture form in the corner of her eye, grow, and spill over the lid to run down her cheek.

A tear. A tear from Kolabati.

Jack was speechless. He turned and stared though the door where Moki was feverishly working like the madman he was. But working on what? And didn't he ever sleep? He'd harangued them for hours, then he'd rushed to the upper floor where he'd gone to work on the shattered pieces of sculpture littering the great room, recutting them, fashioning a new, giant single work from the remnants of all the others. Ba was in there with him now, sitting in a corner, sipping tea and watching him in silent fascination.

"He was wonderful," Kolabati said.

Jack looked at her again. The tear was still there. In fact it had been joined by others.

"You love him?"

She nodded. "I love who he used to be." She turned toward Jack, wiping the tears from her cheeks, chasing the fresh ones that replaced them. "Oh, Jack, you would have loved him too. I only wished you'd known him then. He was gentle, he was so alive and so much a part of his world, these islands. A genius, a true genius who couldn't flaunt his brilliance because he took it for granted. He never tried to impress anyone else, never tried to be anyone else but Moki. And he wanted to be with me, Jack. *Me.* Nobody else. I was happy, Jack. I was in love. I thought I'd found an earthly Nirvana and I wanted it to last forever. And it could have, Jack. You know it could have."

He shook his head. "Nothing lasts forever." He reached out and touched her necklace. "Even with that."

"But so soon? We'd just begun."

He searched her face. Here was the difference. The seemingly impossible had happened. Kolabati, the cool, aloof, self-absorbed, ruthless Kolabati who had sent him out to kill her own brother Kusum, who had walked out with her own necklace as well as Kusum's and left Jack bleeding in a chair because he had refused her offer of near immortality . . . Kolabati Bahkti had fallen in love and it had changed her. Maybe forever.

Amazingly, she began to sob—deep, wrenching gasps of emotional pain that tore at Jack. He'd come here expecting to find the old, cold, calculating Kolabati and had been fully ready to deal with her. He wasn't prepared for the new Kolabati.

He resisted the impulse to take her in his arms. No telling what Moki-The-Unkillable might do if he saw that. So he settled for touching her hand.

"What can I do?" he said. "What will fix it?"

"If only I knew."

"Maybe it's the necklace. Maybe the necklace is part of the problem—maybe it *is* the problem. Maybe if you take it off him—"

"And replace it with a fake?" Her eyes flashed as she dug into the pocket of her muumuu. She pulled out a necklace exactly like her own. "This one, perhaps?"

Since Kolabati was wearing one of the genuine necklaces, and Moki the other, this had to be Jack's fake.

He swallowed. "Where'd you get that?"

"From your duffel bag." Her eyes hardened. "Was that your plan? Steal my brother's necklace and replace it with a fake? It never occurred to you that I might have given it to someone else, did it?"

Time to bite the bullet, Jack thought. Let her know the whole story.

"Kusum's necklace isn't enough," he said, meeting her gaze. "We need both."

She gasped and stepped back, her hand clutching at her throat.

"Mine? You'd steal *mine*?"

"It wouldn't be stealing, exactly. I'd just be returning it to its original owner."

"Don't joke with me about this, Jack. The people who carved the necklaces have been dead for ages."

"I know. I'm not working for them. I'm working for the guy they stole the original metal from. He's still around. And he wants it back. All of it."

Kolabati's eyes widened as she studied him. "You're not joking, are you?"

"You think I could make up a story like that, even if I tried?"

"All those years will rush back upon me without it, Jack. I'd die. You know that"

"I intended to ask you for it."

"And if I refused?"

He shrugged. "I was going to be very convincing."

Actually he'd had no firm plan in mind when he'd come here. Good thing too. He hadn't counted on Moki. Not in his wildest dreams had he counted on the likes of Moki.

Kolabati's hand still hovered protectively over her necklace. She couldn't seem to drag it away.

"You frighten me, Jack. You frighten me more than Moki."

"I know it sounds corny as hell," he said, "but the fate of the whole world depends on this guy Glaeken getting those two necklaces back and restoring them to their original form."

Kolabati gestured to the stinking valley, to the whirlpool beyond. "He can change all this? He can make everything as it was?"

"No. But he can stop the force that's making it this way, that's working to destroy everything we see here. And it isn't bad here, Bati. This is really pretty decent because there aren't many people around. But back on the mainland, in the cities and towns, people are at each other's throats. Everyone's frightened, scared half to death. The best are holed up, hiding from the monsters by night and their fellow humans by day. And the worst are doing what they've always done. But it's the average Joes and Janes who are really scary. The ones who aren't paralyzed with fear are running amok in the streets, looting and burning and killing with the worst of them. You can do something to stop it, turn it all around."

"I don't believe you. It can't be that bad. I've lived for a century and a half. I saw my parents shot down by an English officer, I witnessed the Sepoy rebellion in the 1850s, two world wars, the Bolshevik revolution, and worst of all, the atrocities in the Punjab, Indian killing Indian during the partition. You have no idea what I've seen."

"This is worse," Jack said. "The whole world's involved. And after Thursday it'll be night all over the world, forever. There'll be nowhere to run. Unless you do something."

"Me." The word was spoken in a very small, faraway voice.

"You."

Jack let that sink in awhile, let her stare down at the island she seemed to love so much, let her breathe the reek of its slow death. And then he put the question to her. He'd have never considered asking the old Kolabati, the one he'd known years ago in New York. But this was a new, improved version, someone who'd loved a man, who loved this island. Maybe this Kolabati could be reached.

"What do you say, Bati? I'm not asking you to take it off and hand it to me. But I am asking you to come back to New York with me and talk to Glaeken. He's the only guy on earth who's older than you. Hell, you're a newborn compared to him. You sit down with him and you'll believe."

She turned and leaned against the railing, staring through the door into the great room of her house.

"Let me think about that."

"There's no time to think."

"All right," she said slowly. "I'll come see this man. But that's all I promise you."

"That's all I'm asking," he said, feeling his fatigued muscles begin to uncoil with relief. It was a start. "Now, about Moki's . . . "

She looked at him sharply.

"He's not going to die," Jack added quickly, "or even age appreciably if someone should manage to replace his real necklace with a look-alike." An idea occurred to Jack. It was wild but it might help enlist Kolabati more firmly as an ally. "Who knows? Could be it's the necklace that's making him crazy. Get it off him and maybe he'll revert to his old self."

Before Kolabati could answer, Moki's voice boomed from within the house.

"Bati! *Hele mai!* And bring your ex-lover. See what your god has fashioned!"

Kolabati rolled her eyes and started forward. Jack grabbed her arm, gently.

"What do you say?"

"I'll think about it."

She pulled her arm away and dropped the dummy necklace back into her pocket. Jack followed her.

And stopped inside the door, staring.

The great room had been transformed. All the wood and lava from the broken sculptures had been reshaped, combined, coalesced into a single huge assembly that stretched from wall to wall. And where he'd run out of sculpture remnants, Moki had smashed pieces of furniture and added them to the mix. The assorted stained and bleached wooden fragments were arranged so as to appear to spring from the wood paneling of the walls, forming four spokes in a giant lopsided wheel, weaving crooked paths toward a common center. A lava center. Moki had somehow joined all the red and black lava fragments—the gleam of wire, the dewy moisture of still-drying epoxy were visible within the irregular mass—into a new whole, a jagged, haphazard aggregate that had no coherent shape, no symmetry, no discernible intelligence to it, yet somehow was undeniably menacing and implacably predatory.

"What do you think of Maui's masterpiece?" Moki said, standing near the center, hands on hips, grinning like a caricature of Burt Lancaster.

Ba squatted in the far corner, a gaunt Buddha, silent, watching.

"It's . . . disturbing," Kolabati said.

"Yes!" He clapped his hands. "Excellent! Exactly what it is supposed to be! Disturbing. True art *should* disturb, don't you think? It should challenge all your comfortable assumptions, tip them over so you can see what crawls around on their underbellies.

"But what is it?" Jack said.

Moki's smile faltered, and for the first time since he'd arrived, Jack detected a hint of uncertainty in the man's eyes.

He hasn't the faintest idea what he's done.

"Why . . . it's a vision," he said, recovering quickly. "A recurring one. It's plagued me for days. It's . . ." His eyes brightened with sudden inspiration. "It's Maui! Greater Maui! Yes! The four separate islands—Molokai, Lanai, Kahoolawe, and Maui itself—drawing back to where they belong—together. Forming one seamless mass at the center!"

Jack stared at the construct. This was no island or regrouping of islands. Too bizarre, too menacing. It was something else, but even the artist hadn't a clue as to what.

"Come," Moki said, grabbing Kolabati's hand. "Maui is tired. He needs to rest before the ceremony tonight. And he needs his woman by his side." He stared at Jack, challenging him. "The woman who once loved you now loves a god. She can never go back. She will never want to. Isn't that true, Bati?"

Kolabati smiled and nodded. "Very true, my love."

Jack watched her carefully. Kolabati was not the type to allow herself to be pushed around like this. No one told this woman what to do.

As Moki led her away by the hand, she glanced back at Jack and patted the pocket of her muumuu. The one that bulged with the fake necklace.

Jack nodded. *That* was the Kolabati he knew.

"You kids play nice, now," he called after them.

He watched until she disappeared into the bedroom, then went over to where Ba still squatted.

"What do you think, Big Guy?" he said, leaning against the wall next to him. "You've been watching the whole process. What's it look like to you?"

"It is evil," Ba said.

Jack waited for Ba to elaborate, but that was all he was going to say. So Jack walked around it, ducking under the spokes, crouching, stretching up on tiptoe, looking for a fresh perspective, an angle that would reveal the work's secret. But the more he looked, the more unsettled he became. Why? It was only wood and lava. And it didn't look like anything in particular. If anything, it resembled DaVinci's man in a circle—except the man here was some sort of ugly amoebic embryo.

He had an inescapable sense that more than Moki was at work here. Jack couldn't help but feel that the sculptor's madness had tapped him into something outside himself, outside everything humans knew, and he'd built a crude model of it.

And Ba was right. Ba had said it all.

Whatever it was, it was evil.

Dinu Pass, Rumania

"Look down, Nick. At the ground. Do you see anything?"

Night had come. So had the bugs. The air was dense with them. From the base of the keep's tower, Bill watched their bizarre and varied forms buzzing, darting, drifting in the air a mere half-dozen feet away.

But he and Nick were safe. Though they stood in the open doorway, the bugs kept their distance. As soon as it was dark, Bill had guided Nick back into the depths to the heavy stone door where now they both stared into the hungry darkness outside.

"Come on, Nick," he said. "Take a good look. Do you see any of that glow you saw last night?"

He nodded and pointed straight ahead. "There."

A slow change had come over Nick during the day. He seemed more alert, more responsive to the world around him. Were the effects of his descent into the hole wearing off?

"All right, then." Bill's insides were coiled tight. "I guess this is it."

He turned to the baker's dozen of villagers armed with chairs and torches who waited behind him in the tower base. The thirteenth was Alexandru, standing off to the side.

Through Alexandru, Bill had explained that the red-haired man who'd come here in 1941 was still alive and in America, that if he could recover some pieces of the "magic sword" that had shattered here on these stones, he might be able to close up the hole out there in the pass and bring the sun back. They'd helped him search around the base of the tower this afternoon but their efforts had been no more fruitful than his own in the morning. They'd have to go out at night.

Bill had expected to be laughed off as a madman, or rudely rebuffed at the very least. Instead the villagers had conferred together, then agreed to help him. The women had begun wicker- weaving while the men set about making torches. Now they were dressed in multiple layers of clothing, wicker armor on their thighs and lower legs, heavy gloves, sheepskin hats and vests. They looked ready for an arctic blizzard, but it was a different sort of storm they'd be facing.

Bill nodded to the men. It was time. Their faces remained mostly expressionless, but Bill noticed glances pass between them, saw them begin to breath more heavily. They were scared, and rightly so. A perfect stranger had asked them to put their lives on the line, to perform the equivalent of wading into a piranha-infested river with only a crab net and a spear for protection. If they turned around and headed back up the stones stairs now, he wouldn't blame them.

But they didn't. They filed out through the opening with their shields and torches raised, to form a shallow semicircle of protection into which Bill and Nick stepped. And then, just as they'd rehearsed it inside the keep, they advanced as a group, the end members closing the circle behind Bill and Nick as they moved away from the tower wall.

The bugs assaulted in a wave. The men in the circle around him began to cry out in fear and anger and revulsion as they blocked the swooping creatures with their raised chairs and shields while thrusting at them with their torches. To the accompaniment of buzzing wings and sizzling bug flesh, they inched forward.

Bill crouched next to Nick, his arm over his shoulders, keeping his head down as they moved. He shouted in his left ear.

"Where, Nick? Show me *where!*"

Nick kept his eyes down, searching the rocky ground but saying nothing. Bill had a sudden, awful fear that Nick might not be able to see the glow because of the torches the circle of villagers carried. If daylight obscured the glow, would torchlight do the same?

As if in answer to Bill's unasked question, Nick said, "Here's one."

His pointing finger was directed at a spot two inches in front of his left shoe.

Bill shouted to the group to stop, pulled out his flashlight, and began pawing through the stones with his free hand. He felt the circle constrict around him as the villagers were beaten back into a tighter knot by the bugs. But under the stones there was nothing but dirt.

"There's nothing here, Nick!"

But Nick kept pointing. "There, there, there."

"Where, dammit?"

"The glow. There."

Nick sounded so sure. Out of sheer desperation, Bill began digging through the moist silt. It didn't seem likely, but maybe rains over the decades had buried some of the fragments and the glow was filtering up through the ground. The trip had been a bust so far and they didn't have much time out here, not with the increasing ferocity of the bug attack, so he was willing to try almost—

Bill's fingers scraped on something hard and slim with rough edges, something that felt nothing like sand or stone. He forced his fingers down into the silt, worked them around the object, under it, then pulled it free.

A rusty, dirty, jagged piece of metal lay in his palm. He held it up.

"Is this it, Nick?"

"Can't you see the glow?"

Bill turned the object over and over in his hands. No glow. Just a broken, pitted piece of metal.

"No. Are there more?"

"Of course." He pointed to Bill's left. "Right there."

Bill began to dig again. One of the men shouted something to him. Bill didn't know the language but the meaning was clear.

Hurry!

Bill placed his flashlight on the stones and used the first piece to help dig after the second, throwing dirt in all directions as he dug. He heard a faint clink of metal on metal and was reaching into the hole to feel for it when a chew wasp darted between the legs of one of the men and sank its needle teeth into his arm. Without thinking, Bill lashed at it with the metal fragment in his hand.

The flash of light nearly blinded him for an instant. He blinked, and when the purple after-image faded, he saw the chew wasp flopping on the stones and gnashing its teeth in waning fury, a deep, blackened, smoking wound in its back.

Bill stared at the metal fragment in his hand for a second. Whatever power this blade had once held was not completely gone, not by a long shot.

He threw himself into probing deeper into the bottom of the second hole. He found another piece of metal almost immediately and held it up.

"How about this one, Nick? Quick! Does it glow?"

Nick nodded. "Yes."

"Great. All right now. Where's the—"

Then one of the villagers screamed and fell backward, landing across Bill's back and nearly knocking him flat. Bill thought the bugs might have broken through his defenses and latched onto him en masse, but he was wrong.

It was worse.

Something had the man by the ankle, something that had uncoiled out of the darkness like a long black rope, but alive, tapered, twisting, and powerful. His fall had broken the circle and now the bugs were inside, attacking from within as well as without. The men tried to reclose the circle but wavered as the snake-like thing began to drag their friend from their midst. Some bent to grab his arms to pull him back but the bugs were immediately upon them and they had to let him go to protect themselves. Bill watched in horror as the man was dragged screaming into the darkness, the bugs swarming over him, ripping at him.

Another inky snake uncoiled from out of the night and snared a second villager. And as he was pulled crying to his doom, a third creature caught Nick and pulled him off his feet. Nick made no sound as he landed on the rocks. Bill wrapped an arm around his chest but the snake began to drag them both away. Bill sensed something huge and dark looming in the blackness beyond the reach of the torchlight and realized then that these weren't snakes but the long, smooth tentacles of a single monstrous creature. Glaeken's off-handed comment floated through his mind . . .

The bigger ones tend to be slow; it will take them a while to get here, but they'll get here.

Bill knew from the inexorable pull it exerted on Nick that there was no way he could resist its strength.

In desperation he reached down to the tentacle encircling Nick's legs and slashed at it with the sword fragments. Another blinding, sizzling flash and suddenly the tentacle had uncoiled and was writhing and flopping furiously about on the stones like a beheaded snake.

The villagers were now in complete disarray, stumbling about, swinging their torches and shields wildly in the air.

"Back!" Bill cried. "Back to the keep."

He pulled Nick to his feet and half carried him over the rocky ground toward the base of the tower, flailing about in the air with the metal shards, clearing a path through the bugs. Finally they were there, trailing some of the villagers, just ahead of a few others, stumbling through the doorway into the blessedly empty air of the keep. Bitten, bleeding, burned, they collapsed into panting heaps on the granite floor; compared to the rough stones outside, its smooth surface felt almost soft. Only the elderly Alexandru was standing, exactly where they had left him.

"Where are the others?" he said, his eyes ranging through their ranks. "What happened to Gheorghe? And Ion? And Michael and Nicolae?"

Bill lifted his head and counted. Only eight of the dozen villagers who'd gone out with him had made it back. He went to the door and looked out. Four torches burned smokily on the stones of the gorge. The men who had carried them were nowhere in sight. Behind him, the survivors began to weep and he felt his own throat tighten. Four brave men had sacrificed themselves so a stranger could dig up some chunks of old metal.

Bill looked down at the fragments in his hand, then again at the four sputtering torches.

These had damn well better be worth it.

Outside, something huge and black dragged its enormous weight over the rubble of the gorge.

Bill was ready to go. The two metal shards were settled deep in his pocket, Nick was strapped into the passenger seat, and the villagers had nailed a board across the land-rover's broken rear window. Bill hoped it blocked the bugs half as well as it blocked his rear view.

"I don't want to go."

Bill glanced at Nick and was shocked to see tears running down his cheeks. "Nick . . . ?"

"I like it here. I feel . . . better here. Please let me stay."

"Nick, I can't leave you here. I've got to go back and we may need you back home. But once this is all over, I'll bring you back."

He sobbed. "Do you promise, Father Bill?"

Bill felt a sob building in his own throat. He gripped Nick's hand.

"Yeah, Nicky. I promise."

He felt miserable but hid it as he waved to Alexandru and the others.

"Tell them I'll be back," he told the old man in German. "After this is all over, after the holes are closed and the monsters are gone, I'll be back. And I'll tell the world of the bravery of your people."

Alexandru waved but did not smile. There were tears in his eyes. Bill shared his grief, not only for the dead but for Alexandru's little community. A village atrophying and dying as was his could not afford to lose four of its most vital men.

"I'll be back," he said again. "I won't forget you."

And he meant it. If he survived this, if he was alive to do so, he'd be back.

He threw the vehicle into first, and started out the gate onto the causeway. The bugs swarmed around him. He was halfway across when the headlights picked up the first tentacle. It lay stretched lengthwise along the planks and lifted its tapered tip at Bill's approach, as if watching him, or catching his scent.

Bill stopped and squinted into the darkness as other tentacles pushed forward to join the first. Soon the causeway was acrawl with them. He found the high-beam button on the floor to the left of the clutch and kicked it.

Bill gasped and instinctively pressed himself back in his seat when he saw what waited at the far end of the causeway. The light from his high-beams reflected off a huge, smooth, featureless, glistening black mass, thirty feet high and at least a hundred feet across. He looked for eyes or a mouth but could find none. Just slimy-looking blackness. A huge slug-like creature with tentacles.

And those tentacles were reaching for him, stretching closer.

Bill looked for a way out, a way to get around it, but its massive bulk blocked the end of the causeway. Even if he could run the land-rover over the tentacles, he'd end up against the immovable wall of the thing's flank.

The tip of one of the tentacles suddenly appeared at the end of the hood. It coiled around the hood ornament and pulled. Bill shifted into reverse and backed up a dozen feet. The tentacles inched after him.

I'm trapped, dammit! Trapped until morning!

He pounded the steering wheel in impotent rage and undiluted frustration. He had the shards that he'd come for and he couldn't get them back to Glaeken, couldn't even set off for his return trip to Ploiesti until dawn.

More time wasted. And another night without seeing Carol. He wanted to be with her. Every moment was precious. How many did they have left?

Using the rearview mirror, he carefully backed the vehicle through the gates of the keep, then sat behind the wheel and swallowed the pressure that built in his chest as he stared out at the night. He felt like crying.

"We're back?" Nick said, smiling. "Oh, I'm so glad we're back."

WNEW-FM

FREDDY: Jo's catching a few much-needed Zs, but I'm still here with you, and I'm afraid it's time to get back inside. It's 4:48. Ten minutes to sundown. Get your butts to safety right now.

MANHATTAN

Carol watched the light fade from the sky over the darkened city and thought of how lucky they were to have generators for the building. She thought of Bill. He'd been an integral part of each thought since he'd left yesterday morning, but especially now, with dark coming.

"Where is he?" she said to Glaeken.

He was passing behind her, carrying an empty tray from Magda's room. He paused beside her.

"Still in Rumania, I should think."

She glanced at her watch. Almost five here. That meant it was almost midnight over there. Almost Wednesday.

"But he should have been back by now."

"*Could* have been back, perhaps, but as for should . . ." He shook his head. "I don't think so." He reached out and laid a scarred hand gently on her shoulder. "Don't worry yet. Not until tomorrow. If he's not back by this time tomorrow, *then* worry. You'll have company then—I'll be worrying with you."

He left her and headed toward the kitchen.

Carol continued to stare at the darkening city, wondering about Hank now. The thought of him was a sharp blade sliding between her ribs. He'd deserted her. How could he do that? And yet, strangely, she felt no malice toward him. But where had he disappeared to?

THE NEW JERSEY TURNPIKE

By nightfall Hank was utterly exhausted, but he would allow himself no sleep.

How could he? With darkness the drain pipe had come alive. First the sibilant stirrings, echoing softly around him, ballooning to a cacophony of hard-pointed mandibles clicking a hungry counterpoint to countless chitonous feet scraping against the concrete; then the sinuous shapes, faint and vague in the light of the rising moon slanting through the grate, undulating toward him from left and right, sloshing through the water below, crawling along the ceiling of the pipe directly above him, the thinnest of them as thick as his upper arm, the largest as big around as his thigh, ignoring him as they slid by, weaving over, under, and around each other with a hideous languid grace that seemed to defy gravity, blackening the pale gray of the concrete with Gordian masses of twisting bodies, blotting out the moon as they nosed against the closed grate.

He heard a metallic scrape, a screech, then a clank as the grate fell back onto the pavement above. A sudden change came over the millipedes. Their languor evaporated, replaced by a hungry urgency as they thrashed and clawed at each other in a mad frenzy to join the night-hunt on the surface.

Moments later, the last of them had squeezed through. Once again there was moonlight and Hank was alone.

No . . . not alone. Something was coming. Something big. He knew without looking what it was. And a few minutes later he saw her huge pincered head rise and hover above him, swaying.

Not again! Oh, no, Lord, not again!

He'd worked since dawn on regaining control of his limbs, and for most of the day it had seemed a hopeless task. No matter how he concentrated, how he strained, his body simply would not respond. But he'd kept at it, and as the light had started to fail, he'd begun to achieve some results. He'd noticed muscle twitches in his arms and legs, in his abdominal muscles. Either the toxin was wearing off or he was overcoming it. It didn't matter which. He was regaining control—*that* was what mattered.

But all his efforts would be for naught if the queen dosed him again with her neurotoxin.

She made no move, simply hovered there with her head hanging over him. Did she suspect anything?

Oh, Lord, oh, Lord, oh, Lord, oh, Lord!

He'd spent the entire day willing his muscles to move, now he was begging them to be still. One twitch, one tremor, one tiny tic, and she'd ram her proboscis into his gut again and put him back where he started.

She watched him for what seemed like forever, then she began to move—
No!
—her head lowering toward his belly—
NO!
—and past him. She arched over him, her hard little feet brushing across the skin of his abdomen. He could feel nothing but he saw his abdominal muscles twitch and roll with revulsion and he prayed she wouldn't notice.

She didn't. Her near-endless length finally cleared him and she wound her way up through the drain opening and into the night.

Now he was alone! And now was the time for action.

He strained his arms and legs upward as if fighting against steel manacles. To his delight he saw the muscles bulge with the effort. His fingers didn't move, didn't close into the rebellious fists he willed for them, but he watched the veins in the undersides of his forearms swell as blood coursed into the resistant muscles, watched his abdominals ripple and swell around the wound as he tried to sit up.

But nothing was happening. His veins and arteries continued to swell, stretching against the envelope of skin, his abdomen rippled like the Atlantic in a hurricane, but there was no sign of voluntary movement, only chaos.

And then his eyes snapped to the wound below his navel. Something moved there. Something wriggled within it. This morning's scream built again in his unresponsive throat as two slim black pincers, each no more than an inch long, poked into the air. A multi-eyed head, deep brown and gleaming, followed. It paused, glanced around, fixed Hank with its cold black gaze, then dragged its long, many-legged length from the wound with a crinkling *slurp*. Another identical creature quickly followed. Then another.

Hank's once quiescent and unresponsive body was moving now with a will of its own, writhing, bucking, convulsing, rocking up and down, back and forth in its webbed hammock as his veins and arteries bulged past the limits of their tensile strength and ruptured, freeing more wriggling, pincered, millipedic forms.

Something snapped within Hank's mind then. He could almost hear the foundations of his sanity begin to crack and give way. And that was good. He welcomed the collapse.

Yes. Welcomed it. A whole new perspective. Everyone above ground was dying. Dying and decomposing. Not Hank. No way. Hank was alive and would stay alive through these, his children.

Parenthood at last.

If only I could cry!

He'd wanted it so long, now it had happened. His children. They'd grown within him. Fed off him. Made him part of them. He'd go on living through them while everybody else - including the cop lieutenant and his two renegade underlings—died.

If only I could laugh!

He watched with pride as dozens more of his children broke free of the cramped confines of his body to swarm and crawl with wild abandon over his skin. So good to see them free and moving about, stretching their slender, foot-long bodies, gaining strength before heading to the surface and joining the great hunt. Some of them tangled and began to rake and spear each other with their pincers.

No fighting, children. Save it for topside.

Just then two more broke free from the sides of his throat, trailing remnants of the arteries through which they'd been traveling. They reared up and faced him, swaying back and forth like cobras before a snake charmer.

Yes, my children, he wanted to tell them, I am your Daddy and I'm terribly proud of you. I want you to—

They darted forward without warning, each burying a pincered head hungrily into one of his eyes.

No! he wanted to say. I'm your Daddy! Don't blind Daddy! How can he watch you grow if you eat his eyes?

But they were naughty children and didn't listen. They kept burrowing inward, deeper and deeper.

If only I could scream!

WPIX-TV

dead air

MAUI

Night was falling.

Jack stood in the great room and stared again at Moki's giant sculpture. The closer darkness came, the more repellent he found the piece. The stench of rotting fish from outside only made it worse. Its foulness urged him to smash it back into its component fragments.

He turned at a sound behind him and saw Kolabati emerging from the bedroom. Alone. Finally. Her dark eyes flashed with excitement as she strolled toward Jack. And as she passed she pressed something into his hand—warm, heavy, metal. He glanced down.

The necklace.

"Moki?" he said.

She motioned him to follow her to the lanai.

"He's wearing your fake," she whispered when they'd stopped at the railing. "And he's still . . . ?"

Bitter anguish dulled the animation in her eyes as she nodded. "Still the same."

"I'm sorry."

"Put it on," she whispered, touching the hand that held the necklace.

Jack thrust it into his pocket. "Better not. He'll notice."

"Put it on. You'll need it. Trust me."

Jack shook his head. "I'll be okay."

He looked out over the darkening valley. In the ocean beyond it he saw the white water of the whirlpool fading to gray. The maelstrom was slowing. Soon the geyser would begin and the air once again would be full of dying fish and hungry bugs.

But there was still time to make it to Kahului and take to the air.

He turned back to Kolabati. "What about the rest of it? What about you? Are you coming back to New York with me?"

"*Do* you trust me, Jack?" she said. Her gaze drilled into him. The answer seemed very important to her.

"Yes," he said, not completely sure of the truth here, but saying it anyway.

He sensed the new, improved Kolabati could be trusted further than the old, but how much further he couldn't say. He wasn't quite ready to stake his life on it yet.

"Good. Then I'll return to New York."

Jack couldn't resist wrapping his arms around Kolabati and hugging her. She truly had changed.

"Thank you, Bati. You don't know what this means to me, to everyone."

"Don't get the wrong idea, Jack," she said levelly. "It's good to have your arms around me again, but I'm not giving up my necklace. I have no intention of doing that. I'm going back to New York just to talk to this ancient man you've told me about. That and nothing more."

"That's fine. That's all I ask. I'll leave the rest up to Glaeken. I know he can work something out with you. But let's get moving. We haven't got much time."

"Not so fast. There's still tonight's ceremony."

Jack pushed her to arm's length but Kolabati clutched his forearms, refusing to let him go.

"Ceremony? You're going to let him kill another—?"

And then Jack remembered how last night Moki had let the Niihauan stab him first. Was that what she wanted? To see Moki die? Did she hate him that much for going crazy on her? He looked into her eyes and couldn't read them.

He would never understand this woman. Fine. But could he trust her? Her allegiances seemed as mercurial as her moods.

"That's my condition. After the ceremony, I'll return to New York. You have my word."

"Bati?" a voice called from inside.

And then Moki stepped out onto the lanai. His eyes flared when he saw the two of them touching. He took Kolabati by the arm and pulled her away.

"Come. We'll start the ceremony early tonight." He glared at Jack. "I'm especially looking forward to this one."

As Kolabati followed him into the house, she looked back at Jack and mouthed three words: *Wear . . . the . . . necklace.*

When they debarked from the Isuzu, Moki turned to Jack and jabbed his index finger at his chest.

"We came early because it will be *you* who faces Maui tonight."

Jack smiled. "I don't think so."

"If you can defeat me in the ceremony, you may have her. Otherwise she stays with me and you return to America."

Jack noticed how Moki had said "America" instead of "the mainland." Apparently Maui had seceded from the union, at least in Moki's mind.

Jack looked at Kolabati. She returned his stare coolly.

"So . . . this is what you meant by 'after the ceremony.' Swell."

She nodded. That was all.

"Come," Moki said, gesturing to the crater's edge. "It's time."

Jack hesitated. This was happening too fast. None of it was in his plan. He didn't like surprises, and this was a particularly ugly one. Kolabati had known about it before when they were whispering on the lanai. Had she cooked it up with Moki, or was this all his idea?

At least Jack had one of the necklaces . . .

Or did he?

What was that around Moki's neck? Jack's fake, or the real thing? He cursed himself for not checking the one Kolabati had given him more closely. It didn't feel any different, and if he remembered correctly from years ago, the necklace had caused an unpleasant tingle the first time he'd touched it. But that sensation had dissipated after he'd worn it for a while. Was that why he felt nothing when he touched it now? Or was there nothing to feel because it was the fake?

"What's the matter?" Moki said, his grin broadening. "Afraid?"

"I will go," Ba said, stepping forward.

Jack held up a hand. He couldn't allow that. After all, he'd promised Sylvia Nash he'd get Ba back safely.

"It's okay, Ba. I'm going. But thanks for offering."

"Remove your shirt and follow me," Moki said, then turned and started up to the crater's edge.

Jack followed, removing his shirt as he went. The cold air raised and then flattened gooseflesh on his skin. He tossed his shirt to Kolabati as he passed. Her dark, almond eyes widened when she saw no necklace around his neck.

What had she wanted to do? Rattle Moki by letting him see that Jack wore a necklace exactly like his? Uh-uh. Jack wasn't playing her games.

Jack welcomed the heat from Haleakala's fires when they reached the ridge. Moki stopped and faced him. He looked like a grinning demon in the orange light as he produced two knives with slim, six-inch blades. The flames from below glinted off their polished surfaces. He handed one to Jack, wooden handle first. As Jack gripped it, a chorus of shouting erupted from below. He turned and saw the Niihauans approaching, angrily waving their arms.

"I was afraid of this," Moki said, sighing like an indulgent father watching his unruly children. "That's why I brought you up here early tonight. They want one of their own to defeat me, not some *malihini*. I'll have to tell them not to worry. They'll get their turn."

But he didn't have to. Ba had stepped between the Niihauans and the crater rim. He spread his arms wide and spoke to them. Jack couldn't hear what he said over the roar of the inferno below, but they were looking up at him in awe. Finally they stepped back and waited.

"Good!" Moki said. "Your friend has bought us some time. Let's get on with it." He put his hands on his hips and puffed up his chest. "You strike first."

"Take the necklace off first," Jack said.

"Stop stalling," Moki said. "Is this the brave Repairman Jack Bati told me about? I think you're a coward."

"You won't take it off?"

"My necklace is not a subject for discussion. It is part of me. It will remain with me until I die. Which shall be never."

"Okay," Jack said slowly, "since we're on the subject of courage, let's give ourselves a real test: Each of us will pierce his *own* heart."

Moki stared at him with wide eyes. "You mean . . . I will plunge my knife into my chest and you will do the same into yours?"

"You got it. Simultaneously. It's one thing to stab somebody else, but it takes a *god* to stab himself."

Moki's grin widened. "I believe you are right. You are a worthy rival, Repairman Jack. I'll be sorry to see you die."

Not as sorry as I'll be if Kolabati has suckered me.

Moki positioned his knife over his chest, the point indenting the scarred area just to the left of the breast bone. Jack did the same. His sweaty palms were slippery on the handle. The touch of the point sent a chill straight through to the organ beating barely an inch beneath it. It picked up its tempo in response.

This had to work.

"Ready?" Jack said. "On three. One . . . two . . . " He shouted the last number. *"Three!"*

Jack watched as Moki rammed the blade deep into his chest, saw his torso hunch, his grin vanish, his features constrict with the sudden agony, watched his eyes fill with shock, horror, rage, betrayal as the sick realization of what had just happened to him filtered through the haze of pain.

Moki looked down at the knife protruding from his chest. Blood welled up against the hilt and ran down his skin. Then he looked at Jack's blade, still poised over Jack's chest. His lips worked.

"You . . . didn't . . . "

"You're the crazy one, pal. Not me."

Moki glanced over to where Kolabati stood in the flame- flickered darkness. The hurt in his eyes was unsoundable. Jack almost felt sorry for him, until he remembered the brave Niihauan who hadn't had a chance against him last night and had died the same way. Jack followed his gaze and saw Kolabati staring at him with unmasked fury. Why? Because he hadn't stabbed himself?

Suddenly pain seared across his chest. He staggered back and saw Moki go down on his knees, blood pumping from the slit in his chest, his bloody knife free in his hand. And across Jack's chest—a deep gash. Moki had pulled his own knife from his wound and slashed Jack.

Jack pressed his hand against the gash but it had already stopped bleeding. The pain, too, was gone. And as he watched in amazement, the wound edges closed and began to knit.

He looked up and saw Moki watching too. Moki reached a bloody hand up to the necklace that encircled his neck. Ashen faced now, he looked at Jack's unadorned neck, his eyes pleading for an explanation. He couldn't speak, but he could move his lips.

They said: *How?*

Jack pulled up the left cuff of his jeans to show where he'd wound the true necklace around his ankle.

"Just because they call it a necklace doesn't mean you *have* to wear it around your neck."

Moki pitched forward on his face, twitched, shuddered, then lay still.

Jack looked at the blade in his hand and tossed it onto the hardened lava beside Moki. Another victory for Rasalom, another talented human gone mad, and now dead. Suddenly Jack felt exhausted, empty. Must it have ended like this? Couldn't he have found another way? Was the mad darkness in the air seeping into him as well? Or had he always carried a piece of the darkness within him? Was that what he felt twisting and thrashing against the walls of the cage he'd built for it?

Shouts made him turn. The Niihauans had broken away from Ba and were charging up the slope. Jack backed away, unsure of their intent. But they ignored him, rushing directly to Moki's body. They prayed by it, then lifted him by his hands and feet and tossed his remains into Haleakala's fires.

As the others began to pray, the chief turned to Jack.

"Haleakala," he said, beaming. "The House of the Sun. Now that the false Maui is dead, the sun will return to the path that the true Maui taught it."

"When?" Jack said.

Ba had come up the slope and now stood at his side, looking at the night sky, then at the rumbling crater. He seemed tense.

"Tomorrow," the chief said. "Tomorrow, you will see."

"I hope so," Jack said. He turned to Ba. "But in case he's wrong, I think it's past time we headed back home."

Ba nodded. "Yes. We must hurry. I fear we might already be too late."

"Too late for what?"

A tortured look flickered across his features, all the more startling because of their usual waxy impenetrability.

"I don't know. I only know I must get back to the Missus."

"Okay, Big Guy. We're on our way." He turned toward Kolabati. "All we've got to do is load our lady friend in the Jeep and we're—"

Kolabati was gone.

Jack spun this way and that, searching the darkness. Not a sign of her. The Isuzu was still parked down the slope but no trace of Kolabati. He and Ba searched the entire area but all they found was Jack's shirt, lying on the lava where she had been standing. He pulled it on and hopped into the passenger seat of the car.

"She must have taken off on foot when we were listening to the old chief. You remember how to get back down the trail?"

Ba nodded and started the car.

They picked their way down the trail, Ba driving as quickly as he dared, while Jack scanned the road ahead in the headlights and as far to each side as he could see in the dark. Nothing. Nothing moving but the wind. As they wound down from the crest, the wind abated and the fish and seawater began to rain from the sky, narrowing vision even further. An occasional bug began to harass them.

Finally they came to the house. The lights were on and the generator was running, just as they'd been an hour ago. Jack leapt out and ran inside, stepping over a thrashing tuna and dodging bugs on the way. There weren't many around at the moment. Once inside he ran through the halls, shouting Kolabati's name. He didn't expect her to be here—how could she have beat them back on foot?—but he had to give it a shot, had to assure himself that he'd looked everywhere.

Uncertainty gnawed at him. What if he didn't find her? What if she was hiding from him? Had she lied? Had she had any intention at all of coming back to New York with him? Apparently not.

What a pathetic jerk I am.

He took the stairs to the upper floor, to the great room, but lurched to a stop when he heard the sound. Ahead, bleeding down the hall from the great room, a buzz, the unmistakable sound of over-sized diaphanous wings, hundreds of them, beating madly. Had they caught somebody—Bati perhaps? Were they in the midst of some sort of feeding frenzy?

He wanted to turn and run but forced himself to stand fast. Something about the buzzing . . . not wild and frenzied . . . calmer, smoother, almost . . . placid.

He stepped forward. He had to see what was going on in there. From back here he could see only the front end of the room. The lone lamp that still functioned gave off enough light for him to make out the details of the room. And what he saw sent his skin crawling.

Bugs . . . the great room was full of them, *crowded* with them. They obscured the walls, perched on the furniture, floated in the air. All kinds of bugs, from hovering chew wasps to drifting men-o'-war, and all facing the same direction, away from the smashed windows, toward the interior of the room. Jack's legs urged him to get the hell out of here, but he had to see what held them so spellbound.

Jack dropped to his knees and inched forward. The bugs remained oblivious to him. He stretched out on the bare floor and craned his neck around the edge of the entryway to bring the rest of the room into view.

More bugs. So tightly packed he could barely see through the thick of them. Then a gust of wind sluiced through the windows, undulating the hovering mass enough for Jack to catch a look at the center of the great room.

It was the sculpture, Moki's final work. The only object in the room on which the bugs had not perched. Its long, arching wooden spokes were bare for their entire length, from where they seemed to spring from the walls to their common center, the jagged, unwieldy aggregate of black and red lava fragments. The bugs hovered about it, every one of them faced toward its center like rapt churchgoers in silent benediction.

And the lava center . . . it pulsed with an unholy yellow light, slowly, as if in time with the beat of a massive, hidden heart.

A single glimpse and then Jack's view was obscured again. But that glimpse had been enough to break him out in a sweat and send him sliding back along the floor. Something about that sculpture, the way it glowed, the reverence of the bugs, the entire scene disturbed Jack on a level too deep to comprehend or understand. Something within him, not from his personal experience, but some sort of racial memory, a warning carved on his hindbrain or encoded in his genes, flooded him with circulating fear, leaving him unable to react in any way but flight.

And when he was far enough down the hall, he rose to his feet and ran out of the house to where Ba waited in the Isuzu.

"Drive, Ba!"

The Oriental pointed to the Jeep they'd driven from Kahului.

"Shouldn't we—?"

"Forget it. Let's get out of here! Now!"

Jack sat and shivered as Ba drove downhill through the downpour. He resented the fear crawling under his skin. He prided himself on his ability to govern his fear, channel it, use it. Now it was nearly out of control. He closed his eyes to the night, ignored the thump of fish bouncing off the hood and roof, took deep breaths, willing himself to be calm. By the time Ba had swerved through most of the downhill switchbacks, he was in control again. But his fingers still trembled on their own in the adrenalin aftermath.

The fear was slowly replaced by disappointment, and perhaps some depression. He'd failed. Kolabati had lied to him. Should he have expected any less? *Me, of all people.* He'd spent most of his life lying. He mentally kicked himself for believing she'd changed. But she'd been so convincing.

That's what you get for playing by the rules.

Maybe he and Ba simply should have tied up Moki and taken his necklace, then ripped Kolabati's from her throat and left her back there to die of old age in a few hours. Not that it hadn't occurred to him, yet everything within him balked at the plan. But maybe this hadn't been the time for ethical niceties. Too much at stake here.

Was there any use at all in going back to New York? Glaeken had sent him for two necklaces. He was returning with only one.

He set his jaw. Glaeken would have to find a way to make do with one necklace. He'd given it his best shot and had come up short.

He just hoped it wasn't too short.

When Ba hit the pavement above 377, he picked up speed. The wheels skidded on dead fish and clumps of wet seaweed.

"Easy, Ba," Jack said. "If we crack up, we may never get back to the plane, and then this whole trip will be for nothing. If it's not already."

"I must get back to the Missus. Quickly. She needs me."

Jack studied his grim, intent features in the dashboard glow. Ba was scared too. But not of bugs. Ba was scared for his adopted family. Why? Why now? What was happening back there?

WEDNESDAY

1 • IN THE STILL OF THE NIGHT

WNEW-FM
FREDDY: It's a minute after midnight. A little over nine hours till dawn.
JO: Yeah, you're almost half way home. Hang in there.

MONROE, LONG ISLAND

Alan felt like a vampire.

Why not? He was living like one. Up all night, sleeping when he could during the day. Reminded him of his days as an intern. Many a time he'd gone thirty-six hours straight without a wink. But he was older now, and the stress of the nights—the insane paradiddles on the storm shutters, the incessant gnawing at the outer walls—carried over into the dwindling daytime, keeping his naps fitful and restless.

He was exhausted, plain and simple. But he couldn't let Sylvia know. She was a wreck as it was. The only time she got any rest herself was when she could curl up in the basement with Jeffy and Mess and Phemus, secure in the knowledge that Alan was patrolling the upper reaches of Toad Hall.

Alan was just finishing one of those patrols now, wheeling through the first-floor halls, checking the candles, replacing the ones that were guttering into glowing puddles. The power had failed around midday. He'd thought it might be just a local failure but the radio said LILCO was off line for good. Another time it might have been romantic. Knowing what was outside, straining to get in, made it anything but.

So now with the midnight rounds completed and fresh candles flickering in every room, Alan settled himself down in the TV room and turned on the radio. Strange how a little adversity could change your habits. A week ago he wouldn't have thought twice about leaving the radio on while he'd made his rounds. Now, with the power out and batteries suddenly scarce, he didn't leave it on a moment longer than necessary.

246

Jo and Freddie were still hanging in there, God bless 'em. Their voices were ragged, sometimes they were completely incoherent, and they were broadcasting in shifts with power that at times seemed like it was generated by a collection of frantic, wheel-spinning gerbils, but they weren't giving in to the fear. Neither was a fair share of their remaining listeners.

And neither was Alan.

Only problem was they didn't play doo-wop. They played so- called "classic rock." As far as Alan was concerned, the real classic stuff had been sung on street corners, with popping fingers and the bass voice as rhythm section, and close, soaring three- and four-part harmonies telling the story. That was where it all began. There'd been some great stuff done in the sixties, and even in the seventies, but the heart of it all, the *classic* end of the music, had begun in fifty-five and tapered down into sixty-four when the Brits had begun reinterpreting the classic formulae.

"Eight Miles High" came on. Alan could live with that. The Bryds knew their harmony. He was losing himself in McGuinn's Coltranesque solos when he heard an unfamiliar sound from the front hall. He turned off the radio.

Splintering wood.

He pulled the tooth-studded billy from the pouch behind his back rest, laid it in his lap, and wheeled his chair toward the front of the house. As soon as he entered the foyer he saw the problem. After nights of constant effort, the chew wasps finally had managed to rip off the metal weather strip from the bottom of the front door and were now busily at work gnawing rat holes at the floor line. Sharp-toothed lower jaws were visible in two spots, sawing relentlessly at the wood, gouging off pieces, building piles of splinters.

This wasn't good. In half an hour or less they'd have a couple of holes big enough to wriggle through. And then Toad Hall would be full of chew wasps— and spearheads, too, no doubt.

All looking for Jeffy. But to get to Jeffy they'd have to go through Sylvia. The very thought of it sickened him.

But to get to Sylvia they've got to get by me.

Alan looked around for some sort of back-up defense, something to shore up the weak point along the bottom edge of the door. He spotted the heavy brass etagere to the right of the door.

Perfect.

He rolled over to it, removed all the *netsuke* and piled them gently in the corner, then pulled the etagere over onto its side. He tried to let it down easy but it hit the floor with a clang. He found that maneuvering it against the door from his wheelchair was all but impossible, so he slid from the seat onto his knees and worked from the floor.

As he was guiding the thick brass back of the piece against the door, a chew wasp began to wriggle its head through the hole it had made. As its eyes lit on Alan, its movements became more frantic, its toothy jaws gnashed the air hungrily. Alan grabbed his club and bashed in the creature's skull with two blows. It wriggled for an instant, then lay still, its carcass wedged in the hole, blocking it.

Alan fitted the etagere snugly against the door, then pulled his wheelchair closer. He'd stocked its backrest pouch with the equivalent of a toolchest. Hammer, nails, saw, ax, pliers, screwdriver—anything he might need on short notice during the night. He couldn't run to the workshop for them, so he carried them with him.

He took out the hammer and began driving half a dozen of the biggest nails he had into the seams between the tiles along the outer edge of the etagere. Damn shame to mess up these beautiful marble tiles like this but they could be replaced. The people besieged in Toad Hall could not.

Alan pulled himself back up into his chair and regarded his handiwork. It looked pretty stable. With only wing power behind them, he doubted the bugs were strong enough to push back the heavy brass piece even if he left it unsecured. But now, with nails acting as stoppers, he was certain they'd be frustrated until morning. He heard sharp little teeth scraping against the far side of the metal.

"Let's see you chew a hole in that."

Tomorrow, though, he'd have to find some way to reinforce the outer surface of the door.

Maybe Ba would be back by then. Alan hoped so. As much as he insisted on his own independence and refused to lean on anyone else, Toad Hall was awfully big. Too big to be adequately patrolled by one man in a wheelchair. With the welfare of Sylvia and Jeffy at stake, he couldn't let his pride endanger them. As long as Sylvia insisted on staying here, he'd stay with her and do his best to protect her, but he wished Ba were here to help. Even more, he wished they'd all moved in with Glaeken last Saturday when the old guy had offered.

"Alan?"

He wheeled around and found Sylvia standing in the entrance to the foyer. She wore the loose sweater and baggy old jeans that were serving as her pajamas during the siege. Her face was pale and lined from the pillow case. She did not look like the Sylvia Nash who'd once appeared in *The New York Times Magazine* with her unique bonsai art—her beautiful bonsai, now smashed and broken in the shattered remains of the greenhouse—but Alan thought she was as beautiful now as ever.

"Hi," he said. "You're supposed to be catching some sleep."

"I heard all that banging. I thought something was wrong."

"Sorry. I didn't mean to wake you, but the chewers have started to gnaw rat holes in the door."

She came over and dropped onto his lap; she slipped her arms around him and hugged.

"I wasn't sleeping. I couldn't. I'm worried about Ba. I'm afraid he won't come back. And if he doesn't, if he's . . . dead . . . it will be my fault for letting him go. I'll never forgive myself."

Alan put his arms around her waist. "If anyone can take care of himself, it's Ba."

"But I'm worried about you too, Alan. When I'm down in the basement with Jeffy and you're up here alone I begin to think I've been very foolish, very selfish in insisting that we stay here. And for some strange reason I feel it more tonight than ever. So I've made up my mind. Tomorrow we move in with Glaeken. Hopefully Ba will be back by then and we can all leave here as a family. I want our little family back together again, Alan. Toad Hall is our home, but we've got to survive. That comes first."

"I know what this place means to you," he said, squeezing her against him. "I know how tough it is for you to leave it."

"It's like giving up." He could feel her jaw muscles bunch as she spoke. "I hate to give up."

"But it's not giving up or giving in. It's a strategic withdrawal so you can live to fight another day when you've marshaled your forces."

"I love you," she said, leaning her head against his. "Sometimes I wonder why you put up with me and my stubbornness."

"Maybe its *because* of your stubbornness. Maybe I like a woman who don't take no shit from nobody, not even this Rasalom guy and his bugs."

Sylvia jerked her head up, fluttered her eyelids, and put on her Southern Belle voice.

"Whah, Doctah Bulmuh! Ah don't believe Ah've evah heard you speak that way! Especially in front of a layday!"

"I only speak that way when I'm *under* a lady."

They kissed—simultaneously, spontaneously. Whether it was body language or the kind of telepathy that develops between soulmates, Alan didn't know. And didn't care. All he knew at that instant was that it was time for a kiss. And Sylvia knew it too. So they kissed. Simple.

"When was the last time we made love?" he heard her say as he nuzzled her neck and inhaled the scent of her.

"Too long."

They hadn't had a chance to sleep together let alone make love since last week when the attacks had begun.

"Another good reason to move in with Glaeken," she said. "An excellent reason."

They sat there for a while, Sylvia cradled on his lap, and held each other, listening to the bugs gnaw at the edges of the brass etagere. Alan realized again how much he loved this woman, how attuned he was to her, like no other person he had ever known. The thought of her coming to harm was unbearable. Tomorrow they'd move to Glaeken's and she'd be safe, as safe as anyone could be in this madness.

But first he had to see them through the night.

The Movie Channel:
Joe Bob Briggs' Drive-In Movie—A Special All-Day Edition.
Flesh Feast ((1970) Cine World Corp.
Twilight People (1972) New Worlds
Beyond Evil (1980) IFI- Scope III
The Night God Screamed ((1973) Cinemation
From Hell It Came (1957) Allied Artists
The Unearthly (1957) Republic
Night Of The Dark Full Moon (1972) Cannon
Bug (1977) Paramount
Creatures of Evil (1970) Hemisphere
The Unknown Terror (1957) Twentieth Century Fox
The Day The World Ended (1956) AIP
Scream And Scream Again (1970) Amicus/AIP
It's A Mad, Mad, Mad, Mad World (1963) United Artists

The scrape of metal on metal.

It snapped Alan to full alert. Without hesitating he wheeled out of the game room and rolled toward the foyer. That was where it had come from. It sounded as if the etagere had moved. Alan didn't see how that was possible, but he had his toothed billy out and ready in his lap, just in case.

As he turned into the living room he heard the buzz of wings.

They're in!

His heart pumped dread but he kept on rolling. Maybe there were only a few. Maybe—

Something flashed toward him. He snapped his head back and it blew by his cheek, jaws grinding furiously.

Chew wasp.

Alan's heart was pumping furiously now. He fumbled in his lap for the billy. By the time the bug had banked around for a return run, he had it ready. Visibility wasn't great in the candlelight so he didn't swing at it. He simply held the billy between his face and the bug and braced himself.

The chew wasp ran into the club mouth first. It glanced off to the right and shredded its wing on the club's teeth in passing. Alan left it flopping around on the rug and wheeled into the foyer. It wasn't going anywhere with one wing and he could administer the *coup de grace* later. Right now Alan wanted to kick that etagere back into place before any more of its friends got in.

He smelled them first—that rotten carrion odor. And as he rounded the corner from the living room into the foyer he saw two spearheads and another chew wasp wriggle free from behind the etagere and take flight. Either they didn't see him or they ignored him as they winged up the open curved stairway toward the darkness of the second floor.

Looking for Jeffy.

At top speed he rolled his chair over to the etagere. Not only had it been pushed away from the door, it had been moved with enough force to bend the nails onto their backs and now rested atop them.

Alan shook his head grimly. "How in the world . . . ?"

Time enough later to ponder how the little monsters had done this. Right now he had to plug the hole.

With a quick glance over his shoulder at the stairs, Alan slid off the wheelchair to his knees as he had before and threw his weight against the etagere. A squeaky scrape echoed through the foyer as it slid back over the nails and settled again on the floor, flush against the door. Alan turned and leaned his back against it.

Okay. No more could get in, at least for the moment. Now he had to find a way to secure it here until morning. He glanced at his watch. 6:22. Morning was almost three hours away. Well, he could sit here all night, just like this; that would do it. Three hours on this marble floor wasn't forever; it would only seem that way. The problem with staying here was that he was a sitting duck for the bugs that had already got in. He knew there were at least three. There could be more.

He hefted the billy. At least he didn't have to concern himself with hunting them down. Sooner or later—most likely sooner—they'd come hunting him. He'd have to be—

The etagere bucked against his back.

Startled, Alan half turned and leaned hard against it with his shoulder. The piece slid back into place.

What the hell was that?

Uneasiness prickled Alan's scalp. That was no chew wasp pushing through its hole. There'd been power behind that thrust. Something big was out there. Bigger than—

Alan suddenly remembered the dents in the storm shutter out front, and that long depression in the yard. He had a feeling whatever had been responsible for them was back.

Christ!

He didn't know what it was using to push the etagere but Alan had been able to push it back, so maybe things weren't so bad as they seemed.

And then the etagere moved again, a good foot this time, sliding Alan along with it. He pushed back, his feet scraping along the marble floor, searching for purchase and finding little. And even if they had, he doubted he'd be able to do much.

If only I had two good legs! he thought, his heart pumping wildly as he brought all his upper body strength to bear on the etagere. I could beat this thing!

But what *was* this thing? How was it pushing the etagere?

As if in answer to his question, a smooth black tentacle, glistening in the candlelight, slid up from the other side and unerringly darted toward his face. Alan ducked and swung at it with his club.

And missed. The tentacle had dodged the blow, almost as if it could see. It came for him again immediately and wrapped around his wrist. Its touch was cold and damp, but not slippery; Alan yanked back in revulsion but couldn't pull free. His skin was stuck, as if the tentacle was coated with glue. It began drawing him toward the door.

Thoroughly frightened now, Alan quickly switched the club to his other hand and began pounding on the tentacle. The embedded teeth opened gashes that grew deeper and leaked foul-smelling black liquid with every blow. The traction eased, the grip loosened, and Alan was free again.

But only for a heartbeat. Another tentacle snaked in beside the damaged one and reached for him. Alan fell back, reached into his wheelchair pouch, and fumbled around until he found the ax. It wasn't a big ax—a hatchet, really, with a short handle and a wedged head, no more than three inches along the cutting edge. But it was sharp. Alan got a good grip and swung it at the new tentacle. The blade sank deep, severing it clean through about a foot behind the tip. The proximal end whipped back immediately, spraying the foyer with its ebony equivalent of blood, while the free tip wriggled about.

All right! Alan thought. I can beat it!

He pushed the etagere out of the way and quick-crawled to the door, positioning himself to the right of the hole. The little holes had merged into one hole now—a little arch about eighteen inches wide and about four inches high. He'd barely set himself when a third tentacle slithered through the near edge. He severed it with a single chop and that tip joined its brother on the floor. A fourth tentacle darted in, then a fifth. Alan hacked at them as soon as they appeared and they withdrew, wounded.

"Yes!" he said, the word hissing softly between his teeth. "Keep 'em coming, you bastards! It's circumcision time! Let's see if you've got more tentacles than I've got chops!"

He was pumped. He knew he was acting a little bit crazy, but that was because he was *feeling* a little bit crazy. Maybe he'd been in that wheelchair too long. Whatever, here he was, free of it, weapon in hand, defending Toad Hall. He hadn't felt this alive in years.

Suddenly half a dozen fresh tentacles surged through at once, rearing up, reaching for his arms, his face. He swung wildly at them, catching one in mid air, one against the door. He was taking a bead on another when he heard buzzing wings and gnashing teeth above and behind him.

The bugs!

Instinctively, he ducked, but too late. Pain ripped through his left ear. He touched a hand to the side of his face. It came away red. Alan turned and grabbed the billy. Now he had a weapon in each hand—hatchet in right, club in left—and he was eager to use them. The pain and the blood from his ear had released something within him. His fear was gone, replaced by a seething rage at these creatures who dared to invade his home and threaten the people he loved.

Damn you! Damn you all to hell!

He chopped at an extended tentacle, severing its tip, then heard the buzz again and swung blindly at the air.

And connected. The broken, oozing body of the chew wasp— its jaws still smeared with blood from Alan's ear—bounced off the door and fell to the floor. Immediately, one of the tentacles coiled around its squirming form and yanked it outside.

Alan chopped at a particularly thick tentacle, severing it half way through. As he drew back to finish the job, something slammed against his back, shooting a blaze of pain through his right shoulder. He grunted with the sudden agony. As wings buzzed furiously by his ear, he dropped the billy and reached over his shoulder. When his questing fingers found the horny beak piercing his flesh, he knew a spearhead was trying to make him its next meal. It must have come in at an angle and glanced off his shoulder blade. A direct hit would have put it right through to his chest cavity, collapsing his right lung and leaving him with a sucking chest wound. He had to get it out before it dug itself deeper and finished the job.

Alan wrapped his fingers around the twisting, gnawing beak and yanked. He was rewarded by another eruption of vision- dimming pain, but the spearhead came free. It writhed and twisted and wriggled and flapped madly as he brought it around front. But as he raised his hatchet to chop it in half, the tentacle he'd wounded seconds ago coiled around his right wrist and wrenched it toward the door. He groaned as the sudden movement sent a bolt of pain lancing down his arm from the shoulder wound. His fingers went numb momentarily; he lost his grip on the hatchet handle and dropped it. But he couldn't worry about that now. He had to get his right hand free. *Now.* So Alan struck at the tentacle with the only weapon he had—the bug writhing in his left hand.

Using the spearhead's pointed beak as a knife, he stabbed and slashed madly, repeatedly. Desperate breaths hissed between his teeth. This was out of hand now. He'd lost the high ground and was on the defensive. He spotted a slew of new tentacles sliding under the door—how many did this thing *have?*

He had to retreat. He was going to be in very big trouble if he didn't pull free in the next few seconds and get out of reach.

He took a big swing with the spearhead, angling it so it cut into the open, oozing area he'd previously damaged with the hatchet. As the bug's sharp beak pierced through the far side, Alan pushed it deeper, cramming it into the tissues. It must have struck a vital nerve trunk because the distal end of the tentacle went into spasm, coiling and uncoiling wildly.

Alan pulled free of its grasp and immediately rolled away from the door. Leaving his wheelchair behind, he rose to his hands and knees and scrambled across the foyer floor toward the living room.

He almost made it.

Two strong, healthy legs would have got him to safety. He cursed his legs as they slumped beneath him, slowing him down. His right arm was letting him down too. He had to depend on his arms for a good part of his speed, but the right one was wounded. His left hand was just inches from the living room carpet when he felt something coil about his ankle. Even then, a good strong kick might have freed him, but his legs didn't have a good strong kick in them. He realized then that he should have tried for the stairs. If he'd have been able to reach the newel post of the bannister he'd have had something to hold on to.

As the tentacle dragged him back, Alan clawed at the marble floor, looking for a crack, a seam, anything to hold on to, but there was nothing. It had been too expertly installed. He kicked feebly with his free leg but then felt another tentacle wrap around that ankle and worm its way up to his thigh.

And now he was being dragged back at a faster rate.

He spotted his hatchet where he'd dropped it. He tried to reach it. He stretched his good arm and fingers to the limit, until he thought his shoulder would dislocate, but could not get near it. Like a departing sailor gazing at his home port from the stern of a ship, he watched the hatchet slip further and further out of reach.

Next came his wheelchair. He grabbed at that, caught hold of a foot rest but it simply rolled with him. He clutched it because it was all he had to hold on to.

And then other tentacles, Alan couldn't count how many, looped and coiled around his legs, and he couldn't kick free now, even if he'd had two good legs. He was helpless. Utterly helpless.

I'm going to die.

Although he never stopped struggling against the inexorable tug of the tentacles, the realization was a sudden cold weight in his heart. Fear and dread shot through him, but not panic. Mostly there was sadness. Tears sprang into his eyes. Tears for all the things he'd never do, like walking again, or watching Jeffy grow up, or growing old with Sylvia, but most of all, for the way he'd be dying. He'd never feared the moment, but then he'd always imagined the moment arriving when he was gray and withered and bedfast and that he'd welcome it with open arms.

The tentacles dragged his legs through the opening at the bottom of the door. The jagged wood raked the backs of his thighs and then dug into the flesh of his hips and buttocks as he became wedged into the opening.

He wasn't going to fit through. At least not in one piece.

Oh God, oh God, oh God, I don't want to die like this!

And suddenly amid the fear and the grief and the pain he realized that he had to die a certain way. He'd been given no choice in how death was coming to him but he had something to say about how he met it.

Silently.

He groaned as the traction on his legs increased and the ligaments and tendons and skin and muscles began to stretch past their tolerances.

Quiet!

He reached up and grabbed the thin cotton blanket from the wheelchair and stuffed it deep into his mouth, gagging as the fabric brushed the back of his throat.

Good. Gag. Then he couldn't scream. And he *mustn't* scream.

Oh God, the pain!

He *had* to be quiet because if he let the pain and fear out in a scream, Sylvia would wake and come for him . . . he knew her, knew if she thought he was in danger, she wouldn't hesitate, she'd charge, she'd wade through a storm of bugs and tentacles to get to him . . .

Alan screeched silently into his blanket-stuffed mouth as the ball at the head of his right femur twisted free and dislocated from the hip socket with a grinding explosion of agony, and screamed again as the left one followed.

Quiet, quiet, QUIET!

. . . because it was too late for him and if she came upstairs they'd have her too, and after they got Sylvia, they'd get Jeffy and then Glaeken wouldn't be able to assemble whatever it was he had to assemble and the Enemy would win it all and the bugs would feast on everybody . . . he just prayed he'd bought Sylvia and Jeffy enough time . . . prayed his body would stay wedged in the opening and block the bugs out for a while because soon Toad Hall would be swarming with them and if they had enough time they'd gnaw through the cellar door and all this agony would be for nothing . . . so he had to hold on and keep quiet for just a few more seconds because in just a few more seconds it would be over and . . .

Alan's blanket drank the howl that burst from his throat as his right leg ripped free of his body and slid away into the night and yet he smiled within as he felt his consciousness draining away in the warm red stream pumping from his ruptured femoral artery, smiled because there's nothing quieter than a dead man.

dead air

"Alan?"

Sylvia awoke with a start and stared wildly around her, momentarily disoriented in the darkness. Then she saw the candle flickering on the ping-pong table and remembered she was in the basement. She reached out a hand and found Jeffy's slumbering form curled next to her on the old Castro convertible.

She squinted at the luminous dial on her watch. 7:30. Had she been asleep that long? She must have been more tired than she'd thought. At least the night had gone quickly. Sunrise was due at 9:10. Another long, long night was drawing to a close. She stretched. Soon Alan would be knocking on the upstairs door, telling them all to rise and—

Then she heard it.

On the upstairs door—scratching. She leapt out of bed and hurried to the foot of the steps to listen again.

No—not scratching. *Gnawing.*

Trembling, chewing her upper lip, Sylvia crept up the stairs, telling herself with each tread that she was wrong, that it couldn't be, that her ears had to be playing dirty tricks on her. Half-way up she caught the smell and abruptly ran out of denials. She rushed the rest of the way to the door where she pressed the flats of her hands against the solid oak panels and felt the vibrations as countless teeth scored the outer surface.

Alan! Dear God, where's Alan?

She turned the knob and gripped it with both hands as she leaned her shoulder against the door. *Bugs in Toad Hall.* She had to see. She could hear them and smell them but she had to see them to believe there were that many of the horrors in her house. She edged the door open a crack and saw a sliver of the hallway. The creatures immediately attacked the opening and she slammed the door shut. But she'd seen enough.

Bugs. The hall was choked with them—floating, drifting, darting, bumping, hanging on the walls.

Sylvia began to tremble. If the halls had been taken over by the bugs, where was Alan? To invade Toad Hall they had to get past Alan.

"Alan?" she cried, her face against the vibrating door.

Maybe he got to the movie room and locked himself in there. Maybe he was safe.

But those were only words. She could find no place in her heart and mind that truly believed them. A sob built in her throat and ripped free as a scream.

"ALAN!"

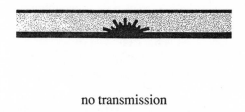

HBO

no transmission

2 • HOMECOMINGS

MONROE, LONG ISLAND

"Go faster, Jack. Go faster, please."

Ba wished he were behind the wheel. As the familiar streets and storefronts of downtown Monroe flashed by, his anxiety increased with every passing block. *Empty* streets, *smashed* storefronts, and only a few frightened people hurrying through the waning afternoon light. The town had deteriorated badly in the two days since he'd left.

"Easy, Ba," Jack said beside him. "I'm doing the best I can. Hell, I'm barely slowing down for stop signs, and none of the traffic lights are working. If we run into someone crossing our path we may not get there at all."

Bill Ryan laid a hand gently on Ba's shoulder.

"Jack's right. Between us we've traveled more than half way around the globe and back. It'd be a shame to crack up and die so close to home. This is, after all, the car that was labeled 'Unsafe at any speed.'"

"A lie!" Jack said vehemently. "Nader's first Big Lie!"

Ba disliked letting other people drive, but this little American car that had been discontinued even before he'd come to America had no space for him behind the wheel. He closed his eyes and willed the car closer to Toad Hall.

He had spent the entire trip home from Maui in this state of anguished fear. He could not escape the notion that something terrible was happening at Toad

Hall without him. He had been unable to get through to the Missus from the phone in the jet. Just a word or two from the Missus, that was all he would have required to ease his mind. But he could not make the connection.

Fortunately the trip had gone well. They had caught the jet stream and made it back to Long Island without a fuel stop in California. Even more fortunate, Bill Ryan and Nick had already arrived and were waiting for them when they touched down.

Ba had tried to call again from the hangar phone but still there was no response. And so now he was being driven toward the scene of a tragedy. He knew it. He should not have left Toad Hall. If anything had happened to the Missus and her family . . .

Here was Shore Drive. Now the front wall of Toad Hall's grounds, the gate posts, the curving driveway, the willows, Toad Hall itself, the front door—

"Oh, shit," Jack said softly beside Ba. "Oh, no."

"Missus!"

The word escaped Ba when he saw how the bottom half of the front door had been smashed through and torn away. He was out the door and running toward the house before the car stopped. He took the front steps in a bound. The door hung open, angled on its hinges. He burst through and skidded to a halt in the foyer.

Carnage. Furniture strewn about, wallpaper hanging in tatters from the walls like sunburned skin, the Doctor's wheelchair sitting empty in the middle of the floor, and blood. Dried blood puddled on the threshold and splattering the outer surface of the door.

Fear such as he'd never known gripped Ba's throat and squeezed. He'd battled the Cong and fought off the pirates on the South China Sea, but they'd never made him feel weak and helpless like the sight of blood in Toad Hall.

He ran through the house then, calling for the Missus, the Doctor, Jeffy. Through the deserted upstairs, back down to the movie room, to another staggering halt before the cellar door. The door stood ajar, its finish gnawed off, its beveled panels splintered, nearly obliterated. Ba pulled it open the rest of the way and stood at the top of the stairs.

"Missus? Doctor? Jeffy?"

No answer from below. He spotted the flashlight lying on the second step. He picked it up and descended slowly, dreading what he'd find.

Or wouldn't find.

The basement was empty. A red candle had burned down to a puddle on the ping-pong table. Ba's finger trembled as he reached out and touched the pooled wax. Cold.

Feeling dead inside, he dragged himself up the stairs and wandered out to the front drive. Jack and Bill were standing by the car, waiting for him, watching him.

Bill said, "Are they . . . ?"

"They're gone," Ba said. His voice was so low, he could barely hear himself.

"Hey, Ba," Jack said. "Maybe they left for—"

"There's blood. So much blood."

"Aw, Jeez," Jack said softly.

Bill lowered his head and pressed a hand over his eyes.

"What do you want us to do, Ba?" Jack said. "You name it, we'll do it."

A good friend, this Jack. They had only met a few days ago and already he was acting like a brother. But nothing could ease the pain in Ba's heart, the growing grief, the bitter self- loathing for leaving the people he loved—his *family*— unguarded. Why had he—?

He whirled at the sound of a car engine starting in the garage at the rear of the house. He knew that engine. It belonged to the 1938 Graham—the Missus' favorite car.

Fighting the joy that surged up in him, afraid to acknowledge it for fear that it might be for nothing, Ba stumbled into a run toward the rear. He had gone only a few steps when the Graham's shark-nosed grille appeared around the corner of the house. The Missus was behind the wheel, Jeffy beside her. Her mouth formed an *O* when she saw him. The old car stalled as she braked and then she was out the door and running across the grass toward Ba, arms outflung, face twisted in uncontrollable grief.

"Oh, Ba! Ba! We waited all day for you! I thought we'd lost you too!"

And then the Missus did something she had never done before. She threw her arms around Ba, clung to him and began to sob against his chest.

Ba did not know what to do. He held his arms akimbo, not sure of where to put them. As overjoyed as he was to see her alive, it certainly was not his place to embrace the Missus. But her grief was so deep, so unrestrained . . . he had never seen her like this, never guessed she was capable of this magnitude of sorrow.

And then Jeffy ran up, and he, too, was crying. He threw his arms around Ba's left leg and hung there.

Gently, gingerly, hesitantly, Ba lowered one hand to the Missus' shoulder and the other to Jeffy's head. His elation at seeing them was tempered by the slowly dawning realization that the picture was incomplete.

Someone was missing.

"The Doctor, Missus?"

"Oh, Ba, he's gone," she sobbed. "Those . . . *things* . . . killed him and dragged him off! He's gone, Ba! Alan's gone and we'll never see him again!"

For a moment Ba thought he glimpsed the Doctor's face peering at him from the shadows in the back seat of the Graham, thought he felt the warmth of his easy smile, the aura of his deep honor and quiet courage.

And then he faded from view and something happened to Ba, something that hadn't happened since his boyhood days in the fishing village where he was born.

Ba began to weep.

As the Change progresses above, so progresses the Change below.

Rasalom's new form grows ever larger. Suspended in its cavern, it is the size of an elephant now. To make room for him, more earth drops away into the soft yellow glow of the bottomless pit below.

With his senses penetrating deep into the earth, Rasalom knows that the Change is progressing unimpeded, and is far ahead of schedule. Chaos reigns above. The sweet honey nectar of fear and misery, the ambrosia of rage and ruin continues to seep through the strata of the earth to nourish him, help him grow, make him ever stronger.

And in the center of the dying city, Glaeken's building stands unmolested, an island of tranquility in a sea of torment. Members of his pathetic little company now rushing back from their trips here and there around the globe with their recovered bits and pieces of the first and second swords All of them, still clinging so doggedly to their hope.

Good. Rasalom wants to let that hope grow until it is the last great hope left for all humanity. Let them think they've been doing something important, something epochal. The higher their hope lifts them, the longer the fall when they learn they've struggled and died for nothing.

But Rasalom senses them taking comfort in their relative safety, drawing strength from their comradeship. Their peace, uneasy though it may be, is a burr in his hide. He cannot allow this to continue unchallenged. He does not wish to destroy them—yet. But he does wish to breach their insulation, unsettle them, vex them, start them looking over their shoulders.

One of them must die.

Not out in the streets, but in the heart of their safe haven. It must be an ugly death—nothing quick and clean, but slow and painful and messy. And to make the death as unsettling as possible, it must befall a dear member of their number, one who seems the most innocent, the most innocuous, one they never would expect him to single out for such degradation.

The new lips gestating within the sac twist into a semblance of a smile.

Time for a little fun.

In the tunnel leading to the cavern, Rasalom's skin, shed days ago, begins to move. It ripples, swells, fills out to living proportions. Then it rises and begins its journey toward the surface.

As it walks, it tests its voice.

"Mother."

Ba should be driving this, Bill thought as he raced along the deserted LIE, aiming the old Graham for the Queens-Midtown Tunnel like a bullet from a gun. He glanced at his watch. 3:32. Less than forty minutes to sundown. He would have preferred the Queensboro Bridge but remembered that was impassable due to the effects of a gravity hole.

Jack rode shotgun—literally. He sat high in the passenger seat with this huge short-barreled thing—he'd called it a "Spas"—held up in plain sight. Ba sat behind Bill with a similar shotgun in plain view. The two warriors were sending a message: Don't mess with this car. Nick sat behind Jack, Sylvia and the boy were squeezed in the middle, their cat on the boy's lap, their one-eyed dog panting on the floor.

That left the driving chore to Bill. He knew he wasn't the greatest driver, but if they ran into one of the roving gangs that had taken over the city during the day he figured he'd do better with a steering wheel than with a shotgun.

He glanced at Jack who'd been strangely silent and withdrawn since their reunion at the airport. He was definitely on edge. Something eating at him, something he wasn't talking about.

Bill gave a mental shrug. If it concerned them, they'd find out soon enough.

The further he drove into Queens, the more obstacles on the expressway; he wove as quickly as he dared around and through the litter of wrecked or abandoned cars. They slowed him and he wanted to fly.

Carol . . . he hungered for the sight of her, for the sound of her voice, the touch of her hand. She consumed his thoughts, his feelings. He wished he could have got a line through to her from the airport, just to let her know he'd made it back and was coming home.

"Better hurry," Nick said from the back.

"Going as fast as I can, Nick."

"Better go faster," he said. His tone was completely flat. He'd reverted to near cataonia since leaving the keep. "It's Carol."

The car swerved slightly as Bill's fingers tightened on the wheel.

"What about Carol?"

"She's in trouble. She needs help."

WNYW-TV

no transmission

MANHATTAN

The head was waiting in the kitchen.

Carol was on her way back from Magda's room, carrying her lunch tray, worrying about Bill and why she hadn't heard from him yet. She screamed and dropped the tray as she rounded the corner and saw it floating in the air. She recognized the face.

"Jimmy!" she cried, then got control of herself.

Not a head, just a face. And not Jimmy. Not her son. She'd almost stopped thinking of him as her son.

Rasalom. It was Rasalom.

The face smiled—an Arctic gale registered greater warmth. Then its lips moved, forming words, but the voice seemed to come from everywhere. Or was it inside her head?

"Hello, mother."

Carol backed out of the kitchen. The face followed.

"Mommy, don't leave me!" The tone was mocking.

Carol stopped retreating when her back came up against the dining room table. She looked around for Glaeken but knew he wouldn't be there. He'd gone out hours ago and had left her with Magda. Carol swallowed and found her voice.

"Don't call me that!"

"Why not? That's what you are."

Carol shook her head. "No. You grew inside me for nine months, but you were never my child. And I was never your mother."

Another smile, as cold as the first. *"I sympathize with your efforts to dissociate yourself from me. I understand them because I've tried to do the same in regard to you. Perhaps you've had more success than I."*

"What are you talking about?"

"The bond of flesh. Since the day I was conceived within you, I've worn the flesh you gave me. It links us. I don't like it any more than you do, but it is a fact, one that won't go away. One we both have to deal with."

"I've learned to deal with it—by not thinking about it."

"But that doesn't cancel it. I've given this a lot of thought and there's a better way to deal with it, a way that allows me to come to terms with my fleshy link to you. A way that can benefit you as well."

The voice in her head was so calm, so soothing. Almost mesmerizing. Carol shook herself.

"I—I don't want anything from you."

"Don't think just of yourself. Think of your friends. I'm offering you and some of them a safe harbor, a haven, a chance to survive the endless night."

"I don't trust you."

The smile again, rueful this time. *"I wouldn't trust me either. But hear me out. You have nothing to lose by listening to my proposal."*

Carol remembered what Bill had told her about a woman named Lisl who'd lost her soul and her life by listening to Rasalom. But what, besides her sanity and her dignity, did Carol have left to lose? Unless a miracle occurred, tomorrow would hold the world's last daylight. By Friday she'd be in the same leaky life raft as the rest of the world.

"What do you mean by 'a haven'? And how many of my 'friends' can I take there?"

"A reasonable number."

"Glaeken among them?"

The face rotated back and forth, the equivalent of a head shake.

"No. Not Glaeken. Anyone else, but not Glaeken. I've waited too long to even my scores with him."

Carol didn't know what to think, what to do. If Rasalom had agreed to allow Glaeken safe harbor, she'd have known he was lying. There was probably no rivalry, no enmity in human history as long and as bitter and as deeply ingrained as theirs. But he had excluded Glaeken. What did that mean? Could his offer be genuine? If she could save Bill and a few of the others . . .

"Come downstairs and we'll discuss it."

"Downstairs? Oh, no. I'm not leaving this building."

"I'm not asking you to leave this building. I'm one floor down. In your apartment."

"How—how did you get in?

"Come now, Mother dear. I can do anything I wish. Anything. Come visit. We'll talk. I'll be there until darkness falls. After that I'll have other matters to attend to."

The face grew dim, became transparent, then faded completely. Gone as if it had never been.

Carol sagged back against the table. *Expect the unexpected.* Wasn't that what Glaeken had said? Easy enough to say, but Rasalom's face—floating in the air, talking to her as casually as if they'd bumped into each other in an aisle at the A&P.

And the ease with which he seemed to have entered the building was bad enough, but knowing he was waiting down in her apartment tied her up in knots.

Should she go? That was the question. And what was this all about? Was she supposed to haggle with him? Barter for lives? The responsibility was numbing.

Maybe she could ask him about Hank—where he was, *if* he was. She should have thought of that when Rasalom was here.

She had to risk it. If she could save even a few people . . .

But she didn't want to go alone. She knew she had to, but she didn't like it. She didn't have much time, either. If only she had a weapon of some sort. But what could she use against someone who could change the course of the sun and anything else he pleased?

As Carol picked up the broken dishes from the kitchen floor and threw them away, she spotted the knife rack over the sink. She pulled out the wide-bladed carving knife and tucked it into the folds of the old cardigan she had borrowed from Glaeken. A laughable weapon, considering who she'd be facing. She knew her best hope was not to need any weapon at all, but the weight of the blade in her hand imparted a modicum of comfort.

She peeked in on Magda and found her sleeping soundly. Carol guessed it would be all right to leave her for a few minutes. Glaeken would be back soon, and Rasalom had said he'd wait only until dark.

She hurried downstairs.

Her apartment had an empty feel. The drapes were open but because the windows faced north, the light was dusky.

Was he here? What was she supposed to call out? Jimmy? Rasalom? Certainly not *Son.*

"Hello?" she said, settling on that. "Are you here?"

She walked through the living room and down the hall. Why didn't he answer? Was this some sort of a joke?

Suddenly he was there, stepping out of the bedroom not three feet in front of her.

He was naked.

Carol cried out in shock and jumped back.

"Hello, *Mother.*" His voice was coarse, raspy, more dead than alive.

He stepped toward her as she backed away. His slim body seemed faintly luminescent, and his genitals . . . he was hugely erect, pointing directly at her face. Suddenly he darted by her and positioned himself between her and the door.

She turned and faced him, her heart thudding, her palm slick on the handle of the knife in her sweater.

"Wh-what's this all about? I thought you wanted to talk."

He smiled. "Isn't it wonderful what desperation will do to people? It paralyzes some, makes others brutish, and makes still others *stupid.* You fall into that final category, *Mother*." He spat the last word. "What's it about? It's about a love note to Glaeken and the rest of you. It's about defilement and slow, painful death, Mother. Incestuous rape and matricide. In other words, you and me."

He leapt at her. Reflexively Carol pulled out the knife and held it before her with both hands. She felt the impact as Rasalom's body struck it, felt the skin part before the point, felt the blade sink deep into his flesh. He grunted and stepped back. He looked down in wonder at the knife handle protruding from his upper abdomen, just below the breast bone. He touched the handle with a finger, then looked up at her.

"Mother . . . you shock me. I guess there are still a few surprises left in this world."

"Oh, God!"

"He won't help you. He was never there. But I am here now. And I am your God. Think of it, Mother. You are about to be raped by God. And afterwards . . . ." He caressed the handle like a priapic tool . . . "I shall use this to skin you alive. Won't that be a nice gift to hang in Glaeken's closet? Your skin."

Carol screamed and tried to dash past him but he caught her with one hand and slammed her back against the wall. The breath wooshed out of her with the impact. As she tried to regain it, the door to the apartment burst open.

"Carol!"

A group of men—some of then armed—burst in, and in the lead was Bill. He leapt to her side and Carol clung to him, sobbing.

"Oh, Bill, oh, Bill, thank God you're here!"

"You!" It was Bill. He was staring at Rasalom who had stepped back and appeared to be surveying the scene with amusement.

Jack stepped forward and faced Rasalom, a shotgun of some sort cradled in his arms. Ba stood by the door, similarly armed, while Nick stood behind him in the hall.

"Who the hell are you?" Jack said.

"I once knew him as Rafe Losmara," Bill said. "But his real name is Rasalom."

Jack's expression was skeptical as he glanced at Bill, then back to Rasalom's slim, naked figure.

"You're kidding. This . . . *this* is the cause of everything that's going on out there?"

Rasalom bowed, unfazed by the intruders. "At your service."

Bill was staring at the handle protruding from Rasalom's abdomen.

"Is that a knife . . . ?"

"Probably," Jack said. The sight of the knife seemed to incite him. Jack appeared ready to explode. "I think I've been through this movie before."

As Carol wondered what Jack meant, Rasalom smiled and yanked the blade free.

"Please don't be concerned, Father Bill. I'm a rapid healer."

"Yeah?" Jack said. His face was tight with rage. In a single smooth, swift motion he had his shotgun extended to arm's length, its muzzle inches from Rasalom's face. "Heal this."

The explosion was deafening. Close against her Bill cried out in shock as Carol screamed and turned away, but not before she saw Rasalom's head disintegrate behind the muzzle flash.

A moment later, Bill's hushed, awed whisper slipped past the ringing in her ears.

"Look at that!"

Carol turned and saw Rasalom's headless body lying on the floor. It seemed to be shrinking, deflating. And then she saw why. Loose soil was pouring from the stump of his neck.

"Dirt," Jack said, nudging the body with his toe. "The guy was nothing but skin filled with dirt." His eyes were more than a little wild above his fierce grin. "A real dirt bag."

Glaeken hobbled through the doorway then.

"What has happened here?"

Carol quickly ran over the events of the past twenty minutes. Glaeken nodded with slow resignation.

"Leave your skin in my closet, he told you?" Glaeken said.

Carol felt Bill tighten his grip around her shoulders.

"Why?" Bill said. "What does it mean?"

"More of his games," Glaeken said. "A diversion while he waits for the Change to be complete, one more thing to confound, confuse, sicken, and terrify. He probably meant to leave Carol's skin and his own. A grisly reminder to me that his Change is far along to completion."

Glaeken went to Rasalom's remains and lifted the skin by both feet. Jack helped. Together they shook the last of the dirt from within. It looked dry and light, almost like an oversized set of a child's footed pajamas. Glaeken rolled it up and tucked it under his arm and started for the door.

"Come upstairs. I want to get rid of this once and for all. Then we have work to do."

Rasalom's skin smoked, curled, browned, blackened, and burned in the fireplace. Carol watched as Glaeken pushed it deeper into the flames with the poker. As the ashes curled and rose up the flue, he turned and surveyed the gathering of his inner circle.

Carol surveyed it as well. The newcomers were Sylvia Nash and her son, huddled against her. Pale, distant, remote in her grief, Sylvia sat quietly in a corner of the huge sofa. Carol's heart went out to her. Alan was missing. Bill had told her what had happened last night in Monroe. She hadn't got to know that man in the wheelchair, but during their brief contact last Saturday Carol had sensed something fine and strong within him. And now, looking at Sylvia, she could sense a comparable rebellious strength within her. This woman had been battered but refused to bow. Ba stood tall behind her like some preternatural guardian.

Carol leaned against Bill; Nick sat stiff and straight but inattentive on Bill's far side.

And at the far end of the sofa sat Jack, aloof, silent, nearly as withdrawn as Nick.

"Well," Glaeken said, jamming his hands into his pockets, "our wanderers have returned. What have you brought back with you?"

Bill reached into a sack and pulled out a few odd-shaped pieces of rusted metal. He dropped them onto the marble-topped coffee table.

"This is the best I could do."

Glaeken picked up the pieces, examined them closely, then nodded.

"Amazing. These are from the blade. How——?"

"Nick helped. I'd never have found them without Nick's help. But are they . . . is it enough?"

"These are fine. We only need a sample of the metal." He turned to Jack. "How did you fare in Maui?"

Jack tossed a heavy, intricately carved necklace onto the table. It rolled and skidded to a stop in front of Glaeken.

"Let's hope you just need a sample of that too."

Glaeken picked it up. He didn't examine it. He seemed to know it was right merely by touching it.

"Very good. Oh, very good. Where's the other?"

"That's the problem," Jack said, keeping his eyes down. "I couldn't get it."

Carol noticed Glaeken's complexion fade two or three shades toward white. He seated himself—carefully.

"Couldn't . . . get it?"

Jack capsulized his travails on Maui.

"I got suckered," he said when he was done. "Kolabati seemed different. I thought she'd changed. I was wrong. Dead wrong. But that's okay, right? You've got enough here to do your thing, right? I mean, you've got the kid, pieces of the old sword, and one of the necklaces. That's enough, right?"

Glaeken sat motionless for an endless moment, then he shook his head, slowly, painfully.

"No, Jack. I wish it were, but we need the combined power within the pair of necklaces to make this work."

Jack shot to his feet and began to pace the room. Carol had learned something about him from Glaeken during the past few days, how he made his living working for people who had been let down by everyone else. She had the distinct impression that here was a man unused to failure, and that his failure here was eating him alive.

"I don't know where she is. She took off, disappeared. She could be anywhere."

"It's all right, Jack," Glaeken sad. "You did your best."

"But I didn't get it done. That's the bottom line: I didn't get it *done!*"

"I doubt if anyone else on earth could have returned with even one of the necklaces."

"All fine and good. But you're telling me one necklace doesn't cut it, so the whole trip was a waste of time. And Bill's trip was a waste of time. And I took Ba with me, and maybe if he'd stayed home . . . "

Jack didn't finish the thought. He stopped and faced the group. His eyes were tortured. It took him a moment to find his voice again.

"I blew it, didn't I? And because of that, there's no way out now, for any of us. I've let you all down. I'm sorry."

He turned and started for the door. Carol tried to think of something to say that would ease his pain, lighten his load, but before she could call out to him, she saw Sylvia reach out and grab his arm as he passed. He stopped and stared down at her. She rose wordlessly, slipped her arms around him, and hugged him.

For a moment Jack stood stiffly, looking baffled, then he lifted his arms and returned the embrace. He closed his eyes as if in pain.

Bill rose to his feet and Carol rose with him.

"It's okay, Jack," Bill said. "Really. We know you gave it your best shot. If you couldn't do it, then it couldn't be done. We trust in that. And if that's the way it is, then that's the way it is. We go on from here as best we can."

He stepped toward Jack and extended his hand.

Jack eased away from Sylvia and gripped Bill's hand, then Carol hugged him, then Glaeken offered his own hand.

His throat working, his voice on the verge of crumbling, Jack stepped back and stared at the semicircle that had formed around him.

"You people . . . you people. Where'd you all come from? Where've you been all my life?"

His voice failed him then, so he simply turned and walked out the door.

When he was gone, they stood and stared at each other in silence.

"There's no hope then?" Carol said.

Glaeken heaved a sigh, slow and heavy, as he shook his head. His eyes were remote, his disappointment palpable.

"If there is," he said, "I don't know where to look for it."

"That's it?" she said. "We've lost? What do we do now?"

"We do what we've always done," Bill said. "We don't back down. And we refuse to be anything less than we are."

Carol looked at him standing tall and defiant. He'd told her what he'd been through in the past five years, and if that hadn't broken him, she doubted anything could. She realized then in a blaze of heat how much she loved Bill Ryan.

Glaeken, too, seemed to draw strength from him.

"You're right of course. We can make Rasalom come for us rather than crumble and fall toward him. That will be a victory of sorts." He extended his elbow toward Sylvia. "Mrs. Nash, if you'll allow me, I'll show you the apartment I've been holding for you."

As they left, Bill turned to Nick.

"Want me take you back to your room, old buddy?"

Nick was staring at the flames in the fireplace. To Carol's surprise, he answered.

"I want to watch the fire. I want to see where all the ashes go."

Carol dared a quick glance at the fireplace, ready to turn away if Rasalom's skin was still there. But it wasn't—at least not recognizably so. Just burning logs.

"They go up the chimney and float away, Nick," Carol said.

"Not all of them. Some are on the window."

Carol turned and for the first time noticed the ashes sticking to the picture window. She gasped and clutched Bill's arm when she realized that they clung there in a gray, feathery pattern—the shape of a headless man, spread-eagled against the dying light.

Bill hurried to the wall and touched a button. The drapes slid closed.

"Maybe I'd better walk you home."

"I can't go back there." The thought of that pile of dirt on the rug, the memory of what he'd planned to do—it sickened her.

"Sorry," he said. "I wasn't thinking."

Carol looked at Bill. She didn't know how else to say this, other than come right out and say it.

"Can't I stay with you?"

He stared at her for a long moment, then reached out to her, pulled her close, and kissed her.

"I've been wanting to do that for days," he sighed. "For years. For decades. Forever, I think."

She looked up at him, into his clear blue eyes.

"It's time, isn't it?"

He nodded. "Yes. Long past time, I think."

He took her hand and led her toward his room.

WXRK-FM:

dead air

Until tonight, Carol had made love to only two men in her life, both of them husbands. Bill was the third and by far the most anxious. His hands trembled as he undressed her, as he helped her remove his own clothes, as he caressed her.

"I'm a virgin," he told her when they were lying skin-to- skin, and even his voice trembled. "Alive for half a century, and I'm a virgin."

"I'm not," Carol said, and drew him into her.

What he lacked in technique he more than made up for with the intensity of his passion. Their lovemaking rocked the mattress. It was hot, it was fierce, and it was over too soon for Carol, but somehow it left her as breathless as Bill. She hugged him tight against her, reveled in his being warm and wet within her.

And then she heard him sobbing softly on her shoulder.

"Bill? Are you okay?"

"No. Yes. I don't know. It's just . . . I keep thinking . . . what a waste. This is so wonderful. I've never felt so close to another human being in my entire life. I'm fifty, Carol. We can all count the rest of our days on one hand, and I'm just learning what it's like to make love. All those years—wasted! My *life*—wasted! What an idiot!"

"Don't you say that, Bill. Don't you ever let me hear you say that!" She shared his hurt, but she was angry at him too. "You did *not* waste your life. Maybe your beliefs were misplaced, but not your actions. You spent your life being a father, a real father, to hundreds of lost and abandoned boys, the first and maybe the best father they ever knew. You couldn't have done that as well if you'd had a wife and children of your own. You couldn't have been there twenty-four hours a day for them like you were. So it wasn't wasted at all. You made a difference, Bill. A big difference. A lot of grown men are walking around who still remember you, who still have a warm place in their hearts for you, who are maybe good to their own kids because you were good to them, because you showed them how it's done. That's a legacy, Bill, one that might have gone on for generations if Rasalom wasn't trying to bring all our generations to an end. So don't you dare say you've wasted your life—at least not in front of me."

After a long pause, Bill lifted his head and kissed her.

"I love you," he said. "I puppy-loved you in high school and then buried it in an unused corner like a bone. But it never went away. I think I've always loved you."

"And I think part of me always loved you, a little bit. But now all of me loves you—a lot."

"Good. Does that mean we do this again? Soon?"

"How soon?"

"Now?"

And then she realized that he was hard again inside her.

"Oh my."

3 • THE FINAL PIECE

WNEW-FM:
JO: It's 4:00 in the afternoon, ten minutes to sunset.
FREDDY: Yeah. And according to the Sapir curve, this is the next to last sunset.
Let's all hope he's wrong, man.

Glaeken had settled Sylvia Nash and her son in her apartment and was on his way back to his own when Julio, the muscular little fellow who owned the bar where he and Jack had shared their first pint of Courage, ran up to him in the hall.

"Mr. Glaeken! There's a woman downstairs looking for Jack!"

"What does she want? You let her in, I hope." It was dark out now. The streets would be lethal.

"Yeah, but I've got somebody staying in the lobby with her. Thing is, I can't find Jack nowhere an' she's real crazy 'bout seeing him."

"Is it the woman he sent into hiding?"

"Gia? No way. I know Gia. This lady's dark. Says her name's Cola-body or som' like that."

Glaeken closed his eyes and steadied himself, making sure he'd really heard that last sentence. Could it be? Could it truly be her? Or could this be another of Rasalom's games?

Well, he'd know soon enough, wouldn't he?

"Bring her to the top floor. Immediately."

A few moments later, Glaeken was waiting by the door to his apartment when Julio ushered a slim, dark, raven-haired woman from the elevator. Her clothes were torn, her hands and face smudged with grime, the dark almonds of her eyes were wide, wild, exhausted. Not at all the way Glaeken had pictured her, but he sensed the years crowded beneath the smooth youth of her skin.

He could barely drag his eyes from the necklace encircling her throat. He had to get it from her. How he was going to do that, he did not know, but he could not allow her to leave here with that necklace.

"Miss Bahkti?"

She nodded. "And you're the man Jack told me about, the old one?"

The old one. He hid his smile. Is that how they speak of me? Well, it's true, isn't it? Truer than they imagine.

"Yes, that would be me. Call me Glaeken. Come in."

He nodded his thanks to Julio and ushered Kolabati into his apartment. She stumbled crossing the threshold and almost fell, but Glaeken caught her under the arm.

"Are you all right?"

She shook her head. "No. Not in the least."

He led her to the sofa. She all but fell into it. She rubbed a trembling hand over her eyes and sighed. She looked utterly exhausted.

"Jack told me what was happening to the world," she said. "I thought he was lying, trying to trick me. It couldn't be as bad as he said." She paused and looked up at Glaeken with haunted eyes. "But it's worse. Much worse."

Glaeken nodded, watching her closely. She appeared to be under extreme stress.

"And worse is yet to come."

She stared up at him. "Worse? Outside . . . one street over . . . something huge and black and slimy . . . so big it had to squeeze against the buildings on both sides to get down the street. It was covered with tentacles and it was reaching into the windows and pulling out anything it found. I heard people—children—screaming."

"A long dark night of the soul for the survivors," Glaeken said.

Kolabati shifted her gaze toward the fire and fingered her necklace.

"Did Jack return with the other necklace?"

"Yes."

"Is it sufficient for your needs?"

"No." Where was this leading?

"Then you still need this one?"

"Yes."

"Will it make a difference?" she said.

"It may. It may be too late now for anything to make a difference, but it is our only chance, our only hope. We must try it."

She continued to stare at the fire. Her voice was barely audible.

"All right then. You may have it."

A wave of relief struck Glaeken. The impact forced him to sit down. But before he could speak, Jack burst into the room.

"It *is* you!" he said, glaring at Kolabati. "Where'd you find the nerve to show up here?"

"Jack—" Her lips curved half way to a smile but Jack was in her face before they reached it.

"You lied to me! You agree to come back here and talk to Glaeken, then you pull a vanishing act."

Glaeken wanted to stop Jack before he said anything rash, but noticed that Kolabati was unfazed by the outburst. So he kept quiet.

"That's true," she said. "And I am here. And I've been talking to Glaeken."

Jack hovered over her, his anger visibly evaporating.

"Oh. Yeah, but you said—"

"I never said I'd come back *with* you. I said I'd come back. And I have—but on my terms, not yours. I am no one's prisoner, Jack. Ever."

"But how'd you get back?"

"Do you really believe you're the only one who knows a pilot willing to fly here from Maui?"

Jack jammed his hands in his pockets. "Obviously not."

Glaeken studied Jack and Kolabati as they faced off. He sensed more going on between these two than met the eye, but he had no time to concern himself with that. He jumped into the momentary lull.

"Jack," he said, "Miss Bahkti has agreed to give us her necklace."

"We already have it. You said it wasn't enough."

"No," Glaeken said softly. "The one she is wearing."

Jack's eyes narrowed with suspicion.

"What's the catch?"

"No catch, Jack," she said, her voice laden with exhaustion. "What I've seen on my journey from Maui has convinced me that you were not exaggerating. Everything is falling apart. This is not a world I wish to live in. If I keep the necklace, I'll go on living in it—indefinitely. That would be horrible beyond imagining. So I've decided to give up the necklace to someone who can make better use of it and to end my life the way I've lived it—on my own terms."

"Charity isn't in your nature, Bati," Jack said. "What aren't you telling us?"

"Please, Jack," Glaeken said, offended by the younger man's unyielding hostility. "She's agreed to give us the necklace, the rest is really none—"

"I've always been up-front with Bati," Jack said, half- turning toward Glaeken. "She knows that. She knows not to expect anything less." He turned back to Kolabati. "What's the rest of it?"

She rose and stepped to the window. She stared into the living darkness for a long moment.

"Karma," she said. "What's happening out there threatens the turning of the Karmic Wheel."

She turned and faced Jack. Glaeken felt as if he'd been forgotten.

"You know the stains on my karma, Jack. Kusum shared those stains. The weight of that karmic burden drove him to the acts that led to his death at your hands. I've long feared dying because I'm terrified of the retribution my karma will earn for me in the next life. Now . . . now I fear living more than dying."

She touched her necklace again. "And perhaps . . . if giving this up will allow the Great Wheel to keep turning . . . perhaps this deed will undo all the others. Perhaps this act will purify my karma of its stains."

Jack nodded his understanding. Glaeken, too, thought he understood: Kolabati was making a deal with her gods— forgiveness of her karmic burden in return for the necklace. Glaeken wondered if truly there might be a Karmic Wheel. He doubted it. In all his many years he had seen no evidence of it. But he was not about to say anything that might dissuade Kolabati from surrendering her necklace.

Without warning, she reached both hands behind her neck, unfastened the necklace, and handed it to Jack.

"There," she said, her voice husky, her eyes glittering. "This is what you wanted."

Then she turned and headed for the door.

Jack stared a moment at the necklace in his hand, then started after her.

"Bati, wait! Where're you going?"

"Outside. It will end quickly there."

Glaeken leapt to his feet and followed Jack. He passed him and caught up to Kolabati at the door. He grabbed her arm and stopped her.

"No," Glaeken said. "I cannot allow you to die like that. Not out there. Not alone."

Her eyes were frightened, terrified of what lay beyond, waiting for her.

"Everyone dies alone," she said. "I'm used to being alone."

"So was I. But I've learned to draw strength from companionship. Let the years take you. It will be gentle—far gentler than out there."

"I'll stay with you, Bati," Jack said. "I'll sit with you to the . . . the end."

"No!" she said, her voice rising. "I don't want you to see me—I don't want *any*one to see me."

A proud woman, Glaeken thought. And vain, too, certainly. But that was her privilege.

He loosened his grip on her arm and clasped her hand. It was cold, moist, trembling.

"I know a place where you can be alone and comfortable. Where no one will see you. Come."

As he began to lead her through the door, Jack stepped forward.

"Wait."

For the first time since Glaeken had met him, Jack looked awkward. His cat-like grace was gone. The necklace hung in his hand like a leaden weight. He seemed at a loss for words.

"Please, Jack," Kolabati said, turning to him, "I haven't much time."

"I know. I know. I just wanted to tell you that I've thought some awful things about you for the past few years, but what you're doing now . . . it takes courage. More courage than I think I'd have if positions were reversed. I think you're the bravest woman I know." He reached for her hand and raised it to his lips. "I . . . we all owe you. And we won't forget you."

Kolabati nodded slowly. "I know I don't have your love, so I guess I'll have to settle for that." She stretched up and kissed him on the cheek. "Goodbye, Jack."

"Yeah," Jack said, his expression stricken. "Goodbye."

Glaeken lead Kolabati down to Carol's apartment—*former* apartment. Carol would not re-enter it. He guided her to the bedroom but did not turn on the light.

"It's quiet here. Safe and dark. No one will disturb you."

He heard the springs squeak as she sat on the bed.

"Will you stay with me?" she said in a small voice.

"I thought—?"

"That was Jack. I couldn't be comfortable with him here. But you're different. Your years stretch far beyond mine. I think you understand."

Glaeken found a chair and pulled it up beside the bed.

"I understand."

His sentiments echoed Jack's: this was a brave woman. He took her hand again as he had upstairs.

"Talk to me," he said. "Tell me about the India of your childhood—the temple, the rakoshi. Tell me how you spent your days before you came to wear the necklace."

"I seems that I was never young."

Glaeken sighed. "I know. But tell me what you can, and then I will tell you of my youth, what little I remember of it."

And so Kolabati spoke of her girlhood, of her parents, of her fear of the flesh-eating demons who roamed the tunnels beneath the Temple-in-the-Hills. But as she talked on, her voice grew hoarse, raspy. The air in the room grew moist and sour as her tissues returned their vital fluids to the world. Her voice continued to weaken until speech seemed a terrible effort. Finally . . .

"I'm so tired," she said, panting.

"Lie down," Glaeken told her.

He guided her to a recumbent position, gripping her shoulders and lifting her knees. Beneath her clothes her flesh felt wizened, perilously close to the bone.

"I'm cold," she said.

He covered her with a blanket.

"I'm so afraid," she said. "Please don't leave me."

He held her hand again.

"I won't."

"Not until it's completely over. Do you promise?"

"I promise."

She did not speak again. After a time her breathing became harsh and rapid, rising steadily to a ragged crescendo. Her bony fingers squeezed Glaeken's in a final spasm—

And then relaxed.

All was quiet.

Kolabati was gone.

Glaeken released her hand and stepped into the hall outside the apartment. Jack was there, sitting cross-legged on the floor next to the door. He looked up at Glaeken.

"Is she—?"

Glaeken nodded and Jack lowered his head.

"Collect both necklaces and the blade fragments and be ready to leave as soon as it's light."

Jack nodded, still looking down. "Where?"

"I'll tell you later. I must remain with her a while longer."

Jack looked up again. His red-rimmed eyes questioned.

Glaeken said, "I promised I'd stay until the end."

Back in the bedroom, the scent of rot was vague in the air. He resumed his seat and found Kolabati's hand again. The skin was cold, dry, as flaky as filo dough. He clasped it until it crumbled to dust and ran through his fingers. And when the sky began to lighten, he drew the curtains, closed the door, and locked the apartment.

THURSDAY

The House at the End of the Road

MONROE, LONG ISLAND

"You sure these are the directions he gave you?"

Jack stopped Glaeken's old Mercedes in the middle of the road and peered about in the gloomy light. Bill Ryan sat in the passenger seat, a pair of shotguns propped between his knees. The two necklaces and the blade fragments sat between them in a carved wooden box. Bill peered at the hastily scribbled note in his hand.

"Positive," he said.

Jack would have preferred to have Ba along on this trek but he'd possessed neither the heart nor the nerve to ask the big guy to leave Sylvia and the boy again. But Bill seemed different today. There was a odd air of peace about him that Jack found strangely comforting.

"You grew up in Monroe, didn't you?"

"Yeah, but I've never been out here. I don't think I ever knew there *was* an out here. This is nowhere."

Nowhere. Perfect description, Jack thought. They were in the far northeast corner of Monroe, on a dirt road leading through the heart of a vast salt marsh. To their left, under a low, leaden, overcast sky, Monroe Harbor lay smooth and flat and still and gray as slate. Somewhere dead ahead was the Long Island Sound. Nothing moved. Not an insect, not a bird, not even a breeze to stir the reeds and tall grass lining the road. Like being caught in the middle of a monochrome marshscape.

The only break in the monotony was the file of utility poles marching along the east flank of the road and what looked like an oversized outhouse near the water at its far end.

"That's got to be the place," Bill said.

"Can't be."

"You see any other place around? We're supposed to follow this road out to the house at its end. That's the place. It's got to be."

Jack doubted it but put the Mercedes in gear again and started forward.

"I still say we made a wrong turn somewhere."

As they approached the shack, Jack noticed smoke rising from behind it. "Whoever he is, he's got a fire going."

"I hope he builds a better fire than he builds a house," Bill said.

"Right. He must be the original crooked man and this must be the original crooked house."

The shack did not seem to have one true upright. The entire one-story structure was canted left, leaning against the peeling propane tank on its flank; its crumbling brick chimney was canted right; and the aerial atop that was canted left again.

But this had to be the place: the house at the end of the road.

An old Torino sat in front. Except for the fire in the back, the place looked deserted.

"You know," Bill said as they neared it, "that's not just a plain old fire in back there. I don't know much about that sort of thing, but it looks to me like he's got some kind of forge going full blast.

As Jack pulled into the small graveled front yard, he noticed that all the screens were ripped and tattered, all the windows smashed—like every other house they'd passed on their way out from the city.

"This doesn't look good."

Bill shrugged. "The fire's going, and Glaeken said . . . "

"Yeah. Glaeken said."

He parked and took the wooden box with him when he got out. Bill accompanied him to the door. To the right was what appeared to be a small vegetable garden, but nothing was growing. The front door opened before they reached the steps and a grizzled old man glared at them through the remnants of the screen in the upper half of the storm door.

"Took your time getting here, didn't you?"

His shock of gray hair stuck out in all directions. He needed a shave like his stained undershirt needed to be washed—or better yet, tossed out and replaced.

"You're expecting us?" Jack said. How could that be? The phones had been out for days.

"Yeah. You got the metal?"

Bill glanced at the note in his hand. "First we've got to know: Are you George Haskins?"

"'Course I am."

"May we come in?"

"I don't think they'd like that. You see—"

Jack heard a garbled babble from somewhere behind the solid lower half of the storm door. Haskins looked down and spoke toward the floor.

"All right, all right!" he said, then looked up at Jack again and thrust his hand through the opening. "They're real anxious to get started. Gimme the metal."

Jack handed him the box. Haskins pulled it inside and handed it to someone down by his feet.

"There! You happy now? You gonna shut up and leave me alone now? Good!" He looked up at Jack again. "They been driving me crazy waiting for this stuff."

"Who?"

"My tenants. I been spending my nights down in the crawlspace with 'em. They been keepin' the cooters out. If it hadn't—"

More babbling.

"Okay, okay. They say come back in about four hours. If they really rush it, they should be done by then."

Curious, Jack stepped up on the stoop and peeked through the opening. He saw maybe a dozen scurrying forms, like midgets, only they couldn't have been more than a foot-and-a-half tall. And they looked furry.

"What the—"

Haskins moved to block his view.

"Four hours. They'll have it for you then."

"Yeah, but who are 'they'?" Jacked remembered Glaeken mentioning something about "smallfolk."

"My tenants. They been with me nigh on twenty-five years now, just waitin' for this day—'when time is unfurled and we're called by the world,' as they put it. Seems to me like time and ev'rything else is unfurled these days. So go away and come back later. They don't want anyone around while they're workin'. See you later."

He closed the door.

"Four hours," Bill said, looking at his watch as they returned to the car. "It's a little after eleven now. That'll be after dark."

Jack sat behind the wheel, unease gnawing at his stomach. Bill was right. According to the Sapir curve, this morning's sunrise had been the last. After four hours and forty-two minutes of light, the sun would set for the last time at 3:01 p.m. No more day forever after. Only night.

And then there'd be no quarter from the "cooters," as Haskins called them.

"How the hell are we going to get back?" Bill said.

Jack started the car. "Drive. How else?"

He pulled out and headed back down the road, wondering how to kill the time. No point in heading back to the city. Maybe they could find something to do in Monroe.

"What is it with this town?" Jack said.

"Village," Bill said. "North Shore towns like to refer to themselves as villages."

"Fine. Village. But what gives here? Every time I turn around, the name pops up. You're from Monroe, Carol's from Monroe, the Doc, the Nash lady and her boy are from Monroe. And now we're back out here again making a delivery to some old coot with a house full of furry dwarves. Why are we always coming back to Monroe?"

"I've wondered about that myself, and I think I know. Take a right at the end of the road down here and I'll show you."

Bill guided him to a residential neighborhood, to Collier Street. They stopped in front of number 124, a three-bedroom ranch.

"This is where it happened," Bill said, his voice strangely husky as he stared at the house through his side window. "This is where Rasalom re-entered the world more than a quarter-century after Glaeken thought he'd killed him. It was in the house that used to stand on this lot—the original was set afire—that Carol conceived the child whose body was usurped by Rasalom. That single event has left a stain on this town, given it some sort of psychic pheromone that draws odd people and creates a fertile environment for weird and strange occurrences."

"Like those dwarves out in the marsh."

"Right. They must have sensed Rasalom's return, must have known they'd be needed, so they've been camped out there with George Haskins for decades, waiting for their moment. Now it's come. Same with the *Dat-tay-vao*. It traveled half way around the world to end up in Monroe where it lived for a while in Alan Bulmer, then moved on to Jeffy. From what I can gather, that journey began about the time Rasalom was reconceived."

"So it must have known that it would be needed too."

"So it seems. But there were other occurrences back in that first year, a cluster of hideously deformed children born in November and early December. No one could explain it then, but now I can see that they all must have been conceived around the same time as Rasalom. His very presence in town must have mutated them in embryo." Bill shook his head. "Major tragedies for the families involved but merely warnings of what was to come."

Jack mulled that as Bill guided him through the town, past the high school where he'd been a football star, past the new house built on the site of his family home, burned to the ground a little over five years ago, killing both of his elderly parents.

"I truly believe Rasalom was responsible for that too," he said in a low voice, thick with emotion. He ground a fist into his palm. "So many others—friends, acquaintances, *children*! My folks, Jim, Lisl, Renny, Nick, and Danny—dear God, Danny! Damn, I've got scores to settle!"

Jack put a hand on Bill's shoulder and gave it a reassuring squeeze.

"We'll get the bastard. We'll make him pay."

Sure we will.

They killed time driving around Monroe. The town—village—seemed all but deserted. No bodies lay about. No bodies anywhere. Probably because unlike the bugs, which merely sucked the juices from their victims, the newer, bigger hole- things devoured their kills. Occasionally Jack spotted fearful faces peering at them from darkened rooms through shattered windows. As they cruised the main drag through the remnants of the downtown harbor front area, a gang of lupine scavengers began to approach the car.

Bill lifted one of the Spas-12s and worked the pump.

"I almost hope they try something," he said through thin, tight lips. "I'm feeling *real* mean at the moment."

At the sight of the shotgun they immediately lost interest and trotted away. Jack stared at him. "Even you."

"What?"

"It's getting to you. Even you're starting to feel the effects of this craziness, aren't you?"

"And you're not?"

"Nah. I've made my living waiting for guys like that to start something. You're just beginning to browse in the neighborhood where I've spent my adult life."

The Movie Channel:
Joe Bob Briggs' Drive-In Movie—A Special All-Day Edition.
   And Soon The Darkness (1970) Levitt/Rickman
   When Time Ran Out (1980) Warner Brothers
   Nothing But The Night (1972) Cinema Systems
   Doomed To Die (1940) Monogram
   Night Must Fall (1937) MGM
   The Dark (1979) Film Ventures
   Dark Star (1972) Bryanston
   Dead Of Night (1945) Universal
   Fade To Black (1980) Compass International
   Don't Be Afraid Of The Dark (1973) TV
   Night World (1932) Universal

By three-thirty they were back at Haskins' place. The fire was still burning in the forge in the back, but not as brightly as before. The air, however, was filled with the clang of metal upon metal.

"You're early," Haskins said at the door, still not inviting them in.

"We know," Bill said, "but it'll be dark soon and we want to get moving as soon as we can."

"Can't say as I blame you. Just as well you did show up. They're almost done. Wait in the car and I'll bring it out to you."

Jack and Bill returned to the old Mercedes. Bill sat inside, fiddling with the radio, trying to find a broadcast of any sort, while Jack paced in front, his gut twisting steadily tighter as the gray sky faded toward black.

He wished again that he hadn't sent Gia and Vicky off with Abe. He needed to see them again, hold them in his arms—one last time before the end.

"Listen," Bill said, sticking his head out the window. "The clanging's stopped."

"Doesn't matter," Jack said. "It's too late. We're not going to make it back. Even if we had a goddam *plane* we couldn't make it back in one piece."

The storm door slammed then, and there came old George Haskins lugging two blanket-wrapped objects in his arms like sick children.

"There you go," he said, dumping them into Jack's waiting hands.

One bundle was square and bulky, the other long and slim. And they were *heavy*. Bill took the smaller one and together they placed them on the back seat, then Jack was diving for the driver seat.

"It's been great talking to you, George, but we've got to run."

"Good luck, boys," Haskins said, heading back to his front door. "I don't know what this all means, but I sure hope it works out."

The rear wheels kicked gravel as Jack accelerated down the road. He glanced at the rearview mirror and saw Haskins standing on the stoop, watching them go. He couldn't be sure in the dim light but he thought he saw a group of knee-high figures clustered around his legs. Then Haskins waved—they *all* waved.

Blinking his eyes to clear them, Jack concentrated on the road.

Somewhere beyond the mists that masked the sky, the sun was setting for the last time.

"We're not going to make it," Jack said. "No way we can get back alive."

"We've got to give it our best shot," Bill said. "We don't have any other options that I can see."

"Oh, we'll give it one hell of a shot, Billy boy. One *hell* of a shot."

But we're not *going to make it.*

WNEW-FM

JO: This is it, Folks. It's 3:01 in the afternoon. Supposedly the last sunset. If Sapir's curve is right, the last time we'll ever see the sun.

FREDDY: Yeah. Nobody's offered us any hope, so we can't pass any on to you. We wish we could, but—

JO: And don't ask us why we're here because we don't know ourselves. Maybe 'cause it's the only thing we know how to do.

FREDDY: Whatever, we'll keep on doing it as long as the generators hold out, so keep us on as long as you've got batteries to spare. If we hear anything we'll let you know. And if you hear anything, call us on the CB and we'll pass it on.

JO: Anyway you look at it, it's gonna be a long night.

Part III

NIGHT

Aaaahh! NIGHT. Endless night. Everlasting darkness.

Rasalom turns within his fluid-filled chrysalis and revels in the fresh waves of panic seeping through from the nightworld above. Darkness reigns supreme. His dominion is established beyond all doubt. A fait accompli.

Except for one flaw, one minuscule spot of hope—Glaeken's building. But that is a calculated flaw. It, too, will fade once its residents realize that all their puny efforts to reassemble the weapon are for nought. It is too late—too late for anything. The juices from those crushed hopes will be SWEET.

All Rasalom need do now is await the completion of the Change at the undawn tomorrow, then break free from this shell to officially lay claim to this world. His world.

And he is nearly there. He feels the final strands of the metamorphosis drawing tight around and through him. And when it is done, he will rise to the surface and allow Glaeken to gaze on the new Rasalom, to shrink in awe and fear from his magnificence before the life is slowly crushed from his body.

Soon now.

Very soon.

End Play

MANHATTAN

"Where can they *be*?"

Carol knew she was being a pest, that no one in the room— neither Sylvia, nor Jeffy, nor Ba, not Nick, not even Glaeken himself—could answer the question she'd repeated at least two dozen times in the past hour, but she couldn't help herself.

"I know I'm not supposed to be afraid, I know that's what Rasalom wants, but I can't help it. I'm scared to death something's happened to Bill. And Jack."

"That's not fear," Glaeken said. "That's concern. There's an enormous difference. The fear that Rasalom thrives on is the dread, the panic, the terror, the fear for one's self that paralyzes you, makes you hate and distrust everyone around you, that forces you either to lash out at anyone within reach or to crawl into a hole and huddle alone and miserable in the dark. The fear that cuts you off from hope and from each other, that's what he savors. This isn't fear you're feeling, Carol. It's anxiety, and it springs from love."

Carol nodded. That was all fine and good . . .

"But where *are* they?"

"They're gone," Nick said.

Carol's stomach plummeted as she turned toward him. Glaeken, too, was staring at him intently.

Nick hadn't answered her all the other times she'd asked the same question. Why now?

"Wh-What do you mean?" she said.

"They're gone," he repeated, his voice quavering. "They're not out there. Father Bill and the other one—they've disappeared."

Carol watched in horror as a tear slid down Nick's cheek. She turned to Glaeken.

"What does he mean?"

"He's wrong," Glaeken said, but his eyes did not hold quite the conviction of his words. "He has to be."

"But he sees things we don't," Carol said. "And he hasn't been wrong yet. Oh, God!"

She began to sob. She couldn't help it. Lying in Bill's arms last night had been the first time since Jim's death that she had felt like a complete, fully functioning human being. She couldn't bear to lose him now.

Or was this part of a plan?

She swallowed her sobs and wiped away her tears.

"Is this another of Rasalom's games?" she asked Glaeken. "Feed us a little hope, let us taste a little happiness, make us ache for a future and then crush us by snatching it all away?"

Glaeken nodded. "That is certainly his style."

"Well then, fuck him!" she said.

The words shocked her. She never used four-letter words. They simply were not part of her vocabulary. But this had leapt from her—and it seemed right. It capsulized the anger she felt. She glanced over to where Jeffy sat reading a picture book with Sylvia. He wasn't paying attention. She turned back to Glaeken.

"Fuck. Him." There, she'd said it again, but in a lower voice this time. "He's not getting anything from me. I won't be afraid, I won't lose hope, I won't give up."

She went to the huge curved sofa, picked up a magazine, and sat down to read it. But she couldn't see the trembling page through her freshly welling tears.

The Movie Channel:
interrupted transmission

"Got to be those things in the back seat," Jack said in a hushed voice.

Bill said nothing. He held his breath and leaned away from the passenger side window as the countless tentacles brushed across its surface.

Hurry up! A giant, tentacled slug blocked their way on Broadway as it squeezed into 47th Street. He mentally urged it to keep moving and get out of their way.

"This happened to me once before," Jack went on. "With the rakoshi. As long as I was wearing one of the necklaces, they couldn't see me. One or both of those things Haskins gave us was made from the necklaces. This has got to be the same kind of effect. I mean, look at that slug. It's ignoring us like we don't even exist." He flashed a smile at Bill. "Isn't this neat?"

"Oh, yeah," Bill said. "Real neat."

The whole trip had been like a dream, an interminable nightmare. The horrors from the holes had taken over— completely. Their movements had lost the frantic urgency of all past nights. Now they were more deliberate, no longer like an invading army, but rather like an occupying force.

Bill and Jack had traveled in from the Island through swarms of bugs and crawlers large and small—but they had traveled unnoticed. An occasional horror would flutter against one of the windows or crash into a door or a fender, but each was accidental contact. Still, their progress had been slow through the dark dreamscape, and when they arrived at the Midtown Tunnel, they'd found it utterly impassable—choked with countless giant millipede-like creatures. They'd finally found their way across the Brooklyn Bridge, which was still intact, and had been making good time heading uptown on Broadway. Broadway had run downtown in the days when it had been a thoroughfare for cars instead of crawlers, but there didn't seem to be anyone writing tickets tonight.

The slug's back end finally cleared enough pavement to allow Jack to scoot around behind it and they were on their way again. Another fifteen minutes of picking their way around abandoned cars and the larger crawlers and they were back at the Glaeken's building.

Bill unlocked his door and reached for the handle as Jack drove up on the sidewalk.

"Better not get out empty-handed," Jack said. "You might not make it to the door."

Good thought. Bill grabbed the boxier of the two blanket- wrapped objects and hopped out. Julio was at the lobby door, holding it open.

"Where you guy's been?" he said as Bill rushed through. "We been worried sick 'bout you."

Bill patted him on the shoulder as he passed.

"Elevator still working?"

"Slow as shit, but it gets there."

Bill hopped in and waited for Jack only because it would have been a slap in the face to leave him behind. The need to be with Carol was a desperate, gnawing urgency. He wanted to see her, hold her, let her know he was all right. She had to be sick with worry by now.

He ran ahead of Jack when they reached the top floor, straight into Glaeken's apartment, and there she was, the wonder and joy and relief in her eyes so real, and just for him. She sobbed when he wrapped his free arm around her and he wanted to carry her back to the bedroom right now but knew that would have to wait.

"Nick said you were dead!"

Bill straightened and looked at her. "He did? Dead?"

"Well, not dead. But he said you were gone—not there anymore."

"Why would he—?"

And then Bill thought he understood. Just as he and Jack had been invisible to the bugs on their trip home, so they must have been invisible to Nick as well.

He realized that he and Carol were the center of attention—Sylvia, Jeffy, Ba, Glaeken—everyone but Nick was staring at them. He released Carol and showed his blanket- wrapped bundle to Glaeken.

"We got it. Those smallfolk you mentioned were there. They took the necklaces and gave us these in return."

Glaeken made no move to take the bundle. He pointed to the coffee table.

"Unwrap it and place it there, if you will."

Bill searched through the many folds of the blanket until his hand came in contact with cold metal. He wriggled it free and held it up.

Bill's gasp was echoed by the others in the room.

"A cross!" Carol said in hushed tones.

Yes. A tau cross, identical to the ones that studded the walls of the keep back in Rumania. But it was the colors that surprised him most. He'd expected something made of iron, a dull flat gray similar to the necklaces they had delivered to Haskins this morning. Not this. Not an upright of solid gold and a crosspiece of shining silver, reflecting the dancing light of the flames in the fireplace.

Bill tore his eyes away from its gleaming surface and looked at Glaeken.

"Is this it? A cross?"

Glaeken had stepped back, placing a section of the sofa between Bill and himself. He shook his head.

"Not a cross. But it is the source, the reason the cross is such an important symbol throughout the world. In truth it is merely the hilt of a sword."

Jack stepped forward, staring at the hilt. He ran his fingers over its surface.

"But what happened to the iron from the necklaces?"

"You're touching it," Glaeken said. "The small folk have a way with metals."

"I guess they do," Jack said. He began unwrapping his own, longer burden. "Then what's in here?"

"The rest of the instrument," Glaeken said. "Be careful. It may be sharp."

Another intake of breath across the room as the layers of blanket fell away to reveal a gleaming length of carved steel.

"The blade," Jack breathed.

The muscles in his forearm rippled as he held it by the butt spike and raised it in the air, turning it back and forth, letting the light leap and run across the runes carved along its length.

The blade was magnificent. The sight of it warmed one part of Bill and chilled another. Something alien and unsettling about those runes. He slipped his arm around Carol and held her closer.

He still held the hilt in his free hand. He'd noticed a deep slot in the center of its upper surface—a perfect receptacle for the blade's butt spike.

"Should we put them together?" he asked Glaeken.

The old man shook his head. "No. Not yet. Please place the hilt on the table."

As Bill complied, Jack lowered the blade.

"This too?"

"Drive that point first into the floor, if you will."

Jack shot him a questioning look, then shrugged. He upended the blade, grabbed the butt spike with both hands, and drove it through the carpet and deep into the hardwood floor beneath. It quivered and swayed a moment, then stood straight and still.

Glaeken turned to Sylvia. His eyes opaque, his expression grave.

"Mrs. Nash . . . it is time."

Sylvia stared at the gold and silver cross gleaming on the table not five feet in front of her and felt all her strength desert her in a rush.

Everything was happening—changing—too quickly. She'd gone to bed last night thinking she'd been freed of the burden of deciding. Jack had returned with only one necklace and it wasn't enough. The instrument could not be reassembled, Jeffy would not be called on to give up the *Dat-tay-vao*. She had been frightened, terrified of the near future, and ashamed at the relief she had felt at being spared the burden of risking her son's mind.

This morning she had awakened to find everything changed. Glaeken had both necklaces and the original plan was back in motion.

Sylvia had been preparing herself for this moment all day but she wasn't close to ready. How could she ever be ready for this?

She sensed Ba looming behind her and didn't have to look to know that whatever she decided he would be with her one hundred percent. But the rest of them . . . she glanced around the room. Carol, Bill, Jack, Glaeken—their eyes were intent upon her.

How could they ask her to do this? She'd already lost Alan. How could they ask her to risk Jeffy?

But they could. And they were. And considering all that was at stake, how could they *not* ask?

Jeffy, too, seemed to notice their stares. He drew his eyes away from the hilt—he'd been fixated on it since Bill had unwrapped it—and turned to Sylvia.

"Why are they all looking at us, Mom?" he whispered.

Sylvia tried to speak but no sound came out. She cleared her throat and tried again.

"They want you to do something, Jeffy."

He looked around at the expectant faces. "What?"

"They want you to—" She looked up at Glaeken. "What does he have to do?"

"Just touch it," Glaeken said. "That is all it will take."

"They want you to touch that cross," she told Jeffy. "It will—"

"Oh, sure!"

Jeffy pulled away from her, eager to get his hands on the shiny object. Sylvia hauled him back.

"Wait, honey. You should know . . . it might hurt you."

"It didn't hurt that man," he said, pointing to Bill.

"True. But it will be different for you. The cross will take something from you, and after you lose that something you . . . you might not be the same."

He gave her a puzzled look.

"You may be like you were before, in the time you can't remember." How did you explain autism to a nine-year-old? "You didn't speak then; you barely knew your name. I . . . don't want you to be like that again."

His smile was bright, almost blinding. "Don't worry, Mommy. I'll be okay."

Sylvia wished she could share even a fraction of his confidence, but she had a dreadful feeling about this. Yet if she held him back, didn't let him near the hilt, then what had Alan died for? He'd gone to his death protecting Jeffy and her. How could she hold Jeffy back now and condemn him—condemn everyone—to a short life and a brutal death in a world of eternal darkness.

Yet the risk was Jeffy losing the light of intelligence in those eyes and living on as an autistic child.

Certain darkness without, a chance of darkness within.

What do I do?

She forced her hands to release him and she spoke before she had a chance to change her mind.

"Go, Jeffy. Do it. Touch it."

He lurched away from her, anxious to get to the bright metal thing on the table. He covered the distance in seconds, reached out and, without hesitation, curled his tiny fingers around the grip of the hilt.

For an instant his hand seemed to glow, then he cried out in a high-pitched voice. A violent shudder passed through him, then he was still.

What is that?

Something disturbs Rasalom. An aberrant ripple races across his consciousness, disrupting the seething perfection of the ambient fear and agony.

Something has happened.

Rasalom searches the upper reaches, sensing out the cause. There is only one possible place it could have originated—Glaeken's building.

And there he finds the source.

The weapon. Glaeken has managed to reassemble it. He has actually recharged it. That is what Rasalom felt.

But even now the sensation is fading.

Such hope concentrated in that room now, an unbearable amount. Yet exquisite misery is incipient there. How wonderful it will be to catch the falling flakes of that hope as it crystallizes in the cold blast of fear and terror when they realize they have failed utterly.

For it is too late for them. Far, far too late. This world is sealed away from Glaeken's ally force. Let him assemble a hundred such weapons, a *thousand*. It will not matter. The endless night is upon the world. A dark, impenetrable barrier. There can be no contact, no reunion of Glaeken with the opposing force.

Let him try. Let his pathetic circle hope. It will make their final failure all the more painful.

There now. The disturbing ripple is gone, swallowed by the thick insulating layers of night that surround it like a shroud.

Rasalom returns to his repose and awaits the undawn.

"Jeffy?"

Her little boy stood stone still with his hand on the hilt, staring at it. Sylvia had jumped to her feet and rushed to his side at his cry of pain. Now she hovered over him, almost afraid to touch him.

"Jeffy, are you all right?"

He did not move, did not speak.

Sylvia felt a rime of fear crystallize along the chambers of her heart.

No! Please, God, no! Don't let this happen!

She grabbed him by the shoulders and twisted him toward her, caught his chin with her thumb and forefinger and turned it up. She stared into his eyes.

And his eyes . . .

"Jeffy!" she cried, barely able to keep her voice under control. "Jeffy, say something! Do you know who I am? Who am I, Jeffy? *Who am I?*"

Jeffy's gaze wandered off her face to a spot over her shoulder, held there for a few seconds, then drifted on. His eyes were empty. *Empty.*

She knew that face. She fought off the encroaching blackness that her mind hungered to escape to. She'd lived with that vacant expression for too many years not to know it now. Autism. Jeffy was back to the way he used to be.

"Oh, no!" Sylvia moaned as she slipped her arms around him and pulled him close. "Oh, no . . . oh, no . . . oh, no!"

This can't be! she thought, holding his unresisting, disinterested body tight against her. First Alan and now Jeffy . . . I can't lose them both! I *can't!*

She glared across the room at Glaeken who stood watching her with a stricken expression. She had never felt so lost, so alone, so utterly miserable in her life, and it was all his fault.

"Is this the way it has to be?" she cried. "Is this it? Am I to lose everything? Why? Why me? Why Jeffy?"

She gathered Jeffy up in her arms and carried him from the room, hurling one final question at Glaeken and everyone else there as she left.

"Why not *you?*"

The heaviness in Glaeken's chest grew as he stood at the far end of the living room and watched poor Sylvia flee with her relapsed child.

Because this is war, he thought in answer to her parting question. And every war exacts its price, on victors and vanquished alike.

Even in the unlikely event we win this, we will all be changed forever. None of us will come through unscathed.

That knowledge did not make him grieve any less for the loss of that poor boy's mind.

A single sob burst from Carol and echoed like a shot in the mortuary silence. Bill slipped his arms around her. Jack stood with his hands in his pockets, staring at the floor. And Ba looked simply . . . lost. And tortured. Anything that hurt his mistress hurt him doubly. His pain-filled eyes reflected the war within—torn between following Sylvia or staying with the others.

"Please don't go yet, Ba," Glaeken said. "We may need you." He turned to the others. "We are ready."

"How can you be so cold?" Carol said.

"I am not immune to their torment," Glaeken told her. "I ache for that child, and even more for his mother. He may have lost his awareness and his ability to respond to the world around him, but he has lost his perspective as well—he doesn't know what he has lost. Sylvia does. She bears the pain for both of them. But there is no time to grieve. If the price the child has paid is to have meaning, we must take the final step."

"Okay," Jack said. "What do we do?"

"Put the hilt and the blade together."

"That's it? Then it's done?"

Glaeken nodded. "Then it is done."

"Then let's get to it."

Jack picked up the hilt, hefted it, and turned to the blade where it rose from the floor.

"Wait, Jack," Glaeken said. "There's something you should know."

The easiest thing would have been to allow Jack to ram the hilt onto the blade's butt spike and have done with it. But it was only fair to warn the man what he was getting into. Glaeken wished someone had warned him countless years ago before his own first encounter with the weapon.

But I was so reckless and headstrong then. Would it have made a difference?

Jack stood by the blade, waiting.

"When you join the two halves," Glaeken said, "you are, in a very real sense, joining yourself to the weapon and the force that fuels it. It's an intimate bond, permanent, one you will not be able to break no matter how much you desire to."

"Just by putting it together?" Jack said. "No spells or incantations or any of that stuff?"

"None of that *stuff*," Glaeken said, allowing himself a tiny smile. "Because that's just what it is—*stuff*. Show biz. This is the real thing."

He noticed that Jack seemed to have lost some of his enthusiasm for joining the hilt to the blade.

"You are free to choose to do so or not, Jack. Just as the weapon is free to decide who shall wield it."

"*It* has a say?"

"Of course. The *Dat-tay-vao* resides within it now. That is not an inert amalgam of metals you hold in your hand, it is very much alive—and sentient."

Jack's gaze dropped to the hilt, then rose again. Glaeken sensed the indecision there.

"What about you, Glaeken? Didn't this used to be yours? Shouldn't you be handling this?"

Glaeken fought the urge to back to the farthest corner of the room.

"No. This is not my age. I'm from another time, a long- dead time. This is your age. I saved mine. Someone from your time must save yours."

"One of *us?*"

It was Bill. The ex-priest released his grip on Carol and approached Jack, hesitantly, as if Jack were holding a poisonous snake.

"Yes. You, Ba, Jack. Each of you qualifies, each of you has risked his life to bring us to this point. One of you is next."

Glaeken watched Jack. He could tell he would have liked nothing better than to hand the hilt to Bill, but his pride would not allow it. The hellish weight of machismo. Jack was burdened with an especially heavy load.

"All right," he said in a low voice. "Unless anyone objects, I'll go first."

Jack glanced around. No one objected. Shrugging, he hefted the hilt and stepped next to the blade. Glaeken was glad it was Jack first. He was almost certain Jack was the one. He had a warrior's heart. He was the perfect choice to wield the weapon.

Jack upended the hilt over the butt spike, then paused.

"What's going to happen?"

"Maybe nothing," Glaeken said. "It may be too late for anything to work. Rasalom may have us sealed off too completely for the signal to break through."

"But if it does work, how will I know?"

"Oh, you'll know," Glaeken said. "Believe me, you'll know."

Jack continued to stare at him questioningly.

Glaeken said, "For one thing, the blade and hilt will fuse. That will be your confirmation that the blade has accepted you."

And that will be the least of it, he thought, but said nothing. *If you're the one Jack, there will be no doubt.*

Jack nodded. Glaeken took a surreptitious step backward and looked away as Jack lined up the hole in the hilt over the butt spike, inhaled deeply, and rammed it home.

Nothing happened.

"Well," Jack said after a few heartbeats, "I don't feel any different." He pulled up on the hilt and it easily slipped free of the butt spike. "And neither does this thing. I guess I've been rejected."

Glaeken cursed softly under his breath. Jack would have been perfect. Why hadn't the instrument accepted him?

Jack glanced around the room.

"Ba—you want to give it a try?"

A good choice, Glaeken thought. Ba was the other warrior in the room. And he had a personal grudge against Rasalom—his friend Dr. Bulmer had died and Jeffy had been harmed because of Rasalom. His righteous fury would further fuel the weapon.

The big Oriental's expression remained calm but Glaeken sensed a tightening in the muscles of his throat. His nod was almost imperceptible.

Jack held up the hilt. "All yours, buddy."

As Ba stepped forward with no hint of hesitation, Glaeken noticed Sylvia slip back into the far corner of the room holding her listless Jeffy by the hand. She must have been listening, must have heard Ba's name called. She watched intently as Ba took the hilt from Jack and slipped it down over the spike.

Again—nothing.

Glaeken ground his teeth and hid his frustration. Not Jack, not Ba. Who?

Without a word, Ba removed the hilt and turned to Bill.

"Me?" Bill said.

Ba held it out to him.

"But I can't . . . I mean, I'm not . . . "

"But perhaps you are," Glaeken told him. "In a way, you've been Rasalom's nemesis since his rebirth—since *before* his rebirth. Is there anyone alive today—besides me—who Rasalom hates more? Anyone Rasalom has tried to harm so dreadfully? Is there anyone else from this age who has actually harmed Rasalom? No. Only you, Bill."

Yes. It was Bill. It had to be Bill. He was perfect—a holy man's soul and a warrior's heart. Bill had drawn first blood and had withstood the death, misery, and horror of Rasalom's vicious campaign to break him.

They were *made* to face off against each other.

Although at the moment Bill looked anything but the fearless standard bearer.

"Yeah," Jack said, smiling tightly. "It's you, Bill. I should've seen it."

Carol was clutching Bill's arm, but she let go as he moved forward. She stood back with her eyes fixed on the hilt and both hands pressed tight against her face, covering her mouth.

Slowly, hesitantly, Bill reached out with trembling hands and took the hilt from Ba.

"It can't be me," he said.

Ba stepped aside, clearing the path to the blade.

Like a sleepwalker, Bill shuffled to the blade, fitted the tip of the spike into the opening—and paused. He looked around.

"It's not me," he said. "I know it's not." But his hoarse voice lacked conviction.

Bill didn't shove the hilt down, he merely let it fall upon the spike. Once again, Glaeken averted his eyes . . .

But nothing happened.

Bill stepped back from the instrument, his entire body trembling.

"I—I don't know whether to laugh or cry."

"Well, then, who is it?" Carol said in a high voice verging on anger. "It's got to be somebody!" She turned to Glaeken. "And who said it has to be a man?"

Glaeken had no answer for that, and Carol wasn't waiting for one anyway. She stepped forward, lifted the hilt, and rammed it back down.

Nothing.

"Don't tell me we went through all this for nothing!" she said. "It's got to—"

She spotted the watcher at the far end of the room. "Sylvia! Sylvia, you try it. Please."

Sylvia wiped away a tear. "I don't . . . "

"Just come over and do it."

Leading Jeffy by the hand, Sylvia approached the instrument. She made eye contact with no one.

"This is a waste of time," she said.

The words proved too true. She released Jeffy, lifted the hilt, and rammed it home with no more effect than anyone before her.

How pathetic they are.

Rasalom has watched the members of Glaeken's circle stride up to the odd conglomeration of metals and spirit standing in the center of the room, each so full of hope and noble purpose, and watched each of them fail. He relishes the growing despair in the room, thickening and congealing until it is almost palpable.

And something else growing there . . . anger.

When their trite little totem fails, they will begin to turn on each other. Luscious.

Glaeken watched Sylvia tug the hilt free of the spike and turn in a slow circle. This time she made eye contact—and her gaze was withering.

"This is it?" her voice bitter, brittle. "This is all we get? Alan loses his life, Jeffy sinks back into autism, all for what? For nothing?"

"Maybe it's Nick," Bill said.

"No," Sylvia said disdainfully. "It's not Nick."

"Maybe it wasn't refurbished right," Jack said. "Or like Glaeken said, maybe it's too late. Maybe the signal can't get through."

"Oh, it's too late all right," she said, continuing her slow turn. "Too late for Alan and Jeffy." Finally her turn brought her around to Glaeken. She stopped and glared at him. "But it's not too late for you, is it, Glaeken?"

"I'm afraid I don't understand."

"Yes, you do." She lifted the hilt higher, straining against its weight. "This is yours, isn't it?"

"It's predecessor was, before it was melted down and—"

"It's *still* yours, isn't it?"

Glaeken felt his mouth going dry. Sylvia was trespassing along a path he dearly wished her to avoid.

"Not anymore. Someone new must take it up now."

"But it wants you."

"No!" What was she *saying?* "I served my time—*more* than my time. Someone else—"

"But what if no one but Glaeken will do?"

"That's not possible."

She lifted the hilt still higher. Her expression was fierce.

"Try it. Just try it. Let's see what happens. Then we'll know for sure."

"You don't understand," Glaeken said. His arthritic lower back was shooting pain down his left leg so he eased himself into the straight-back chair against the wall directly behind him. "I served my time. You can't ask me to serve again. No one has that right. No one."

He saw Jack step closer to Sylvia. He kept his voice low but Glaeken made out the words.

"Chill, Sylvia. Look at him. He's all rusted up. Even if he's the one it wants, what can he do against all that's going on out there?"

Sylvia stared Glaeken's way a moment more, then shook her head.

"Maybe. But there's something else going on here. Something he's not telling us." She handed the hilt to Jack. "You figure it out."

She took Jeffy by the hand and led him from the room.

Jack glanced down at the gold and silver hilt in his hand, then looked at Bill.

"Only one other person left to try."

As they led Nick to the blade, wrapped his hands around the hilt, and guided it over the butt spike, Glaeken rose stiffly to his feet and walked down the hall to the rear of the apartment. He needed to be alone, away from the oppressive despair in the living room.

He stopped at Magda's bedroom and looked in. She was sleeping. That was all she seemed to do these days. Maybe that was a blessing. He took a seat at her bedside and held her hand.

Sylvia and the others didn't—couldn't—understand. He was *tired.* They didn't know how tired one could be after all this living. To have engineered one last victory, or merely to have launched a final battle against Rasalom would have been wonderful. He could have gone blissfully to his death then. But that was not to be. He would die in the darkness like everyone else.

No, he couldn't risk even going near the instrument. Who knew what the reaction might be? It might start everything over again, and once more he would be in the thrall of the ally power. Forever.

I've done my part. I've contributed more than my share. They cannot ask for more.

Someone *else* had to carry on the fight.

"Where's my Glen?"

Startled by the words, spoken in Hungarian, Glaeken looked down and saw that Magda was awake, staring at him. Their litany was about to begin. Her memories were mired in the Second World War, when they both had been young and fresh and newly in love.

"I'm right here, Magda."

She pulled her hand away. "No. You're not him. You're old. My Glen is young and strong!"

"But I've grown old, my dear, like you."

"You're not him!" she said, her voice rising. "Glen is out there in the darkness fighting the Enemy."

The darkness. Some part of her jumbled mind was aware of the horrors outside, and knew Rasalom was involved.

"No, he isn't. He's right here beside you."

"No! Not my Glen! He's out there! He'd never let the Enemy win! Never! Now get away from me, you old fool! Away!"

Glaeken didn't want her to start screaming, so he rose and left her.

"And if you see Glen, tell him his Magda loves him and knows he won't let the Enemy get away with this."

The words stung, setting their barbs into the flesh of his neck and shoulders and trailing him down the hall toward the living room.

The living room . . . it looked like a wake. The five silent occupants were separated by a few feet of space, but were miles apart, each closed off, locked behind the walls of their own thoughts. And fears.

Even here.

Ba sat cross-legged against the far wall, eyes closed, silent. Jack and Sylvia stood at opposite ends of the long room, each staring out at the eternal blackness. Even Bill and Carol were apart, sitting silent and separate on the couch.

And here am I, he thought, separated from them and from my wife, as cut off from the rest of humanity as I've ever been.

Rasalom had won outside, and he was beginning to win in here.

And then Glaeken saw Jeffy. The boy was on his knees before the coffee table, his hands gripping the hilt where it lay on the table top, his cheek pressed down against it, as if some part of him knew that what he was missing was locked within the cold reaches of the metal.

All their sacrifices . . . all their faith in him . . . Rasalom eternally victorious . . .

Anger erupted within Glaeken like one of the long dormant volcanoes in the Pacific, exploding in his chest, engulfing him in its fiery heart.

Rasalom winning . . . having the last laugh . . .

It comes down to that, doesn't it? Me against him. That's what it's always been.

And suddenly Glaeken knew he couldn't allow Rasalom to win. If there was one chance, no matter how slim, he had to take it.

He found himself moving, crossing the room toward Jeffy, lifting him gently away from the hilt.

"Sylvia," he said, keeping his voice calm. "Take him and stand back."

Sylvia rushed over and pulled Jeffy away.

"Why? What's happened?"

"Nothing yet. And perhaps nothing at all will happen. But just in case . . . "

Glaeken stared down at the hilt, hesitating.

This is what you want, isn't it? he thought, speaking silently to the power he had served for millennia, wondering if it could hear him. *You want me back. You let me go and now you want me back. Will no one else do?*

The hilt was silent, gleaming coldly in the flickering light of the silent room. Wondering which he hated more, Rasalom or the power to which he had allied himself ages ago, Glaeken reached down and wrapped his gnarled fingers around the hilt.

Memories surged though him at the metal's touch. Yes, the hilt was alive. The entity that had been the *Dat-tay-vao* welcomed him back. The smallfolk had done their job well.

And as much as he hated to admit it, the hilt felt as if it *belonged* in his hands.

He turned toward the blade.

"Everybody back."

What is that?

Rasalom is disturbed by another ripple through the enveloping chaos above. Bigger. A wavelet this time.

He spreads his consciousness. It's that instrument again. And this time Glaeken himself is holding it. It's the reunion of the man and the living metal that is disturbing. No matter. A minor disturbance, and short lived.

"Too late, Glaeken!" he shouts into the subterranean dark. "Too late!"

"Don't look," Glaeken said.

But Carol had to look. As soon as Glaeken had touched the hilt the air of the living room became charged.

She'd risen and followed Bill to the far side of the sofa where they now stood with their arms wrapped around each other and watched as Glaeken poised the hilt over the butt spike.

Something was going to happen. How could she turn away?

She watched the old man set his feet, take a deep breath, then ram the hilt downward.

! ! ! ! ! LIGHT ! ! ! ! !

Light such as she had never seen or imagined, *light* like the hearts of the Hiroshima and Nagasaki and the Bikinis and all the Yucca Flats bombs rolled into one, *light* like the Big Bang itself exploded from the hilt, engulfing Glaeken and searing the room. Hot light, cold light, new light, ancient light, it blasted through the room in a wave.

In that initial flash Carol saw Glaeken's bones silhouetted through his flesh and clothes, saw the springs and inner supports of the sofa before her, then the *light* was upon her and her retinae screamed and her irises spasmed and her lids clamped down tight to shut out the *light* but it was no use because the *light* would not be denied and it poured through her, suffusing each cell of each tissue in a perceptible wave of warmth as it passed.

She heard cries of wonder and astonishment from the others in the room and was startled by a deafening crash as the glass in the picture windows blew out. Gusts of night air stormed through the room as Carol fought to open her eyes against the glare.

The light was still there, more diffuse now, and splotched with purple from the afterburns on her retinae. It had stopped expanding and had begun to contract, rushing back from the edges of the room to concentrate again at the center, coalescing into a column with Glaeken at its heart. Carol had to raise a protecting arm across her face and half turn away as it consolidated and amplified its power into a narrower beam, shooting upward, burning through the ceiling, through the roof, into the blackness above. And faintly through the brilliance she could still make out the figure of a man standing in the heart of the light.

She turned to Bill. "The roof! We've got to go up on the roof!"

He blinked at her, half-dazed. "Why?"

She didn't know why exactly. A deep part of her was responding to the light, almost as if she recognized it. Whatever the reason, she felt compelled to be up there on the roof to watch this beam of light challenge the darkness.

"Never mind why." She grabbed his hand. "Let's go!" She turned to the others in the room. "Everybody—the roof! The roof!"

Rasalom writhes in his chrysalis.

What is happening? A sudden squall of light in the upper reaches of Glaeken's building.

The instrument! He's activated it!

Rasalom remains calm. The light being shed is a discomfort, a painful irritant. No more.

This is not a setback. Glaeken may be able to cause some trouble with this, but he can be no more than an inconvenience. The Change is too far along. It cannot be reversed.

Carol led the way to the roof, throwing her shoulder against the door at the top of the stairs and bursting out into the cold night air. She was vaguely aware of the hungry buzz and flutter of the night things swooping through the darkness beyond the edges of the building; she barely heard the rooftop gravel crunch under her feet, or noticed the others crowding out behind her. She was locked on the bright beam spearing into the heavens—straight and true, unwavering, a narrow tower of light shooting upward, ever upward until it pierced the sky.

And then it faded.

"It's gone," Bill said close behind her.

"No!" She pointed up. "Look. There's still a bright spot up there. Like a star."

The only star in the sky.

"Never mind the star," Jack said. "Check out the roof."

Carol wished he'd be less mundane at times but looked at the roof anyway. A smoldering hole was left where the light had burst through. She approached it cautiously and looked down through it into the living room below, afraid of what she might see there, afraid that Glaeken had been harmed somehow by the blaze of light.

There were no charred, blackened remains crumbled on the rug below. But Glaeken wasn't there either. Instead a stranger stood in his place—in Glaeken's clothes—clutching the hilt that sat upon the blade.

"Look!" Carol whispered. "Who's that?"

He was taller than Glaeken and had the old man's broad build, but this man was much younger, younger even than Sylvia. Perhaps Jack's age. And his long hair was fiery red. His shoulders and upper arms stretched the seams of the shirt he wore. Who—?

And then she caught a glimpse of his blue eyes and knew beyond all question—

"It's Glaeken!"

She felt an arm slip around her shoulder as she heard Bill's hoarse whisper beside her.

"But he's so young! He can't be more than thirty-five!"

"Right," she said as understanding grew. "The same age as when he first took up the battle."

Carol could not take her eyes off him. The way he moved as he tore the blade free of the floor and swung it before him. He was—she could find no other word for him—magnificent.

And then he looked up at them through the opening and Carol recoiled at the grim set of his mouth and the rage that flashed in his eyes. He lifted the weapon and reduced the coffee table to marble gravel and kindling with one blow, then he strode from sight. Seconds later they heard the apartment door shatter.

"He is *pissed*," Jack said. "And I hope it's not at us."

"No," Bill said. "It's at Rasalom. It's got to be Rasalom."

"Then I'm glad I'm not Rasalom."

Carol shivered in the cold wind and looked back up at the point of light the beam had left in the sky. It was brighter— and bigger.

"Look!" she said, pointing up. "It's growing."

"I think you're right," Bill said, squinting upward at the rapidly expanding spot. "It almost looks like—" Suddenly he was pulling her backward, away from the hole in the roof. "Run! It's coming back!"

Carol shook him off and stood waiting for the light rushing down from the heavens. It wouldn't hurt her—she *knew* it wouldn't hurt her. She spread her arms, waiting for it, welcoming it.

And suddenly she was bathed in light—the whole rooftop was awash in brilliant, white light. Warm, clean, almost like—

"Sunlight!"

The entire building stood in a cone of brilliance that broached the darkness from the point source far overhead, as if a pin hole had been poked into the inverted bowl of Rasalom's night and a single, daring ray of sunshine had ventured through.

Carol ran to the edge of the roof and leaned over the low parapet. Down below, on the bright sidewalk, the crawlers were scuttling away into the darkness of the Park across the street, fleeing the glare.

She heard a crash as bright fragments of glass exploded onto the sidewalk. And suddenly Glaeken was there, striding across the street toward the Park, his red hair flying as he swung the blade before him, as if daring something to challenge him. And as he stepped from the light into the darkness beyond—

"Bill!" Carol cried. "Oh, God, Bill, come look! You've got to see this!"

The light was following Glaeken, clinging to the sword and to his body like some sort of viscous fluid, trailing after him, creating a luminescent tunnel through the darkness.

"Where's he going?" Bill said as Jack, Ba, Sylvia and Jeffy joined her at the edge.

Carol thought she knew but Jack answered first.

"To the hole," he said in a low voice. "To the first one, the Sheep Meadow hole. The one he's after is down there."

They quickly lost sight of Glaeken, but together they stood on the roof and watched the tube of light channel its way into the inky depths of the park.

WNEW-FM:

FREDDY: *Something's happened out there, man. We just got a call on the CB that there's a beam of light coming out of the sky on Central Park West. We can't see it from here so we don't know for sure if it's true.*

JO: *Yeah. This guy who called has been pretty reliable all through this mess, but you know we've all been getting, like, a little funky since the sun went out, man, so if you've got a CB and you're anywhere near Central Park, peek out what's left of your window and let us know what you see.*

Rasalom relaxes within his chrysalis.

Only a pin hole, nothing more. All that effort expended by Glaeken's circle and to what end? A pin hole in the night cover. Nothing. And it changes nothing.

Except Glaeken. He's been changed, returned to the way he was when he and Rasalom first squared off against each other. Little did either of them know that they would be locked in battle for ages.

But Rasalom cheers Glaeken's rejuvenation. It would have been almost embarrassing to crush the life out of that feeble old man he had become. Destroying the reborn Glaeken—young, agile, angry—will be so much more satisfying.

And best yet, he doesn't even have to seek Glaeken out. The idiot is coming to him. How convenient.

It shall end as it began—in a cavern.

Glaeken stood in the dark on the rim of the hole and looked down into deeper darkness.

Somewhere down there, Rasalom waited. Glaeken could feel him, sense him, *smell* his stink. He would not be hard to find.

But he had to hurry. A rude, insistent urgency crowded against his back, nudging him forward. In spite of it, he turned and stared back at the cone of brilliance that pinned his apartment house like a prop on a stage, at the worm of light that had trailed him from the cone. Because of it, the night things had avoided him on his trek to this spot. He almost wished they hadn't. He wished something had challenged him, blocked his path. He hungered to hurt something—to slash, cut, maim, crush under his heel, destroy.

I was free! he thought. *Free!*

And now he was caught again, trapped once more in the service of—what? The power he'd served had no name, had never presented a physical manifestation of itself. It was just *there*—and it wanted him *here*.

The rage seething and boiling within him was beyond anything he had ever experienced in all his many years. It was a living thing, like a berserk warrior, wild, deranged, psychotic, slavering for an object—anyone, any*thing* on which to vent the steam of its pent-up fury. His whole body trembled as the beast within howled to be let loose.

Save it, he told himself. *Save it for Rasalom.*

He was sure he'd need it then. All of it.

He turned back to the pit and swung the weapon. Damn the power, but it felt good to feel good, to have his muscles and joints feel so strong and lithe, to be able to fling his arms freely in all directions, to twist and bend without stiffness and stabs of pain.

And the weapon—he hated to admit how *right* it felt in his grasp, but a deeper part of him remembered and responded to the heavy feel of the hilt clutched tight against his palms and fingers. The warrior in him smelled blood.

No more time to waste.

He slipped the weapon through the back of his belt, lowered himself over the edge, and began his descent.

WNEW-FM
*JO: All right, man. We've had confirmation. A few other good people have CBd
in to tell us that yes, there is some heavy light coming out of the sky on
Central Park West up near the Sheep Meadow.*
*FREDDY: Yeah, and if you remember, that's near where the first of those nasty
holes opened up. We don't know if there's a connection so you might want
to be careful, but a lot of the folks who've contacted us say they're going to
try to get over to it to check it out.*
*JO: We'll keep you informed. As long as we've got juice for the generator, we'll
be here. So keep us on.*

Carol pointed into the dark blob that was Central Park. The thread of light
that wove through the blackness there had not lengthened in the past few
minutes.

"Glaeken must have stopped moving," she said. "Do you think something's
wrong?"

"I don't think we'll see it move any further," Bill said. "It looks like it's gone
as far as the hole. He's probably out of sight now, moving down."

"I hope the light's still following him."

Carol glanced down at the sidewalks below in time to see a battered car skid
to a halt against the curb. It was covered— smothered—with night things, but
they slipped away when the car lurched to a stop on the edge of the light. The
door flew open and half a dozen people—a man, two women, and three kids—
tumbled out. They began to run for the door of the building but slowed to a stop
as they realized they were no longer being pursued. They looked up at the light,
spread their arms, laughed, and began to embrace each other.

Another car suddenly flew out of the darkness and bounded over the curb
before it came to a stop. Another group of people jumped out. They were greeted
with cheers by the first and they all embraced.

"I don't know if I like this," Jack said.

"They're coming to the light," Carol said.

"Yeah," Jack said, shaking his head. "And that could be trouble. Maybe I
ought to get downstairs. You coming, Ba?"

The big Oriental stood behind Sylvia and Jeffy. He shook his head.

"Okay," Jack said. "I understand. But we might need you later." He waved and trotted for the stairs.

"I don't think there's anything to worry about, do you?" Carol said to Bill. "I mean, I think we should share the light."

"I do too," Bill said. "Jack's just being Jack. He doesn't like surprises."

Carol looked down again. More people had reached the light, some apparently on foot from neighboring buildings. She noticed something.

"Bill?" she said. "Remember when we first looked down? Wasn't the light just to the edge of the sidewalk?"

Bill shrugged. "I don't know. I didn't notice."

Carol stared down at the rim of shadow the encircled the building. It was now a couple of feet beyond the curb on the asphalt of the street.

Glaeken found the mouth of the lateral passage a hundred or so feet down the western wall. A dozen feet across, it was the only break in the wall of the hole. Glaeken swung inward and landed on his feet. He pulled the weapon free of the back of his belt and started walking. He needed no signpost to tell him that Rasalom lay ahead. He knew.

The light followed, filling the tunnel behind him, stretching his shadow far ahead, sending dark things scuttling and slithering and fluttering out of the way.

He pushed on, not running, but moving swiftly with quick, long strides. The sense of urgency was still at his back, propelling him forward. He swung the blade back and forth, splashing the air ahead of him with bright arcs of light, then waded through them.

But as he progressed deeper and further along the tunnel, he noticed a dimming of the light. He turned and looked back along his path. The light seemed as thick and bright as before back there, but down here it was attenuated, diluted, tainted . . .

It could only mean he was nearing his goal, the heart of the darkness.

Not much further on, the light loosened its embrace and pulled free of him; it hung back, deserting him, abandoning him to penetrate the beckoning blackness of the tunnel ahead alone.

Glaeken kept moving, slower now, stepping more carefully. Only the blade was glowing now, and that faintly, struggling against the thickening blackness that devoured its light. Soon its light failed too. Glaeken stood in a featureless black limbo, cold, silent, expectant. The darkness was complete. Victorious.

And then, as he knew it would, came the voice, the hated voice, speaking into his mind.

"Welcome, Glaeken. Welcome to a place where your light cannot go. My place. A place of no light. Remind you of anyplace from the past?"

Glaeken refused to reply.

"Keep walking, Glaeken. I won't stop you. There's light of sorts ahead. A different light, a kind I choose to allow here. No tricks, I promise. I want you here. I've been waiting for you. The Change is almost complete. I want you to marvel at my new form. I want you to be the first to see me. I want to be the very last thing you see."

Glaeken felt his palms dampen. He was in Rasalom's country now, where he made all the rules. Tightening his grip on the hilt, he stepped forward into the black.

WNEW-FM:

JO: *Okay. We've had somebody CB us from right inside the beam of light over on Central Park West and they say it's the real thing. Bright, warm, and the bugs won't go near it. Nobody knows how long it'll last, but it's there now and these folks think it might be there to stay.*

FREDDY: *So look, here's what we're gonna do. We're gonna make this loop and set it going, then we're outta here. We're heading there ourselves. We'll have a message on the tape, then we'll follow it with a Travelin' Wilburys song, and the whole deal will play over and over.*

JO: *And here's the message: Get to the light. Get over to Central Park West any way you can and get into the light. Get moving and good luck. And while you're gettin' there, here's some appropriate traveling music. See you there, man.*

Cue: "Heading for the Light"

Dim light ahead, oozing around the next bend in the passage.

Unhealthy light. A sickly, wan, greasy glow, purulent green, clinging to the tunnel walls like grime, casting no shadows. There was no hope to be found in that light, no succor from the night, merely a confirmation of the dark's superiority.

As Glaeken moved toward the feeble glow, the air grew colder; a bitter, acrid odor stung his nostrils. He rounded the bend and stopped.

In the center of a huge granite cavern, a hundred feet across, Rasalom's new form hung suspended over a softly glowing abyss. Four gleaming ebon pillars reached from the corners of the chamber, arching across the chasm of the abyss to fuse over its center. A huge sack, bulging, pendulous, nearly the size of a small warehouse, hung suspended from that central fusion. Glaeken could make out no details of the shape that floated within the inky amnion of the sack. He didn't need to see Rasalom to know that it was he, undergoing the final stage of his transformation.

"Welcome to my uterus, Glaeken."

Glaeken did not reply. Instead, he leapt upon the nearest support where it sprang from the wall and strode along its upper surface toward the center where Rasalom hung in his amniotic sack.

"Glaeken, wait! Stop!" Rasalom's voice took on a panicky edge in his head. *"What are you doing?"*

Glaeken kept moving toward the center, the weapon raised before him.

"There's no need for this, Glaeken! I'm so close! You'll ruin everything!"

Glaeken had progressed to within a dozen feet of the sack when the surface of the support suddenly softened and erupted in hundreds of fine tendrils that wrapped around his ankles, snaring them, encasing them in a squirming mass, then recrystallized to rock-like hardness. He pulled and strained at them but his feet were locked down to the support. He chopped at them with the blade but he remained trapped like a fly on a pest strip.

He stared down at the sack hanging within spitting distance below him. A huge eye rolled against the inner surface of the membrane and stopped to stare back at him.

"That is quite far enough," Rasalom said.

"Perhaps you're right," Glaeken said.

He shifted his grip on the hilt and raised the weapon over his shoulder like a spear, its point directed at the eye. Rasalom's voice screamed in his brain.

"No! Glaeken, wait! I can help you!"

"No deals, Rasalom."

He reared back to hurl the weapon.

"I can make her whole again!"

Glaeken hesitated. He couldn't help it.

"Whole again? Who?"

"Your woman. That Hungarian Jewess who stole your heart. I can give her back her mind—and make her young again."

"No. You can't. Not even the *Dat-tay-vao*—"

"I'm far more powerful than that puny elemental. This is my world now, Glaeken. When I complete the change I can do whatever I wish. I will be making the rules here, Glaeken. All the rules. And if I say the woman called

Magda shall be thirty again and sound of mind and body forever—forever—
then so it shall be."

Magda . . . alert, young, healthy, *sane* . . . the vision of the two of them
together as they used to be . . .

He shook it off.

"No. Not in this world."

*"It doesn't have to be this world. You can have your own corner of the globe,
your own island, your own archipelago. All to yourselves. You can even take
some of your friends. The sun will shine there forever. You can live on in idyllic
splendor."*

"While the rest of the world . . . ?"

*"Is mine. All you have to do is acknowledge me as master of this sphere and
drop your weapon into the abyss. After that I shall see to all your comforts."*

For a heartbeat he actually considered it. The realization rocked Glaeken.
Did he want Magda back that much? And Magda—she'd never forgive him.
He'd have to live on with her abhorrence, her loathing of him.

He tightened his grip on the weapon.

"No deals."

Putting all his arm and as much of his foot-locked body as he could behind
it, Glaeken hurled the weapon at the sack. The huge eye ducked away as
Rasalom's voice screamed in his mind.

"NOOOOOOOOOOOOOOOOOOOO!"

The point of the blade pierced the membrane of the sack, penetrated about
a foot, then stopped, quivering. Rasalom's voice became a howl of pain as inky
fluid spurted out around the blade, coating it, congealing around it, sealing the
wound and encasing the weapon until the entire blade and all but the pommel
of the hilt were mired in a hardening tarry mass.

And then Rasalom's howl of pain segued into a peal of laughter. The single
huge eye once again pressed against the inner surface of the membrane and
regarded him coldly.

*"Ah, Glaeken. Noble to the end. Just as well, I suppose. You probably knew
you'd never see the tropical idyll I promised you. But did you truly think you
could hurt me? Here in the heart of my domain, in the seat of my power? Your
arrogance is insufferable at times. It is too late to harm me, Glaeken. It has been
too late for a long time."*

Glaeken tried once more to pull his feet free but they would not budge. He
took a deep breath and stood quietly, waiting, listening to the hated voice in his
mind.

*"You knew it was too late, Glaeken. You must have known all along. Yet
knowing it was useless, still you took up the weapon and came to me instead of
waiting for me to come to you. I don't understand that. Can you explain your
madness, your arrogance? We have some time. Speak."*

"If the answer is not apparent to you," Glaeken said, "no amount of talking
will make you understand. Where do we go from here?"

"We wait. I'm almost ready. At the undawn I will be complete. When I emerge from my chrysalis I shall leave you here and move to the surface where I shall deal with your little circle of allies. And as I gut them I shall let you see it all through my eyes. And as for your wife, I shall keep my promise to you: I will restore her youth and her mind before she dies—after all, we wouldn't want her to die without knowing exactly what is happening. And when all that is done, I'll return for you. And then the fun shall truly begin."

Glaeken said nothing. There was no use in asking for mercy for himself or the others—there was no mercy to be had. So he closed his eyes and willed his insides to stone to inure them from the sick fear coiling through him.

"And while we wait, I believe I'll close that tiny wound in my perfect night. Too many people are taking undue pleasure in it. Imagine their fear when it starts to fade and they realize that they are naked prey to all the night things encircling them. Yes, I like that idea. I should have thought of the pinhole myself. Allow a little cone of light through here and there about the world, let the locals run to it like moths to a flame, let it shine long enough to lift hopes, and then douse it. Thank you, Glaeken. You've given me a new game."

"Look at them all," Bill said. "Must be thousands down there."

Carol had returned with the others to the living room of Glaeken's apartment and now she gazed down through the broken windows at the crowd below, listening to the noise floating up as each new arrival was greeted with cheers and hugs. It was a good sound, the noise of people taking a break from unrelenting fear. Some of the more daring revelers were following the channel of light that wound into the Park—but not very many and not very far.

"It's the radio," Jack said. "The only station in town still on is playing a message sending everybody here."

Suddenly it was quiet below.

"What happened?" Bill said.

Carol's heart thudded with alarm and she clutched his arm.

"I think the light just dimmed. Tell me I'm wrong, Bill. Tell me I'm *wrong!*"

Bill glanced at her, then back out the windows.

"No . . . I'm afraid you're right. Look—it just dimmed a little more!"

"It's Glaeken's fault," said a familiar voice.

They all turned. Nick was still sitting on the couch where they'd left him, still facing the dead fireplace.

"Glaeken has lost. Rasalom is ascendant."

"Glaeken is . . . dead?" It was Sylvia, stepping forward, hovering over Nick.

Carol was surprised at her concern. She'd thought Sylvia blamed Glaeken for Jeffy's condition.

"Not yet," Nick said. "But soon. We'll die. Then he'll die. Slowly."

Carol heard a new sound well up from the crowd outside—murmurs of fear, wails of panic. She turned back to the window and had the sudden impression that their cries of despair seemed to chase the light. She watched with growing dread as it faded from midday glare to twilight glow.

They're afraid again.

"Afraid!" she cried. "Maybe that's it." Suddenly she knew what had to be done—or thought she knew. "Bill, Jack, everybody—downstairs. Now!"

She didn't wait to explain and she didn't wait for the elevator. Filled with a growing excitement and a desperate urgency, she galloped down the dizzying flights to the ground floor, dashed through the lobby, and out into the crowd on the twilit sidewalk.

Bill was right behind her, then Jack. Ba brought up the rear, carry Jeffy and guiding Sylvia through the restless, panicky people. Carol led them to the edge of the fading light, right to the shadow border facing the Park, then grabbed Bill's hand in her right and took a stranger's—a frightened looking black woman's—in her left.

"I won't be afraid anymore!" Carol shouted at the huge outer darkness that tried to stare her down. She squeezed the woman's hand. "Say it," she told her. "I won't be afraid anymore! Grab somebody's hand and say it as loud as you can." She turned to Bill. "Shout it, Bill. Mean it. Take a hand and get them to say it!"

Bill stared at her. "What's this—?"

"Just do it. *Please!* There's not much time."

Bill shrugged and grabbed someone's hand and began repeating the phrase. She noticed that the black woman to her left had taken a young man's hand and was repeating the phrase to him. Carol turned and saw a very grim Jack standing behind her, his arms folded across his chest. Sylvia was beside him, equally stone faced.

"Come on, Jack," Carol said.

He shook his head. "This is nuts. It's—it's hippy bullshit. Like those peaceniks back in the sixties trying to levitate the Pentagon. You can't chant Rasalom away."

"I know that, Jack. But maybe we can put a kink in his plans. His whole thrust has been to isolate us from each other, to use fear to break us up into separate, frightened little islands. But look what's happened here. One little ray of light and we've suddenly got a crowded little island. What if we refuse to play his game anymore? What if we refuse to run screaming in fear back to our hidey holes? What if we stand here as a group and defy him? There's a defect up there, a hole in Rasalom's endless night. Maybe we can keep it open. Maybe we can even widen it. What have we got to lose that's not already lost?"

"Not one damn thing!" Sylvia said. She pulled Jack's arm away from his chest and grabbed his hand. "I won't be afraid anymore!" she said through tightly clenched teeth as she clutched Jeffy's hand in one hand and Jack's in the other. "Do your worst—I *won't* be afraid anymore!"

Carol felt her throat tighten at the defiance in Sylvia's voice.

"Come on, Jack," Sylvia said. "I'm not a joiner, either. But this is one time you can't hang back. Say it!"

"All right, dammit," Jack said. He looked uncomfortable as he repeated it in unison with Sylvia, but then he reached for a stranger's hand and got her to join in.

The chant was becoming more organized, picking up a rhythm as it spread through the crowd, growing in volume as more and more voices chimed in . . .

And then the light around them brightened. The increase was barely noticeable, but it *was* noticed. A cheer rose from the crowd and suddenly *everyone* was a believer. The chant doubled, tripled in volume.

Carol laughed as tears sprang into her eyes. She heard Jack's voice behind her.

"It's working! I'll be *damned*! It's working!"

Everyone in the crowd was involved now, shouting at the tops of their lungs. And the light continued to brighten. Carol had no doubt of that now. The light was growing stronger. Even the light in the bright channel that had trailed Glaeken into the Park was growing brighter.

But more than that, the cone of brightness was growing *wider*, inching across the pavement toward the Park, pumping pulses of brightness along the luminous channel that led to the Sheep Meadow hole.

And more people were coming, running to the light, swelling the crowd, swelling the sound of defiance.

Something was happening.

Rasalom had been uncharacteristically silent. And his huge new form did not lie quiet in its amniotic sack. The membrane rippled now and again, like a chill running over fevered skin, and occasionally it bulged in places as Rasalom shifted within.

Glaeken closed his eyes and tried to sense what was happening. He stood perfectly still, listening, feeling.

Warmth.

Light . . . there was light above. Not visible here, but he sensed it. Light and warmth, seeping into the earth above the cavern. And behind . . .

He turned and looked down the passageway. Where there had been perfect darkness, there was now the faintest glow. An illusion? Or the harbinger of a tiny dawn?

Glaeken turned back to his ancient enemy.

"What's happening upstairs, Rasalom? Tell me!"

But now it was Rasalom's turn to be silent.

Sylvia watched the scene from a second-floor window. The noise, the press of people had begun to frighten Jeffy so she'd brought him inside.

The cone of light had returned to noontime brightness and was widening steadily now, creeping uptown and downtown along the street, invading the Park. The crowd, too, was swelling steadily, the light and the noise attracting thousands more. The Manhattan mix was there, red, yellow, Central African ebony to Norwegian white and every shade between.

The chant Carol had started still reverberated loud and clear, but here and there in the crowd Sylvia noticed pockets of people singing and dancing. A couple of ghetto blasters had appeared and different kinds of music, from rap to salsa, were each attracting their own fans. A couple of guys were singing "Happy Together." She guessed that was just as effective. You didn't have to proclaim your lack of fear when you were singing and dancing. How could you sing and dance if you were afraid? And from directly below her window, uncertain doo-wop harmonies drifted up as a rag-tag group tried to find a comfortable key for "The Closer You Are."

Sylvia thought of Alan then and how he'd loved the oldies and suddenly she was crying.

Oh, Alan. My God, how I miss you. You belong here, not me. You loved people so much more than I. I should be dead and you should be here.

Alan . . . after he'd pulled out of the coma he'd been left in by the *Dat-tay-vao,* she'd come to think of him as indestructible. An indisputable assumption: Alan would be around forever. She'd never even considered the possibility of life without him. And now he was gone—no body, no grave, no trace, just *gone*—and she hadn't even had a chance to say goodbye.

She hugged Jeffy closer. It was all so damn unfair.

For a while she had blamed Glaeken, but she knew now that he, too, was paying a terrible price. She'd seen it in his eyes as he'd picked up the hilt and told her to get Jeffy clear—the anger, the frustration, the vulnerability, the weary resignation. All in a single glance. The weight of the responsibility he once more was reluctantly shouldering had struck her like a blow. She'd instantly regretted the all angry things she'd said to him.

And now maybe he was gone too.

She watched the arc of light edging through the Park. It was well into the Sheep Meadow now, almost to the rim of the hole. Did that mean they were winning, or was this just a false hope?

Sylvia closed her eyes and hugged Jeffy tighter.

If you're still alive down there Glaeken, please know that you're in our thoughts. If there's anything you can do, do it. Get him, Glaeken. Don't let him get away with what he's done to us. GET HIM!

Yes, there was light down the tunnel. Glaeken was sure of it now. Growing steadily. And Rasalom . . . Rasalom was thrashing about in his amniotic sack.

What was happening up on the surface? The weapon was here, useless, encased in hardened fluid from the sack. What in the name of anything could exert such a disturbing effect on Rasalom?

Suddenly a thunderous rumble from the tunnel behind him. The support shuddered beneath Glaeken's feet. He twisted and saw the growing glow disappear as the roof of the tunnel collapsed, choking the passage with rubble. As the tunnel mouth belched a cloud of dust, Rasalom's voice returned.

"Once again you've chosen a vexing group of friends, Glaeken."

A warm glow of pride lit within him, along with a glimmer of—did he dare?—hope.

"They're a tough bunch. What have they done?"

"Nothing that will matter in the long run, but for the present they've created an annoyance, an inconvenience."

"What?"

"They've enlarged the pinhole in the night-cover made by your puny little weapon."

Glaeken steadied himself, choked down the shout of triumph that surged against his vocal cords. He maintained a calm exterior.

"How?" he said.

"How is irrelevant. Their success is irrelevant. The entire world is in darkness. A single cone of sunlight, no matter how bright, is laughably insignificant."

Glaeken sensed the weight of all that Rasalom had left unsaid.

"Sunlight, Rasalom? Since when have you been afraid of sunlight?"

"I am afraid of nothing, Glaeken. I am master of this sphere. It fears me."

"It's not sunlight, is it, Rasalom. It's another kind of light. Light from your enemy. And it comes at a time and place that's more than 'inconvenient,' doesn't it? It's shining directly above your little nest, and it has arrived at a time when you're vulnerable, before your new form has matured."

"Nonsense, Glaeken. Pure wishful thinking on your part. When my gestation is through, and that is only a matter of hours now, I shall personally plug that hole in my perfect night. Then you will see how 'vulnerable' I am."

Glaeken noticed a growing warmth at his back. He twisted again toward the rubble-strewn tunnel. Something was happening there. Something he'd never dreamed. The light was working into the rubble, determinedly worming its way through, as if it had a mind of its own.

And then he saw it. A gleaming pinpoint, a tiny bead no larger than a grain of sand, glowing amid the rubble, growing bigger, growing brighter.

"Don't allow yourself to hope, Glaeken. It cannot harm me."

Yet Glaeken did allow himself to hope, could not help but hope when he saw the bead brighten suddenly and shoot out toward the pit in a narrow beam of brilliance, like a needle-thin blue- white laser streaming toward Rasalom. But it came up short against the support under Glaeken's feet, spraying and splashing like water against a stone wall.

The beam of light persisted, though. Like a living thing with a will of its own, it split, one half sliding upward, the other down around the support. The light crept to the top just inches ahead of Glaeken's trapped feet. As soon as it crested the support it raced downward to rejoin its other half. They fused and once again shot out toward Rasalom's amniotic sack.

But the beam did not strike the sack. Instead it flashed toward the weapon, igniting the exposed pommel of the hilt. The pommel blazed with blinding fire, and dimly, through the encrustations, Glaeken could see bolts of light flashing along the length of its blade.

Rasalom howled in Glaeken's mind as he writhed and thrashed within his sack. Glaeken had a feeling that this time it was no act.

The weapon began to vibrate, the encrustations began to crack and fall away like an old skin, and suddenly the weapon was free, blazing with white light.

Another beam of radiance broke through the rubble and flashed across the cavern. It too found the weapon and added its power to it.

As Rasalom's howl rose to a shriek, Glaeken felt the tendrils wrapped around his legs begin to soften, their hold on him weaken. He bent and tore at them, straining to pull free. There was no time to lose. Rasalom's thrashings were shaking the weapon within the wound it had made. The beam of light stayed with it, moving whenever it did, but if the weapon slipped loose it would fall into the pit. And then Rasalom's victory would be assured.

With a final surge, Glaeken yanked his legs free and leapt to the central disk where the four arched supports fused. He dropped to his belly, hung precariously over the edge, and reached for the weapon.

Cold-fire eternity beckoned below.

Glaeken fought a surge of vertigo and stretched his right arm to its limits, violently thrusting it down to force the ligaments to give him the tiny extra increment of length he needed to reach the jittering hilt. His fingertips brushed the pommel twice, and then with a final, agonizing thrust, he hooked two fingers around it. At his touch the weapon seemed to move on its own, slamming the body of the hilt against his palm. Power surged up his arm and throughout his body and once more the weapon was his.

And he was the weapon's.

He stood and looked about. The beams of light from the rubble stayed with the blade, fueling it, following wherever he moved it. He couldn't reach Rasalom or his sack, so he decided to try the next best thing.

Reversing his grip, he lifted the weapon high and drove the point down into the center of the nearest of the supporting arches. A blinding flash lit the cavern as the blade cut deep into the flinty substance. The material of the support began to bubble and smoke as the blade melted its way through it like a hot knife cutting frozen butter. The smoke was greasy, foul, reeking of seared flesh. More flashes followed as Glaeken worked the blade back and forth, widening the gash as he deepened it, strobing the cavern with bursts of light and stretching weird shadows against its walls.

"*No, Glaeken!*" Rasalom howled. "*I command you to stop! Stop now or you'll pay dearly. And so will your friends!*"

Without pausing an instant in his labors, Glaeken glanced down at the huge eye pressed furiously against the membrane.

"You've already promised that, Rasalom. What have I got to lose?"

"*I* won't *kill you, Glaeken! I'll let you live on, just barely. I'll make you witness, see,* feel *everything that happens in my new world.*"

Glaeken said nothing. He had almost cut through the first arch. With a final thrust, the blade angled through the underside and came free.

The central portion suddenly sagged a half a foot under him. Glaeken hurried to his left, toward the next support.

"*Glaeken, NO! That island I promised you—you and the woman and your friends—*"

Glaeken shut his mind to Rasalom's rantings and drove the blade into the second arch. More flashes and oily smoke. He worked the blade ferociously, gasping with the stench and the exertion, and eventually it worked its way through.

The center sagged again, its free edge lurching downward almost two feet this time. The two supports he had cut wept dark fluid from their truncated ends as they remained suspended above the void like severed arms reaching for something they would never again possess.

Supported now on only one side by the two remaining arches, the center tilted at a steep angle. Glaeken's feet slipped on the smooth surface as he hurried toward the nearer remaining arch.

And again he drove the blade deep into the substance. As he worked it through, he felt an impact on his right leg. Reflexively he pulled away as searing pain flashed up to his hip. He caught a flash of movement and he rolled away from the center.

It was a huge hand, but it resembled a hand only in the vaguest sense—black as the night above, and only three fingers, each as thick around as Glaeken's waist, each terminating in a sharp yellow talon. Blood dripped from one of those talons—his own.

Rasalom—it had to be. Rasalom in his new form. Glaeken could not see the rest of him, most of which was no doubt still in the sack below. Had his new form finally matured, or was he breaking free before the process was completed in order to stop Glaeken?

It made another swipe, blindly, in his direction. Glaeken ducked under the talons. The sudden move sent a fresh surge of agony through his wounded leg. As it came for him again, he slashed at it with the weapon and felt the blade dig deep into the inky flesh.

Light exploded above him, a flash of brilliance that dwarfed all those before it. In his mind he heard Rasalom cry out in shock and pain. When his vision cleared he saw the taloned hand waving above him, one of its thick fingers swinging madly back and forth as it dangled from its smoking stump by a few remaining intact tendons.

Glaeken straightened and limped to the other support. He had been able to cut only part way through the third and it was unlikely he'd get a chance to finish the job within Rasalom's reach. He'd attack the fourth—but not near the center.

His move must have surprised Rasalom because he was half-way along the arch before the voice sounded in his brain.

"Don't run off, Glaeken. We've only begun to play."

Glaeken didn't look back. He continued his torturous trek toward the far end of the arch. Within a dozen feet of its origin he stopped and turned.

Rasalom's amniotic sack still hung from its lopsided platform like a gargantuan punching bag, but now a sinewed arm with a wounded hand protruded from the rent made by the weapon. It raked the air above it with its two remaining talons. And the eye . . . that malevolent eye was still pressed against the membrane, glaring at him.

"I'm not running far," Glaeken said.

With another burst of light and bloom of oily smoke, he drove the weapon deep into the arch beneath him and began to work it back and forth. The support was thicker here near its base, but he could afford the extra time it would take because he was out of Rasalom's reach.

"Glaeken," Rasalom said to his mind, *"you'll never learn. You are forcing me to . . ."*

Ahead, over the center of the pit, another arm clawed free of the membrane, then ripped a talon down the surface of the sack, opening it like a zipper. Tons of black fluid poured from the rent, spilling into the bottomless glow of the depths below. The rent parted, widened, and then . . .

Something emerged from the sack.

Glaeken knew who it was, but could not be certain *what* it was. It had arms, that he knew. And a huge eye at its upper end. But in the dim glow leaking up from the pit below he could be sure of little else as it crawled from the sack and hoisted itself up onto the sagging central platform. Legs . . . now he could see legs, very much like the two arms, but the rest of it was encased in an oozing gelatinous mass that dripped off the platform in amorphous globs and tumbled into infinity. There was a larger shape within the mass, something with a head and a torso, but Glaeken could make out no details. And now a pair of thick tentacles wriggled free of the gelatin below the arms to twist and coil in the air.

It began moving his way, crawling upward toward him along the fourth arch.

Glaeken redoubled his efforts with the weapon, widening, deepening the cut in its upper surface, thrusting the blade through to the underside. Rasalom's incomplete new form was cumbersome, his progress slow, but he was sliding steadily closer. He soon would have Glaeken within reach of those talons.

Suddenly an explosive crack echoed through the cavern as the fourth arch shook beneath Glaeken's feet and broke part way through like a green sapling. Its distal segment sagged. Glaeken paused and watched Rasalom claw frantically for purchase as he slipped back along the decline toward the central disk. He gave the monstrous form no time to recover, however; immediately he renewed his hacking assault at the remaining splinters holding the arch together.

"Give it up, Glaeken! This is an exercise in futility! You cannot win!"

Rasalom's voice was no longer in his mind. His new form was speaking in a startlingly powerful voice. Even muffled by the gelatinous coating, it was still loud enough to shake the walls of the cavern.

Glaeken ignored it and forced his wearying arms to maintain the assault on the arch. The reflexes were still there, the arms knew what to do, but the unconditioned muscles were sagging with fatigue. Yet he couldn't rest, couldn't even slow his pace. He closed his eyes to blot out all distractions and kept hacking.

"GLAEKEN!"

The stark terror in the voice and the ripping sound that accompanied it jolted Glaeken. He looked up.

Rasalom was near, clinging to the arch, his outstretched talons only a few feet from Glaeken's face, yet he was receding, falling away. And then Glaeken saw why. He'd cut through the remnant of the fourth support and now Rasalom was dangling over the pit, clutching frantically with arms, legs, and tentacles to the swiftly tilting remnant.

The entire structure—the new Rasalom, the central disk, and the remnant of his sack-like chrysalis—was now supported entirely by the third arch. And Glaeken had already damaged that near its union with the disk.

After all these ages, Rasalom's end was at hand.

Or was it?

Rasalom was suspended head down over the pit, but he was scrabbling backwards along the remnant of the arch, up toward the disk.

"You cannot win, Glaeken! Not this time! It cannot happen! I won't allow it! I'm too close!"

His movements were shaking the entire structure, exerting enormous pressure on the lone arch. It began to bob like a fishing pole that had hooked an enormous Great White. As Glaeken hobbled back to the rim of the cavern and made his way toward the final arch, he heard it begin to crack where he had started a cut near its distal end.

Rasalom must have realized it too, because even in this dim light Glaeken could discern a frantic desperation in his movements. But it was too late. The end of the arch was splitting, angling down at its wounded tip. Breaking . . .

A cannonshot crack signaled the end. The disk lurched downward suddenly to a vertical angle, twisted crazily. Rasalom was there, clutching the disk's upper edge with his taloned fingers. Other appendages, spiny, rickety arms with clawed tips had broken free of the gel along his flank and were blindly questing for purchase while his tentacles stretched toward the end of the arch, reaching.

And then the final threads of the final arch gave way and the disk, the sack, and Rasalom plunged into the abyss.

No—not Rasalom.

Glaeken groaned as he realized that Rasalom was still there. The rest had fallen away but he was clinging to the final support by one of his tentacles—and pulling himself up!

Glaeken forced his wounded leg to move, to half run, half stagger to the base of the third arch, climb upon it, and hobble along its wavering length. He didn't have time to cut through this one. He had to meet Rasalom at its terminus and stop him there before he regained his footing.

"This is what it's always come down to, hasn't it, Rasalom. You and me. Just you and me."

Rasalom's reply was to snake his other tentacle upward and loop it around the shaft of the arch next to the first. He used them to hoist himself higher until his taloned hands could grip the arch. That done, new tentacles began to spring from the great gelatinous mass of his body to join the others in coils around the shaft.

He's going to make it!

Glaeken clenched his teeth against the pain in his leg and increased his speed. He didn't hesitate when he reached the first tentacles—he slashed at them with the weapon. Blinding flashes, greasy smoke, and thick, dark fluid spurting from the amputated ends. The world narrowed to Glaeken, Rasalom, the arch, and the weapon. Closing his eyes against the flashes, choking on the smoke, he slipped into a fugue of pain and motion, moving in a fog, operating on reflexes as he severed coil after coil and kicked their writhing remnants aside, then moved on the next group.

From below him came a thunderous roar as Rasalom kicked and thrashed in inarticulate pain and rage.

Spiny, spidery, pincer-tipped arms rose on both sides and snapped at him. Glaeken lashed out left and right, scything them down as he kept pushing forward.

Until finally he was at the end of the arch and Rasalom swung below him, suspended only by his yellow-taloned hands, one of them already missing a finger.

"Glaeken . . . no . . . please!"

And in the instant of that plea Rasalom yanked his body upward and lashed at Glaeken with the three fingers of his good hand. Glaeken ducked as the talons raked the air inches above his head. He swung the weapon upward, over his head. The impact with Rasalom's wrist and the simultaneous detonation of brilliance as the blade sliced through skin and muscle and tendon and bone nearly knocked Glaeken off the arch. He threw himself flat and hung on as Rasalom thrashed and howled and waved his partially severed, black-spurting wrist in the air.

Up ahead, near the shattered tip of the arch, Glaeken saw that Rasalom's only remaining hold on it was the two surviving fingers on his damaged hand. He crawled quickly forward and slashed at the nearest with the weapon, severing it with another flash of light. The talon of the last digit scraped along the surface of the arch, scratching a deep furrow as it slipped slowly toward eternity. Then it caught in a small pit near the edge.

"Glaeken!" came the muffled, agonized voice from below. "You can't! This can't be happening! Don't!"

Glaeken was about to raise the weapon and sever that last digit but thought better of it. Instead he rolled over and swiveled his body around; he flexed his good leg all the way to his abdomen.

His foot shot out and knocked the talon over the edge.

No final farewell to Rasalom, no verbal send off. Nothing more than a contemptuous kick.

Rasalom's scream was loud, almost painfully so. It echoed up from the glowing depths long after his tumbling, mutilated form had been swallowed by the mists.

But Glaeken did not wait and watch and listen as he dearly would have loved. Instead, as soon as the arch slowed its bobbing from the release of Rasalom's enormous weight, he began crawling back toward the cavern rim as fast as his limbs would allow

Rasalom was falling into eternity. When he passed the point where his presence no longer influenced this sphere, the old laws would begin to reassert themselves. Nature would awaken from the coma Rasalom had induced and begin its recovery, regain its control.

And this cavern had no place in nature.

As he reached the end of the arch, the walls began to shake. The rubble choking the side tunnel began to tumble free, revealing the opening. If he could reach that granite passage, he might survive.

He was almost there when the roof caved in.

The crowd quieted as a new sound overwhelmed their chants and songs. Carol's voice had given out a while ago, so she was already quiet.

They'd spilled across the street and into the illuminated sections of the Park, and were swelling further. But the sound had frozen them all in their tracks; and now they stood half crouched, looking up, looking around, looking at each other. Carol hushed those near her.

A basso drone, a thunderous buzz, a monstrous flapping in the air all around the widening cone of light, growing louder, vibrating the streets, the sidewalks, the buildings.

"It's the bugs!" someone cried. "They're coming back! Coming to get us!"

"No!" Carol cried, her voice a ragged blare above the growing fearful murmur of those about her. "Don't be afraid. They hate the light. As long as we stay in the light they won't come near us."

She, too, was afraid, but she hid it. What was happening? She glanced at Bill and he shrugged and held her close.

Then she saw them. Bugs. An immense horde of them, thickening the air and swarming along the ground around the cone of light. Some of them were forced to dip into the light by the crowding but their wings and bodies began to smoke where the light touched them and they darted back out.

No concerted attack, no suicidal kamikaze bug rush to wipe them out. Rather, a mad, blind, panicked dash toward the hole. The cone of light had reached the edge of the bottomless opening and she could see the countless horrors diving into the depths beyond the light, the winged ones spiraling down, the crawlers leaping from the edge.

"They're going back!" Carol said, as much to herself as to Bill. "They're going back into the hole!"

As a cheer roared from the crowd and she pressed forward for a better look, the earth began to shake—violently. Cheers turned to screams as people were knocked from their feet and thrown to the ground. Carol's hoarse shout of alarm rose with the others as she was hurled to the pavement with Bill atop her.

From the blown-out windows of the top floor, Sylvia watched the pandemonium below with growing alarm. Jeffy had soiled himself and so she and Ba had brought him upstairs for a change of clothes. Now she held onto the sill with one hand and Jeffy with the other as the building shook and creaked and groaned around them.

An earthquake! she thought. She'd never been in one, but this had to be how it felt.

And there, down on the near edge of the Sheep Meadow. The earth was cracking open.

Another hole!

This was it, then. The growing light, the sense of impending victory, the return of the bugs en masse to the original hole—it was all a false hope, an empty promise. A new hole, unafraid of the light, was opening closer to the building. And what new horror was going to issue from that?

The sudden changes could mean only one thing: Glaeken had failed.

The tremors worsened as a deep rumble issued from the first hole in the center of the Sheep Meadow. Clouds of what looked like dust or smoke were spewing from the opening. Sylvia reached for the field glasses and focused on the hole. The edges looked ragged—they seemed to be crumbling, breaking away, sliding into the opening, choking it.

Yes! It was closing! And below—she shifted the glasses—what was happening with the new hole?

But it wasn't a hole yet. Maybe it never would be. More like a depression, a cave-in of some sort.

The tremors stopped.

Then silence. Sylvia lowered the field glasses and paused, listening. Silence like no silence she could ever recall. Not a bird, not an insect, not a breeze was stirring. She could hear the rush of her own blood through her arteries, but nothing else. All the world, all of nature paused, frozen, stunned, afraid to move, afraid to breathe.

It lasted one prolonged agonized moment. And then, for the second time tonight, the light began to fade.

The silence was shattered by a burst of cries of renewed terror from below, then the chant began again. She heard Ba begin to repeat the words behind her. Sylvia joined him, whispering the litany as she raised the glasses and scanned the roiling crowd for Carol or Bill or Jack—anyone she knew.

The chant was failing this time. Despite thousands of throats shouting the words at the tops of their lungs, the light continued to fade.

We've lost!

Somehow in the dying light she managed to pick out Carol's familiar figure at the edge of the new hole, or depression, or wherever it was. She wanted to shout down to her to get away from there. That was where the new threat would arise. But Carol was right on the edge, pointing down at the bottom of the depression. She was jumping up and down, hugging Bill, hugging everyone within reach. What—?

Sylvia refocused on the bottom of the pit. Something moving there, struggling in the loose dirt. She strained to see in the last of the light.

A man. A man with red hair.

Glaeken? Alive? But he couldn't be. If he survived down there it could only mean—

Suddenly Ba was at her side, pointing across the Park toward the east side. "Look, Missus! *Look!*"

In all their years together, she had never heard such naked excitement in his voice. She looked.

The crowd below couldn't see it yet, but from this elevation there could be no doubt. Sylvia didn't need the field glasses. Straight ahead, down at the far end of one of the concrete canyons, a bright orange glow was firing the sky over the East River.

"The sun, Missus! The sun is rising!"

Part IV

DAWN

FRIDAY

IN THE BEGINNING ...

Carol stood on Glaeken's rooftop in the bright morning sunlight and wished she had the nerve to remove her blouse. Jack and Bill had pulled off their shirts as soon as they'd stepped out the door. Carol envied the males their casual ability to expose so much surface area to the warm light pouring through the cloudless sky.

Why not me? she thought, reaching for the top buttons on her blouse. After all we've been through together, what difference would it make?

But she stopped after two buttons. If it was just Bill, maybe. But not with Jack here.

I know I've been changed by all this—but not that much. An uptight Catholic girl was still alive and well somewhere within her.

"Still hard to believe it's over," Jack said.

"What a mess," Bill said, looking over the city.

Carol followed his gaze. There didn't seem to be an unbroken window in the city. Ruined buildings were everywhere, some torn apart by gravity holes, some crushed by debris falling from other gravity holes. Above them, pillars of smoke rose from fires still raging here and there about the city. Below, a rare car picked its way through the cluttered streets. Dazed looking people wandered the sidewalks or stood around the huge depression that only hours ago had been the Sheep Meadow hole.

"It's not all bad," Jack said. "When was the last time midtown air smelled this clean?"

Bill nodded. "You've got a point. I'm just wondering how we'll ever rebuild this."

"Who said we should? And anyway, it won't be 'us' doing the rebuilding— it'll be *them*. And believe me it won't be long before we're all back to the same old shit."

Carol stepped between them. "Do you think anyone down there knows what you two did?"

"No," Jack said sharply. He suddenly seemed uneasy. He began slipping back into his shirt. "And let's leave it that way."

"Don't want to be a hero?" Bill said, smiling.

"I don't even want to be *noticed*." He turned toward the door.

"Leaving?" Carol said.

"Yeah. Soon as I find a car with gas I'm heading out to Pennsylvania." A light glowed in his eyes. "Abe's bringing Gia and Vicky back. I'm going to provide the escort."

"Good luck," Bill said.

Carol watched Jack leave. "Heaven help anyone who tries to block the return of the two women in *his* life."

Bill slipped his arm around her waist and turned her toward the ruined cityscape before them.

"I doubt heaven helps anybody."

"Just a figure of speech. But I do wonder who or what will get the credit for the sunrise."

Bill laughed. "I heard a bunch of guys singing 'Here Comes the Sun' over and over. I'll bet that becomes a new religious hymn. But you're right. A whole new mythology could rise out of this. A new round of sun worship, that's for sure. It'll be interesting to see what develops."

"But whatever it is, it will be wrong. They'll be looking for some deity to praise and thank."

"That's nothing new."

"But what about you? You deserve part of the credit."

Bill shook his head. "No. I just ran an errand." He looked into her eyes. "You're the one who found the real key and put it to use. You saw that the answer was inside us rather than outside."

"It's always been that way, hasn't it? We've always been in charge but we've never taken control. We just let ourselves get pushed this way and that."

"Fear is like a disease, and I guess some of us have better immune systems than others. Sometimes we need a little help from others, but we all have the power to step aside and say I'm not going to be a part of this anymore."

She locked her arms around his waist and smoothed his wind- ruffled gray hair.

"Do you think things will be different?"

He shook his head. "I like to think I'm more optimistic than Jack, but I fear he's right. There'll be lots of talk about a new world and a new brotherhood but in no time it'll be business as usual: the truly capable people, the ones you'd be proud to call leader, will be devoting all their time to the actual rebuilding, while the usual crew of blowhards who are incapable of building anything will be generating hot air and pretending to lead. Nothing changes."

"That's not true, Bill. I'm changed, you're changed, we've all been changed by this."

"Especially Glaeken."

Yes, she thought with a pang of anguish. Especially poor Glaeken. What would he do, where would he go when Magda was gone?

And Sylvia and Jeffy—what about them?

So many questions, so many uncertainties.

She locked her arms around Bill's waist and snuggled against him.

At least there were a few things of which she could be sure—her love for Bill, for one, and the certainty that no one alive today would ever again take sunrise for granted.

And beneath their feet, in the apartment directly below, a young red-haired man with an ageless thirty-five-year-old body was spoon- feeding applesauce to the twisted, feeble-minded woman he loved so dearly and with whom he had hoped to grow old.